Outcast
of Redwall

'Eeulaliaaaaaa!'

The camp came to life instantly. Two vermin fell under the club as the badger threw himself at Swartt. Before the ferret had half drawn his sword the badger's club thudded hard against his foe's sixclawed paw. Swartt screeched and fell back injured, yelling to his creatures, 'Stop him! Kill him!'

Skarlath saw the badger disappear under a crowd of vermin as they tried to bring him down, and he hurtled in, ripping and stabbing with beak and talons. Though the badger was weighted by foebeasts, none could fell him. He stood like a mighty young oak, flailing the club, his deep-throated warcry ringing through the forest.

'Eeulaliaaaaa!'

Also by Brian Jacques in Red Fox

Redwall
Mossflower
Mattimeo
Mariel of Redwall
Salamandastron
Martin the Warrior
The Bellmaker
Seven Strange and Ghostly Tales

BRIAN JACQUES

Outcast of Redwall

Illustrated by Allan Curless

RED FOX

A Red Fox Book

Published by Random House Children's Books
20 Vauxhall Bridge Road, London SW1V 2SA

A division of Random House UK Ltd
London Melbourne Sydney Auckland
Johannesburg and agencies throughout the world

Copyright © Text Brian Jacques 1995

Copyright © Illustrations Allan Curless 1995

1 3 5 7 9 10 8 6 4 2

First published by Hutchinson Children's Books 1995

Red Fox edition 1996

This book is sold subject to the condition that it shall not,
by way of trade or otherwise, be lent, resold, hired out, or
otherwise circulated without the publisher's prior consent
in any form of binding or cover other than that in which it
is published and without a similar condition including this
condition being imposed on the subsequent purchaser.

The right of Brian Jacques and Allan Curless to be identified
as the author and illustrator of this work has been
asserted by them in accordance with the Copyright,
Designs and Patents Act, 1988.

Printed and bound in Great Britain by
Cox & Wyman Ltd, Reading, Berkshire

RANDOM HOUSE UK Limited Reg. No. 954009

Papers used by Random House UK Limited
are natural, recyclable products made from wood grown in
sustainable forests. The manufacturing processes conform to
the environmental regulations of the country of origin

ISBN 0 09 960091 9

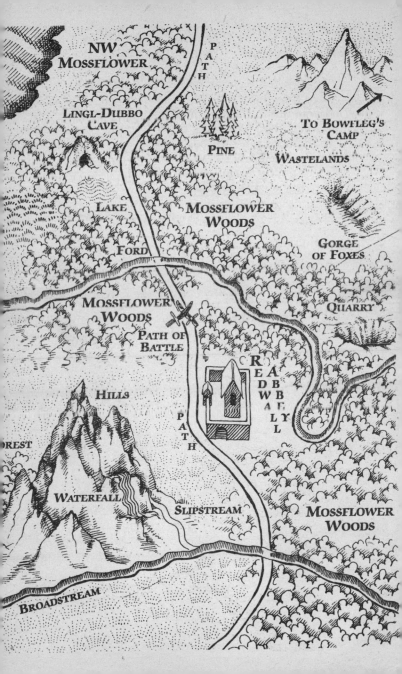

'When blood of weak meets blood of strong,
Reap the whirlwind you have sown,
Beware the lightning summer mark,
Of one whom you have known.
To the Lord who scorns all pity,
Open wide Dark Forest gate,
There a little flower awaits,
One day to seal your fate.'

Nightshade the Seer

It was a warm old autumn afternoon of russet and gold, a time for legends and stories of seasons long gone. Blue haze on the far horizon blended sea and sky into one. On the pale sands of a silent shore, ebbing waves had carelessly strewn a broken necklace of shells and pebbles along the tideline. Standing tall and mysterious was the mountain, like some huge beast guarding the coast. Salamandastron! Stronghold of Badger Lords and fighting hares. Once when the earth was young, it had spouted fire and molten rock. But the winds of time had long since banished smoke from the monolith, cooling its stones. Now Salamandastron was home and fortress combined, run through and honeycombed with halls, caverns, corridors, chambers, tunnels and secret places.

Midway up the west face on a broad rocky ledge, tufted with shrubs and wildflowers, a picnic lunch was set, close to the mouth of a tunnel entrance. Half a score of leverets, young hares, attended by a fully grown harewife, sat watching an ancient otter. Stooped and greyed by many seasons, he stood leaning on an ashpole, shaking his grizzled head in disapproval, as old creatures often will when faced with the young. When he spoke, his voice was surprisingly strong for an oldbeast.

'Hmph! Wish I was at the Abbey, those young uns at Redwall have proper manners. Instead o' layin' about gawpin', first thing they'd do would be help a body sit down!'

Stifling a smile, the harewife watched the leverets scurrying around the aged otter, doing their best to show respect and concern as they assisted him.

'A seat y'say, nothing simpler, old chap, er, I mean, sir.'

'Pop y'self down here, sir, grass is nice an' soft, wot!'

'Whoops a daisy! Easy does it, ol' sir!'

'Lean y'back on this rock, that's the ticket!'

'Righto, ancient one, comfy enough now?'

The venerable beast nodded slowly. 'Well enough, thank ye. Now, are you all goin' t'stand there watchin' a pore creature starve?'

There followed a further scuffle as the young hares set food and drink before their guest.

'Enough tuck to kill a duck here, sir!'

'Summer Salad an' a beaker of Old Mountain Ale.'

'How about freshbaked carrot'n'leek flan?'

'Some scones with gooseberry jelly, very good y'know!'

'Rather! Give the old chap a hot pastie!'

When the old otter was served, the harewife beckoned the young ones back to their seats. 'Good show, chaps, but mind y'manners or Mister Rillbrook won't tell you a story.'

Beneath fuzzy brows, Rillbrook's old eyes glinted mischievously. He broke open a steaming pastie, and said, grumpily, 'Story? Just stopped here t'rest awhile, marm, wasn't intendin' t'do no storytellin'.'

A fat, cheeky leveret piped up indignantly, 'Scoffin' a load of our grub an' not tellin' a story? I say, what a bally swizz!'

The harewife cuffed his long ear lightly. 'Burrbob! That's quite enough from you, m'laddo. I don't think you deserve a story after such impudence!'

Rillbrook took a deep draught of Mountain Ale, smacked his lips and wiped a paw across his mouth. 'Oh I dunno, marm, a good story often teaches rotters an' rogues to be better creatures.'

The leverets shouted encouragement eagerly.

'Rather, tell on, old chap!'

'I'll say! Anythin' to make us better creatures, wot?'

'Do us the world o' good, doncha know!'

The ancient otter waited until silence fell and they were watching him expectantly, then he began.

'They call me Rillbrook the Wanderer, son of Rillbrook the Wanderer, my grandsire was called Rillbrook the Wanderer . . .'

The cheeky Burrbob could be heard muttering, 'I s'pose his great great auntie was called Rillbrook the thingummy, we know that, get on with the yarn. Yowch!'

This time the harewife's quick paw did not descend so lightly on the impudent leveret's ear. She fixed him with a frosty glare, and said, 'One more word from you, sir, and it's bed with no supper!'

Burrbob took the hint, becoming the very model of silence.

Rillbrook started from where he had left off.

'I have wandered all the seasons of my life, near and far, sometimes under forgotten skies, along hidden streams, across silent forests. I have seen many things: mountains topped with snow, hot wastelands where creatures would kill for water. I have eaten among strangebeasts, listened to their songs, poems and stories, words that have brought tears and laughter to these old eyes. I have heard tales so mysterious that they trouble my memory and still return to roam my dreams on lonely nights.

'Listen now, and I will relate to you a mighty saga. It

concerns a Badger Lord who once ruled this mountain and his mortal enemy, a Ferret Warlord. The destiny of these two was entwined with many creatures, but mainly with two young ones who dwelt at the Abbey of Redwall. They were a pair thrown together by chance, for good or evil.

'Each of us is born to follow a star, be it bright and shining, or dark and fated. Sometimes the paths of these stars will cross, bringing love or hatred. However, if you look up at the skies on a clear night, out of all the countless lights which twinkle and shine, there will come one. That star will be seen in a blaze, burning a path of light across the roof of the earth, a great comet. Think on these words as my tale unfolds. Mayhap you will learn something valuable, not about stars, but of the value friendship brings.'

BOOK ONE

A Friendship Made

1

Skarlath the kestrel fledged later than his brothers and sisters; the autumn was almost over when he left the nest never to return. This is the way with hawks. They are fierce and independent, free spirits who love to soar high.

So it was with Skarlath, but being young and reckless he flew north and was trapped by winter. Howling gales from the very edges of the world bore him away. The young kestrel was held captive by a whirling mass of snow that swept him over hill, dale and forest. Shrieking winds drove him along, a bundle of wet feathers in a tight cocoon of damp white flakes that built on to his plumage in small drifts. Helpless, Skarlath was shot like an arrow into a forest. His body smashed against the trunk of an old hornbeam. Relentlessly the storm plunged onward, keening a wild dirge, leaving in its wake the unconscious young kestrel.

Skarlath regained his senses slowly. It was night, still, with not a breeze about the forest. The cold was bitter and intense, and frost glittered and twinkled on snow-laden tree boughs. Somewhere close he could see the glow of a fire, but could not feel its heat. Voices and raucous laughter came from the lighted area, drawing

7

him, but when he tried to move, the young kestrel squawked aloud in pain. His whole body was pinioned by ice; he was frozen tight, spreadeagled to the trunk of the hornbeam.

Swartt Sixclaw sat closest to the fire. He was a young ferret, but obviously the leader of the threescore vermin who made up the band. Tall, vicious and sinewy, Swartt had made himself Chieftain, because he was quicker and stronger than any who dared challenge him. He was a fearsome sight to friend and foe alike, his face striped with a sloping pattern of purple and green dye, teeth stained glistening red. Round his neck hung the teeth and claws of dead enemies. His left forepaw bore six claws – it rested on the hilt of a long curved sword thrust through a snakeskin belt.

The kestrel's agonized cries brought Swartt upright. Kicking a nearby stoat, he snarled, 'Trattak, go and see what's makin' that noise.'

The stoat scuttled obediently off into the snow-laden trees. It did not take him long to find Skarlath. 'Over 'ere, some stupid bird got itself froze to a tree!' he called out.

Swartt smiled wickedly at a young badger, tied to a log by a halter. It was a creature about the same age as himself, painfully hobbled and muzzled with rawhide strips. On its head was a broad, golden-coloured stripe. Drawing his sword, the ferret touched its point to the rare-coloured stripe. 'Get up, Scumtripe, and give your master a ride over there,' he said.

The vermin crowding round the flames jeered and laughed, as Swartt sat upon the badger's back and goaded it forward, raking with his claws and slapping it with the flat of his swordblade. Hobbled close, the young creature could only take small stumbling steps. Anguished growls issued from its bound mouth as it fumbled through the snow.

Swartt thought it no end of a joke, shouting aloud for

the benefit of his band, 'Giddy up, Scumtripe, y'great lazy stripedog, move!'

Skarlath eyed the ferret fearfully, as Swartt brought his face close, leering and licking his lips. 'Well now, what 'ave we 'ere? A kestrel, not as tasty as quail or woodpigeon, but young and tender I'll wager. Stuck fast by the ice are ye, bird? That'll keep y'nice an' fresh until you join me at breakfast!'

Then, dragging the badger cruelly up, he tied the halter attached to its muzzle to an overhanging limb of the hornbeam. 'Here's a good job for ye, Scumtripe – guard my breakfast until mornin'! Yer gettin' too fat'n'lazy lyin' by the fire.' Swartt Sixclaw strode off chuckling to rejoin his band round the flames, leaving the unfortunate pair fastened to the tree.

An hour passed, when all that could be heard was the crackling of pine logs as flames devoured them; the vermin camp was silenced in sleep. Suddenly, in one swift, silent movement, the badger flung his body close against the kestrel, trapping the bird between himself and the bark. At first the young kestrel thought he was to be smothered, but the warmth from the soft fur of the badger's chest started to melt the ice. Slowly, Skarlath felt the blood begin to stir in his veins. Although the badger was tethered and muzzled he clung on tightly with all his strength until at last Skarlath was able to move his head and wings. Skarlath jerked his head around until he found himself looking into the dark eyes of the golden-striped creature. Both young ones stared at each other, communicating in silence. Then the badger held still as the hawk's beak went to work. With short, savage movements Skarlath tore into the rawhide muzzle strips that bound the badger until they were ripped to shreds. The badger clenched and unclenched his teeth, testing his jaws, then bowing his great gold-striped head he devoured the rawhide hobbles that

9

bound his paws, chewing and swallowing the strips in his hunger. They were both free!

'Come, friend, we go, escape, get away!' said Skarlath, keeping his voice to a hoarse whisper.

But the badger acted as if he had not heard his companion. Fierce anger burned in his eyes. Stretching his powerful young limbs, the badger seized a bough of the hornbeam and snapped it from the tree with a single wrench. Smashing the bough against the treetrunk, he broke it in two then, casting aside the thin end, he gripped the heavier piece with both paws. It was about half his own height, thicker at one end than the other, like some huge rough club. Roaring out his challenge, he charged the unwary vermin around the fire.

'Eeulaliaaaaaa!'

The camp came to life instantly. Two vermin fell under the club as the badger threw himself at Swartt. Before the ferret had half drawn his sword the badger's club thudded hard against his foe's sixclawed paw. Swartt screeched and fell back injured, yelling to his creatures, 'Stop him! Kill him!'

Skarlath saw the badger disappear under a crowd of vermin as they tried to bring him down, and he hurtled in, ripping and stabbing with beak and talons. Though the badger was weighted by foebeasts, none could fell him. He stood like a mighty young oak, flailing the club, his deep-throated warcry ringing through the forest.

'Eeulaliaaaaa!'

Skarlath decided then that his friend was totally mad. The vermin numbers would tell soon and the badger would be brought down to be slain. Fighting his way through, the kestrel landed upon the badger's shoulder and cried into his ear, 'Come away or we'll both be killed. Escape!'

The badger struggled to the fire's edge and, using his club, he scattered the blazing logs into the ranks of his enemies. Flames whirred and sparks showered as

10

he battered burning wood everywhere. It sizzled and steamed in the snow, throwing up choking clouds of smoke and wood ash. Then the two friends were away, the young badger bounding through the night forest with Skarlath perched upon his shoulder. Bursting with the energy of freedom they travelled tirelessly, crashing through bush, briar and bramble in a welter of flying snow.

Back in the ruined camp, all was confusion, smoke, ashes and freezing dark night. A weasel called Muggra extricated himself from a snowdrift where the badger's club had bowled him. Rubbing his aching back he crawled over to where an older vixen named Nightshade was ministering to Swartt, binding his sixclawed paw with a poultice of herbs and snow. Muggra sneaked a pawful of the herbs and rubbed them on his own back, asking, 'Shall we follow them an' slay 'em with arrows?'

The vixen answered without looking up from her task. 'Aye, best do it right away, before they get too far.'

Bad temperedly, Swartt made as if to raise his sixclawed paw and swipe out at them both, but the movement caused him to snarl in agony; his paw hung limp and throbbing. 'Idiots! Get the fire goin', quick, before we freeze t'death in the dark here,' he spat. 'Follow them? With me paw smashed an' ruined, an' five slain, another five, maybe, wounded or injured? I give orders round 'ere, mudbrains, we follow 'em when I'm ready, an' not before!'

With lightning speed he shot out his good paw, and seizing the weasel Muggra by the neck he pulled him close, his hot breath vaporizing on the weasel's face as he hissed, 'But when this paw's fixed an' I've rested by a good fire, there'll be noplace that badger can hide from Swartt Sixclaw. I'll follow that one to the edge of the world or to Hellgates, and he'll take a long time t'die at

11

the blade of my sword. I'll hunt him t'the death an' slay him bit by bit, if it takes me ten seasons!'

The vixen Nightshade continued binding Swartt's paw, fixing the herbs and snow tight, with mud from the earth where the fire had been, and strips of aspen bark. 'If you leave it later than this night it will take you a lifetime,' she said as she worked.

Swartt winced as the dressing tightened. 'Shut yer slimy mouth, fox, always seein' the future, or sayin' that y'do. I could fix your future with one swing of me sword, that'd keep you quiet!'

Muggra was choking under Swartt's grip. The ferret looked at the weasel as if just noticing him. 'What're you doin' gurglin' there, didn't I tell y'to get a fire goin'? Trattak! Halfrump! Gerrout an' forage for dry timber! The rest of you, get shot of those deadbeasts an' clear this place up!' He flung the weasel aside.

Later, as fresh flames licked hungrily around resinous pine boughs, Swartt lay back gritting his teeth, and muttering savagely: 'We'll meet again, badger. Make the best of these few days y've got left – I'll find ye, Scumtripe!'

2

The badger did not stop running until it was broad daylight, cold and crystal clear. He halted in a small clearing at the forest edge. Skarlath fluttered to one side as the hefty young badger threw himself down in the snow and lay panting, tongue lolling, as steam rose from his thick coat. After a while he sat up, cramming pawfuls of the cooling snow into his mouth and gulping them down.

Skarlath hopped about, testing his wings with short swoops, noting gratefully that his pinions were undamaged. Glad to be alive he shook his plumage and spread his wings. 'Heeeeh! Rest, friend, then we go far away!' he cried.

The badger stood and picked up his club. 'You go where you want. When I've rested and found something to eat I'm going back there to slay that vermin Swartt Sixclaw!'

The young kestrel took flight and wheeled round the badger's head, his wings brushing his friend's gold-striped muzzle. 'Heekeeer!' he cried. 'Then you are a deadbeast, my friend. Swartt has too many vermin, you will surely be slain!'

The badger clenched his jaws as his body trembled

13

with rage. 'For many seasons that ferret held me slave, dragging me around hobbled and muzzled, starving, beating, making fun of me. Scumtripe, that was his name for me – Scumtripe! I'll make him repeat my name tenscore times before I slay him with this club. But what *is* my name?'

Whirling his club, the badger charged a dead elm stump and struck the rotting wood a mighty blow ... Whumpff! A hole appeared in the elm stump as Skarlath shrieked out, 'Kreeee! Look, food!'

Hazelnuts, chestnuts and acorns poured out onto the snow, the forgotten cache of some careless squirrel. Anger was momentarily forgotten as the two friends laughed aloud at their good fortune and fell upon the life-giving treasure. Sitting on the stump, the badger cracked shells in his strong teeth and placed the nuts before his friend. Soon they were both crunching and munching.

The kestrel spoke around a beakful of chestnut: 'I am Skarlath, I was alone, but you saved my life, now I am with you. Where come you from, friend?'

Scratching his golden stripe, the badger chewed thoughtfully. 'I'm not sure, I think I had a mother, Bella or Bellen or something, it's hard to remember. I must have been very young. Boar the Fighter, that's a name I recall, maybe he was my father, or my grandsire, I'm not certain. Sometimes I dream about home, or maybe it's my imagination, but it feels nice. Then there's the mountain, was that my home? It is all very mixed up. But Swartt Sixclaw, I won't forget him ...' The young badger looked quizzically at his friend the kestrel. 'Maybe Swartt was right, perhaps my name is Scumtripe. He gave me that name. What do you think my name should be, friend Skarlath?'

The kestrel felt fierce pity for the young badger well up in him. He hopped up onto the strong dark furred shoulder, and cried, 'Kreeeee! Your name I don't know.

But I know you are a great warrior, slay five and injure many, like a lightning bolt! There is none so quick or strong with a mace as you!'

The badger picked up his hornbeam limb and hefted it. 'So this is a mace, is it? I never knew a mace looked like this!'

Skarlath looked at the hulking young beast with his tree limb. 'If you call it a mace methinks nobeast would argue the point. Warriors like you can be anything they want to be. You are unsure of your true name. I will give you a good name. The mark of the sun is on your face, your speed is that of lightning, you have your own special weapon . . . You are Sunflash the Mace!'

The badger laughed happily and, standing at his full height, he spun the formidable hornbeam in his paws and roared: 'I have a name! It is a good name! I know who I am! Sunflash the Mace! Eeulaliaaaaaaa!'

Skarlath took wing and circled high, calling wildly, 'Kreeeeeeee! Sunflash the Mace! Kreeeeeeeee!'

When the kestrel flew to earth again, Sunflash was away, already backtracking swiftly through the forest. Skarlath winged between the trees after him. 'Sunflash, where do you go?' he called.

The warrior blood was rising in the badger's eyes as he brushed past Skarlath. 'Out of my way,' he growled. 'I am going to settle accounts with the ferret!'

'So, you go to your death!' said Skarlath, as he found his perch on the big shoulder and clung doggedly. 'I have told you Swartt has too many vermin, even for you. No matter, I have sworn to stay by your side. I go with you, and we will both be slain!'

Sunflash halted. 'But what else can I do?' he said, a bewildered look on his young face. 'Sixclaw is my enemy!'

Skarlath was wise for a young kestrel. He rapped his beak lightly against the skull of Sunflash, saying, 'We can think! You are brave, but headstrong. Why risk your life against the odds when, if we take our time, we can be certain victors one day.'

Sunflash sat down in the snow, leaning his chin on the mace as he gazed at his companion. 'Tell me how we will do this? I will listen and learn.'

Thus began the education of Sunflash the Mace. Skarlath outlined his plan, which was simple and should be effective. 'Why run after Swartt? He will be coming after us. The ferret will lose face in front of his vermin if he lets you live. Let Sixclaw wear himself out chasing us, while we leave this cold land and find warm country, where it is green and there is plenty of food. There we can rest and grow strong.

'I will be your eyes and ears, flying high, watching for Swartt, listening for information. When the time is ripe, then we strike cleverly, my friend, like wasps we worry the ferret and his band. In and out, sting and disappear, slay one or two at a time, strike like Sunflash, vanish like smoke. Then Swartt will come to fear us, he will realize that you will not disappear – that one day he will turn round and you will be there, waiting. This will trouble his mind, haunt his sleep. That is my plan. What do you think?'

A broad smile spread across Sunflash's face. 'It is a great plan, Skarlath. I will learn to think like the kestrel. Lead on!'

That day the two friends began travelling south and west on a journey that would last many seasons. Sunflash strode over hill, valley and plain, whilst Skarlath soared and circled overhead, scouting out the land. Winter passed into spring as the two friends journeyed onward, growing up together, getting wiser, seeing and learning as they went. Sunflash could not stand injustice, and wherever he saw creatures being oppressed or enslaved, the big badger, remembering his own enslavement by Swartt, meted out terrible retribution to their tormentors.

16

His name and fame began spreading. Songs and poems sprang up in the lands he and Skarlath travelled through. Most were heroic, and some, like this one, were humorous:

I met with six weasels one warm summer night,
And I feared for my life I'd be beaten and slain,
But their faces were fearful, all ashen with fright,
They jibbered and whimpered like they were insane.
'O save us, preserve us, O hide us from him,
The one with the mark of the sun on his face,
In one paw he carries a great hornbeam limb,
He's the Warrior Lord they call Sunflash the Mace!'
Of a sudden the earth seemed to tremble and shake,
And the verminous weasels passed out in a swoon,
As he came like the wind, with a hawk in his wake,
There he stood strong and tall 'neath the moon.
I'll never forget what he told me that night,
While he looked at the weasels, stretched out where
    they fell.
'You're a very brave beast to down six in one fight,
For a small baby dormouse you've done very well!'

But as more seasons passed and time went on, things did not quite turn out as Skarlath had said they would. Swartt Sixclaw had tracked them as predicted, and Sunflash and his friend worried them, striking at them many times. Each attack was successful, and the ferret lost quite a few of his vermin to the lightning strikes of Sunflash. But Swartt was no fool. The realization of the badger's guerrilla tactics came home to him one sunny morning in low hill country to the north of Mossflower Woods. Two vermin whom he valued highly, Spurhakk the stoat and Bulfie, a ferret like himself, both hardened and skilful warriors, had vanished overnight. Swartt sat hunched over a small fire, massaging his damaged paw. From shoulder to elbow the limb was as strong as ever, but the sixclawed paw was rigid and unmoving. It ached every morning, reminding him of the winter night when the young badger smashed it with a piece of hornbeam. Nightshade approached with three others who had been out searching for the missing warriors. Swartt quickly pulled a gauntlet onto his dead paw. It was a heavy affair, meshed brass mail, with two weighty copper fasteners, and it made a very formidable weapon. He glanced up at the vixen and snarled, 'Well, didyer find 'em?'

Nightshade squatted down on the other side of the fire. 'Aye, both sitting up against a sycamore in a copse over yonder, stone dead, each holding one of these.' She tossed over two long-stemmed water plants.

Swartt picked them up and inspected them. 'Bulrushes?' he said.

Nightshade was a healer, and she knew every plant by name. 'That's right, bulrushes. They are also called reed mace, or just mace in some parts of the country.'

Swartt Sixclaw flung them on the fire and watched them smoulder. 'Mace! It doesn't take a genius to work out who did this.'

The vixen narrowed her eyes against the smoke of the fire, saying, 'You should have caught him and slain him the night he escaped.'

Swartt leapt up. Drawing his sword, he scattered the fire, and shouted, 'Should have! Might have! Would have! That's in the past! Get those idlers up off their tails, we travel east!'

The vixen sprang aside to avoid the burning embers. 'East? But my scouts tell me Sunflash still travels south by west. What is there in the east?'

'Bowfleg!'

Nightshade raised her eyebrows questioningly. 'Bowfleg the Warlord?'

Swartt thrust the sword back through his belt, sneering, 'Bowfleg the Warlord, hah! You mean Bowfleg the Old, Bowfleg the Fat, Bowfleg the Glutton!'

Nightshade shrugged. 'Still, he leads a great horde.'

Swartt chuckled evilly as he marched off. 'Not for long!'

3

The far northwest fringes of Mossflower Woods are broken by rocky outcrops, gullies and hills. One could wonder why creatures bothered living there when the woodlands further inward were so lush and bounteous. But home is home and often creatures do not like to move away from the familiar surroundings of their birthplaces. So it was with the hedgehog family of Tirry Lingl and the mole kin of Bruff Dubbo, who had shared the same dwelling cave for untold generations. Tirry and his wife Dearie had four small hogs, scarce a season and a half old. Not counting his old Uncle Blunn and Aunt Ummer, Bruff had his wife Lully and two little molemaid daughters Nilly and Podd to provide for.

However, the dwelling cave of both families was not a happy place. It was a hungry and dangerous time for them, for outside in the grey drizzling afternoon another family waited, a family of five foxes. The old vixen with a hulking son covered the back exit, whilst the father, an equally old dogfox, sat outside the front entrance with a fully grown son and daughter who towered over him. They had been there nearly half a season, laying siege to the dwelling. It was quite easy to relieve one another for the purposes of eating and sleeping, and still keep up a presence, taunting and reasoning by turns, knowing they had the hedgehogs and moles prisoners in their own home until hunger forced them out.

'Don't be foolish, come out, there's food here, friends,' the vixen wheedled.

Tirry Lingl shouted back at them, 'Garn, shift yoreselves, vermin, you ain't welcome 'ere!'

The hulking fox son sniggered as he called into the back exit, 'Heehee, there'll be something tasty here when you come out. Heeheehee. You!'

The vixen nipped him sharply on his ear. 'Shuttup, acorn brain, do you want to scare 'em to death?'

The old father fox cajoled at the front entrance. 'Come on, be reasonable, we just want to talk. You don't think we'd hurt yer liddle ones, do yer?'

Inside the dwelling, Bruff Dubbo helped Tirry to shore up the barricade they had made from furniture and the bit of earth they could scrabble from the cave's rocky interior.

Bruff shook his dark furry head sadly as he spoke in quaint mole dialect to his companion. 'Hurr oi wish't oi 'ad moi ole bow'n'arrers, they vurmints'd soon shift they'm selves, hurr aye!'

Tirry Lingl peered through a gap between an armchair and a table at the foxes sitting outside. 'They've got time on their rotten ole side, Bruff, we ain't. Liddle uns drank the last o' the water this mornin' an' there's nought but a stale rye crust stannin' atwixt us an' starvation.'

Uncle Blunn's quavery voice piped up behind them. 'You'm rarscalls! Oi'm a cummen owt thurr to beat ee with moi gurt stick, ho urr, so oi am!'

Bruff turned the old fellow round, patting his back. 'You'm a fierce ole h'aminal, Nuncle Blunn, but et be toime furr ee noontide nap. Hurr thurr, go'n lay ee daown.'

Back in the cave, the little hedgehogs began weeping for food and a drink, and the two wives, Lully and

Dearie, shushed them soothingly. The small group slumped dejected, knowing what their inevitable fate would be.

Sunflash the Mace sat amid the pines and shrubs on a neighbouring hillside, invisible to the foxes as he watched the scene below. Rain dripped from the edges of an old green cloak draped over his head. The warrior looked up now and then, searching the skies for the familiar figure of Skarlath to break through the drab curtain of drizzle, and then rested his chin on his mace handle. Over the seasons he had shaped it into a weapon that would last throughout his life. The handle had a tight binding of whipcord which formed a loop to go over his paw, and the rest of the club had been fire-hardened, oiled and polished. Several arrowheads and speartips were half buried in the wide, rounded head of the mace. Only Sunflash had the skill and strength to wield such a formidable weapon.

Skarlath had seen the foxes, too. He landed out of their sight and crept silently up until he was at Sunflash's side.

'Friend Skarlath, what news of Swartt Sixclaw?' said the badger, keeping his eyes on the foxes below.

The kestrel edged under Sunflash's cloak, out of the rain. 'Gone east three sunrises back, mayhap we were thinning his ranks too fine for him to follow us safely.'

Sunflash never once moved his eyes from the foxes. 'I think you're right, but he'll be after us again someday, a little older, angrier, and with a lot more help. His ruined sixclaw won't let him forget us. Maybe we'll wait here for him.'

The kestrel's keen eyes began watching the foxes closely. 'They look like they're all one brood, what are they up to?'

Sunflash pointed a huge paw at the cave entrance. 'I think they've got some likely victims bottled up in there. I was waiting on your return. The foxes are just bullies, I would not feel justified in slaying them, but they must be taught a lesson. If they see me, they'll be frightened off. Would you go down and speak to those foxes for me, my friend?'

The young vixen and her brothers were running out of patience, and they began hurling stones through the cave entrance and shouting, 'Get out here, you stupid beasts!'

'I'll count to ten and then we're coming in after you . . . One!'

Skarlath fluttered to earth between the cave and the foxes. 'Kreeeeee! You must go from here!'

The old fox did not appear at all disturbed. 'Who are you, bird, what d'yer want?' he said, indignantly.

The kestrel treated him with lofty disdain. 'Who I am matters not. I was sent here to tell you to go quickly and stop persecuting whoever lives in yonder cave.'

The hulking son and his vixen mother came dashing round from the rear entrance, and he picked up a stone and made to hurl it at the kestrel.

Skarlath spread his wings wide. 'Throw the stone and you will not see nightfall!'

'The bird's bluffing,' the vixen snarled nastily. 'There's only him! Come on, rush him!'

Before they could move the mace came hissing through the air and thudded upright in the wet ground. A voice like thunder froze the foxes in their tracks.

'Be still or die! Eeulaliaaaaa!'

They watched astounded as a huge badger came bounding down the hillside. Taking a rock ledge in his stride, he gave a mighty leap and landed among them with a roar.

'I am Sunflash the Mace!'

The vermin had heard the name; they crouched against the earth, trembling.

Sunflash nodded to Skarlath. 'See who lives in the cave. Tell them they are safe.'

Peering through the barricade of furniture, Bruff's wife Lully called out, 'Yurr, 'tis an 'awkburd!'

Old Uncle Blunn roused himself from his noontide nap. 'Did ee say an 'awkburd? Wait'll oi gets moi gurt stick, oi'll give'm billyoh!'

Tirry clambered to the top of the barricade, crying, 'Lack a day, first foxes, then 'awks, wotever next? Well, my friend, d'you want to eat us too?'

Skarlath kept his voice gentle and tried a smile. 'No, I don't want to eat you, I am your friend. Do you know of one called Sunflash the Mace?'

Tirry's wife Dearie poked her spiky head through a gap in the barricade. 'Sunflash the Mace, d'you say? I've 'eard of that one – a great warrior, they say. Is he outside? I'd be 'onoured t'make his acquaintance!'

It took a great deal of fussing and persuading to get old Uncle Blunn and Auntie Ummer out, but the little ones had no fear at all of the majestic badger warrior. Tirry and Bruff were completely awestruck. The foxes lay face down in the dirt, Skarlath keeping a fierce eye upon them. When Uncle Blunn was eventually coaxed out, he brought his 'gurt stick' and began laying about at the foxes. Bruff took the stick from the old fellow, saying 'Yurr, Nuncle, doan't ee beat yon vurmin round, ee gurt zurr Sunflash moight want t'do that hisself, hurr!'

The badger warrior listened carefully as Tirry, acting the part of spokesbeast for both families, explained how the foxes had besieged and starved them. Sunflash listened, stifling a smile as he felt the two tiny molemaids licking rainwater from his paw. Then, grasping his club, he winked at Skarlath, and said, 'Stand those vermin upright, friend! Let me look at their scurvy faces while I decide what to do with them!'

The mudfaced foxes wept and shivered as they faced the scowling warrior.

'So these are the tormentors of babes and old ones,

these are the terrorizers of the defenceless. Well, what have you to say for yourselves?'

The father fox was about to speak when Skarlath's wing buffeted him into silence. The kestrel knew the part he had to play. Scowling murderously, he strutted up and down, saying, 'Lord Sunflash, these scum are not fit to speak. They are villains and foebeasts, I say we kill them!'

'Whoooaaa no, please Lord, spare us, we meant them no harm!' The entire fox family flopped down and grovelled on the wet earth, wailing piteously.

Skarlath winked at Sunflash, and the badger twirled his mace thoughtfully. 'Hmm, if we slay them here it might upset these little ones, then there's all that digging holes and burying carcasses . . .' Sunflash winked at Tirry, who had caught on to the idea. 'What do you think, sir? It was your family that suffered.'

Tirry Lingl paced pensively across the backs of the foxes' necks, driving them face down into the earth as he ruminated. 'You 'ave a point there, sir, but if you 'adn't come along these blaggards would've slain us. P'raps you'd best take them somewhere out of sight and finish them off, they surely deserve no better. But I leave it up to you, Lord Sunflash.'

The foxes' blubbering rose in a crescendo, and Sunflash had to shout aloud to be heard. 'I think I'll do it right here and now if this noise continues!'

The fox family were suddenly struck dumb, pressing their quaking bodies against the earth. Bruff Dubbo's old Auntie Ummer shook a paw at them. 'Burr, you'm villyuns, see 'ow you'm loikes a ladle of ee own medicine, hurr hurr, surve ee roight!'

Sunflash produced a good-sized lilac leaf and, making a slight split in it, he folded the leaf in two. Then he locked it between both paws, put it to his lips and blew.

'Phweeeeeeeeerrrrr!'

He passed the leaf to Tirry Lingl, saying, 'Can you make a noise like that?'

The hedgehog did, making an even louder noise than Sunflash. 'Makin' leaf whistles an' blowin' on 'em, that was one of my favourite pastimes as a young un, why d'you ask?'

Sunflash turned to the foxes, his voice stern. 'All of these good creatures are going to learn that noise, and then they will always carry a leaf with them, night and day. The kestrel can hear it almost a day's flight away, and if he does not, then other birds will hear it and tell him. Now listen carefully, foxes, because your lives depend on it. You must leave here and travel north. Never, I say never, must you return. Should you ignore my words and come back to these woods, the creatures you threaten will signal and I, Sunflash, swear a solemn oath upon my mace, that I will seek you out and destroy you. Understood?'

Thoroughly cowed, the foxes bobbed their heads up and down, nodding furiously, too scared even to speak. Then Sunflash began spinning the deadly hornbeam mace from paw to paw, his voice rising menacingly to a full-throated roar.

'I have given you your unworthy lives, but if you are still standing here by the time I have finished speaking I am certain I will regret my decision. So I want to see how fast you can run, due north. Now!'

Wet earth, pebbles and grass flew as the five former bullies scrabbled into a headlong takeoff. In a very short time the sound of their speeding paws was gone. Silence reigned outside the Dubbo–Lingl cave, and then suddenly all present broke out into hearty laughter.

'Hohoho! They went like scalded frogs!'

'Hurr hurr! Gurtly afeared an' muddy nosed, burr aye!'

There followed a round of introductions, congratulations and thanks from both families. The four baby hogs and the two little molemaids had never seen anything as big and furry as Sunflash. They clambered all over him, smiling into his face and stroking the broad golden stripe on his muzzle.

'Ee'm be a mounting wid furr on!'

'Big wunnerful aminal!'

The badger stood stock still, fearing to move lest he upset the tiny creatures or trod on them. His huge face was wreathed in a pleased grin; he had never encountered beasts so small and affectionate. Tirry's wife Dearie and her friend Lully the molewife fussed about, throwing their aprons over their faces in embarrassment as they chided the babes.

'Do come away now, leave the gennelbeast alone. Lack a day, sir, wot must you think o' us all?'

'Hurr aye, you an' ee 'awkburd be welcome to rest awhoil in our dwellin' cave. Us'n's be back at eventoide with vittles aplenty, then us'll all make ee well fed, bo urr aye!'

Both families fled into the surrounding woodland to forage for food, leaving Sunflash and Skarlath the hospitality of their cave. The two friends shifted the barricade and took their ease on thick woven rush mats. Surrounded by the peace and quiet of the homely atmosphere they were soon deep in slumber.

In his dreams, Sunflash could hear waves lapping against the shore; he saw pale sand, sea, and the mountain. A great feeling of longing swept over him, and he wanted so badly to be there, yet it seemed distant and intangible. Somewhere a deep voice, that of a grown male badger, was chanting:

'Find me one day 'neath the sun,
Guarding the land and the seas.
Streams to the rivers must run,
Telling their tales to the breeze.
You are Lord, by the blood of your sires,

27

From dawn 'til the daylight dies,
As the sun burns the sea with its fires,
And stars pin night's cloak to the skies.
Find me whenever you will,
Seek me wherever you may.
All of your dreams fulfil,
'Ere time like the mist rolls away . . .'

Reality seeped back slowly: a warm glowing fire, tantalizing odours and the mole and hogbabes stroking his headstripe and tickling Skarlath's wing feathers.

'Wake ee upp, zurrs!'

'Vittles be yurr aplenty.'

'Mum says you two'n's will take some feedin'!'

Tirry shooed the babes off. 'Come away, you liddle rogues, let the pore creatures up now.'

Around the fire in the cave's centre various concoctions were cooling on flat rock slabs. Bruff Dubbo presented them with beakers which he filled from a pottery jug. 'Yurr, friends, 'tis on'y dandelion an' burdock cordial, but et be noice an' cool t'drink, ho aye!'

It was dark, sweet and delicious, and the two friends slaked their thirst. Dearie Lingl pushed two of her brood forward, saying, 'Standee up straight, 'oglets, an' say your piece. C'mon now, stop suckin' those quills or they'll never 'arden. Speak out!'

Both the small hedgehogs shuffled about, tugging their headspikes respectfully as they recited:

'Thankee sir 'awk an' sir badger . . .'

'For savin' all in this cave . . .'

'From the naughty foxes . . .'

'Aye, naughty, naughty foxes!'

'Bad verminy foxes!'

'Rotten uckypaw stinky ole foxes!'

Dearie wagged a paw at her little ones. 'Tut tut! That's quite enough thankee!' She turned to the two friends, who were hiding smiles by burying their faces in the beakers, and said, 'Wot my liddle ones was sayin' is that our families would like to thank you for rescuin' us from the vermin. You must stay 'ere as long as you wish, our cave is yours. Come now, friends, enough talkin', 'elp yourselves to food.'

Sunflash and Skarlath had never tasted such good cooking. There was young onion and leek soup, hot brown bread spread with a paste made from beechnuts, a woodland salad and a huge apple and greengage crumble. The crumble was a great favourite with the little ones, who spread it thick with honey.

Old Uncle Blunn sipped piping hot soup from a wooden bowl gratefully. 'Oi wurr feared oi'd waste away to an ole shadow. Gurr! Vittles do taste gudd arter all that 'unger!'

Sunflash had an enormous appetite, but the goodwives of Tirry and Bruff would not hear of him stinting himself.

'Allus plenty more, zurr, thurr be an 'ole woodland full o' vittles for us'n's to choose from now ee've set uz free!'

And so Sunflash the Mace did full justice to the spread.

It was late into the night when he and the kestrel sprawled by the fire, warm, rested and, for the first time in many a season, unable to eat another mouthful. The old mole, Auntie Ummer, hunted out a curious-looking instrument, a stout pole with bells, two strings and a pawdrum attached to its base. She plucked the strings, jangled the bells and tapped the drum with a footpaw. The babes, who were far too excited to sleep, began jigging and hopping around the fire, clapping their paws.

'Whurrhoo! Play ee gurdelstick! Whurrhoo!'

Old Uncle Blunn began tapping his paws and chanting:

'Willy Nilly Nilly, Pod Pod Pod!
All you'm 'oglets stamp ee ground,
Moi ole paws b'ain't young loike yores,
Show us 'ow ee darnce around!'

The gurdelstick music speeded up and the little ones
whirled and leaped, jigged and tumbled until they collapsed in a giggling heap, yelling for dandelion and
burdock cordial. Tirry invited the friends to sing, but his
guests declined, Skarlath being too shy and Sunflash
explaining that he had never learned a song, being in
captivity most of his young life.

The homely hedgehog patted Sunflash's massive paw.
'By me spikes, that is a shame! No matter, my Dearie 'as
a voice like a lark at morn in a meadow, she'll cheer you
up!'

Dearie Lingl had a jolly, clear voice, and she sang
happily.

'I once 'ad a cattypillar come t'live with me,
We was both the best of friends as ever there c'd be,
He'd wiggle round upon the ground, he'd smile an'
    Shake my paw,
An' every time that I went out, stop in an' guard my
    door.
But then one time when I returned I cried out "Lack
    a day!"
My little cattypillar he had left an' gone away,
An' there upon my mantelpiece, a butterfly I saw,
Far too proud to speak to me, he flew right out the
    door.
Coloured bright in warm sunlight, that creature
    winged away,
I've never found my cattypillar to this very day,
Which makes me say unto myself, now I am old and
    wise,
I do like cattypillars, but I can't stand butterflies!'

Laughter and applause greeted Dearie's song. The two families were used to entertaining themselves, and there followed a whole repertoire of songs, poems and dances. Then, as the fire was allowed to fall into embers, they took their rest in the warm, dim cave.

Sunflash had never been so happy and contented in his life. He hummed along as one of the small hedgehogs sang herself to sleep drowsily with a curious little chant:

'Arm not alas sand, 'way south in the west,
So star land a mat, there's where I love best,
Sand not as alarm, lone seabirds do wing,
And alas most ran, list' to me whilst I sing.'

Each time the babe reached the end of this strange ditty she went back to the beginning and sang it again, her voice growing drowsier and drowsier until it was silenced by sleep. Something about the jumbled, meaningless words and the sad tune kept going round in Sunflash's mind. Finally, he shook Tirry gently, and said, 'I'm sorry to disturb you, sir, are you awake?'

'Hm, mm, just about, friend, d'you need ought?'

'That song your little daughter was singing, what is it?'

'Oh, you mean the one with all the funny mixed-up words and the nice tune. It's an old thing that my Dearie learned from her mother, she prob'ly learned it from her mother and so on, way back. All our hoglets know it, pretty tune, silly verse.'

Sunflash gazed into the glowing embers through half closed eyes, and said, 'I don't know why, but I'd like to learn it.'

Tirry smiled as he settled into a comfortable ball. 'I'll tell the babes tomorrow, they'll be only too happy to oblige ye, sir.'

4

The seasons turned through spring and summer to a mellow autumn. In the highlands of the far east, Bowfleg's drums beat out their message of warning, whilst Swartt and his ragged band of vermin traversed over tor and scrubland. The pounding drums sent word to three rat runners from Bowfleg's camp, who took off at a swift lope, heading for a long cliffrange which puckered the land like an old scar.

At the foot of the cliffs, bunched close like dirty thunderclouds, lay the tents of Bowfleg the Warlord. The runners halted beneath the purple pavilion awning of the sprawling tent at the hub of it all, and prostrated themselves in front of the circular dais. Bowfleg lolled on his throne, peering at the messengers through the puffy eyelids of his swollen features. The old ferret grunted as he leaned his gargantuan bulk forward, and asked, 'H'wodd do de dromms say?'

At the sound of the Warlord's strange accent the senior rat looked up and made his report. 'Mighty One, the drums tell of Swartt Sixclaw coming hither with a band numbering not more than twoscore.'

Bowfleg dismissed them with a snort. 'Chah! Dadd one, de runaway, met'ink 'e be longdead!'

A stoat Captain standing nearby leaned close to Bowfleg. 'Sixclaw was always spoken of as a wildbeast, a strong fighter, even when he was very young. I would watch that one, Lord.'

Bowfleg grabbed a roasted thrush from a side table and wrenched off a mouthful. 'H'Swartt, 'e can join my 'orderanks, de gudd fighter iss always of use. If nodd, I crosh 'im, like dis!' The Warlord flattened the thrush carcass against his throne with a single blow of his clenched paw. 'Bring 'im 'ere when 'e arrive!'

The stoat Captain, whose name was Greenclaw, saluted smartly and marched off.

At mid-noon Swartt Sixclaw entered the camp of Bowfleg bearing gifts – a carved spear, two belts studded with bright stones, a flagon of fine wine and a drinking cup of silver. Swartt's small band were disarmed and kept outside under guard by a detachment of swordbeasts, each of whom wore a crimson tabard bearing Bowfleg's insignia, a single white fang in a green circle. Greenclaw escorted Swartt into Bowfleg's presence. The ferret knelt respectfully, noting the giant weasel who stood behind the Warlord's throne.

The gifts were placed before Bowfleg, who turned them over with the point of his sceptre. 'Leave us now,' he ordered Greenclaw. With a snort of contempt he looked at the young ferret kneeling before him. 'When you young an' cheeky, you t'ink you better'n Bowfleg, liddle runaway, gonna bring back mooch plunder. Nobeast cudd tell Swartt anyt'ink den. Ho no, 'e knew everyt'ink. Chah! Nodd mooch for one who be's away so long, eh?'

Swartt could be a charmer when required. Smiling disarmingly, he looked up at the Warlord and shrugged. 'I can go many places an' see many things, but to learn real wisdom an' courage I return to the master.'

Bowfleg's vast bulk shook as he laughed. 'Kyahaha! Dadd's gudd, you still know who be's master!'

Swartt stretched forward and kissed Bowfleg's footpaw. 'How could I forget, Lord – you taught me all I know. I was young and foolish when I ran away from here. I am wiser now.'

The Warlord beckoned Swartt to stand upright. 'H'I'm glad to see you godd more sense, budd don't t'ink you be wiser dan me. Anybeast feel like dadd soon be's dead!'

Sixclaw turned aside so the other could not see his eyes. 'I must remember that, Lord – too much wisdom can be the death of a creature, very good!'

The old Warlord waved his sceptre at the gigantic creature standing behind his throne, saying, 'You see dis wizzel? 'E be Wurgg de Spinecracker, dis one guard me night'n'day, 'e slayed many manybeasts. You watch!'

At a nod from his master, the giant weasel stooped and lifted the throne with Bowfleg sitting on it. Showing no sign of strain or effort he held it chest high, then lowered it slowly at Bowfleg's signal.

'H'wodd you t'ink o' dadd, eh?' the fat old ferret wheezed.

Swartt was impressed. Cleverly he let his mouth fall open wide, shaking his head as if in disbelief. 'Never did I see a beast of that size or power! Lord, you have both wisdom and strength on your side, nobeast would dare to oppose you.'

Bowfleg cocked his head on one side, staring at Swartt pensively. 'Den why do you comm 'ere?'

Swartt Sixclaw sat on the top step of the dais. 'Only to serve you, Lord, and to tell you of the rich lands that lie to the south and west. Maybe one day I can travel there with you, as a Captain in your horde.'

Bowfleg rubbed a fat paw across his stomach and began to laugh. 'Kyahahakyukyuk! I don't travel nowheres, dis iss my land. H'wodd I wanna travel for,

34

godd everyt'ink right 'ere. I like you, Swartt, you young, full of de big ideas. 'Ere you come oud of nowheres, raggedytaggle! H'an' wodd you bring me, eh? Spear? I godd many spears. Belts? Nodd bigg enough. Cup an' wine? Who nidd dem?'

'The spear is a symbol of your power, Lord,' said Swartt, indicating the gifts one by one. 'The belts are a sign of my support, but the wine is special, fit only for great ones.' He uncorked the wine flagon and sniffed it delicately. 'The oldest wine of the southlands, dark and sweet with the juice of elderberry and plum, specially for you.'

He offered the bottle to Bowfleg. The Warlord sniffed it and smiled craftily. 'H'you t'ink I be stupid. 'Ere, I want to see you drink.'

Swartt took the flagon, pausing as he held it to his lips. 'You see, Lord, I learn from you all the time. If this wine were poison then I would be a deadbeast . . .' Tipping the flagon he drank deep. 'But I would be the stupid one if I offered you poisoned wine. It is good wine, the best, that's why I brought it to you.'

Bowfleg watched Swartt a moment, on the look-out for ill effects, then said, 'Give me somm, I tell you if it iss gudd wine!'

Swartt offered the bottle, then, as if remembering his manners, he pulled back and filled the big silver drinking cup, which he passed to Bowfleg.

The Warlord smiled over the rim of the cup at him. 'I still be's watchin' you. 'Ow you feel, eh?'

'Never better, sire,' Swartt chuckled, 'but if you still doubt me, then try the wine on your giant there.'

The Warlord patted the massive weasel's paw. 'Ah yiss, my h'fait'ful Wurgg, comm drink.'

The weasel lifted the chalice like an eggcup between two of his thick claws. He emptied it with a loud sucking noise and gave the cup back to his Lord with a smile and a single word: 'Good!'

Bowfleg put on a face of mock indignation as he looked up at Wurgg. 'Hoi! I say h'wodd's gudd, give me somm a dis wine!'

Swartt filled the cup three times before the greedy Warlord was satisfied. Bowfleg lounged back on the throne, confident that the new arrival posed no threat to his leadership. 'Zo, h'you back now, Sixclaw, gudd, gudd! You go now, find you'self a tent, inna mornen we spikk more togedder.'

Swartt knew he had been dismissed. He made an elegant leg, and bowed before he left the tent, saying, 'Sleep well, Lord Bowfleg!'

5

Dawn arrived wreathed in soft white mist, promising a mild sunny day. The drums beat out again over the scrub-scarred highlands, but this time the rat runners did not raise the alarm, for only one creature approached the camp. It was the vixen Nightshade, whom Swartt had purposefully instructed to follow him, leaving one day's gap between their arrivals.

The rat runners kept their distance from the fox, considering her some kind of wild mystic. Nightshade did nothing to disabuse them of the idea, indeed, she had dressed to look the part. A tatty feather-trimmed cloak swirled about her painted and mud-daubed body, and she carried a long staff decorated with bones, hanks of hair and shells. It clanked and clattered as she shook it at the runners, chanting in a reedy quaver:

'Gurgling, rattling, final breath,
Brings me from Dark Forest gate,
I, the messenger of death,
King of Darkness, Lord of Fate!'

Fires from the previous night's embers were being blown into life by a few early risers, as the runners escorted the vixen into Lord Bowfleg's hordecamp. Spying the main tent with its prominent pavilion, she made her way straight to it. Two stoat sentries guarding the closed tentflap moved nervously aside as the odd-looking fox grimaced and shook her staff at them. Nightshade stood in front of the entrance and howled a long eerie call.

'Hawoooooooo! I am the Seer! Ayaaaaaaaaaai! Death has been here!'

The runners and sentries were obviously frightened of the ragged vixen, who was now performing a crazy shuffling dance in front of the main tent. They huddled together, muttering.

'I wonder why Lord Bowfleg hasn't heard her?'

'Aye, it's strange that he hasn't sent Wurgg out to snap 'er scrawny neck an' stop 'er caterwaulin' like that.'

'Well, I'm not goin' to try an' move 'er!'

'But we can't just stand 'ere, what's t'be done?'

'I say we go an' rouse the Captains, let them sort it out.'

'Aye, good idea, mate, come on!'

As word of the vixen's arrival swept through the camp, the hordebeasts deserted tents and cooking fires en masse to follow the group of officers heading to the main tent. Two stoat Captains, Greenclaw and Aggal, together with a rat named Scraw, who was a senior Counsellor, heard all the sentries and runners had to say. They watched the vixen dancing and chanting in front of the closed pavilion entrance.

'Mightier than the Warlord,
Who must come to his call,
I am but a messenger,
Death rules over all!'

Greenclaw was made of stern stuff. He drew his sword, and rapping out orders, pushed the vixen to one side. 'Seize this one and hold 'er, I'll get t'the bottom o' this!' Greenclaw ripped the flaps aside, and strode boldly into the tent. The other officers followed him in a bunch.

Lord Bowfleg sat slumped in his chair; the giant Wurgg was seated on the top dais step, his back against the throne legs. Both creatures looked as if they were merely sleeping, but the rat Scraw could see different. He put his face close to Bowfleg's, at the same time touching his footpaw to Wurgg's limp form.

A short inspection was sufficient for Scraw. He turned to the assembly, shaking his head. 'Dead, both dead! Not a mark on either of 'em. Who could have done this?'

Greenclaw voiced his opinions so that all could hear. 'I left Lord Bowfleg and Wurgg alive and well with Swartt yesterday – let's ask him!'

The sixclawed ferret was dragged into the tent by four armed guards. He struggled free, shouting, 'Getcher claws off me or I'll flay yeh alive!'

Greenclaw had appointed himself official interrogator. 'Answer me, Swartt. What took place here yesterday when you were alone with Lord Bowfleg and Wurgg?'

'I gave Lord Bowfleg gifts,' Swartt sneered at the officious Captain, 'and he said he'd accept me into his ranks as a Captain, nothing else.'

Scraw picked up the gifts of spear, belts and wine. He shook the flagon; wine swished inside. 'Was this wine one of the gifts you brought? Did the Lord drink any?'

Swartt chuckled knowingly. 'He certainly did!'

'Did you drink the wine also?'

'No, it'd be churlish t'bring wine as a gift and then drink it.'

'Did Wurgg?'

'No, Lord Bowfleg said that the wine was too good for a clod like him, only Bowfleg drank that wine,' Swartt lied.

Scraw was nodding and smiling grimly as he thrust

the flagon towards the ferret. 'I think this wine is poisoned. Prove that it's not – take a sip.'

Swartt grabbed the flagon and drank it empty. 'Anything else y'want me t'do, rat?' he sneered.

Anger was rising in Greenclaw. He snatched the flagon from Swartt and hurled it away, growling, 'You're too smart for your own good, ferret. Why did you come here in the first place, tell me?'

Swartt spoke loud, so that the hordebeasts crowded outside the tent could hear him. 'I had no need to come here, I was doing well with my own band. Then one night I had a dream. Lord Bowfleg appeared to me and implored me to come to his side with all speed – he said that he needed my help.'

Greenclaw curled his lip derisively. 'A likely story. Bring in the fox!'

Nightshade was prodded in at spearpoint by several soldiers, who did not want to get too close to her. Greenclaw asked Swartt, 'Have you ever met this vixen before?'

'Never in the light o' day, though I often see her in dreams.'

'This is all nonsense!' snapped Greenclaw, as he paced the dais steps angrily.

The vixen shook her staff warningly at him. 'Do not mock what you cannot understand. None have seen me in this camp before, yet I knew of Lord Bowfleg's death long before I came here. I am the messenger of Death and Fate. I see visions in the stars, the wind, and the eyes of many!'

Greenclaw had heard enough. Drawing his sword, he came at the vixen. 'Did your visions tell that you'd end up dead today?'

Scraw stepped in the way, knocking the sword aside. 'Put up your weapon, stoat. The fox is a seer. It is bad luck to slay one with gifts like hers.'

'A seer, huh!' sneered Greenclaw, as he sheathed his sword with bad grace. 'Well, tell us what you see, vixen!'

Nightshade shook her staff until the shells and bones attached to it clattered ominously. She shut her eyes and wailed:

'Seasons of glory will come to the horde,
Nobeast will lack plunder while Sixclaw is Lord!'

Greenclaw was furious. He turned on Swartt, but the ferret was ready, and before the stoat Captain could unsheathe his sword, Swartt grabbed the carved spear from Aggal and slew Greenclaw.

Nightshade was still chanting and wailing:

'Allbeasts who challenge the Sixclaw will die,
Dark Forest gates will reflect in their eye!'

Swiftly she moved among the Captains, staring wildly into their eyes. To a beast they believed the seer's words, and all looked the other way, avoiding Nightshade's mad stare.

Then Swartt Sixclaw strode dramatically forward and, holding the vixen's face between both paws, he stared steadily into her eyes, saying, 'You shall be my eyes and see all for me, nobeast will be able to hide secret thoughts against me!'

Thus it was that the ferret Swartt Sixclaw became Warlord of the great horde, with only a few gifts: two belts, a spear, a good flagon of wine, and one other thing – a silver drinking cup whose rim and inside had been smeared with deadly poison!

With that and a clever vixen he had won the day.

The entire horde gathered around a small hillock to hear their new Warlord announce his plans. Swartt had repainted the green and purple stripes upon his face and coated his fangs with fresh red dye. Drawing his curved sword from the wide snakeskin belt he whirled in a circle, and a magnificent bright blue velvet cloak, which he had plundered from Bowfleg's belongings, swirled around his muscular body. He pointed the sword at the main tent, which still contained the bodies of Bowfleg and Wurgg, and cried aloud, 'Burn!'

From high on the cliffs a score of weasel archers fired flaming arrows down into the brushwood-laden tent. In moments the whole thing was ablaze. The firelight danced in Swartt's eyes as he held up his sixclawed paw for all to see.

'This is what you follow from now on, Sixclaws! No more lying about in these hills and scrublands, no more idling under a fatbeast who was too lazy to move! Take down your tents and pack them for travel: today we move west and south to the lands of plenty. Food, plunder, captives! All of these you will have if you follow me into the sunwarmed lands. Aye, me, Swartt Sixclaw the Warlord!'

The earth trembled as the massive horde stamped their footpaws and hammered down their spearbutts. A mighty roar rose up like thunder as it echoed from the cliffs.

'Sixclaaaaaaaw!'

Tents were flattened and rolled, drums beat ominously, and banners with the new Sixclaw symbol unfurled on the autumn breeze.

The ferret bared his reddened teeth at the vixen by his side. 'Now let's see if Sunflash the Mace can pick this lot off one by one. Hahahahahaaaaa!'

6

The year turned, and bright spring became bounteous summer. Sunflash the Mace straightened up from his labours, arching his mighty back. The two little mole-maids Nilly and Podd imitated his movements impishly.

'That's enough potatoes for one day, good work!' he said, winking at them.

'Hurr, an' thurr be lots o' taters left furr another toime.'

'Ho aye, leave'm in ee ground t'get 'ooj an' gurtly tastyful.'

The big badger looked around at the neat rows he had created last autumn, clearing bush and moving rock until a sizeable food garden bloomed in the forest amid the hills and woodland. Bordered by several fruit trees, plum, apple and pear, already growing there, plus a couple of horse chestnuts further back, the crops cut straight furrows. Leek, onion, potato, turnip, peas and cabbage all thrived, with mushrooms to be found every few days in the dark shelter of a rocky slab to one side of the chestnuts. There would be berries later, redcurrant, blackberry, raspberry and strawberry. Sunflash had worked hard alongside his friends, and they had taught him about growing things. He liked cultivating the land, finding he had a natural flair as a farmer.

Sweeping the tiny molemaids up with both paws, Sunflash deposited them on top of the basket of vegetables they had gathered. With a single swing he lifted the basket onto one shoulder and strode off towards the dwelling cave of the Lingl and Dubbo clan. Sunflash's deep voice blended harmoniously with the two moles' as all three sang the riddle song:

'Arm not alas sand, 'way south in the west,
So star land a mat, there's where I love best,
Sand not as alarm, lone seabirds do wing,
And alas most ran, list' to me whilst I sing.'

Skarlath was sunning himself in the rocks above the cave, watching Dearie Lingl, Aunt Ummer and Bruff's wife Lully preparing lunch on the grass. Old Uncle Blunn came coughing out of the cave in a cloud of dust, followed by the four small hoglets with Tirry and Bruff. They sat on the grass, dusting their coats down.

Tirry sneezed and blinked, saying, 'Bright ole day out 'ere, ain't it!'

Sunflash marched up, nodding to one and all. Carefully he lifted the basket down, with the two molemaids sitting atop. 'Some nice button mushrooms in here for you, Dearie,' he said. 'How's the store chamber coming along, Bruff?'

The mole pawed dust from his eyes as he answered, 'Near dunn, zurr, we'm jus' abowt finished. Lined et wi' those rock slabs you'm found larst wintur, lukks 'andsome, bo urr!'

Lully used her apron to protect her paws as she gingerly removed a large flat pie from the rock oven Sunflash had made. 'Us'n's got lots o' things dunn since ee been yurr, zurr. Lookit, apple'n'blackb'rry pie, yore fav'rite!'

Sunflash sniffed the aroma, his gold-striped face alight with pleasure.

44

'Come away, 'oglets, you'll burn yore snouts agin' that 'ot thing.' Dearie shooed the four hoglets off as they crowded round to smell the pie. 'Wait'll it cools an' I'll give ye a big slice each.'

Old Uncle Blunn took the hoglets and the two mole-maids off to the stream, which was only a short walk away. Flagons of dandelion and burdock cordial, brewed by Blunn, were submerged in the streamwater to keep cool.

'Wash ee dusty pawo'n'snouts in yon stream, ee mucky liddle vurmints, aye an' ee too, Blunn Dubbo!' Aunt Ummer called after them.

Dearie bustled about preparing salad from the fresh vegetables whilst Skarlath waddled off behind Lully, who was going to test a cheese she had been turning since early last winter. The good molewife smiled fondly at the kestrel, whom she considered to be her special friend. 'On moi loif, zurr, oi never see'd an 'awkburd oo luvved cheeses more'n ee. Cumm naow, us'll try et furr taste, hurr.'

Skarlath eagerly assisted her to roll the cheese out of the cave's dark recesses, where it had been maturing. He had helped make the oval-shaped cheese, right from the greensap milk stage, pounding tirelessly at the fat white grass stems and special tubers, which only true woodlanders knew of. They had gathered nuts together in late autumn, hazel, almond and chestnuts, to stud their cheese with. Between them, the kestrel and the molewife peeled off the thin layer of damp crack willow bark which protected the cheese. It had no rind and was a delicate pale yellow colour. A fragrance of almond drifted faintly about them.

Skarlath hopped from talon to talon, his fierce eyes shining. 'Kraaaah! Is it ready, marm, shall we taste it?'

The good molewife shook as she chuckled, 'Aye, you'm surpintly shall taste et, zurr, hurr hurr hurr!'

Taking a thin, greased twine from her apron pocket,

45

Lully wound the ends round her digging claws and looped the twine over the cheese just below its top, then, placing both footpaws flat against the base of the cheese, she leaned backward pulling evenly on the twine. The molewife was well experienced in all aspects of cheese-making. Skarlath watched fascinated as the strong twine travelled smoothly through the cheese, neatly cutting a large oval piece from the top of their creation. Standing on its edge the slice resembled an oddly-shaped harvest moon, with the white of the nuts and thin slivers of their brown skins highlighted against the buttercup hue of the cheese. Breaking two small pieces off, Lully gave one to her friend. They nibbled daintily, commenting.

'Bo urr, ee be noice'n moist wi' gudd flavour, aye!'

'Mmm, wonderful nutty taste, good and firm!'

'Ho aye, none too solid, none too soft, us'n's dunn well!'

Paw shook talon as the cheesemakers congratulated each other.

On the sward outside the dwelling cave the older creatures lay about watching the young ones play. It had been a satisfying lunch: summer salad served with Lully and Skarlath's new cheese, and fresh oatfarls baked by Auntie Ummer, followed by the magnificent apple and blackberry pie which Lully and Dearie had cooked, all washed down with beakers of old Uncle Blunn's dandelion and burdock cordial, brought specially cooled from the stream. Sunflash stretched luxuriously and set his back against the sunwarmed rocks as he watched the babes trying to lift his mace between them.

Tirry smiled at their efforts as he sprawled beside the big badger. ' 'Twill be many a long season afore they lift that thing, friend.'

Sunflash shook his massive head. 'Tirry, let us hope that they never have to. Learning the trade of a warrior and living in times of danger can rob a young creature of all its happy seasons, and make it grow up fast and hard, as I did. Peace is a precious thing.'

'You brought peace here for our families,' said the hedgehog, as he patted Sunflash's paw. 'You look peaceful an' well content, Sunflash. Mayhap you like our life?'

The badger had a distant look in his dark eyes. 'Oh, I do like the life here. I am happier in this place than I have ever been and I wish dearly that I could live out all my seasons with you and your families on this very spot.'

Tirry Lingl spread his paws at the happy scene surrounding them. 'Then why not? You are greatly loved here – make this your home.'

It was a tempting proposition. Sunflash thought of the crops and the garden he had created, and the dwelling cave, which was larger now and more comfortable due to his help. Fondly he watched the little ones, laughing and rolling about in the bright noon sun. The older ones too, Aunt Ummer, Uncle Blunn and the rest, were all firm friends, trusting creatures, taking their ease together. His loyal companion Skarlath, a hawk, was happy to learn the simple life. It was idyllic. He knew it could not last.

Weighing his words carefully, he explained to Tirry. 'Listen to what I must say, friend. If I stayed here it would mean great trouble, possibly death for those around me. I have told you of Swartt Sixclaw, the evil ferret. Make no mistake, if I make this place my home, then he will turn up here one day with his band. But even if he did not, my warrior spirit would grow restless and I would need to go and seek him out. We are sworn lifelong enemies, he and I.

'However, beside all that there are my dreams. Always I see the mountain of fire looming through my slumbers, and strange voices of other badgers, Warrior Lords whose names I do not know, call me. Why I must go to the mountain, where it is, what name it goes by, I do not know. But I am certain that my fate and destiny are bound to the mountain. Each night I dream, and the urge to travel there goes surging through me. One morning you will wake to find me gone. I am as sure of it as the turning of seasons, Tirry.'

Hiding his sorrow and disappointment the hedgehog murmured, 'I knew all this afore you told me, I felt it every time I looked at your face. You have worked hard here, but only to put things from your mind. But enough o' this, mate, we're gettin' so gloomy we'll 'ave it rainin' afore nightfall! You're still a youngbeast with a great life ahead of ye, Sunflash. But promise me this – you won't go without sayin' goodbye.'

'I promise you, Tirry Lingl, I won't leave without a goodbye!'

All through that afternoon they took their well earned leisure, often joining the young ones at play. Skarlath took off to go on one of his high-flying, wide-ranging patrols, leaving word that he would be back by supper. Sunflash took himself off to the stream where he sat cooling his footpaws in the warm shallows, trying to fathom out the riddle song.

'Arm not alas sand, 'way south in the west,
So star land a mat, there's where I lo—'

Bruff Dubbo's voice interrupted his musings. 'Ho, zurr, you'm see'd ought o' those two liddle 'ogs Gurmil an' Tirg?'

Sunflash stamped his footpaws dry in the grass. 'Haven't seen them since lunchtime. Why?'

Bruff scratched his head with a heavy digging claw. 'Seems loik they'm got theyselves losted, hurr!'

Back at the cave, Dearie was questioning the other babes, without much success. Gurmil and Tirg were the two little malehogs. Their sisters Bitty and Giller had been playing with the small molemaids Nilly and Podd, and none of the four were making much sense, as is usual with babes.

Dearie was worried but patient. 'Now think careful, liddle uns, where'd they two scamps go to?'.

Bitty pointed at the sky. 'Flied 'way, up there!'

'No, no, they never, that was Mister Skarlath the 'awkburd. Lack a day, I do wish 'e were 'ere now. Nilly, do you know where Gurmil'n'Tirg might be?'

'Hurr, a playen in ee water, oi think.'

'No, that was Sunflash, 'e was at the stream. Oh, where 'ave those two liddle villains run off to?'

She stared up at Sunflash beseechingly. The big badger radiated calm and confidence as he patted Dearie's headspikes gently. 'Never fear, marm, I'll find 'em. Tirry, you circle to the east. Bruff, take a wide loop west. I'll go due south, and we'll meet up where the big clearing is, the one with the pond, you know it.'

Lully threw her apron up over her face to hide her upset. 'Burr, they'm rascals, oi do wish't zurr 'awkburd was 'ere!'

Bruff twitched his nose comfortingly at her. 'Doan't ee fret, moi damsen, us'll foind em. You'm stay by yurr wi' Dearie an' watch t'uther liddle uns.'

Sunflash did not travel directly south. The late afternoon sun played through the leaves, casting mottled shade patterns on his broad back, as he weaved through the woodlands on either side of the faint south path, searching wherever he thought the two little hoglets might have strayed. Birdsong trilled in the stillness of the noontide heat, butterflies fluttered their quiet way from shrub to bush, and bees droned lazily amid clumps of bramble, honeysuckle and dogrose. But the tranquillity of nature was lost upon the badger as he strode anxiously about, his great mace swinging from one paw, searching for signs of the hedgehog babes.

At last he found something. It was only small – a

fragment of apple and blackberry pie crust – but it proved that they had passed this way. They were roaming south. Further on, Sunflash chased away a bold blackbird that was pecking at a small morsel of cheese. He quickened his stride. Gurmil and Tirg had to be somewhere hereabouts.

Suddenly a welter of cries and shouts broke upon his ears. Sunflash went thundering and crashing through the woodland and came bounding out into the clearing where he had arranged to meet with Bruff and Tirry. His quick eyes took in the dangerous situation at a single glance. There were the two little hoglets, frightened speechless, clinging on to each other, standing shoulder deep in the pond at the far side of the clearing. Bruff and Tirry, in company with an old squirrel, were circling and shouting. And a short distance from the water's edge, between them, barring their way to the babes, two fully grown adders coiled and reared menacingly. The snakes had not yet seen Sunflash, who slowed his pace immediately and signalled to his friends not to look directly at him and betray his presence to the reptiles.

Tirry Lingl was terrified, but willing to sacrifice his life for the hoglets. He picked up anything close to paw – twigs, soil, grass – and flung it at the big scaly adders, his voice shrill with panic. 'Leave my liddle uns alone, serpents! Don't you go near 'em! Gurmil, Tirg, stay in the water, stop there!'

The old squirrel joined in the shouting. He obviously knew the snakes and hated them. 'Gah, you cold-'earted slimers, leave the babes alone!'

One adder faced the three creatures, menacing them as the other snake began sliding slowly towards the little ones in the water. Cold evil glittered in the snake's eyes, and its forked tongue quivered as it hissed, 'Leave here fasssssst, while you ssstill have livessssss!'

Suddenly, Sunflash made his move. Dropping the

mace, he ran into the lake from one side, pounding in a straight line across the shallows towards the hoglets. The adder who had been sliding towards the water speeded up; it was fast, but not as speedy as Sunflash the Mace when his warrior blood was roused. The badger reached the babes ahead of the snake, snatched them both out of the water with a single movement, and carried on hurtling straight across the shallows. The adder was after Sunflash, zipping through the roiling waters in his wake, as duckweed and rushes broken off by the badger's storming speed flopped wetly on the pond's surface. The other snake turned away from the three creatures on the bank, its coils bunching and stretching as it raced to intercept the badger.

Sunflash leapt from the water and, bursting onto dry land, he rolled the babes, who had tucked themselves up into the refuge of their soft prickles. They skimmed over the bank like twin orbs, coming to rest way out of danger. Sunflash turned as the adder launched itself from the water and buried its sharp fangs in his side. Its companion wrapped itself round one of the badger's footpaws. Roaring aloud, Sunflash grabbed the snake that was biting him around its neck and plunged back into the water with the other adder still wrapped round his footpaw. Tirry grabbed the hoglets, hugging them to him as Bruff and the old squirrel raced about in the shallows. Unable to help the badger, they splashed and shouted.

Sunflash did not come to a halt until he was in deep, the water lapping near his shoulders. Feeling the snake unwinding itself from his footpaw, he stamped down hard several times until he trapped its head, flat beneath his big blunt claws on the bed of the pond, and held it there. The other snake had struck him twice, once in the side and once on his back, and now it slid off him into the water. But Sunflash caught it by the tail and began whirling it round above his head. Round and round it

went, the creatures on shore hearing the whirr it made
as it cut the air in blurring circles. Sunflash roared.

'Eeulaliaaaaa!'

He flung the adder far and high, and it sped through
the air straight out like an arrow from a bow. Tirry
looked up and saw it strike an elm tree limb. The snake's
body wrapped round it several times, then it was still,
resting draped across the high bough like a soggy piece
of rope.

Sunflash ground down hard with his footpaw for a
long time, until the wriggling coils beneath the water
went limp and still for ever. Then, slowly, painfully,
he began wading back to land, his side and back one
throbbing, agonized mass. The big badger tottered in
the shallows as Tirry, Bruff and the squirrel dashed
in and helped him out.

Bruff wrung his paws agitatedly as Sunflash collapsed
on the bank. 'Yurr, ee been bited by ee surrpints, oi
knows et!'

The old squirrel grabbed Sunflash's face between both
paws and shouted as the badger's eyelids began flickering shut. 'Where did yon serpents bite thee?' he cried.

Sunflash was sinking into a black pit; he heard the
words coming from far away. Making an effort, he
answered, 'Bitten . . . twice . . . side . . . back . . .'

Then darkness overtook Sunflash the Mace completely.

7

The sun broiled the flatlands mercilessly, drying up
streams to a trickle, baking the earth and raising dust
swirls on the hot wind. It was a hostile waste where
even scrub, gorse and broom barely survived in the
parched heat.

Things were not going well for the new Warlord
Swartt Sixclaw; there was a murmur of discontent running through the great horde. Swartt sat in his tent pon-
dering the dilemma facing him: too many soldiers and
not enough food or water, and worst of all, they were
lost! The mighty cavalcade had started out on the wrong
paw. Some had wanted to go, swayed by Swartt's promises of plunder and plenty, but others had wanted to
stay, knowing they could get by in the semi-fertile cliff
shadows, where there was at least water and a certain
amount of vegetation, birds and eggs. The whole project
had been too unwieldy from the outset, with tents, trap-
pings and camp followers, most of the hordebeasts
having mates and families.

Sometimes Swartt felt as though he were merely the
figurehead of a great travelling settlement; and as if that
were not enough, he had found himself landed with a
wife. Swartt had not known that Bowfleg had a

daughter. It was the tradition and unwritten law that she became wife to the new Warlord as a matter of course. Bluefen was her name, and she was quiet and pretty enough. Swartt marvelled that such a fat ugly creature as Bowfleg could have sired her. Bluefen largely kept out of Swartt's way, as she had with her father, knowing the angry moods and great rages Warlords were capable of.

Swartt dismissed his wife from his mind and concentrated his thoughts on horde problems. How they had lost direction on the desert-like flatlands was anybeast's guess, but he blamed the vixen Nightshade. She should have been calculating their direction while his time was taken up dealing with more important horde matters. Swartt had berated her soundly, sending her off three nights back to find water and food and to get them back on the right trail, south and west. To make doubly sure, he had sent his two killers with her, the weasels Scarback and Marbul. When he had taken command of the horde, these two had immediately caught the eye of Swartt. They were ambitious and ruthless, cold-hearted assassins, just the types he needed to do his secret biddings.

Outside the tent Swartt could hear the horde as they pitched camp. Travel on the hot windswept plains was impossible at noon – they would move again when eventide cooled the land slightly. Bluefen slipped quietly into the tent, placed a flagon at Swartt's side and hurried out. The Warlord hardly noticed she had been and gone; absently, he knocked the stopper out of the flagon and sipped from it. Pulling a face, he spat out the brackish-tasting water, which hit the footpaw of the stoat Trattak as he entered the tent. Swartt beckoned him inside swiftly, saying, 'Shut the tentflap, I don't want everybeast seein' you report t'me. Are they still at it?'

Trattak pulled the tentflap closed.

'Aye, Lord, it's as you said. Wildag the ferret Captain

and his toady, the rat they call Lardtail, they're the two. I hung about close to them, all's they do is go from tent to tent talkin' about you be'ind yore back.'

Swartt placed the flagon on the ground and sat down by it. 'What do they say, tell me? Speak, don't be afraid.'

Trattak swallowed hard and crouched close to his master. 'They say you've got us all lost and y'don't know where yore goin',' he said in low, halting tones. 'Also they say you ain't fit t'be Warlord an' that you eat all the best food an' drink fine wines from silver goblets while good 'onest 'ordebeasts are starvin' . . . an' . . .'

Swartt Sixclaw nodded understandingly. 'Go on, what else? I know it's their words an' not yours.'

Trattak continued, a little more confident. 'They say that a dagger between yore ribs'd solve a lot o' problems, then they could go back an' live by the cliffs where things were a lot better. Any'ow, Wildag's called a meetin' secret like, tonight. All the Captains'll be there.'

Swartt patted Trattak, noticing the stoat eyeing the flagon. 'You did well. Take this if yore thirsty – it ain't fine wine, only muddy water, but it'll do to wet yer throat with. Send Nightshade t'me the moment she gets back. Go on now, keep an eye out for 'er.'

The vixen returned at twilight. Swartt had not given the order to move on; the horde had stayed camped in the same place since noon. Leaving the two weasel assassins outside the tent, Nightshade went in to make her report.

Swartt watched her as she laid a lumpy sack in front of him. 'The news better be good, fox – speak!' he snarled.

Words spilled from the vixen's mouth like water from a pitcher. 'The word is good, Lord, I have found the southwest trail again – two days' trek should take us out of these desert lands. There is a broad stream, fresh water, small copses with trees and grassy hills. There is food there, fish, birds, and fruit. Look!'

She emptied out the sack, which contained roots, tubers and a couple of russet apples, plus a dead bird which the vixen held up for Swartt's inspection.

'Your weasels Scarback and Marbul killed this bird with slings and stones,' she said. 'There are many like it where we have been.'

Swartt munched on an apple as he turned the carcass with his swordpoint. He shook his head in disgust. 'It's a crow, and an old one at that. You tryin' t'poison me?'

Before the vixen could answer, Swartt shoved the dead crow back into the sack and laughed wickedly. 'Never mind, it'll come in handy before the night's through. Well, at least we ain't lost any more. Go an' get some sleep, I'll be movin' the horde out at the double tomorrow. Send the weasels in here.'

The ferret Wildag was older than Swartt, though not as big, and his ally Lardtail was a grumpy, fat, oversized rat. By the light of a flickering fire at the outer edge of the camp, the two faced a sizeable gathering of Captains and assorted hordebeasts, all of whom were disaffected with the leadership of Sixclaw. Wildag addressed the meeting, backed up by Lardtail's whining comments.

'Well, how does it feel t'be lost an' starvin', buckoes?'

Lardtail stepped up. 'Aye, all I've had since dawn is a few roots an' a mouthful o' dirty water – it's not good enough, mates!'

A voice called out of the crowd, 'There's nought out 'ere but sand an' wind, but if we starve then at least Sixclaws will too!'

Wildag's paw jabbed the air as he shook his head vigorously. 'Swartt Sixclaw starve? Huh, that's a good un, tell 'em, Lardtail!'

'I seen that vixen of his sneakin' into camp this evenin'. She went straight to Swartt's tent, carryin' a sack of vittles!'

Wildag waved his paws to silence the outraged

hubbub. 'Did you 'ear that, friends, a sack of food! I'll wager the scum's sittin' in 'is tent right now, drinkin' wine an' stuffin' a roasted duck down his greedy gullet!'

Amid the uproar that followed a sack flew through the air, and struck Wildag in the face. Furiously he grabbed the sack and shook it at the assembly. 'Who threw this?' he yelled.

Swartt stepped into the firelight, his painted face and redstained fangs highlighted by the flames. Silence fell instantly upon the gathering. Showing no fear or concern, the Warlord winked at the two conspirators and rubbed his paws together in front of the fire. 'Gets a bit chilly 'ere at night when the sun goes in. You cold, Wildag, hungry maybe?'

The Captain was at a loss for words and, sensing something awful was about to happen, Lardtail began shuffling backward.

'Stay where y'are, rat, or I'll gut ye!'

Lardtail froze, noting that Scarback and Marbul, the two assassins, had materialized out of nowhere and were flanking him.

Swartt spoke to the would-be mutineers in a reasonable tone. 'I've heard that some are sayin' we're lost? Now what sort of a Warlord would get his horde lost? Two days from here is a broad stream of fresh water, food, fruit growin' on the trees. Would I be lost if I knew this? An' I tell you somethin' else, the further on we travel, the better it gets – greener, fatter, richer. I don't tell lies, you'll see.'

He picked up the sack and faced the ferret Captain. 'But as for you, my friend, I don't think you was tellin' the truth when you said I was drinkin' wine an' eatin' roast duck. If I was, then I'd make sure everybeast got the same as me.'

A sob escaped Wildag's lips, and he began to tremble. Swartt patted the Captain's back reassuringly. 'Oh come on now, bucko, cheer up, ole Sixclaw don't like to see anybeast unhappy or 'ungry. I'm willin' t'share my vittles with you, but to show you I'm a real comrade I'll let you 'ave it all for yoreself.'

He tipped the old dead crow out of the sack, smiling companionably at Wildag. 'As y'can see, it ain't no roast duck, but yore welcome to it.' Then, pinching Lardtail's ear cruelly in his claws, Swartt marched the rat over to the crow carcass. 'Pick it up, matey, there's a good rat,' he said. 'D'you want some?'

Hauled up on tip-paw by his ear the rat whined, 'No, Lord, I ain't 'ungry!'

Hordebeasts are fickle creatures at best, and now some of the gathering began chuckling as they realized what Swartt was up to. The Warlord winked at them, knowing they would be firmly on his side after he had asserted his power. Wagging his chain-mailed sixclaw in the rat's face he explained firmly, 'Wildag's yore mate, so I want you to feed this to 'im right now, all of it. Meat, bone, claws, feathers, beak, the lot! Show Wildag that Swartt is a real friend. I ain't just sharin' it with 'im, I'm givin' 'im it all out of the goodness of me 'eart.'

Roars of laughter from the pitiless hordebeasts rang out as the two assassins grabbed Wildag in preparation for his awful meal. Swartt silenced them with a wave of his mailed paw. 'I'm goin' to my tent now. I'll eat at the same time we all do, in two days' time, or sooner if we march fast. Meanwhile, don't go mutterin' an' meetin' among yoreselves, come to me. If you have anythin' to complain about I'll always listen.'

Cheers rang in the Warlord's ears as he strode off into the night. He smiled to himself. The horde were with him once more.

The following morning was hot as usual, though not as windy. Swartt waited until the tents were packed and the last rations issued before he stood to address the horde. They gathered around, banners fluttering in the light breeze, drums beating until the entire army stood waiting. Swartt knew that if he was to stay Warlord the one thing he must do was to instil fear of his powers into the hordebeasts. He did not want their affection or comradeship – to Swartt that was mere weakness. Respect and loyalty were only gained by one thing in the ferret's mind. Fear! He demonstrated it fully on that morn in front of his horde.

The rat Lardtail cringed on the ground, flanked by Scarback and Marbul, the two weasel assassins.

'I don't see our Captain Wildag about, where is he?' Swartt Sixclaw's voice rang out commandingly.

Marbul, so called because one of his eyes was a sightless white orb, spoke for the trembling rat. 'Wildag's dead, my Lord!'

Swartt managed to look both concerned and astounded. 'Dead, how did he die?' he asked.

Scarback kicked the quivering Lardtail contemptuously. 'This stupid blunderer killed him by feedin' him a dead crow – beak, feathers, claws, the lot! Pore Wildag choked.'

Swartt shook his head in disbelief. 'Choked eh? Somebeast is goin' to pay for chokin' a Captain!'

Lardtail's voice was a strangled sob of protest. 'But Lord, you told me to feed the bird to Wildag. I was only carrying out yore orders!'

The mailed sixclaw pointed accusingly at the unfortunate rat. 'You liar! I never ordered you to kill Wildag, only to feed him. The penalty for slaying a horde Captain is death!'

Lardtail screamed and grovelled in front of the Warlord. 'No, Sire, please! Spare me, Lord Sixclaw!'

Swartt turned his back on Lardtail, nodding to Scarback and Marbul as he did. Their daggers flashed in the morning sunlight. Turning back to the horde, Swartt did not even bother glancing down at the slain rat. A chilling silence fell over the mighty army.

Swartt hammered the lesson home with harsh callousness. 'Lardtail's learned his lesson, so has Wildag. I am Swartt Sixclaw, Warlord of all this horde! I see all, I know all, I hear all! Look at the beast standin' next to you – he could be one of my spies. I have many, this is the lesson you must learn. Even thoughts cannot be hidden from me, I can read your mind just by your eyes. I see some of you lookin' away from my gaze, but that won't help. My vixen seer Nightshade can read thoughts with her eyes closed! Listen now, every slab-sided, droolin', misbegotten mother's whelp of yeh! Yore mine to the death, everybeast! Wherever we go I will conquer all. Bowfleg was ruler of the east scrublands. Hah! I will be Warlord of the whole country! None will stand in my way and you will see to this! If I say march, starve, fight, die! – you will do it without question. This means everybeast, females, young and families! It is two days' march to food and water, and we'll do it by tomorrow noon. There'll be no stragglers – keep up or die. Drummers, beat double march time. Now!'

The drums beat a fierce tattoo as the entire horde moved forward at double their normal marching pace. Heavy cooking utensils and cumbersome possessions were littered in the wake of the marchers as each tried to keep up with the other. Swartt strode out in front, the vixen at his side showing him the route. At the rear of the horde Marbul and Scarback trotted, blades at the ready to deal with stragglers or deserters. The lesson was being learned, and Swartt had added another title to his name – the Pitiless One!

8

High above the dustclouds of Swartt's army, far out of range from arrow or slingstone, four crows flew like ragged black specks against the sky. Two of the birds broke off and wheeled south, leaving the other two watching the horde of Sixclaw. Soaring on the high thermals and using the breeze, the first two crows were out of the desert regions and into the fertile hill lands by noon. Circling swiftly, they dropped into a copse of pines.

Krakulat, Ruler of the Crow Brethren, sat immobile on a pine stump, his plumage covered in earth, dust and pine needles. The huge bird was grieving for his mother, and none dared come near him. The two scouts landed a respectful distance away and waited until Krakulat's wife Bonebeak waddled up to them before making their report.

'Rakkaaa! The vermin are as many as grains of sand blown by the wind, they come this way. Tomorrow when the sun is this high we will see them, Lady Bonebeak.'

The fierce female called to her husband. 'Yaggaaa! Did you hear that? The ones who slew your mother are coming to this place!'

Krakulat's talons sunk into the bark of the pine stump

with rage; his bloodshot eyes widened with anticipation as he rasped hoarsely to the trees about him, 'Harrkaa! Tomorrow will be the dying day for many vermin, do you hear me, my Brethren? Krakulat has spoken!'

A deafening din arose from the copse as hundreds of savage crows set up a mighty cawing. Krakulat shook his feathers until dust and needles flew about him. Blueblack and beautifully iridescent, the mighty bird nodded his frightening beak up and down in a stabbing movement, screaming, 'Karraaaa! There will be many vermin for our eggchicks to pick over as the sun whitens the bones of those who slew my mother!'

Sunflash the Mace saw the gates of Dark Forest. He lay on the ground as they began opening before him, slowly, oh so slowly; without sound of a creak, the mistshrouded timbers moved. He felt his body being drawn towards them and could not resist, did not want to resist; the burning pains within him eased as he felt the desire to enter Dark Forest and rest. As the gates opened wider he saw two mighty Badger Lords, fully armoured. One carried a fearsome sword, the other a double-headed axe. Now a third badger joined them. This one was simply clad and carried no weapons; he smiled at Sunflash.

'My little Sunflash, do you not know me?' he said.

Sunflash smiled back through the tears that welled in his eyes. 'Father!'

'Yes, my son, I am Barkstripe, husband of your mother, Bella of Brocktree. These two Badger Lords are Boar the Fighter, your grandsire, and Lord Brocktree, your great grandsire. Listen to them now, they have something important to tell you.'

Boar the Fighter and Lord Brocktree barred the gate entrance with sword and axe and spoke as one.

'You cannot enter here, Lord!'

Sunflash felt a great sadness come over him. He wanted to join his sires, not to be rejected by them. He felt alone and helpless. 'Why do you refuse me entrance when I am weary and wish to sleep, and why do you call me Lord?' he asked

Again the sepulchral tones of the Badger Warriors rang out: 'There are many long seasons to be lived before you come here. Do not surrender, rise up, the mountain awaits you! It is in need of a Badger Lord!'

Inside the cave dwelling, the squirrel, who was called Elmjak, rubbed his back ruefully. 'Mine old bones be yet stiff from all that dragging and pulling, 'twas the hardest day's work in many a long season, friends, thanks to thy rush mat, goodwife Lully.'

The molewife peeked over her apron top. 'Hurr, ee ole rush mat'll be wore'd out arter draggen it all that way wi' zurr badger layin' on et, aye, wore'd out loik us'n's be.'

Outside, the little molemaids and hoglets played on the sward under a soft morning sun. Unaware of how close to death Sunflash lay, they had invented a new game, as infants will, fighting off adders. The two little molemaids clung to each other shrieking, 'Eee! 'Elp 'elp, ee surrpints be a goin' to eat us'n's oop!'

Gurmil and Tirg were jointly pretending to be Sunflash. 'Stop still – we'll save ee!'

Bitty and Giller the two little hogmaids stood on the sidelines, yelling, 'Better save'm quick afore they get etted up!'

'Gurr! Go 'way, nasty ole snakers!' Gurmil and Tirg roared, as they thrashed imaginary adders. 'Yah, slinky stinky ole slimy snakes, take tha'!'

Dearie Lingl hurried out with a paw on her lips. 'Shush, 'ush now, liddle uns! Keep yore noise down, we got a very sick badger to nurse in there, do be quiet, please!'

The babes halted their game and clung to her apron.

'Whoi do ee gurt Sunflasher be sicked, marm?'

'Badgers be too big to get sicked!'

'Ee surrpints bited 'im, twenny 'undred toimes!'

'Will Sunflasher get deaded?'

'Ee squirrel make 'im better oi thinks, hurr!'

Dearie rummaged in her apron pocket until she came up with some dried apple pieces, which she gave them, saying, 'Sunflash'll only get well if you keep very quiet. Be good beasts now, try not to make too much noise, my liddle buttons.'

They sat in a row on the grass, watching each other as they ate.

'You'm chewen orful loud, Maister Gurmil!'

'I can't 'elp it, 'tis a noisy apple piece I got.'

'Hurr, then keep ee mouth shutted!'

'Then I won't able to talk!'

'Gudd, that keep ee soilent, hurr hurr!'

Elmjak the squirrel was old and wise. He sat at table with Tirry, Lully and Bruff, and all four took a breakfast of mint tea and wild oat scones spread with honey. They ate in silence, watching the badger. Sunflash lay on his pallet of rushes and fragrant dried grass, and Skarlath hovered over him. The kestrel had not moved from his friend's side for two days and nights.

Dearie crept softly in and tugged Skarlath's back plumage gently. 'Come an' eat now, sir 'awk, or we'll end up nursin' you too.'

Skarlath followed her reluctantly and they joined the others.

Sunflash moaned softly and tried to turn over. Elmjak hurried to his side and calmed him, bathing the badger's fevered brow with dampened dock leaves. He checked the poultices which he had applied to his patient's wounds, saying, 'This one will live, mayhap. Never did I see a beast of such strength; no creature known to me could live through even one adder bite. Look at him now, friends, sleeping like a babe!'

Tirry poured a beaker of the fragrant mint tea for Elmjak. 'More power to yore good poultices, sir, they seem to work right well indeed. You must tell us 'ow t'make them.'

The recipe for the poultices had been in Elmjak's family for long generations, and now he recited it for his new friends:

'If beast be bit by fang of snake,
And lying near Dark Forest gate,
This ancient poultice you must make,
To thwart the paws of fate.
Find berries from the rowan tree,
Add one small green pine cone,
With young leaf of raspberry,
Pounded flat beneath a stone.
Heat o'er a flame 'til coloured dark,
Stir fast to make a paste of it,
Bind hot and tight with aspen bark,
Unto the limb the serpent bit.
Change oft from dawn until nightfall,
Make sure the beast lies still,
Mayhap he'll live to thank us all,
If he be strong of will!'

Bruff Dubbo wagged a sizeable digging claw in the big badger's direction. 'Burrhoo! Nobeast be stronger than ee gurt zurr Sunflash!'

Dearie Lingl agreed wholeheartedly with him. 'Great seasons! Who ever heard of a beast so mighty that he slayed two poisonteeth after bein' struck twice by 'em?'

It had been hard and wearisome getting Sunflash from the pond back to the cave and caring night and day for him, and sleep had only been snatched in fits and starts.

Now, with the badger resting peacefully, there was some long overdue slumber time. Mid-morning was calm and warm, and the friends relaxed on the grass outside. Tiring of their games, the little ones sprawled beside their elders. It was not long before gentle summer cast its spell and, amid distant birdsong and the lazy hum of bees, they were soon dozing off.

However, Gurmil and Tirg did not take kindly to sleeping all day. Shortly before noon they were wide awake. Whispering and chuckling to each other, they tip-pawed past the slumbering elders and made their way into the cave. But they had not gone unnoticed: their sisters Bitty and Giller, followed by the molemaids Nilly and Podd, came hurrying after them.

They threw their little aprons over their faces in imitation of their mothers.

'Gurt seasons, you'm villyuns, wot be ee a doin' in yurr?'

'Come away now, you'm wake Sunflash!'

But Gurmil and Tirg were determined to visit their hero. 'Garr, we b'ain't wakin' 'im, on'y come'd to sing the song nice an' quiet. Sunflash likes the song.'

They gathered round the huge form of the sleeping badger. Nilly twitched her button nose cautiously, saying, 'Us'n's best be singen quiet, lest ee 'awkburd 'ears an' eaten us'n's all oop wi' ee gurt beak!'

Tiny paws stroked the great golden-striped muzzle as the babes sang soft and low.

Dark Forest and its dread gates had receded from Sunflash's dreams; now he wandered lonely through sunlit vales and flower-strewn hillsides. Lying down in the cool shade of a great oak, he looked up at the sky. A shadow passed over him and a face appeared; Sunflash found himself staring into the most beautiful face he had ever seen. It was a badger, wise beyond dreams and calm as a still lake in the dawn. He knew instinctively it was Bella, his mother. In that moment he felt sadness and joy, yearning and fulfilment. Comfort and serenity shone through her smile as she stroked his golden stripe and began singing:

'Arm not alas sand, 'way south in the west,
So star land a mat, there's where I love best,
Sand not as alarm, lone seabirds do wing,
And alas most ran, list' to me whilst I sing.
I'll walk alongside you, my lost little one,
We'll find the mountain . . .'

'Salamandastron!' bellowed Sunflash, finishing the song.

Wakefulness hit the creatures sleeping outside like a lightning flash and a thunderbolt all in one. They leapt upright, fur and spikes bristling at the sound of the booming roar from within the dwelling cave. Skarlath shrieked with shock and took off into the air like an arrow, and the babes came tumbling and howling into the open as the mighty shout reverberated once more:

'Eeulaliaaaa! Salamandastron!'

Limping slightly and supporting himself on his hornbeam mace, the badger appeared in the bright sunlight. Tears flowed openly from his great dark eyes, yet he was smiling. Casting the mace aside he scooped the petrified babes up in both paws.

'Salamandastrooooooon!'

Sunflash executed a great whirl, circling crazily until he fell on his back with an earthshaking thud. Caught up in the wild excitement of the moment, hogbabes and molemaids yelled aloud with their badger friend.

'Salamandastrooooooon!'

9

The fire burned bright and late in the dwelling cave that night as the homely celebration went on. A great cauldron of woodlanders' stew steamed thickly, its wondrous aroma tickling the noses of all who fancied a second helping, or even a third, or in Sunflash's case, a fourth and fifth. Elmjak and old Uncle Blunn had ranged far and wide for the ingredients. Potatoes, leeks, turnips and mushrooms had come from the farm patch, but the special touches like watershrimp, wild onion, fennel, and a delicious addition they had never seen before that Elmjak called southbeans, had taken some finding. The babes greatly enjoyed a summercream pudding that Skarlath and Lully had concocted between them; there was nutbread and even some early strawberry cordial.

Sunflash had told the story of his dream over and over again. Tirry smiled indulgently as his friend recounted the tale once more. Sunflash ladled himself another bowl of stew, saying, 'You're laughing at me, Tirry Lingl.'

The good hedgehog smiled even wider. 'Nay, not laughin' at you, big feller, I'm laughin' for you. Yore parents an' grandsires, you know their names, you've seen 'em, you know who you are now, aye, an' even where yore bound. Hoho! Salamandastron, eh, who'd 'ave thought it?'

The badger's huge paw rapped the tabletop as he repeated, 'That's what I've been telling you, the words of the song all became clear when my mother sang them. Arm not alas sand, So star land a mat, Sand not as alarm, And alas most ran They are all jumbled-up forms of the word Salamandastron!'

Gurmil climbed onto the table, and impudently began helping himself to Sunflash's portion of summercream pudding. 'Hahah! But yore mum wouldn't 'ave knowed the song if we 'adn't started singin' it!'

The badger stroked the soft spikes of his small friend's head. 'That's right enough, mate. I might not have recovered if it hadn't been for you young uns!'

Podd licked her spoon absently. 'Burr aye, zurr, best day's wurk ee surrpints ever did, bitin' ee!'

The badger sat looking slightly puzzled, but the others fell about laughing at the molemaid's innocent remark.

Auntie Ummer waddled to her corner of the cave and sought out her gurdelstick. Old Uncle Blunn banged his beaker on the tabletop in time to the jangle, rattle and bump of the instrument, calling, 'Coom on, moi ole duckyburd, give us'n's a tune, hurr hurr!'

Nilly smiled endearingly at Blunn. 'Do ee sing a song, Nunc, sing Wurpldown Dumm.'

The old mole chuckled as he patted her velvety head. 'You'm gotten oi twisted round yore liddle diggen claw, missie. Roight ho, hurr oi go!'

Old Uncle Blunn soon had them laughing at his song.

'Oh, oi knowed a mole called Wurpldown Dumm,
Ee wurr a rascal, a villyun boi gumm,
An' ee 'ad the plumpest an' fattest ole tumm,
As ever was see'd in yon wuddland.

69

For brekkist ee eated a duzzing gurt pies,
They say that 'is tumm wurr as big as 'is eyes,
Ee kept 'is mouth opened so ee cudd catch flies,
Ee ett everythink in yon wuddland.

One day as ole Wurpldown Dumm lied asleep,
Ee Lord o' Dark Forest came wi' a gurt leap,
An' carried 'im off furrever to keep,
Ole Wurpldown in ee Dark Wuddland.

An' all ee dead vurmints cried, "Coom an' see mates,
O boggle us seasons, an' lackaday fates,
Yon fat mole ee's eatin' gurt Dark Forest gates,
O get 'im back up to ee wuddlands."

Ee said, "Oi've eated butterflies, oi've eated bees,
Oi've drinked lots o' soups an' cordials an' teas,
But gates o' Dark Forest tastes just loike gudd cheese,
One day oi'll go back to those wuddlands!"'

The merriment continued with more songs and dancing until the babes fell to snoring and had to be carried
off to their beds. When all was quiet, Tirry struck a more
sober note, saying, 'Well, Sunflash, I suppose you'll be
leavin' us soon?'

The badger nodded his great golden-striped head
slowly. 'Aye, Tirry, I'll be setting off an hour before
dawn.'

Dearie patted his paw. 'You've got to go, friend, you
always knew that. We'll think kindly of you an' all
you did for our families.'

Skarlath hopped down from the ledge he always liked
to perch on. 'Tomorrow 'twill be the start of autumn
days. I will stay here awhile with you and make cheeses.
Though I will divide my time between, sometimes flying
off to watch for Swartt Sixclaw and other times keeping

70

an eye on you, Sunflash. So, badger, you may go with a light heart, knowing these families have a protector.'

Sunflash stretched out his heavy paw, running it lightly down Skarlath's plumed back. 'What creature ever deserved such a friend as you, my hawk!' he said, his voice trembling audibly.

Lully threw her apron up over her face to hide her distress. 'Oi'll make ee oop a gurt pack o' vittles, zurr, ee woan't be 'ungered on ee journey, an' may'ap 'twill remoind ee of us'n's.'

She and Dearie were overcome with tears, and they hurried off. Sunflash stretched out both paws to Tirry and Bruff, and they shook firmly, blinking and nodding a lot. 'Go to your beds now,' said Sunflash. 'I told you I wouldn't leave without saying farewell. So goodbye, Tirry Lingl, and goodbye to you, Bruff Dubbo, my very good friends.'

The mole and the hedgehog wiped their eyes and went to their beds.

In the hour before dawn the dwelling cave was still and warm, and its occupants, all save one, were asleep. Without a backward glance Sunflash picked up his mace and the sack of provisions; moving softly, he was off on his quest. Outside in the dim light, he started at a sound. Elmjak crept up, a paw upon his lips. The badger nodded, and together they cut into the woodlands, going south and west. Neither beast spoke as they carefully picked their way through bush and undergrowth until they reached the brow of a small knoll. Amber and lilac washed a pale swathe through the eastern skies; woodpigeon, thrush and blackbird could be heard as they rose to herald the dawn; the earth felt tranquil, green and dew-laden.

Suddenly the old squirrel halted and, grasping his companion's mighty paw, he shook it firmly. 'Thy path and mine part here. I walked this far with you so that you would not be leaving the dwelling of friends alone.'

Sunflash was careful not to squeeze Elmjak's paw too hard. 'Thank you, my friend. I would be dead were it not for you. But where do you go now, what path will you travel?'

Looking back the way they had come, the squirrel smiled. 'My wandering days are done. I will return to the dwelling cave and live happily in peace and plenty with those two families of innocents. Methinks they will have need of my special skills. So worry not, Sunflash – like your kestrel, I will watch over our friends gladly.'

The badger touched his golden stripe as a mark of respect. 'You are a goodbeast. My heart is lighter knowing you are protecting the families of Tirry and Bruff. We will meet again someday, I feel it. Send a message by Skarlath should you ever need me. Goodbye, Elmjak.'

Reaching into his herb bag, the old squirrel drew forth a turquoise stone. It was flat, intricately carved into the shape of a sycamore leaf and strung on a thin cord. He looped it around Sunflash's paw, saying, 'This amulet may be of use to you sometime. Show it to any squirrel or otter you may encounter. Tell them it comes from the oakdens of Firjak and was given to you by his son Elmjak. It will make your path easier by bringing you help. Fare you well, Sunflash the Mace. Find your mountain, defeat your enemies and grow great in the land!'

Then with enviable agility in one so old, the squirrel went bounding off through the trees.

10

Morning sun evaporated the damp and dew, clothing the woodlands in a brief gauze of mist. Sunflash trudged steadily onward as the trees and foliage became more luxurious and dense. Digging his footclaws into the loamy ground, the badger descended a steep wooded hillside, noting a warm decaying odour and the earth growing squelchy as he progressed downward. Upon reaching the bottom, Sunflash was forced to balance between a rock and a rotting beech stump. Seating himself, he unpacked oat scones and a flask of dandelion and burdock cordial. He ate and drank slowly as he evaluated the land, the great swamp he would be forced to cross. In front of him, and as far as he could see from left to right, dark treacherous ooze showed between the tall foxgloves, fungus-like growths clung parasitically to half-sunken logs, and clouds of midges swarmed about the mosses and liverwort which abounded everywhere.

From the shelter of clumped elderbushes the badger was being watched. Many reptilian eyes stared unblinkingly from their hiding places. Sunflash was stoppering his drink flask when a strange sound reached his ears; looking around swiftly he identified the source of the odd noise. It was a reed flute, played by a small skinny newt. The creature had painted itself orange and bright blue with plant dyes. It hopped and frisked about with scant regard for the treacherous surface of the morass, skipping from plant to twig, from rush to flower, tootling and twiddling tunelessly. It popped up alongside Sunflash, virtually pushing his footpaw off the rotten log as it made room for itself.

The badger greeted the newcomer. 'Good day to you, little sir . . .'

Further conversation was interrupted as the newt scrabbled to get inside Sunflash's provision sack. The badger nipped the invader neatly by its baggy neckskin and held it aloft. Indignantly, it kicked in mid-air, snarling nastily in a high-pitched nasal squeal, "Ey yew, 'ey yew, gerroffofme an' giz me vikkles, 'urryup!'

Sunflash gave the impudent reptile a warning shake to silence it. 'Hold hard there, cheekyface, who d'you think you're talking to?'

It tried to strike at the badger with its reed flute. 'Stripeydog thicky'ead badjerpadjer daftdog . . . !'

Sunflash had put up with enough. He stunned the newt with a tiny flick of his free paw beneath its chin. Unknown to him the myriad of reptile eyes still watched from the cover of the elderbushes. Sunflash laid the newt carefully out on the stump and waited for it to recover, and when it stirred and opened one eye he trapped it gently with a footpaw and lectured it.

'Now don't say a single word or I'll squash you like a gnat! Right, listen to me. Didn't your parents ever teach you any manners? You come here, diving into my bag, demanding food and then you start insulting me. Have you got no respect for others? Keep a civil tongue in your head, I warn you!'

The little reptile swallowed, its throat rising in a gulp. 'A wiz 'ungry, yew got vikkles, giz Smerc sum . . . pleez.'

'That's better!' said the badger, opening his sack. 'My name is Sunflash the Mace. You want food – good, tell you what I'll do. Obviously you know your way about this swamp, and if you agree to lead me through it I'll feed you. Is it a bargain?'

The newt wriggled out from beneath the badger's footpaw. 'Barrgin, barrgin! Giz Smerc vikkles, I show yadda way!'

Sunflash broke an oatcake in half, twirled a leaf into a cone and filled it with cordial, and gave them both to Smerc. The skinny little creature ate as if it had lived through a seven-season famine, sucking the drink noisily and chomping at the oatcake until crumbs flew. To the badger's amazement it demolished the food and finished the drink.

Holding out the conical leaf cup, Smerc shook it in Sunflash's face. 'Yehhhh! A like it, goodgood, giz me summore!'

The badger eyed it coldly until he heard the word.

'Pleez!'

Refilling the leaf cone, Sunflash gave it to Smerc with the other half of the oatcake. The newt's table manners were totally appalling. When it had finished eating, it grabbed at the amulet which Sunflash had hung about his neck, hissing, 'Luvly meggle giz me it, for showyer across swampy!'

Sunflash understood Smerc completely. He had spent a lot of his young life in a vermin camp where creatures behaved like that as a matter of routine. The only thing such creatures respected was brute force, and now he decided to show the newt a bit. Picking Smerc up, Sunflash set him on a low laburnum branch.

'So then, your name is Smerc. Watch and I'll show you why I'm called Sunflash the Mace!'

Sunflash seized the great hornbeam mace and swung it.

'Eeulaliaaaaa!'

One sweeping sideways blow at the rotten beech stump caused it to disintegrate, exploding into a shower of damp wood, powdery dust, slugs and woodlice. When the debris settled there was no sign of the stump. Smerc stood open-mouthed, quivering all over with fear. Sunflash shouldered his mace, saying, 'I've fed you, that's my half of the bargain. Now you will guide me through this swamp. Move, Smerc!'

Slow worms, eels and newts in a silent slithering procession followed as Sunflash negotiated a passage through the wide morass. He followed Smerc, sometimes waist deep as the newt skipped carelessly over lily pads, other times gripping the moss-covered limbs of long-submerged tree trunks. It was tough going. At the centre of the swamp a jutting oak branch stuck up at an angle. As he moved towards it, the badger felt the shifting ooze gripping and sucking at his body. He floundered, tasting the foul mud in his mouth, unable to wipe it from his eyes as it flopped and splodged with his wild efforts.

Smerc's voice rang out from somewhere nearby. 'Grab 'old o' d'branch, stripeydog, or yer sink!'

Summoning his strength, Sunflash made a mighty surge forward, grabbing blindly at where he knew the tree limb to be. There was a moment's cold panic, then he felt his paw grip wood. Looping the cord of his mace handle over a gnarled burr, he pulled himself from the sticky morass. After what seemed an age his limbs came clear of the swirling sucking mud.

Sunflash clung to the wobbly limb shaking with exhaustion; it had been a formidable task pulling his huge bulk from the swamp. Feeling slowly about him he was surprised to find his provision sack, still hanging from the old cord which served him as a belt. He dug his paw into the sack and pulled out the flask of dandelion and burdock cordial, then, biting out the stopper, the badger tilted his head back and poured the fragrant liquid into his mud-blinded eyes until they were free of swampdirt. Gratefully he cleared his throat by drinking what was left in the flask, then he looked up to see

Smerc and the band of reptiles who had been following him. The wicked newt was perched on the head of a big eel, obviously the leader.

Sunflash tried ignoring them as he reasoned with Smerc. 'Come on, be fair, you haven't completed our bargain. Get me out of this swamp. Which way do I go now?'

The eels, slow worms and newts remained silent, fixing the badger with a concentrated basilisk glare. Smerc, however, was delighted that he had lured the badger into a trap. He pointed at Sunflash and giggled insanely, 'Yeeheehee! Which way ya go now, stripeydog? Yeeheeheehee! This's yer deepest part o' th'swamp, on'y one way t'go, badjerpadjer. Yeeheeheehee! Down!'

Hot rage engulfed Sunflash the Mace, and he hurled the empty flask at the sniggering newt. Had his aim been tempered by calmness the missile would have slain Smerc, but as it was, the flask struck a glancing blow to both the newt and the big eel on whose head he was perched. Smerc flopped senseless on the eel's head, which was now sporting a livid bruise and a rapidly rising bump.

The eel reared up, opening its mouth to reveal two rows of greeny-yellow, needle-pointed teeth. 'Sssssink 'im!' it hissed.

The whole mass of reptiles moved backward and the oak limb began turning on its side. Sunflash threw himself flat, clinging tight to the branches. To his horror he saw a thick vine hawser rise clear of the mud. It was attached to the underneath of the oak limb and the reptiles were pulling on it.

The badger was helpless. He hung on to the turning limb shouting, 'Stop! Stop! What do you want?'

The big eel sank back and, wrapping itself around the hawser, it pulled with the others as it answered, 'Want you . . . Sssssink!'

The awful realization that there was nowhere to go

swept over Sunflash; he held on to the tree limb as it was pulled down, turning slowly, into the fathomless depths of mud.

11

Krakulat withdrew his Crow Brethren to a place where the horde of Swartt Sixclaw could not see them. They settled behind low hillocks, waiting for nightfall. The Crow Leader had been off hunting with his Brethren when the weasels Scarback and Marbul had slain his mother with slingstones. Fearfully the old ones reported the murder to Krakulat on his return, and the savage crow's rage and grief had been awesome, more so when his scouts reported back to him on the dreadful end his mother's body had met. Krakulat decided to take his vengeance without regard to life and limb, and once his initial rage had subsided he planned the time and place his Brethren would strike.

Swartt had suddenly become a great Warlord and the toast of the horde. Never, not even in the eastlands, had the hordebeasts known such a delightful spot. There was a broad stream, fruit trees and an abundance of edible vegetation. The fact that no birds were to be seen was forgotten when Aggal the stoat Captain speared a large fat chub in the stream. The vermin soldiers and their families flocked to the water, and drank, sported and splashed, some catching watershrimp, others hunting caddisworm and tadpoles. Fires were lit, tents were

79

pitched and a holiday atmosphere prevailed. Using a tent canvas under the vixen Nightshade's supervision, a team of soldiers dragged the stream, bringing in a goodly catch of chub, dace, perch and even a big old pike.

The sixclawed ferret sat beneath a shady tree, painting glowing pictures of the good times ahead to his officers. Swartt's unobtrusive wife, Bluefen, scurried about serving fruit and fish. Swartt hardly noticed her.

'This is only the start,' he said. 'Give me one good season travellin' south'n'west an' everybeast in the land'll be flockin' to my banner, you'll see.'

'Hmm, southwest, eh? Is that where the badger is?' Scraw, the rat, now a Captain, mused idly.

The good mood of Swartt Sixclaw suddenly dissipated, and his voice became a questioning snarl. 'Who told you about the badger?'

Scraw was not intimidated by the Warlord's ill humour. 'Some o' those beasts you were running with before you came to the tents of Lord Bowfleg,' he answered. 'They say the badger is young, but a great warrior, fearless in battle . . .'

Swartt leaned forward anxiously. 'What else do they say? Tell me.'

'They say he was the one who ruined your sixclawed paw, made it dead for ever and that you have sworn to slay him.'

Swartt upturned his metal drinking cup, and suddenly dealt it a swift blow with the chain-mailed and copper-bound gauntlet he wore over the withered sixclaw. The vessel crumpled, flattened beneath the force of the blow. Swartt stared at Scraw. 'Don't ever make the mistake that my sixclaw paw is useless. It's slain more foebeasts than you've had hot dinners, rat. As for the badger, I hear he calls himself Sunflash the Mace now, take it from me, that one's a walkin' deadbeast!'

Aggal the stoat Captain made bold enough to ask, 'How'll you know where to find this Sunflash the Mace?'

Swartt nodded to the vixen. 'Tell him.'

'Searats, some seasons back we met them on the coast,' Nightshade explained briefly. 'They told us of a place, far in the southwest, a mountain ruled by badgers and hares, it has a strange name I cannot remember. The searats said that any badger travelling south and west will eventually arrive at this mountain, something to do with the destiny of badgers, who knows?'

Aggal shrugged dismissively. 'Huh, searats! Who can believe that lot of floatin' rogues? We slew a few up on the east coast last season; before they died some of them said they knew of a great redstone Abbey that had been built in the mid-south. Liars, they'd have said fish had wings if they'd thought it'd save their miserable lives.'

Swartt lied with a straight face to his officers. 'I have spoken with a wise old owl, he knew of the badger mountain. You all know that owls don't lie, so gather round and I'll tell you somethin'.'

The officers gathered closer to Swartt. Information from wise owls was rare, but always true. The ferret Warlord spoke low. 'The mountain of badgers and hares, this owl said, was also a storehouse of fabulous treasure, jewelled swords, golden daggers, and shields mounted with pearls and gems. We'll take it by force of arms with this great horde. Then I'll split this treasure, but only with my brave Captains. What I tell you now is not for other ears, it will be our secret. None of the ordinary hordebeasts need know. Are you with me?'

The Captains looked from one to another, their eyes shining with greed. Scraw acted as spokesbeast for them, as he said, 'We're with you, Lord Sixclaw, you can depend on us!'

The remainder of the day passed happily for the horde, as they fed, played and napped among the tents that had been set up on the streambanks. Late night found the fires burned to embers. A soft breeze moved the tentflaps and rippled the stream as the horde slept deep, tired out after their forced march from the flatlands. Even the sentries slept. That was when Krakulat the crow made his move . . .

Scarback and Marbul were sleeping in the open, outside the Warlord's tent. It was their job to guard him, but the two assassins were as tired as any. They did not feel the thin twine made from animal sinews until it began tightening upon their necks, and by then it was too late. Four crows dug their talons into the earth as they strained and pulled in opposite directions on the strangling loops. Meanwhile, Krakulat stirred the embers of a fire at the edge of the camp into leaping flames. Silently, Krakulat's wife Bonebeak dipped her wing in signal to the army of waiting crows; and the Crow Brethren went to work.

Each of them winged silently over the fire, carrying in their talons a long string. At the end of each string dangled a mass of dried moss and grasses dripping with pine resin. As they passed over the flames the fireballs ignited. Speeding like dark phantoms they flew upward, dropping their blazing burdens onto the tents of Swartt's horde. As soon as this was done they circled high out of range of the flames, waiting.

Three ferrets dashed screaming from a burning tent. Krakulat and his crows dived and slew them as they tried to escape the flames. Now others could be seen against the patches of firelight that had sprung up, illuminating the landscape below. The Crow Brethren took no prisoners; the vengeance of Krakulat was swift and unmerciful.

Swartt hurtled from his tent, ignoring his coughing, choking wife who staggered behind him. He grabbed the vixen as she dashed past, yelling, 'What'n the name of blood'n'fur is goin' on, who set all these tents alight?'

Nightshade pointed at four dark shapes attacking a squealing rat in the firelight. 'Crows! They're all over the place . . . Yaaaagh!'

A crow fastened its talons in the vixen's back; Swartt clubbed it flat with his mailed paw. Drawing his sword he roared, 'The stream! Everybeast into the water, archers an' slingbeasts, rally to me!'

The Warlord stood in the shallows, flaying about him with the flat of his swordblade as he rallied his troops. 'Fire arrows an' rocks! There, you dummies, there! Can't yer see 'em in the firelight when they fly down? There ain't so many of 'em! Come on, move yerselves, shoot!'

A withering hail of stones and arrows whizzed into the night sky, followed by another and yet another. Krakulat saw the destruction the missiles wreaked on his Brethren, and wheeled upward out of range cawing, 'Kraawkaa! Follow me, we will show them the Brethren have no fear, higher, my warriors, higher!'

Nightshade found Swartt and pointed upward. 'Lord, they're out of range, but they're going to dive down upon us!'

The Warlord acted quickly, passing word to his Captains. 'Spears an' pikes, hold 'em low 'til I give the signal!'

Swartt's quick thinking ended the encounter. Krakulat sent his crows zooming down like thunderbolts and, unable to stop themselves in time, the last thing most of them heard was Swartt yelling, 'Spears an' pikes up!'

The Crow Brethren's ranks were so drastically thinned by this sudden action that they were forced to take flight.

Morning light found Swartt and his officers seated on the streambank surveying the smouldering ruins of the hordetents. Soldiers, some with fur badly scorched, kept bringing in reports.

'We've found the two weasels Scarback and Marbul, they were strangled to death, Lord.'

Swartt dismissed them with a wave of his sword. 'Just as well, I'd have throttled 'em meself if they'd lived, for not warnin' me of the crow attack. Any more sentries left alive?'

Aggal pointed out a pair of rats. 'Only those two, Lord.'

Swartt's face was expressionless as he pronounced sentence. 'Slay 'em, they're no good to me sleepin' on duty. Make sure the rest see yer do it, teach 'em a lesson!'

A weasel called Grayjaw came running up breathless. 'Sire, we've seen the crows, they're in that grove of pines over yonder. Give the word an' we'll attack!'

Swartt shook his head as if in despair.

'Listen to her, give the word an' we'll attack. Blockhead! They've probably got an ambush set up for us if we go near those pines. Leave 'em, there's no profit in losin' more of us by stayin' in this place an' wagin' war on a lot of crows.'

Nightshade slid to the Warlord's side and whispered in his ear. Swartt brightened slightly, nodding approval, and, standing up, he called so that all could hear: 'Salvage what y'can, pack all gear, we're leavin'!'

The horde broke camp at mid-morning. As they turned to march south and west, Swartt nodded to the line of archers standing round a fire. 'Give 'em back what they gave us. Fire!'

Burning arrows sped into the pine grove. It was a natural firetrap, with thick layers of dead pine needles providing a floor and old pines leaking resin, supporting half-fallen trees, dry as tinder and highly inflammable. Swartt had lost over three score hordebeasts to the crows, but it did not make much of a dent in his horde, many of whom mourned the loss of their tents more than that of their dead comrades in arms. Black smoke belched skyward as the Crow Brethren tumbled out like a pile of old dark rags to take refuge on the streambanks.

Krakulat watched the pine grove burn, saying, 'Kchaakah! We will follow them and kill them one by one. Come!'

The first the horde knew of it was not long after midday. A horderat marching slowly at the rear was seized by a score of crows and lifted screaming into the air. The birds flew as high as they could with their wriggling wailing burden, then they dropped him. He left a dent in the landscape; other hordebeasts leapt to one side to avoid being hit by the falling rat.

After that a whole company of archers were ordered to march at the rear facing backwards, their bows ready strung against further attacks. Next the crows picked another rat off the middle right flank, and the archers at the rear could not fire for fear of hitting their comrades. Before sundown a third rat was lifted off, this time from the front left flank of the marching horde. Swartt's bad temper descended once more, and he ordered the vixen to march alongside him. Repeatedly treading on her footpaws and digging her in the side with his mailed paw, he upbraided her. 'Burn 'em out of the pines, Lord? Shortsighted stupidity! What've yer made me look like, eh? A slop'ead like yerself! Those birds'll follow us until we're dead or they are. Righto, my blight seer, see me a way out o' this, an' quick about it!'

Chaos was beginning to break out in the horderanks as the rats, realizing that they were the only ones light enough for the crows to lift into the air, started panicking. Pushing and shoving at weasels, stoats and ferrets, the rats tried to occupy the centre of the marching masses, where the crows dared not fly down upon them. Hordebeasts fought the rats viciously, claiming the centre spot for themselves and their families, some with young ones. The crows, however, did not have it all their own way. Archers and slingbeasts began a relentless barrage of stones and shafts at the dark winged harassers.

As night fell Swartt was forced to make camp. A burning ring of fires in the open surrounded the horde, stopping the crows picking off anybeast on the fringes. Half the soldiers were ordered to stand upright, pointing spears, javelins and longpikes at the sky, while their comrades rested until it was time to relieve them. Swartt ordered Nightshade to sneak off under cover of darkness and scout ahead for a possible solution to their dilemma. Krakulat and his Brethren squatted out of range of the campfires. Bonebeak gave her husband no peace, as she constantly berated him.

'Rakaaah! Vengeance is a fool's idea, what good will it do us when we are all dead? You have slain enough of the landcrawlers to pay for your mother's life ten times over. Our Brethren must get on with the business of living, we must find new homes. If you get us all slain, who will be left to say what brave birds we were, what a courageous fool Krakulat was? Kchaah!'

She followed the Crow Commander as he waddled angrily between the sleeping Brethren, trying to shake her off.

'Agga! Give your feathers a rest, and your nagging beak too!' he snapped. 'I will say when I have had my revenge on the vermin. The Brethren follow me, my word is law here. Now leave me alone!'

The night wore on with both sides fitful and uneasy, the horde unable to rest because of their guard duties, whilst the crows were kept awake by the constant tirades of their leader's wife.

It was still several hours to dawn when Nightshade slipped back into camp with news for Swartt. 'Lord, there is a deep winding ravine not far from here. A stream runs through the centre of it, and I think there are caves on the streambank. I saw no sign of other creatures there.'

Swartt stood and drew his sword decisively. 'Right,

tell the Captains t'get this lot movin'. We'll get to the shelter of this ravine an' take cover in the caves. Then I can figure out what to do about these crows!'

The horde entered the gorge in darkness, stumbling over the rocky defile at the shallow end of the ravine, still beset by the crows. It was a scene of chaos. Swartt and his Captains yelled commands at the hordebeasts above the cawing din of the birds, vermin fired arrows and slung rocks willy nilly, others jabbed at the night sky with spears. Splashing through the stream, they bundled into the shaded gloom of the caves. There was not room for all the horde soldiers, and many were forced to shelter amid the lupin and brambles of the steep ravine sides. Swartt had managed to light a fire in one of the caves. He looked about at the rushes and dry grass pallets in the corners, then said to the vixen, 'So, you saw no sign of any other creature, eh? Well, who lives in these caves, tell me that?'

Screams and terrified cawing from outside saved the vixen having to answer awkward questions. 'Lord, listen, something strange is happening outside!' she cried.

The Warlord peered outside, taking care to stay away from the cave entrance. 'Well, it'll be dawn soon, then we'll find out.'

The agonized choking cry of a hordebeast rang out, causing Swartt and the vixen to start. Nightshade slunk to the rear of the cave, avoiding Swartt's glare. He shook a mailed paw at her threateningly, snarling, 'By rights I should send you out there, yer cringin' cur! Sometimes I think yer more trouble than yer worth.'

After a while it went quiet outside, and all that could be heard was the odd moan of vermin who were obviously wounded.

Dawn arrived grey and patched with lowering cloud. A fine drizzle caused the gorge to glisten wetly. Swartt poked his head out of the cave to see half a dozen foxes come splashing through the stream shallows towards him. The leader was a large, tough-looking vixen, and like the others of her escort she carried a bolas, four thonged, with rounded pebbles fastened to its ends. The Warlord tried to hide his surprise when the vixen spoke, for her tongue was a bright purple, unlike any he had seen.

'Be ye the leader of this motley array?' she barked.

Swartt could see hordebeasts peeping cautiously from the other caves, and scrambling down the gorge sides. His quick eyes took in the number of slain vermin draped over the rocks. More foxes, maybe fifty, were collecting dead crows and heaping them in a pile. The ferret drew his sword and put on a bold face, saying, 'I'm Swartt Sixclaw, Warlord of all this horde. I see you've slain some of my soldiers. Why?'

The vixen spun her bolas idly, clacking the big pebbles together rhythmically. 'Folly'n'fie! 'Twas a mishap; did I not rid ye of the crows?'

Looking up, Swartt had to agree. There was no sign of a crow flying anywhere about. He saw a young fox plucking feathers from the carcass of Krakulat to decorate his brush with. 'Aye, the crows are gone, sure enough,' he said. 'What do they call you, friend? Never mind the few of mine you slew, those crows were becomin' bothersome.'

The fox's purple tongue showed vividly as she answered. 'I am Shang Damsontongue, and this is my gorge. Ye may stop awhile, Swartt Sixclaw . . .' Shang's eyes glistened covetously as she watched Swartt's sword. 'Ye have many fine metal weapons,' she continued. 'Thy beasts carry spears and good daggers. I see shields too, much metal.'

Immediately Swartt was on his guard, though he took it as an advantage that the foxes seemed only to be armed with the primitive stone and thong bolases.

Obviously metal arms were considered precious by the foxes of the gorge. Swartt sheathed his sword, the beginnings of a crafty plan forming in his mind.

12

The reptiles hissed joyfully as they hauled on the vine hawser. Sunflash wallowed helplessly, and his great weight was sucked under as the tree limb submerged slowly into the ooze. By spreading his paws and holding his head back he tried to halt his descent into the swamp, but it was useless. He gave a final battle cry before he was lost for ever in the murky depths.

'Eeulaliaaaaaa!'

Skarlath arrived like a bolt of lightning. In seconds the big eel was writhing in mid-air, clutched tight in the kestrel's savage talons as he pecked sharply at its head.

'Kreegaah! If my friend sinks, you die! Tell the slimy ones to get beneath him and buoy him up, quick now!'

Though he was trapped fast by the neck the eel hissed aloud, 'Sssssstop, do not let him ssssssink!'

Sunflash felt the mud well into his mouth, then suddenly he was pushed upward from beneath, the wriggling mass under his footpaws acting as a raft. Skarlath forced the eel to clench the vine hawser in its mouth, then, beating the air furiously with all his wingpower, the kestrel flew slowly upward, gripping the eel. Beneath him the reptile latched hard on to the vine hawser, knowing its life was at stake.

Fortunately the hawser was long, and Skarlath managed to reach a dry bank with lime and alder trees growing on it. Flying as high as he could, the kestrel dropped the eel among the topmost branches of an alder and grabbed the vine from it. Leaving the eel stranded high in the alder, Skarlath took three turns around the lower trunk, then, securing the hawser, he flew back to Sunflash calling advice. 'Kreeeeh! Feel around for the vine and pull yourself out!'

Letting his paws sink, the badger felt about until he touched the oak limb beneath the swamp's surface. Sunflash groped wildly, knowing it was his only chance. At one point his head vanished completely under the mud. Skarlath felt a surge of panic, then sudden relief as his friend appeared like some slime-covered primeval monster, rearing up as he pulled and hauled on the hawser that he had found. Blinded by swampdirt and spitting mud left and right, Sunflash dragged himself paw over paw, the vine hawser tautening as it rose and slapped against the viscous surface. Skarlath hovered overhead calling encouragement, while the reptiles, who had all risen to the surface, watched unblinkingly as the swamp-covered giant hauled and pulled, grunting and gasping, until he emerged on the dry bank with a final sucking gurgle.

Sunflash the Mace lay completely exhausted, the mud plastering him turning to a grey, cement-like coating in the hot sun. Skarlath strutted around him, carefully pecking the mess from his friend's ears and eyes. Spitting out the gritty substance, Sunflash nodded weakly at the reptiles.

'That lot look disappointed. I would have fed them for three seasons after they'd suffocated me,' he said.

The slow worms, newts and eels were lying offshore, still watching intently. Nobeast was more surprised than the badger when Smerc staggered up, one side of his jaw swollen out of shape as he grinned lopsidedly and jeered, "Ello, stripeydog, see yer 'scaped from d'swamp. Heeheehee!'

Sunflash made a half-hearted grab at the cheeky newt, but he was too slow. Smerc tottered quickly off into the shrubbery. A moment later he was heard shrilling, 'Gerroff me yew! Lemmego, I di'n't do nottink!'

Two otters hove into view, one hauling Smerc by a back leg. Both beasts looked plump and well fed; they moved with the sure-pawed grace common to otters. Nodding to Skarlath they peered intently at Sunflash, and then the larger of the two spoke.

'Aye aye, matey, we 'eard the commotion over this way so we cruised over to take a glim. I'm Folrig Streampaw an' this fat frogwalloper is Ruddle Banksnout.'

Ruddle promptly passed possession of Smerc's leg to Sunflash. 'Ahoy, just 'ang on t'this bucko for a tick, matey!'

Ruddle hurled himself upon Folrig, and they wrestled and kicked, buffeting each other all over the ground.

'Frogwalloper is it, you bottle-bottomed flotsam, us Banksnouts was always ten times more 'andsome than you Streampaws!'

'Haharr! Did yer say 'andsome, yore mother wouldn't let yer swim in the water 'cos you frightened all the fishes!'

They rolled over and over, locked together, pummelling each other as they laughed uproariously and traded insults.

'Yore father tried t'swap you fer a toadbabe when you was a pup, he said it was nicer lookin' by far! Hohohoho!'

'Harrharrharr, matey, my ole granma used t'say, show me a good-lookin' Streampaw an' I'll die 'appy. She's still livin'!'

Sunflash sat up, still with the writhing Smerc in one paw, and said, 'Would you two like to stop fighting for a moment, I'm getting weary just sitting watching you!'

They quit tussling straight away and stooped, staring closely at the mud-caked Sunflash.

'Blow me down, is that a badger be'ind all that swampmuck?'

'Aye, so 'tis, an' he looks prettier than you, even with all that muck on 'im. Sit still, messmate, I'll soon 'ave you clean an' shipshape with a drop o' clear water.'

Ruddle dashed off to find water, and Folrig took Smerc from the badger, shaking him by his loose neckskin. 'You rotten liddle scumslimer, I'll wager a willow'erb to a watershrimp yore be'ind all this!'

The newt kicked and squealed, pointing upward to the eel draped in the alder branches. 'No, no, streamy-dog, not me, it was 'im up there!'

Folrig grinned broadly at Skarlath. 'I s'pose you put ole squirmskin aloft up there. Why don't y'take this whimperin' whelk up to join 'im, they're mates y'know, shame to keep 'em apart.'

Weeping and wailing piteously, the newt was borne up to the high branches and deposited there next to the eel, who was clinging grimly to the thin branches complaining, 'Ffffeel sssssick up here.'

Skarlath waggled a talon in his face. 'Eelscum, feel grateful this bird let you live!'

Ruddle could find only a bit of wet grass, but he cleaned Sunflash's eyes and nostrils as best he could. 'There y'are, mate, at least y'can see an' sniff proper now. Come with me an' ole ugly mug there, we'll navigate yer back to good dry land away from this swamp. May'ap you'd like to visit our den an' take a bite with us, eh?'

Sunflash thanked them and pulled himself upright slowly.

Folrig was looking this way and that. 'Hold 'ard, where's yer pal, the kestrel bird?'

Powdered mud fell dustily from the badger as he began walking. 'Oh, Skarlath comes and goes as he pleases. No doubt he knows I'm safe with you, so he decided to take off for a while. By the way, what about the newt and the eel up there? Hadn't we better let them down? They might starve and die.'

Ruddle chuckled. 'Not them two, when we're gone they'll slither down one way or another, a bit o' penance don't do rogues like them no 'arm.'

It was nearly twilight when, after a long and perilous trek, they cleared the swamplands and came to a wooded terrain backed by mounds of smooth ancient rocks. The otters made their way towards the rocks; Sunflash heard water splashing as they skirted the fern-fringed bank of a stream. Looking further up to where the rounded rocks reared their massive forms, he saw a beautiful waterfall.

Folrig stepped out jauntily, calling back to Sunflash, 'We'll soon see if yore a badger underneath yore swamp-coat, an' I 'ope yore a prettier sight than ole rot-the-apples there!'

Fighting and chortling the two otters dived beneath the falls, letting the torrents batter them. Sunflash was a bit apprehensive at first, but after gingerly stepping beneath the cascade he revelled in the feel of clean, icy water drenching him after the long hot trek through the swamps. Weariness fell from the badger's limbs, and a marvellous sense of wellbeing enveloped him. With a playful roar he joined the otters in their game, seizing them both in a hug.

'Eeulaliaaa! I'm Sunflash the Mace and I'm better looking than both of you put together, you nut-nosed, boulder-headed beasts!'

Retaliating, Folrig and Ruddle got Sunflash in a double headlock between them, shouting: 'Drown 'im quick afore he scares the young uns!'

'Wot an 'orrible sight, mate, a badger with a butter-dipped nose!'

The three fell about laughing in the water, then

suddenly Ruddle plunged deeper into the thick cascade and vanished. Sunflash pawed water from his eyes and looked at Folrig. 'Where's Ruddle gone?' he asked.

'Into the den, matey. 'Ere, give me yore paw an' I'll show yer.'

It was a cave at the back of the waterfall, completely hidden from view. Stepping from beneath the falls onto a raised ledge, Sunflash followed Folrig around a slight bend and there they were, in a dry, rush-strewn cavern. Ruddle had already put flint to tinder and set a small fire.

'Welcome in, messmate,' he said, 'it ain't much, but 'tis 'ome fer two 'andsome streamdogs such as us.'

Sunflash dried himself by shaking off and rubbing vigorously with aromatic dried grass. Ruddle produced beakers and a big gourd jug full of pennycloud and rosehip squash. Folrig busied himself chopping leeks and white turnips into a cauldron, eyeing Sunflash's hornbeam limb as he did. 'That's a mighty big 'ead-bonker, matey, did you make it?'

Sunflash hefted the weapon fondly. 'Aye, it's my mace,' he said.

The irrepressible otter pointed to a bundle of thick red roots. 'Mace, eh? Well, if you don't fancy smackin' ole Ruddle in the chops to improve 'is looks, p'raps you'd like to pound up those hotroots fer the soup.'

Using the head of his mace the badger pulped the roots to shreds. Folrig tossed them into the cauldron along with some dried watershrimp, young nettles, mushrooms and carrots.

They sat round the fire until the soup was ready, when Ruddle served it steaming hot with chunks of barley bread. The taste was delicious, though the spiciness almost took the badger's breath away. Hurriedly he poured a beakerful of squash down his burning throat. 'Phwooh! I feel as though I'm on fire, what soup is that?'

Folrig began singing.

95

'When I was just a liddle beast,
I was so small an' weak,
I'd often fall flat on me tail,
An' I could 'ardly speak.
I scarce could totter round the floor,
Me whiskers used to droop,
'Til granma made a great big pot
Of good ole hotroot soup!
An' now I'm brisker than a bee,
More fitter than a mole,
Most every day I 'ear granma say,
"Give 'im another bowl!"

I'll live a thousand seasons,
Grow strong as any tree,
Give me a spoon an' fetch it soon,
Good hotroot soup for me.'

As the evening wore on Sunflash began to enjoy the
tangy dish, in fact he ate more than either of his two
friends. They sang and recited, ate and drank until all
three fell asleep where they sat, around the glowing
embers, with the soothing sounds of the falls in the
background.

13

Sunflash did not know whether it was night or day
when he woke. Folrig had put more wood upon the
embers and blown a fresh fire into light. The badger
yawned, stretched and took a mighty draught of squash
from the gourd jug.

For the first time he noticed an opening at the back of
the cave. 'Ruddle, where does that lead to? Is it a backway out?' he asked.

The otter licked a paw and held it up. 'It used t'be,
messmate; feel that breeze, keeps the cave nice'n'fresh
when the wind's blowin' in the right direction. Aye,
'twas once our secret way out, until a boulder shifted in
the meltin' snows an' blocked it. But a little draught still
comes through when it blows southerly.'

Whilst the two otters prepared breakfast Sunflash
went to investigate the secret exit. Sure enough, a sizeable boulder had blocked it, and all that showed through
were a few small cracks of sunlight from outside. The
badger worked at clearing the rocks and debris which
had lodged round the great stone until Folrig called him.
'If y'don't like arrowroot biscuits an' honey with 'ot mint
tea, then stay where y'are, matey, me'n'ole frightface'll
eat 'em for you!'

Sunflash needed no second bidding. He enjoyed a hearty breakfast, while explaining what he had in mind.

'Move what bits and pieces you need to the side walls of this cave – I'm going to unblock your secret backway. I'll push the boulder into the cave from the outside – and when you hear the boulder shifting you'd best stay clear of this place. Better yet, come and show me the backway from outside.'

The two otters followed him, scoffing and chortling at the idea that any creature could clear the obstruction.

'Nobeast'll budge that ole boulder, it's there to stay. We both worked at it right through the spring with nary a scrap of luck, 'tis wedged there for good, Sunflash.'

'If anybeast livin' could move yonder stone, why, we'd give 'im a mighty feed an' call 'im 'andsome. Hohohoho!'

From the outside, the backway was a natural tunnel in the rock above the falls. Sunflash climbed in and started pulling out slabs and shards of stone which had become wedged around the boulder. These he passed back to his friends for disposal. Once it was reasonably clear he set his shoulder to the big rock and began to push, grunting and straining as he sought for proper purchase with his footpaws. Folrig and Ruddle sat outside the tunnel, concern evident in their voices.

'Sunflash, matey, come out o' there, 'tis no use!'

'You'll 'urt yoreself, friend, it ain't worth it fer a daft ole boulder like that'n!'

The large gold-striped head poked from the tunnel opening and glared at them; warrior blood was beginning to rise in the eyes of Sunflash.

'Listen, you two ugly mugs, I'd advise you both to shut up! You're my friends, see – I've been guided through the swamps, been cared for, fed and bedded in your home. So now I'm repaying you by clearing this secret way out. Now both of you, sit tight here and not another word!'

Thoroughly chastened, Folrig and Ruddle watched their friend disappear back into the tunnel.

Setting his back full against the boulder, Sunflash lodged his paws into the walls either side of him, his footpaws flat on the stone floor as he began to push. Muscles bunching and sinews strained, he concentrated all his mind on defeating the mighty boulder jammed squarely into the passage. The powerful jaws clenched vicelike and froth bubbled around his lips as he strained, veins bulging and claws scarring deep into the rock walls.

There was a slight creak, and dust powdered from the boulder edges to mingle with the sweat dripping from Sunflash's muzzle. Straining and pushing even harder the badger shut his eyes tight, as a red mist enveloped his senses. Then the four badgers were with him in spirit, his father, mother and both grandsires, speaking as in one echoing voice.

'Through wintercold and summerheat,
The Badger Lord knows not defeat!
Point of spear or blade of sword,
Nought can stop the Badger Lord!'

A thunderous battle cry ripped from the very depths of the badger's cavernous chest and blood coursed through his frame in a torrent as he slammed his back into the boulder.

'Eeulaliaaaaaaa!'

The huge stone rolled forward, free of its constraints. Lying stretched upon his back, Sunflash opened his eyes and watched as the boulder rumbled off down the passageway. Picking up speed on the slope it boomed its way through the cavern, swerving around the corner of the otters' dwelling and crashing into the cascading curtain of the waterfall. Folrig and Ruddle had heard the commotion; they dashed to the edge of the rocks, following the course of the noise.

'Blisterin' barnacles, mate. Look!'

The boulder came catapulting out of the cataract's centre to crash into the stream below with a terrific splash. Folrig and Ruddle danced about wildly on the rock's edge.

'Hohoho, bucko, Sunflash did it, I told yer he would!'

'On me oath, messmate, I never doubted 'e would!'

Sunflash cleansed himself of the dust and perspiration by taking a final refreshing shower beneath the green-gold, sunlight-laced waters of the falls. When he had washed he stretched out to dry on the grassy banks of the stream below. Folrig and Ruddle bounded up, both carrying travelling staves and bearing three haversacks of food.

The badger sat up and shook himself. 'Hmm, and where do you two frogs' nightmares think you're off to, if I may make so bold to ask?'

Ruddle answered for them both. 'With you, of course. O good-lookin' one.'

Sunflash picked up his mace and one of the haversacks. 'Huh! That's what you think – I'm not having two mudfaces like you pair following me about and scaring off the birds.'

Folrig shouldered his haversack, grinning. 'Belay that talk, butterstripe, we're bound to go with you. You wear the sign of Firjak's Oakden; we must follow it.'

Sunflash remembered the greenstone sycamore leaf talisman given to him by Elmjak which still hung about his neck. The resolute expressions on his friends' faces told him that argument was useless. As they tramped southward he took the greenstone symbol in his paw and inspected it, musing, 'This must be a very powerful omen. Elmjak told me that all squirrels and otters would aid me if I wore it. But why?'

As they pressed deeper into dry heavily wooded

forestland Folrig explained the significance of Firjak's talisman. 'One time o' day the squirrels an' otters in these parts kept themselves to themselves, never botherin' with each other. Except for two liddle uns. They were, Firjak, son of the Squirrelqueen, an' Bankrose, daughter of a great Skipper of Otters. These two were great liddle pals, they played t'gether often. But one day they was both taken by searats, captured an' marched off, far from these woods. Well, Firjak, he bit through 'is bonds an' escaped, then the liddle feller followed the rats, an' one night while they slept 'e slew two sentries an' liberated Bankrose. Firjak was wounded in the scuffle, an' even though 'e was but no more'n a babe, 'e carried Bankrose up into a big ole sycamore an' kept those rats at bay with a tiny sling an' some pebbles until a trackin' party of otters'n'squirrels arrived an' rescued 'em both. Young Firjak was sore wounded, down to 'is last pebble too, a big flat green one, too large t'fit the sling. That's the one yore wearin' round yore neck, matey – the Skipper of Otters carved it to look like a sycamore leaf. After that the squirrel an' otterfolk became allies. So now y'know why anybeast wearin' that leafstone commands the respect an' loyalty of all otters an' squirrels.'

Sunflash looked at the talisman with new respect. 'A tale of great courage. What happened to Firjak?'

'Oh, Firjak recovered, but 'is footpaw was so lamed they say 'e rarely climbed a tree after that. Learned to swim 'e did, somebeasts say 'e was more otter than squirrel in the finish.'

Sunflash was curious about the capture of Firjak and Bankrose. 'You say they were taken by searats. I never knew that searats came this far inland.'

Ruddle pointed westward, saying, 'What d'you mean, we ain't that far inland, the great waters are only a few days over yonder.'

'Then that's the way we'll go,' said Sunflash, changing

his course. 'Once I reach the sea I'm sure I'll only have to keep travelling south. Come on, you beauties!'

Folrig seemed rather hesitant. 'Er, it wouldn't be advisable to set a course that way, mate, searats an' Corsairs 'ang about the coast like ants in honey.'

Sunflash kept walking, calling back to Folrig, 'If a squirrelbabe could defeat the searats they shouldn't be too tough for us. Besides, you two could panic them with your faces. Hahaha!'

The following two days passed uneventfully; the going was not too difficult, the weather fine, and food plentiful. Towards evening of the second day the travellers found themselves scaling some very steep wooded hills, each one seemingly higher than the last. Amid the stunted trees and shrubs of the final rocky tor, Sunflash called a halt. In the last rays of daylight he noticed a faint westerly gleam on the horizon.

'Aha, it's the sea at last, my pretty ones!' he cried.

Ruddle was still panting as he lit a small sheltered fire. 'Well ain't that nice, clamberin' up all them 'ills so ole stripey 'ooter can see the water!'

'Huh, 'ills y'say, matey, if they was 'ills I'm an owl's uncle,' said Folrig, unpacking supper from the haversacks. 'It's mountains we've been climbin', bucko, an' none bigger'n the one we're atop of right now!'

Sunflash chuckled at his two companions. 'Well at least we don't have to climb any higher, it'll be all downhill tomorrow, or should I say down mountain. Come on, you two frogfaces, dig out those turnip'n'mushroom pasties.'

Supper was laid on green twigs to warm over the fire. Ruddle dribbled honey onto three thick fruitcake slices, whilst Sunflash poured out beakers of cold cider.

They lay about round the fire eating supper, enjoying the faint breeze. Folrig winked coaxingly at Ruddle. 'I votes you take first watch, matey, yore the ugliest.'

Ruddle made as if to rise, then slumped back, saying, 'First one can't solve a riddle takes first watch. What goes up an' up an' up an' never leaves the ground?'

Folrig answered without batting an eyelid, 'This pesky mountain we're on, that's an old un. Er, er, what's under the water an' over the water an' never gets wet?'

Sunflash licked honey from his paws as he answered, 'An egg inside a duck's tummy, even I know that one! Righto, what falls every day and breaks every night?'

Ruddle sniffed. 'Huh, dusk an' dawn, what else? What goes buhurr owch! Buhurr owch! See if y'know that'n.'

'Two moles fightin' over a damson pudden.'

Ruddle glared at Folrig. 'How did you know?'

'Well I should know, matey, 'twas me that made it up!'

They fell to wrestling and insulting each other until Sunflash pulled them apart. 'Stop this fighting, you two, I'll go first watch.'

Suddenly Folrig and Ruddle wanted to take first watch.

'No, no, matey, I'll go watch.'

'Oh no y'won't, I will.'

Sunflash tossed his mace from paw to paw menacingly, 'I said I'll go first watch, anybeast care to argue?'

The two otters threw themselves flat, eyes closed tight.

'Can't 'ear yer, mate, I'm fast asleep.'

'Me too, needs me beauty sleep I do.'

Chuckling quietly at the irrepressible creatures, Sunflash strode softly off around the edges of their camp. He settled on a boulder from where he had a good view all round.

The early part of the night was uneventful. Sunflash stayed alert, enjoying the silence of the balmy darkness. He sat thinking of his friend Skarlath and the happy seasons they had spent with the Bruff Dubbo and Tirry Lingl families at the cave. Intermingled with these thoughts were the dreams of his family: father, mother and grandsires, and of course, the mountain, always the mountain, waiting for him somewhere in the southwest. The campfire had gradually reduced to embers and gone dead; there was no moon, only the wide star-strewn darkness above. Gradually, little by little, the badger fell under the soft spell of night's mantle. His eyes began to droop, and small sounds receded into the background, merging into a faint, comforting whisper.

Then a weighted net was flung over Sunflash, pulling him backwards off the boulder. Before he had a chance to break loose or lift his mace, the badger felt cold steel at his throat, at least a dozen sword or knife points. A gruff voice grated in his ear. 'One move an' you're a deadbeast!'

The net tightened as stakes were driven through it into the ground.

'Munga, are those two others taken care of?' the gruff voice called out.

A reply came back out of the darkness: 'Out cold the pair of 'em, Chief!'

Sunflash began to struggle against the confining net. A swordpoint pricked him under the chin and a higher-pitched voice grated angrily: 'Let me finish him off, Chief!'

14

Shang Damsontongue was even easier to deal with than Bowfleg had been. Swartt Sixclaw promised her joint leadership of the horde, plus many fine metal weapons, and she was eager and greedy. They sealed the bargain with fine wine from the south, Swartt drinking from the bottle and allowing his new partner the honour of drinking from the poisoned silver chalice. The sixclawed Warlord could scarce suppress an evil snigger. Would they never learn, these so-called leaders, that none was more deadly and pitiless than him?

Once again he was Warlord of all the great horde. Shang's former band of foxes was only too happy to follow Swartt; issued with good metal weapons to take the place of their former crude arms, regaled with promises of lavish booty to come, they joined gladly. But Swartt had not reckoned with Balefur!

The big dog fox had been only loosely attached to Shang Damsontongue's band. He was more of a loner – tough, independent and fearless, Balefur answered to nobeast. Swartt had noticed him as the march southwest had continued, standing out, bigger than the rest, striding confidently, neither asking or giving help to anybeast. Moreover, Balefur had armed himself with a large double-headed battleaxe, and he carried it with the easy grace of one who knew how to use it.

On the second night's camp Swartt decided to meet with the big fox. Being one of the few left with a tent, the Warlord had it set up, guards posted around it, and a fire burning outside. Cushions were scattered around inside and Swartt's wife Bluefen set out a good array of food and drink. The Warlord was out to impress any potential friend or enemy with a show of splendour and power.

Four armed vermin were sent to bring the fox into Swartt's presence, but from the start the interview went badly. Balefur sauntered in, battleaxe slung nonchalantly across his shoulder, completely ignoring the four guards around him. He winked casually at Swartt and leaned up against the tentpost.

Swartt studied his guest before speaking, then he crooked a claw at Aggal the stoat Captain. 'Aggal, relieve our friend of that great heavy weapon.'

Balfour toted the axe, shaking his head at the Captain. 'Nay, laddie, this's mah weapon, nobeast takes et from me, d'ye ken?' He laughed openly at the hesitant Aggal. 'Besides, et's no heavy, ah kin wield et wi' nay fuss!'

Taking a quick pace forward, Balefur swung the axe in a swift arc. Aggal jumped backward, but not before the axeblade had sheared through his swordbelt. The fox picked up the severed belt and sheathed sword lightly on his double-headed axe and tossed it to the speechless Captain.

'Och, yer no' hurt, stoat. If ah was aimin' t'slay ye they'd be buryin' ye in two pieces now!'

Swartt got up from his chair; striding forward he faced the fox imperiously. 'I am Swartt Sixclaw, Warlord of this horde!'

Balefur looked away insolently as if dismissing him. 'Aye, so ah've heard, what else is new, ferret?'

Swartt fought inwardly to control his rising anger. 'So

you're Balefur, I can tell by your speech that yer from the far northlands. How did y'get this far south?'

The fox shrugged, smiling patronizingly at the Warlord. 'Och, that's a long story, but nae doubt ah'll be goin' farther a bit wi' ye, if we're t'believe all yer talk o' great booty an' mighty plunder.'

Knowing the fox was getting the better of the confrontation, Swartt decided to change his tack. He smiled and clapped the big beast's back, saying, 'I like you, mate, yer a beast after me own heart. How'd y'like to be a horde Captain in my army?'

Balefur chuckled, shaking his head. 'Not fer me, polecat, ah'll leave that tae the wee beasties who like t'dress up an' play soldiers. Mah business is takin' care o' maself, not lookin' after otherbeasts.'

Seething inwardly, Swartt pasted a smile on his face. 'Don't take or give orders, eh, a good idea. Come sit with me, Balefur, let's eat'n'drink together, friend.'

The big fox laughed openly.

'Yer a canny creature, Swartt, ye drink from the bottle an' ah drink from the silver cup, eh? Is that what yer thinkin'? Well et'll no' work, ah ate an' drank afore ah came here an' ah'm off tae take mah rest now, so ah'll bid ye goodnight.' Without waiting permission from the Warlord, Balefur shouldered his battleaxe and strode off.

When Balefur had left, Swartt leapt at one of the guards standing nearby and felled him with a mighty blow from his mailed paw.

'There! That'll give yer somethin' to smile about! Anybeast want some of this, speak up an' I'll give it to yer!'

At a nod from Nightshade, the guards and Captains hurriedly left the tent. The vixen hovered behind Swartt's chair. 'That one is dangerous, Lord, he knows we poisoned Shang Damsontongue. But we will have to be careful. Balefur is much admired within your horde; we will watch and wait.'

Swartt gritted his teeth until his jaw ached. 'I'd like to finish the blaggard tonight, while he's sleepin'!'

'It would not be easy, Lord, he is a northlander, experienced in the art of battle. 'Twould be no simple task to slay that one. If you missed then you would be made to look foolish in front of the horde.'

Swartt studied his sixclawed paw in its metal gauntlet, and said, 'I suppose you're right, vixen, we'll watch an' wait. Nothing must happen t'make me look foolish in front of my horde. I want you to go ahead and scout the land for three days. Make sure we're on the right course, I don't want them mutterin' that we're lost again, Balefur'd just love that. Travel alone and let nobeast know where you're goin', d'ye hear?'

Nightshade stuffed provisions in a sack. 'I'll go now. Don't worry too much about Balefur, he does not figure in your fate, Lord.'

Swartt drew his curved sword and tested its edge. 'No, but I'll figure in his fate sure enough. There's more ways of shellin' an acorn than hittin' it with a rock. Go now.'

The following days were not easy for Swartt. Tales, enlarged by rumour, had spread through the horde, telling of his encounter with the fox Balefur. The stories grew more fantastic as they passed from one to another.

'I tell yer, mate, Swartt's terrified of ole Balefur.'

'Who told yer that?'

'One of the guards who was in the tent, 'e said that Balefur chopped Swartt's belt in pieces with that battleaxe of his.'

'So, what did Sixclaw do about that?'

'Never did a thing, jus' stood there tremblin', then Balefur goes an' lays Cap'n Aggal out with a single blow.'

'It must've been a good blow, that Aggal's a tough un!'

'Hah, none of 'em are as tough as the fox. 'Ave yer seen the size of 'im? I wouldn't like to chance me paw with that one!'

'Me neither, not if 'e did wot you said.'

'Well 'e did it, true as I stan' 'ere. I'll wager that ole Balefur 'll be leadin' this 'orde atore long.'

Swartt could hear the murmurs, he heard the stifled chuckles also, though he could never identify the oul prits from out of the marching horde. Luckily the going was easy, over copse-dotted grasslands criss-crossed by small gurgling streams. Alone in his tent at nights, the Warlord noticed that his Captains were hardly bothering to come in and report at the end of each day. When he slept his dreams were visited by visions of the badger Sunflash. Each morn he would wake, and the one thing driving him on, even in his present precarious position, was to slay his enemy, the badger who had ruined his sixclawed paw.

Balefur however was enjoying his notoriety, and courting popularity with his admirers. There were a great number of hordebeasts who favoured the big fox; some were only too glad to serve him food, erect a tent for his use and obey his whims. The horde Captains were plainly frightened of him, and Balefur took every oppor tunity to belittle them by making sideswipes at their authority. His prowess with the battleaxe was becoming something of a legend around the campfires. Often he would chop an officer's spearhandle in two pieces and pretend it was an accident.

'Whoops! Sorry about that, laddie, ye must've stepped in mah way jist as ah was practisin', still, nae harm done, eh?'

Some days he would deliberately hold about half of the horde back, by taking a rest in mid-march. He would sit at the edge of a stream, bathing his paws and calling out so that Swartt could hear every word clearly, 'Och, ye march on wi' yer badger-chasin', we'll catch ye up by nightfall, mebbe!'

Grim-faced and silent, the Warlord marched onward, afraid to challenge Balefur's easygoing insolence in case he lost to the fox, yet knowing that while the challenge remained unanswered, he was losing the respect of both horde and Captains. It was a dilemma he would have to face sooner or later.

It was in the dark of a moonless night when the vixen returned. The Warlord sprang up from the cushions where he had lain sleepless through the long hours. 'Where in the name of fur'n'blood have you been all this time, vixen? Make yer report, an' it better be good!'

It was good. Swartt's agile mind weighed up the possibilities as Nightshade explained what she had found.

'Lord, you are marching south now and have been for the last few days, but no matter. Two days from here a great river runs to the west. If we follow it to the shores of the sea then we only have to go due south.'

Swartt nodded impatiently. 'Yes, yes, y'did well, vixen, we won't get lost followin' a river. But there's somethin' else you've seen, I know there is! Tell me.'

Nightshade leaned close, her voice low, relishing the role of conspirator. 'A little way east before I found the river I discovered two old stoat hags living not far from a great hole in the ground, a quarry they called it. Funny thing though, these two old ragbags of stoats, they were living in a hovel made of grass sods, but it was ringed about by many thick ropes lying flat on the ground . . .'

'Thick ropes on the ground, what for?' Swartt interrupted.

'I asked them that very question, Lord. They told me it was because of the snakes – they said that serpents won't cross over a rope laid flat on earth . . .'

Swartt stared hard at the vixen in the gloom of the

tent. 'Snakes! How many snakes were they talkin' about?'

'They said a great nest of adders live down in the quarry, where the stone is dry and sandy in places. I stood at the edge of the quarry with them and they showed me the entrance holes to the serpents' lair. Anybeast going into one of those holes would meet a horrible death for certain.'

Swartt scratched his painted chin thoughtfully. 'A great hole in the ground full of snakes, eh? I wonder how they got there?'

There was disbelief in Nightshade's voice as she explained. 'Those two old hags said that the quarry was made by many mice, squirrels, moles and woodland creatures, who needed the red sandstone to build. When they left, the snakes took it over. I think those two stoat hags are as crazy as weedfed frogs!'

Swartt waved her to silence with his mailed paw. 'Never mind all that, if the hole in the ground is there and full of serpents as they say it is, then I've got a great idea. Listen carefully now, I want no slip-ups!'

15

The following day was light and breezy. Patches of sun and shade stippled the grasslands as Swartt stood on a small knoll, his face and teeth freshly painted, cloak swirling on the wind. The Warlord's tone had a fresh ring of confidence as he addressed the horde in a loud voice: 'I've been travellin' due south because I know a great river runs west not two days from here. We'll march to that river and follow it west, and if we make it to the river in good time I'll allow you a couple of days' rest, eatin', sleepin' and doin' what you like. Now break camp and let's move!'

A half-hearted cheer went up, but most of the horde did not seem in any hurry to march. From somewhere in the centre of the horde, Balefur's voice could be heard clearly. 'All those who want tae chase badgers, follow the ferret!'

'If you think Swartt Sixclaw came all this way just to chase a badger then you're slow in the head, fox.'

Balefur stared at Nightshade curiously. 'What makes ye say that, do ye ken somethin' I don't?'

Nightshade smiled craftily, tapping her muzzle with one paw. 'I know more about Swartt Sixclaw than any beast living. Don't you believe he's down here on a badger hunt. Follow me if you want to know the real truth.'

Balefur followed the vixen as she picked her way through the vermin throng until the two of them stood alone in an ash grove. She sat and patted the grass indicating that Balefur join her. The fox inspected the area, then sat in a place of his own choosing, back against a tree, axe lying close to paw. 'Ye dinna fool me, lassie,' he said, 'ah know ye t'be Swartt's creature.'

Nightshade's eyes were bitter and her voice shook as she answered, 'For too many seasons, my friend, but now I'm sick of being treated like a pawrag – vixen do this, vixen do that, fetch, carry, yes Lord, no Lord.'

Balefur smiled as he toyed with the axe haft. 'Och, then what changed yer mind all o' a sudden?'

Nightshade leaned forward and grasped his paw. 'You did! Swartt's afraid of you, it's plain to see his days as Warlord are numbered. I want to be on the winner's side. Everybeast knows you are the next horde leader!'

Balefur pursed his lips shrewdly. 'Tell me more, ah'm beginnin' tae like the sound o' this.'

Nightshade's voice held an undercurrent of greed and excitement. 'The badger story is just a ruse. Swartt wants power and wealth. The position of Warlord is his power, but the wealth lies hidden southeast of here. searats sailed up the great river long seasons ago and hid their treasure in a secret place!'

The big fox immediately became very attentive. 'Aha! Treasure ye say – where?'

'Only Swartt and I know. We fought the searats and slew them many seasons ago on the east coast. Before their Captain died we squeezed the location of the loot out of him. However, I know now that Swartt has grown too powerful to share any loot with me. What I'm looking for is somebeast I can trust, a fox like myself to share both the treasure and command of the horde.'

Balefur spat upon his paw and held it out. 'Play me

false an' I'll gut ye, but take my paw, tell me where yon treasure lies, an' ye've got a bargain. I give ye my word, lassie!'

Nightshade spat on her paw and joined it with the big fox's.

'Fox and fox together act,
Here's my paw and here's my pact!

Right, when we reach the river Swartt is giving the horde a couple of days' rest, that's so he can slide off and get the loot. He wants the horde to move west, but if you follow the river east and come back north a bit you'll see a great hole scooped out of the earth, a quarry. That is where the treasure lies. Go carefully, and avoid an old sod dwelling where two stoat hags live. They act as sentries for the treasure, guarding the quarry. Those old hags are dangerous, they have knowledge of great spells, magic and poisons. Keep away from them, and enter the quarry secretly from the opposite side of their dwelling. You will find many holes lowdown in the pitface – choose the biggest. Follow down the hole, it is a tunnel, and at the end of it you will find the treasure if you dig straight down. Take two trusty friends with you to carry it back, for it is a great hoard that took the searats many, many seasons to steal and plunder. They say there is a great jewelled axe made from gold there, bigger even than the one you carry.'

Though Balefur's eyes shone covetously at the thought of such riches, still he asked the question, 'An' what'll ye be doin' whilst ah'm gettin' yon booty?'

The vixen nodded approvingly. 'Good, I thought you'd ask that! I'll be convincing Swartt that you've deserted with a couple of your mates; meanwhile I'll be slipping a potion in his food that'll weaken him a bit. No sense in taking stupid risks, then when you challenge him for the leadership you'll be sure to win. Now get going, take two of your foxes with you, if you leave now you'll set paws on the treasure a full day before we arrive at the river. I'll meet you at the cave to split the spoils.'

Balefur called back as he ran off towards the moving horde, 'Ah'm glad tae have ye as a friend on' not a foe, Nightshade!'

The vixen smiled and waved, knowing she was linked by destiny to serve only one. The Warlord Swartt Sixclaw!

Balefur chose two dogfoxes, young and completely in awe and admiration of him. Without telling them too much he shepherded them away from the marching horde, and they slipped off south and slightly east, away from the main body.

Swartt was joined by the vixen as they forded a small brook. 'Well, did our big-mouthed fish take the bait?' he asked.

The vixen scooped up a pawful of water and sipped lightly. 'Hook, line and sinker, Lord; it was like telling a hungry ratbabe where cook hid the apple pie.'

There was no breeze that night. It started to rain, with a slight rumble of thunder from the west getting closer. Balefur had travelled hard and fast, the two foxes panting to keep up with him. Completely drenched, they halted on a hill of shale and scree overlooking the quarry. Lightning crackled from the sky, illuminating the huge pit scooped out of the earth. Wiping rainwater from his eyes, one of the foxes stood back a bit from the edge, saying, 'It looks too scary, I don't like it!'

One hard prod from the battleaxe haft left him sprawling and nursing aching ribs. The big fox snarled contemptuously. 'Ah'm no bothered whether ye like et or no, laddie buck, up on yer paws now. Look down yonder, ye two, when lightnin' flashes again, then tell me if ye see a big hole in the quarryside.'

Thunder boomed and a bolt of lightning cut the wet night sky.

'Aye, there it is, just off t'the left, see!'

It was clear enough; all three saw it at once. There was a series of small holes, but one larger than the rest stood out like a great dark mouth, gaping wide. Balefur pushed the two young foxes ahead of him. 'Shift yersel's, mates, that's where we're bound!'

Still rubbing his ribs, the young fox protested, 'We could do with a lighted torch to see the way . . .'

Balefur's claws dug into neckscruff as he shook the protestor. 'Are ye daft, laddie, where's dry wood tae be found? Ah've flint an' tinder wi' me, d'ye want me tae dry yer tail out an' set a light to et, eh? Now move yersel's!'

The lightning became more frequent and their descent to the quarry floor was unpleasantly rapid as they skidded and slipped over rainslicked stone and through patches of wet clay. Muzzle over brush they landed, soaked and dizzy on the quarry floor. Suddenly lit by lightning the whole place looked unreal, a crater of banded pink and red stone enveloped by lancing rain. Balefur shouldered his axe, saying, 'Keep those wide daggers close, ye'll be needin' em to dig.'

'To dig? What for, Balefur?'

'Ach, never ye mind. Come on – we haven't all night!'

The hole entrance loomed dark and forbidding, but before either of the foxes could hesitate Balefur had pushed them inside with his axeshaft. Once in, it was surprisingly dry and silent, and they took a moment to shake and wipe rainwater from their faces and paws.

'Och well, at least 'tis warm an' dry,' the big fox remarked cheerfully. 'If ye feel anythin' around that'll do fer a torch let me know an' we'll light one.'

One of the two foxes sniffed the air and shuddered. 'Ugh! What's that smell, it's awful!'

Balefur sniffed several times before pronouncing. 'Ah don't know what et is, but mind, laddie, anyplace searats have been is bound tae stink a bit. Right, hang on to mah tail, yer pal can hang on to yours. Follow me.'

The moment Balefur began to suspect that all was not right was when the tunnel took several twists and turns. Attempting to find his way back through the total darkness to their original entrance, he found himself caught up in a maze of chambers, cross tunnels and dead ends. The two young foxes began whimpering.

'L . . . let's get out of here, I'm scared!'

'Aye, we should never have left the horde!'

Using his free paw, the big fox cuffed about in the darkness until he had soundly buffeted them both. 'Shuttit! D'ye hear me, belt up yer snivellin' gobs!'

They went quiet. Balefur squatted in the darkness, trying to get his bearings, then he heard the noise.

Plip . . . Plop . . . Plip . . . Plop!

'Hear that, et might be the rain's stopped an' 'tis drippin' from the rocks. Sounds like et's up ahead, right, let's go!'

As they groped their way further along the passage one of the foxes yelled joyfully, 'Light ahead, look!'

Sure enough, there was a pale light to be seen dimly ahead. They dashed towards it, tripping, stumbling and shouting, 'It must be moonlight, I'll bet the rain's stopped!'

It was a cavern, a vast, high-ceilinged chamber in the natural rock. Limestone stalactites and stalagmites could be seen everywhere, some of them reflected in the pale green luminous light given off by a massive pond in the centre of the cavern. The three foxes stood disappointed but spellbound at the glowing scene before them. The smell grew stronger – sweet, dry, cloying. Balefur had caught that odour before on the battlegrounds of the northlands. It was the scent of death!

Sssssssssssssssstttttttt!

It started gradually until the whole chamber echoed to the sinister hissing noise. Then they saw the snakes. Every exit from that dreaded place was blocked by them: adders, writhing and hissing, baring fangs as they slithered forward. Scaly, cold-eyed, olive and black-chevroned reptiles; long, short, thick, fat, poisontoothed and sinuously evil. Rearing, bunching and swaying, they came. Balefur had never witnessed anything like it, not even in his worst nightmare. The battleaxe slid from his nerveless paws as he felt himself fixed by a thousand hypnotic eyes. One of the foxes at his side screamed and threw himself into the pool.

'Eeeeyaaaaagh!'

There were only ripples on top of the bottomless pool to show where he had broken the icy surface, and a dark shape could be traced for several moments going down . . . Down . . . Down!

Then, without a sound, their faces frozen masks of terror, eyes and mouths wide open, Balefur and the remaining fox slid silently into the rustling, many-coiled embrace of the serpents of the cavern.

16

As the metal point broke the skin under Sunflash's chin, he felt its holder knocked aside and the weapon wrenched away. Then a gruff older voice growled, 'Let it be, Gring, this is too big for a searat. Musko, make a light and bring it here. Let's see what we've caught!'

Flint struck metal and a torch was lit. A raggy-furred shrew wearing a coloured headband pointed his small rapier at Sunflash. 'This ain't no searat, comrades, this's a badger, a big un too!'

Sunflash began pawing the net aside, angry at being caught napping. The fixing stakes flew from the ground as he stood. 'Huh! I thought you lot were the searats. If you've harmed those two otters I'll make you sorry you were born!'

A young shrew ran forward threateningly, sword drawn. 'I don't trust this one, he could be with the searats, kill him!'

The older shrew neatly tripped the young one, then, relieving him of his sword, he thwacked him smartly across the rump with the flat of the blade. 'That's enough out of you, Gring. I'm Log a Log round here. I'll say who gets slain and who gets spared. Now behave yourself!'

Turning to Sunflash, the shrew leader made a brief

salute with the sword. 'Sorry about that, friend. Hi, Munga, how are those otters?'

The reply came back with a deep bass chuckle. 'Comin' round fine, Chief. It's those two thick-skulled uglies Folrig an' Ruddle – good job we only sandbagged 'em!'

A small fire was lit on the lee side of a protruding rock. The otters rubbed their heads as they sat around with Sunflash, Log a Log and some older shrews.

Ruddle introduced Sunflash to the shrews, wincing as he touched a bump between his ears. 'It's a season or two since our paths crossed, matey. What're you shrews doin' up in these high hills?'

Log a Log pointed in the seaward direction. 'Taking a short cut to head Warpclaw an' his searats off. We were off clearin' a dam from the broadstream, few days back, and when we got home to our camp that villain Warpclaw had sailed his ship *Gutprow* clean up our river from the sea an' carried the liddle ones off for galley slaves. The old ones managed to run off an' hide – what else could they do?'

Sunflash thought of the Lingl and Dubbo babes, and a wave of anger swept over him against the searats for stealing little ones.

'How many babes were taken, Log a Log?' he asked.

'Thirty an' four t'be exact.' Log a Log stopped mid-sentence. For a moment his eyes filled with pain. 'And that includes my own little daughter, barely more than a season old.'

Sunflash picked up his mace. 'Come on then, there's no time to be lost. We're with you!'

The shrews gaped open-mouthed as the huge badger went pounding off down the steep slopes towards the distant shore. They were amazed at his agility and strength. Where he could not climb he took great leaps, where it was too steep to walk he threw himself into a roll, and any rock or hindrance that barred his way was pulverized beneath the mighty mace.

Folrig and Ruddle bounded after him calling to the shrews in their wake, 'Sunflash'll get yore liddle ugly mugs back if anybeast will! Hoho, bet yore glad t'be on the same side as this badger!'

They made the beach an hour after dawn. Sunflash gathered them behind a rocky outcrop from where they could see the broadstream flow across the shore and into the sea. Folding a leaf he began blowing a high-pitched signal.

Log a Log looked at him strangely. 'What're you doing, friend?'

Sunflash stopped blowing. 'Just a chance a friend of mine might be around. Right, we need a plan. You otters, swim upstream and see if you can sight the searat ship coming this way. Log a Log, have you got any ideas how we can slow them up or stop them reaching the sea?'

The shrew Chieftain scratched his scrubby chin as he gazed out over the beach, then he pointed to one spot. 'See there, that's where the sand forms in a bump on the tideline. The river flows shallowest over that part. Musko, Floom, go an' check it out for depth.'

The two shrews dashed out to the spot and plunged into the water. A moment later they were out and running back dripping. 'Neck high, Chief, just about neck high!'

Log a Log turned to Sunflash. 'That should be enough. How strong are you, friend?'

Sunflash shrugged. 'Strong enough. Tell me what you want me to do and we'll see how strong I am.'

Captain Warpclaw of the slaveship *Gutprow* was a true Corsair searat, tattooed from face to claws, decked out in tattered silks and brass earrings, with a broad scimitar thrust in his waistband. He stood perched on the stern behind the tiller rat, leering down at the huddle of terrified shrewbabes crowding together around the mastpole in the shade of *Gutprow*'s huge single green sail. The dull-eyed slaves chained at the oarbanks pulled steadily, keeping their faces down. They pitied the young captives, who would be condemned, like them, to a life at the oars of some piratical galley, but they were afraid to offer them any comfort.

Warpclaw ducked his head and, breaking a green twig from an alder tree as it brushed the ship's side, he fanned himself with the leafy twig, breathing deep of the good morning air. He was in a rare good mood, happy to be sailing seaward after a successful raid that had netted him a good cargo of young ones from the shrew settlement upstream. Warpclaw called up to the lookout high on the masthead, 'Ahoy, Bilgesnout, any sign o' blue water yet?'

'Not yet, Cap'n, may'ap we'll catch a glim o' the sea round the next bend – can't be far now!'

Warpclaw stalked down the steps from the stern into the midship well. Turning to a fat-bellied stoat who wore a broad leather belt and carried a braided sinew whip, he said, 'Too fair a mornin' t'be dawdlin', Bulgorn! Tickle yer rowers up a bit, let's see a turn o' speed out of this craft.'

Grinning cheerfully through a mouthful of blackened and broken teeth, the stoat cracked his long whip across the naked backs of the rowers. Painfully they increased their oar strokes under the vicious swish and crack of Bulgorn's lash. The shrewbabes had to crouch low to avoid being hit by the whip's backlash; they whimpered and squeaked with fear.

Warpclaw was having fun. He leapt down among them and, thrusting his face forward, he snarled cruelly, 'Yahaharr, me liddle beauties, I'll 'ave yer guts for ratlines if I 'ears one more moan out of ye!'

The little shrews went into a terrified silence, clinging pitifully to each other. They were still not fully aware of the horrors that awaited them on the open seas.

Bellowing orders, the searat Captain livened his crew up as the ship rounded a bend in the broadstream. 'Haul in them fenders! Make fast yer mainsail ends! Lookout, where away the sea now!'

The rat lookout leant out from his perch, shading his eyes with a paw as he called back smartly, 'Main dead ahead, Cap'n, I kin see the sun on the water atwixt these rocks'n'trees now!'

Folrig and Ruddle had been watching the slaveship from a safe distance for some time. Shooting ahead like twin arrows through the broadstream waters, the two otters outswam even the small fish as they sped towards the shore. Sleek and shining from the water, they arrived safely at the hideaway behind the rocks at the beach edge.

'Hearken, mates, the searat vessel ain't far behind us,' said Ruddle. 'What've you been up to, ole goldie nose?'

Log a Log shook his head as if in disbelief as he patted the badger's sturdy shoulder. 'This beast has carried two great boulders that a score of shrews couldn't budge. See over there where the sand humps up at the tideline? Sunflash dumped those boulders in the water right at that spot. I tell you, no ship'll be able to pass them an' make it to the open sea.'

Sunflash took out his split leaf and blew one last loud call with it. He shrugged as the shrews and otters stared at him curiously. 'It's worth one last try, though I can't risk that noise again. Maybe he heard it; then again, he might've been too far away.'

Log a Log shook his head; he was not about to start asking silly questions at a time like this. The big badger's business was his own, no explanations asked.

Cool shrewbeer, oatbread and cheese were passed

around, and they ate as swords were given a last edge upon the rock surfaces, and slings were loaded with flat heavy pebbles. Sunflash tightened the mace cord around his paw, and all was ready.

As the *Gutprow* came clear of the rocks to the open shore the broadstream ran slightly more shallow. The oarslaves were made to stand and punt with their long paddles, digging them into the sandy shallows to push the vessel along. Warpclaw was jubilant at the prospect of the high seas in front of him after a trouble-free raid. A fair breeze from the east bellied the big single mainsail, hurrying the ship across the shoreline towards the white-flecked main.

The searat Captain ran for'ard and, standing with his back to the bowsprit, he faced the crew. He waved his scimitar and roared, 'Ahoy, buckoes, who's the best Cap'n on land or sea?'

They cheered and shouted his name. 'Cap'n Warpclaw!'

Sunlight glittered and twinkled on his brass ornaments and shining scimitar as Warpclaw threw wide his paws triumphantly.

Whump!

The searat was thrown flat on his back as the ship stopped dead. Two crewrats sitting on the after gallery were shot backwards into the water and the oarslaves fell sidewards like a load of tenpins. A stricken-faced lookout came sliding down a rope and shot past Warpclaw, who was staggering upright and rubbing at the back of his skull with both paws.

The lookout hung over the bows yelling, 'She's trapped 'ead on atwixt two dirty great rocks! They wasn't 'ere when we sailed up this way! Eeeeyyaaarrgg!'

With a hefty kick from Warpclaw, the lookout went straight over into the water. Still massaging his aching head, the Corsair looked over at the spluttering rat in the water. 'Guts'n'tripes! Who stuck them there?' he snarled.

'Give the babes back, Seascum!'

Warpclaw whirled around. Sunflash was striding across the beach, flanked by the two otters and backed by sixty shrews. The badger's voice was like thunder as he hefted his mace.

'I won't tell you twice, rat! Deliver those little ones back. Now!'

Warpclaw was a quick thinker. Forgetting his throbbing head, he leapt down amidships and came up with a shrewbabe, then, holding the tiny creature upside down by a single footpaw, the searat pulled out his scimitar and swung it aloft.

'Stop right there or I'll slay this'n!' he bellowed.

Sunflash and the rescuers ground to an immediate halt. The badger pointed with his mace at the wriggling, weeping babe. 'I warn you, rat, touch one hair of him and you'll die!'

Warpclaw knew it was a standoff, but he had the upper paw. 'Shift those boulders or I'll kill 'em all, every last one!'

The crew of *Gutprow* sprang to arms; suddenly the rails bristled with armed vermin. Log a Log looked at the two otters, despair stamped on his scrubby face.

Warpclaw chuckled; he knew how soft woodlanders were about their young. 'Well, stripedog, you look big enough. Are yer goin' to move the rocks?'

Sunflash could not stop his voice trembling as he answered, 'Give the babes back and I'll free your ship.'

The Corsair knew he had won. Drawing the scimitar further back, as if ready to chop, he called down to the badger, 'Tell yer wot I'll do, we'll call this liddle maggot number one, then I'll keep slicin' 'em until you move those rocks!'

The wide blade glittered in the sun as he swung at the babe.

'Kreeeegaaaaaar!'

Skarlath hit the searat like a thunderbolt from out of

the sky! One set of talons buried itself in the swordpaw whilst the other took Warpclaw round his throat. He fell backwards, dropping the babe into the water. Then Sunflash the Mace was aboard the ship in a flash, blood-wrath of the Badger Warrior Lords filling his eyes.

Skarlath knew what was about to happen; he was powerless to stop it. Seeing the shackle that connected the slave chain he wrenched at it madly until it clattered free, then he shrieked at the oarslaves, 'Kreeeh! Grab those little ones! Get clear of this ship!'

One paw at his throat, the other scrabbling for his scimitar, Warpclaw rasped hoarsely at the crew of the *Gutprow*, 'Kill the badger, rip 'im, tear 'im to shreds!'

As the crew advanced on Sunflash the oarslaves splashed overboard, clutching the yelling shrewbabes.

Skarlath swooped down beside Log a Log as the babes and their rescuers were hauled from the water. 'Kreeeh! Stay clear of the ship!'

A blood-chilling roar rang out from the deck.

'Eeulaliaaaaaaaaa!'

Log a Log drew his rapier, saying, 'But we must help him!'

The kestrel knocked the blade from his paw. 'If you value your lives, stay clear of the ship, all of you! The sight of that rat nearly slaying the little one has set off the bloodwrath in him; Sunflash is berserk! I have seen it before, though never like this. He will slay anybeast in his path, he is a Badger Lord. Stay clear I beg of you!'

The gathering on the shore stood in shocked silence as roars, screams and chaos echoed from the *Gutprow*. Sunflash the Mace was visiting death upon the searats who had stolen babes from the shrews.

17

With his back against the mast, Sunflash faced the searats six at a time. Daggers stabbed, blades slashed, but nought could stand before him. The mace swung and fell, whirling in arcs, sweeping like a scythe, smashing like a sledgehammer. The searats fought back with desperation, but their swords snapped like twigs as the Badger Warrior wielded his mace, so fast that it was hard for the eye to follow. His speed and strength were unmatched.

On shore, the shrews covered their babes' eyes and ears as they looked away from the swaying vessel. The oarslaves, however, stood watching, grim satisfaction stamped on their thin faces. The vermin of the waves were being paid back in full for every lashmark, every chainscar, every day of near-starvation, every night separated from their loved ones. An old squirrel raised a clenched paw and shook it at the hated *Gutprow*, crying, 'Let them reap the whirlwind they have brought upon their own evil heads!'

Not one searat or wave vermin left the ship alive. When his terrible task was at an end Sunflash let slip the mace from his paws and fell down in a stupor by the mast.

Folrig, Ruddle and Skarlath had long since herded the shrews back behind the rocks at the shore's edge, where they ate and stayed resting until sunset's scarlet fires began lighting the horizon. Then the kestrel flew out over the silent ship.

Sunflash was wakened by the lonely cry of seabirds. Lowering himself over the ship's side, he washed all traces of battle from his body and cleaned off his mace in the cold water. The badger's eyes were normal now, back to their usual mild, dark-brown hue.

Skarlath landed nearby and watched as Sunflash took his mace and smashed two gaping holes in the *Gutprow*, one each side, amidships, just above the waterline. Placing his mace to one side he waded into the broadstream and, bending his back and grunting with exertion, he loosened the two boulders from the streambed and rolled them ashore. The water had been building up behind the vessel, and now it was free of the restraining boulders the ship sprang clear. Night winds caught the sail, billowing it out; the *Gutprow* was off on its last voyage.

Sunflash sat down on the sand beside Skarlath, his shoulders bowed wearily, saying, 'She will sail out into deep waters until the waves find those holes, then she will go to the bottom.'

A great fire was lit on the beach; shrews sat round it with their backs to the rocks, and a cauldron of soup made from watershrimp, herbs and leeks bubbled away merrily. Bread and cheese was shared, shrewbeer was poured, with blackberry cordial for the little ones.

Sunflash sat alone, apart from the festivities. Log a Log brought him food, and said, 'Lord Sunflash, we of the Guosim thank you. Words do not come easily to show our gratitude for what you have done for us, but our hearts are full for you. The name Sunflash will live for ever with the Guosim.'

The badger echoed the curious word, 'Guosim?'

Log a Log explained. 'Guerilla Union Of Shrews In Mossflower, first letter of each word. We are warriors, we honour you!'

Sunflash nodded his thanks, but still he sat alone, knowing the first real feelings of being a Badger Lord, fearing his own bloodwrath, shuddering at the sight he had been granted of his own dark side.

Skarlath sat perched by the fire, watching Sunflash from a distance. The shrewbabes were too excited to sleep; they played and danced, laughed and sang with boundless energy. The kestrel knew how little ones affected his friend, so he called them over. 'Poor old Mister Sunflash, doesn't he look sad,' he said. 'Why don't you go and say thank you to him for saving you from the searats? Go on, maybe he'd like to play with you!'

When the little shrews had run off to Sunflash and there was peace around the fire, two shrewmaids began singing. One of them played a small stringed instrument not unlike a mandoline. It had a sweet tinkling tone, and to it they sang a ballad that they had written that very day, a song that would become a great favourite around shrew campfires for countless seasons to come.

'Oh 'twas all in the summertime,
Our hearts did sadly grieve,
The searats stole up in the night,
And with our babes did leave.
Full four and thirty little shrews
Were taken to be slaves,
To live in misery or refuse
And die in watery graves.
But then a mighty warrior
Did come along our way,
We knew what fate had sent him for,
When these words he did say:
"Come follow me down to the sea,

Across the mountain track,
And I will set your young ones free,
I'll bring those babies back."
And then with mighty chunks of rock,
He dammed the great broadstream,
And gave those foul searats a shock,
Which caused them all to scream.
He came with death held in his paw,
Which no rat born could face.
Oh woe to those who break the law,
Of Sunflash and his mace.
Take warning all you bold searats,
Who plough the raging main,
Steal not our babes, and come not near,
Our peaceful shores again,
For fear you meet the Badger Lord,
He of the gold-marked face,
For you'll meet death once you have met
The Warrior with the Mace.'

Folrig raised his beaker in admiration. 'Here's to a great ballad sung well by pretty maids!'

Ruddle and Log a Log were chuckling. The shrew pointed, and said, 'Aye, look, here comes a big babe playing with little babes.'

There were six shrewbabes riding on Sunflash's back as he ambled up and shook them off, then collapsed on the sand, begging, 'Enough, enough! I'd sooner do battle with ten shiploads of villains than fight you lot off!'

Another group arrived panting, dragging the mace along the sand by its corded handle. A plump, serious-faced infant held up a pebble in one paw and addressed Log a Log. 'See dis peggle, I make it get stucked inna star, watch!'

Smiling broadly, Sunflash picked up his mace and held it like a bat, calling to the infant, 'One, two, three. Now!'

The little shrew flung the pebble and Sunflash struck it with his mace, sending it straight up into the night. He crouched and held out one paw, and the infant stood solemnly on it and was lifted high.

'Where has that pebble gone?' the badger asked him.

A little paw pointed straight at the sky. 'Way up der, it stuck inna star now!'.

Yelling and laughing, the big badger dashed off across the beach with a horde of little ones clinging to him.

'Cummon, let's go'n paggle inna water!'

Skarlath looked up from a bowl of soup and shook his head. 'Shame on him, he's worse than the babes!'

The Guosim slept on the shore that soft autumnal night, and never had they felt more safe. The presence of Sunflash drove away all fear of trouble. Next morning, Log a Log stood on the rocks that skirted the broadstream. Cupping his paws around his mouth he warbled a long ululating call upstream.

'Logalogalogalogaloooooog!'

It was answered so faintly that at first Sunflash thought it was an echo, but the shrew Chieftain put him right.

'That is our elders coming downstream with the logboats. We of the Guosim don't care to do too much travelling by paw.'

In a short while the boats appeared. They were long logboats carved from pinetrunks, punted skilfully by old shrews.

Log a Log took Sunflash's paw. 'You'll like our settlement; we'll lay on a feast for you that'll make your fur curl, matey.'

The big badger shook Log a Log's paw firmly. 'No thank you, friend. I have my own path to follow.'

Folrig and Ruddle nodded in agreement. 'Aye, matey, we're bound a long ways from here.'

Sunflash grabbed the two otters and, tucking one

beneath each elbow, he walked to the broadstream and dropped them into the nearest logboat.

'You two ugly mugs are going back with Log a Log,' he said. 'This part of my journey I must make alone. I can feel it in my bones; the mountain of Salamandastron is not far away now.'

By the look on Sunflash's face, the otters knew there would be no room for argument, so they slipped back into their old insulting ways.

Ruddle stretched out in the stern and waved. 'G'bye, ole frog frightener, hope yore mountain doesn't crack down the middle when y'look at it, what d'you say, nastynose?'

Folrig flicked streamwater at the badger. 'Right, me ole bulgebelly, at least I won't have t'wake up an' think I'm havin' nightmares when I see yore great big badger-butterbonce starin' at me. Take care of yoreself, 'cos nobeast else will, yore not pretty enough!'

Skarlath and Sunflash stood on the shore, waving as the logboats loaded with Guosim disappeared around the broadstream bend with the shrews paddling and chanting:

'Shrum a too rye hey, shrum a too rye hey,
Dig those paddles deep today,
Where the alders shade me overhead,
And trout swim on the broadstream bed.
I'm a Guosim to the water wed,
Shrum a too rye hey, shrum a too rye hey,
I'll see you one day to make,
O'er any stream or pond or lake,
A good ole logboat's ripplin' wake,
Shrum a too rye hey, shrum a too rye hey, shrum
    shrummmmmm.'

The sounds died off into the far shady reaches of broadstream.

Sunflash turned to Skarlath as he set off, saying, 'Straight south to the end of autumn, I dreamed it last night. But what of you, my hawk, have you no affairs of your own to fly off to and attend?'

The kestrel circled his companion's head. 'I'll stay with you for a score and a half days, until you reach your dream mountain, then I will fly off and see to my own business.'

Sunflash tried to focus on Skarlath as he swooped and wheeled. 'How do you know it is a score and a half days away?'

Dipping low, the kestrel brushed the gold-striped head with his wings, and flew off high, calling, 'Because I have flown south until I saw it rearing to the sky. Go now, see for yourself, Badger Lord of Salamandastron!'

The autumn was, if anything, as warm as the summer. Sunflash travelled the shores moving south. He saw little of Skarlath during this time, but he knew his friend was not far off, watching, ever watching. Misty mornings dissolved into golden noontides and crimson sunsets, and the big badger found peace, walking alone, making solitary camp at night, thinking and reflecting on both the past and the future. Often he was visited in dreams by his mother, father and grandsires; they imparted much wisdom to him, as if preparing him for the role he was to play.

The last day of autumn was hot and bright as midsummer. Still as a millpond, the sea reflected a cloudless blue sky. Seabirds wheeled and called, soaring lazily on the warm thermals above the sun-baked sands of the shore.

Sunflash stood for a moment, his breath taken away by the majesty of the great mountain that lay ahead of him.

Two hares stood shaded by a cave entrance, watching a fully grown male badger plough his way wearily across the beach towards them. He was big and dangerous looking; the fierce light in his eyes glinted off the metal tip of an immense war club which he carried easily in one paw.

When the two hares stepped out from the shadows, Sunflash could see that both were of a very great age.

'What do they call this place?' he asked.

The older of the hares, a male, answered him, 'Salamandastron, the place of the fire lizard.'

The badger gave a huge sigh. Leaning against the rock, he rested his club on the sand.

'I feel as if I've been here before,' he said strangely.

The female hare produced victuals from within the cave entrance. 'Rest awhile. Eat and drink. I am called Breeze, and this is my brother Starbuck. What do they call you?'

The badger smiled. He touched one of his headstripes, which was yellow rather than white.

'Some call me Sunflash the Mace. I am the son of Bella and Barkstripe. I'm a traveller.'

Starbuck nodded in satisfaction. 'Your travelling is at an end, Sunflash. You are the grandson of Boar the Fighter and great grandson of Old Lord Brocktree. It is written on the walls of our mountain that you would come here someday.'

Sunflash straightened up. He stared hard at the hares. 'Written, you say. By whom?'

Breeze shrugged. 'By whoever wrote that other hares will follow after us. That is the way it has always been and always will be.'

Both hares stood in the cave entrance. They bowed to the badger.

'Welcome to your mountain, Sunflash the Mace, Lord of Salamandastron.'

The high sun above watched as the badger and the hares went together into the mountain on the shores below.

Skarlath the kestrel had watched all from the crater peak of the mountain fortress. Fierce pride welled in his breast for the badger who had given him back his life all those long seasons ago in a winter forest. Then, without a backward glance he soared off into the blue, winging northeast to seek out Swartt Sixclaw.

BOOK TWO

A Broken Trust

18

Nobeast in living memory could recall a winter as long and harsh as the one that followed the brief, hot autumn, though some had predicted it earlier, judging by the great number of berries that were seen on tree and bush at harvest time. Shrieking northeast winds drove the snow into deep drifts, and great, ancient trees were riven, split from root to tip, felled by ice which sought out any weakness in their trunks. Overnight, the west-flowing river stood still, frozen solid. Bushes lining both banks poked bare skeletal twigs at the hostile sky, as if pleading for the release of spring. Bitter and intense, the cruel season took savage toll of anybeast weakened by its ravages. It was a winter of death, hunger and despair.

The great horde of the Warlord was held prisoner, trapped amid a freezing world of whiteness. They erected crude shelters in the woodland surrounding the riverbank. Sustenance and morale were at their lowest, stifling any ideas of desertion or mutiny as effectively as the snows that shrouded the earth. Bluefen, daughter of Bowfleg and wife of Swartt, gave birth to a ferretbabe, after which she faded and died, like a delicate spring flower suddenly embraced by severe frost, though it was said that she had never been a strong creature. Unlike the babe, a young male, tough as a deep-rooted weed and marked with the legacy of his father Swartt, six tiny claws showing on the left forepaw. The Warlord lived up to his title the Pitiless One, neither grieving after his wife, nor caring for his son. Bluefen was buried with scant ceremony in a shallow hole hacked into the stone-hard earth, whilst the babe was given to an old female rat to nurse and guard. Swartt acted as though the whole thing was no concern of his.

Nightshade, the vixen seer and healer, had erected a separate shelter, as far from the vicious-tempered Warlord as she dared, though she was constantly on call, applying heated poultices and nostrums to her master's damaged sixclawed paw, which pained him agonizingly in cold weather. Hordebeasts crouched and trembled in their own meagre dwellings, listening at night to Swartt's anguished cries as winter tortured his withered paw. Any horde soldier with a grain of sense kept clear of the Warlord when he was like this, for the ferret's temper was unpredictable. Once the pains had subsided, Swartt would sit in his fir bough leanto, staring into the fire, sleepless, cursing the name of Sunflash the Mace. Revenge was what kept Swartt Sixclaw alive through that winter. The thought of vengeance upon his foe was like food, drink and sleep to him, as he planned what he would do on the day he had the badger at his mercy. And so the horde existed through that long winter, starving, freezing, and waiting for spring.

Skarlath spent his winter among friends. Snug in the warmth and good cheer of the Lingl–Dubbo cave, the kestrel enjoyed himself hugely. Knowing Sunflash was safe inside the mountain of his heart's desire and that no horde could march in such a terrible season, the faithful bird had no worries. His time was spent making cheese with the help of the molewife Lully, playing with the young ones, brewing ale with Uncle Blunn, helping

Tirry and his wife Dearie to cook wonderful meals with the food they had stored in their supply chamber, and eating, always eating. The fierce bird even learned to sing a few songs and dance to the gurdelstick, though as one of the little molemaids remarked, 'Hurr, you'm a gettin' so gurtly fattinged 'twill be a wunner if ee be able to fly cumms ee spring toime, hurr hurr hurr!'

Skarlath chased her twice round the cave. 'Kreeh! Impudent little rip, if I am too fat to fly then I'll fall right out of the sky on top of you!'

The old squirrel Elmjak bustled in, carrying two pails of snow to be melted down on the fire. He stamped his paws as Aunt Ummer unwound a long heavy scarf from his neck. 'Yurr, zurr Ellumjakky, 'ow be et owt thurr today?' she enquired.

Elmjak seated himself by the fire, allowing the molemaids Nilly and Podd to towel the snowdamp from his bush and back. 'Well, let me tell thee, good friends, I think winter has now done its worst and spring will soon be here.'

Tirry Lingl looked up from a bowl of barley broth. 'What makes you say that? Have you seen a sign, Elmjak?'

Opening his paw, the squirrel presented two tiny flowers to the delighted molemaids. 'See, little missies, the best sign of all – two new snowdrops. I found them right outside the cave in a bare patch sheltered by the rock, mayhap the cave's warmth must have helped 'em a bit, but there they are, two tiny beauties, just like you pair.'

Dearie Lingl poured water into a small jug. 'Ooh, ain't they just about the prettiest, most welcome sight after a long winter, snowdrops! Put 'em in the jug 'ere, it'll please our eyes t'watch 'em open. Come on, Auntie Ummer, out wi' yore gurdelstick an' sing of spring to the liddle flowers!'

Skarlath preened his wing feathers, a bit self

consciously. 'Er, er, I've thought up a springsong. If I sing it could you manage to pick up the tune, Auntie Ummer?'

The fat old mole winked as she twanged her gurdel-stick's string. 'You'm sing et, zurr 'awkburd, oi'll catch ee up!'

The kestrel had often joined in choruses, but this was his first solo attempt, and he clacked his curved beak nervously.

'I went off to my bed on one dark winter's night,
When the ground was all snowy and covered up
   white,
And snug in my blanket I started to dream
That the ice had all melted away from the stream.
   Ooooh! Plip plop, hear the water drop,
   And larks take wing as the buds go pop!
   And the sun do shine as the birds do sing,
   Throw open wide the gates of Spring!

Then I dreamt that I felt all the earth come awake,
And the sky was as blue as a clear mountain lake,
And through that old dream a good sound ringing
   true,
'Twas the heralding song of a happy cuckoo!
   Ooooh! Plip plop, hear the water drop,
   And larks take wing as the buds go pop!
   And the sun do shine as the birds do sing,
   Throw open wide the gates of Spring!

Fol de rol de lair oh lair oh,
Hail the newborn day,
Spring has made the weather fair oh,
Winter's gone away!'

Skarlath buried his head modestly in his wing feathers as he bowed, and they cheered him to the echo, encouraging him to sing his song twice over. The small hoglets and molemaids danced as the gurdelstick kept rhythm with the singing kestrel.

In the days that followed, Elmjak's prediction proved true. The sun showed itself, weakly at first, then the cheeping of the hardy birds, who had borne winter's brunt, began. Warmth started to pervade the land, unlocking the streams to chuckle over the stones with gladness, causing the icicles to weep tears and shorten their lives, melting the crusted white from limb and bough, lengthening the happy hours of daylight.

For the first time in many moons Swartt felt the lancing pains recede from his paw. He repainted his face and teeth, put a new edge on his sword and emerged from the crude pine bough shelter roaring, 'Up on yer stumps, you lousy layabouts! Nightshade, take six scouts an' see what it's like up ahead! Aggal, Scraw, Muggra, kick some life into this skinny slobjawed mess! We break camp now! Westward with the river! Keep up or be slain!'

Like a single great beast the horde moved west, churning up mud on the banks of the racing river, grabbing anything that came to paw in their hunger, grass, green twigs, withered roots, worms, dead frogs and any insect that moved. Somewhere at the rear of the marchers, the ferretbabe whom nobeast had bothered to name tore greedily at a pawful of dead grass, as it bobbed and swayed in a bark sling on the old rat's back. Tiny sharp teeth gnawing, quick sly eyes darting to and fro, making never a sound as it watched for the opportunity of its next meal.

Four days later, Skarlath sighted the horde below as he ranged the northeastern skies. His brief sojourn with old friends cut short by the arrival of spring, the kestrel was once more soaring the breeze, searching, watching, nothing below missing his keen gaze. He had gone in search of the enemy and, unerringly, he had found them. The horde had arrived at a place where a wide, well-trodden path intersected the river. The path ran from north to south; there was a ford at the river junction.

Perched low down in a horse chestnut tree, the kestrel kept himself well hidden and listened to a dispute which had sprung up between the Warlord and his Captains.

The weasel Muggra was all for following the river. 'You said yerself, foller the river west, that way we don't go gittin' lost again.'

Swartt's hand was straying dangerously close to his sword hilt. 'Lost? Who ever said that I got me own army lost? Well, speak up, fatmouth – was it you?'

Muggra wanted to back down, he wished he had never spoken, but Swartt was not letting him off easily. Muggra shrugged. 'I never said you got us lost, not me, all's I said is why go down that path when you said t'foller the river.'

Swartt drew his sword casually, glancing at the other Captains. 'What d'you lot say, foller the river with Muggra, or go south down the path with me? Or would you like to go and find that traitor Balefur and see if he survived the winter?'

All silent, they directed their eyes at the ground. Rumours of Balefur's coming to a horrible end had been circulating.

The Warlord smiled nastily at his weasel Captain. 'Not much support from yer mates there. Righto, let me settle this argument. I'm Warlord, I command you all, an' I say we go south down the path. Is that all right wid you, Muggra?'

The weasel was nodding dumbly when Swartt struck, slashing him across his footpaw with the curved sword. Muggra screamed and sat down hugging his injured footpaw.

Swartt lifted the chin of the Captain on his swordpoint until their eyes met. 'So you win. If yore against marchin' down the path, then you don't 'ave to, mate, y'can hop! Now up on yer paw an' let's see yer hoppin' out front there. I'd hop fast if I was you, 'cos if y'don't I'll use me blade agin, but next time it won't be on yer paw!'

Without further argument the entire horde started marching south down the path. Swartt shot a glare in the direction of Nightshade, whose face was the picture of disapproval, and snarled, 'Now don't you start, vixen, one word from you an' y'can join ole Muggra fer a hop!'

Skarlath had seen and heard enough. In time he would report the horde's movement to Sunflash, but first he felt it important to warn others, particularly the occupants of the big redstone building he had sighted some days back as he was searching for signs of Swartt. It was a large construction and looked newly built, a fine dwelling place for whatever creatures chose to live there. Unfortunately it stood square on the pathside. Swartt Sixclaw and his horde could not possibly miss it if they marched four days south down the path.

19

Extract from the writings of Barlom, Recorder Mouse of Redwall Abbey and grandson of Timballisto who was friend to Martin the Warrior.

I wish that I had known Martin the Warrior, but alas he is gone with the other heroes who helped to build this beautiful Abbey. My grandfather Timballisto (peace be upon his memory) used to tell me tales when I was a tiny Dibbun, stories of the wild old times. He would often sing songs or recite poems about the warriors who fought and helped to form our order, battled against tremendous odds and made this Redwall, this way of life for all of us whom they would never live to see. But that is the way of things, and we revere their names now, knowing they sleep in peace after a task well done. Only one remains amongst us, they say she is a living miracle, Bella the Ancient of Brockhall.

I had always known that female badgers have a great life span, but I have heard even the most senior of our elders say that the silver badger will go on for ever. Poor creature, she is the most loving of beasts, almost blind with age now, a snail could move faster than her. Bella never talks of the old days. Abbess Meriam says that is because it is too painful for her. Long ago Bella lost a son of her own; nobeast knows what became of him. Now she cares for our young, the Dibbuns, and all the Abbeybabes are very fond of her. I myself have seen her send a wailing babe to sleep with merely a stroke of her paw upon its head. I hope that she will be with us for many long seasons yet; they say a badger may live almost four times as long as others, let us hope this is so.

Tonight there is to be a feast; we will be celebrating the memory of the great ones, Martin, Gonff the Mousethief, Columbine, Dinny the mole, Abbess Germaine, Ben Stickle, my own grandsire Timballisto and a list of heroes, friends and Redwallers too long to mention. There will be no sadness, but great joy in our Abbey – how could we be unhappy to recall those who live for ever in our minds? It would shame their memories for us to weep at table!

But enough of my ramblings. I'm so absent-minded that I missed lunch today, but that is soon to be remedied, for I hear the gruff tuneless singing of my friend Togget, grandson of Dinny. He never forgets to bring me a snack if he misses my face at table.

'Ho a bumblybee ee'm a wunnerful burd,
Sings a song loike you'm never hurrd,
Ho a fuzzbuzz fuzzbuzz fuzzbuzz buzz,
That's all ee'm ever duzz duzz duzz!'

Togget trundled into the gatehouse bearing a tray covered with a cloth, then, bowing low, he whisked off the cloth neatly. 'If'n 'tweren't furr oi, maister Barlom, ee'd starve'n'unger gurtly. Veggible zoop, 'Tober Ale, apple'n'cheese furr ee!'

Barlom took them gratefully from his friend. 'What would I do without you, Togget? How can I repay you for your constant kindness to a dusty old Recorder?'

The mole's heavy digging claw reached out for Barlom's quill. 'Let oi make writin' marks in ee gurt book, zurr.'

'Hmm, well all right, just one, right here at the bottom of the page where nobeast will notice. Dip your pen, Togget.'

Togget licked the quill point several times before dunking it deep into the inkwell. Smiling broadly, the little mole flourished the quill and bent to write at the foot of the page. Barlom smiled as he watched him. Eyes scrunched, tongue sticking from the side of his mouth, Togget concentrated on writing a big scrawling X. He dotted it with a full stop.

'Thurr, that be et, moi name!' he announced.

Barlom shook his head as he retrieved his quill pen. 'That's not your name. You're called Togget, that says ex.'

The mole nodded sagely. 'Aye, h'ex, that be moi mark, oi be gudd at makin' et, hurr!'

Alongside the cross Barlom wrote the name Togget. 'There, that's how you write your name, see.'

The mole patted his friend's paw sympathetically. 'Sumtoimes oi wunner why they'm callen you a cleverbeast, maister Barlom, you'm no gurt writer o' moi name, hurr no! Ho well, oi'm off t'wake ee Friar oop now. Gubbye, zurr.'

As soon as Togget was gone Barlom burst out laughing.

Young Bryony watched Togget approaching as she sat sunning herself against the great Abbey wall. The pretty little mousemaid wore a mob cap askew and her white apron was stained with berry juice. She patted flourdust from her paws as she rose to meet her friend, complaining, 'Ole Bunny's still snoring, I can't wake him.'

Togget waved a paw in the air as if creating a spell. 'You'm leave thatbeast to oi, moi dear.'

Friar Bunfold was sleeping in his favourite place, an old wheelbarrow in the orchard. His bulging stomach rose and fell with each snore, the leaves of an overhanging pear tree trembling with every exhalation of his breath. Bryony covered her mouth to stifle a giggle as her molefriend shook the fat mousefriar by his sleeve urgently. 'Coom on, ole zurr, wakey oop, ee toald oi to wake ee if'n ee gurt cake was a burnen in ee h'oven!'

Bunfold fell out of the barrow with a start. 'Cake burning, where, what cake?'

As Togget and Bryony ambled back off to the kitchens the mole nodded ruefully. 'Dearie me, but oi do tell whackin' fibbers, tho' et did wake ole Bunny oop, hurr hurr, that et did!'

Cheerful Redwallers called out to Bunfold as he bustled through Great Hall on his way to the kitchens.

'Good afternoon, Friar, what's for dinner tonight?'

Exercising his dry wit, Bunfold gave a mock scowl at a young squirrel. 'Boiled frog an' toasted clouds for you, Brugg, m'laddo!'

Brugg pulled a face, playing along with the Friar. 'Yukk! Sooner have lightnin' soup an' ditchwater!'

Togget managed to pull Brugg's tail as he passed. 'Loightnen zoop'n'ditchwatter, oi'll see wot oi c'n do for ee, maister, bo urr!'

Bryony giggled helplessly at the face Brugg pulled, and gasped, 'Don't be sad, Brugg, I'll see if I can bake a little thundercake to dip in your lightnin' soup, hahahaha!'

The Abbey kitchens were all abustle, clouds of steam wreathing the woodlanders as they dashed to and fro. A huge hedgehog wife called Myrtle waved a ladle at a large cake which lay on a stone cooling slab, saying, 'D'you want to slice it now, Friar? It baked well.'

Selecting a flat, thin slicing knife, Bunfold winked at her. 'Burnt cake eh, well let's see. Togget, bring the cherry conserve. Heartwood, is that meadowcream ready yet?'

Heartwood, a reliable old otter, dipped his spoon into a pottery bowl and sampled the golden mixture. 'Stirred gently to a turn, Friar matey, ready as ever!'

Lifting the bowl, Bunfold was forced to execute a nimble sideskip for two tiny otters scooting past with a laden trolley, both yelling in deep olderbeast voices, 'Gangwaaaaay, watch y'backs there, mates!'

Bunfold arrested their progress, catching both by their aprons as he halted the trolley with a quick footpaw. 'Whoa there, steady up, Dibbuns, what's all this?'

The otter twins, Blatt and Scrimmo, waggled their tails respectfully at the Redwall Friar.

'Butt'n mushrooms, matey, sir!'

'Aye, an' watershrimps too, sir, matey!'

Bunfold sorted through the snowy white mushrooms and inspected the netful of almost transparent watershrimp. 'Good work, Dibbuns, did you gather these?'

'Sir, this very mornin' out in the woods, matey.'

'Our mum 'elped us too, she said to bring 'em straight t'you.'

Bunfold rummaged in his apron pocket and, pulling forth two candied chestnuts, he gave the otters one each. 'Champion stuff! Don't forget an' thank your mum for me. They'll make great pasties for the feast this evenin'. Want to stay and watch me cut'n'fill this big cake?'

Blatt and Scrimmo nodded furiously. Myrtle lifted both and stood them on the cooling slab, for a good view of the proceedings.

Togget stood by, tottering wearily, both paws latched firmly on to the handles of a sizeable jar. 'You'm gunner chatter'n'jaw wi' they two h'otters or fix oop ee cake, maister? This'n ain't gettin' much loighter, burr no.'

With swift sureness Bunfold sliced through the sides

of the pale fawn cake, and then sliced again. The little
otters watched wide-eyed as the Friar worked, separat-
ing the cake into three flat circles, moist and gently
steaming. Bryony closed her eyes, savouring the aroma.

Heartwood smiled at the otters. 'By 'okey, mates, it
do smell good!'

Blatt and Scrimmo were allowed to wield flat beech-
wood spreaders, covering the bottom layer until it was
one thick smooth circle of dark red conserve. Then
Togget and Bryony took their turn, layering the middle
tier even more thickly with meadowcream. Heartwood
and the Friar carefully placed the three circles together
in their former positions, and coated the cake generously
with the remainder of the meadowcream.

The six cakemakers began decorating, working around
the sides and top with a random pattern of hazelnut and
almond flakes, sliced early strawberries and tiny young
rose leaves crystallized in honey. The finished cake
attracted great attention. Redwallers gathered round to
admire and comment on the masterpiece that had been
created in their kitchens.

'It's the very picture of a spring afternoon!'

'Bo urr, et surpintly lukks wunnerful cool'n'cream-
loike!'

'Yes, shame it has to be eaten, really.'

'Haht! Y'mean 'twould be a shame not to eat it!'

'Bet I could eat the lot, all on my own!'

'Greedyguts, you'd be sick for two seasons!'

'But it'd be well worth it for a cake like that!'

'Hush now, here comes Mother Abbess!'

All work in the kitchens stopped as Meriam Abbess of
Redwall entered; never appearing to walk, she glided in
like a swan crossing a still lake. Meriam was tall for a
mouse, slender and of middle seasons, though her great
wisdom and serenity would have done credit to one
twice her age. Clad in a simple long robe of pale green
belted by a soft white cord, paws folded into her wide

sleeves, the Mother Abbess of Redwall radiated calm and respect to everybeast about her. A rare fleeting smile hovered about her hazel eyes as she viewed the confection, and said, 'A truly beautiful cake, Friar Bunfold.'

Bunfold bowed, his chubby face glowing with pleasure. 'Thankee, marm, I had lots o' good help t'make it.'

A brief nod passed between Bryony and the Abbess, who said, 'I would not doubt the truth of that, Friar. It might have spoiled in the oven whilst you were napping in the orchard, had it not been for the vigilance of Togget and our little flower Bryony.'

The surprise on Bunfold's face was forestalled as Meriam continued speaking, lowering the tone of her voice. 'You are a good old Friar – a little rest each noontide is not begrudged you, Bunfold. Leave this now, I am sure your helpers can prepare the festive food well enough. I need the wise counsel of yourself and Heartwood. Please accompany me to the gatehouse, Barlom has a visitor waiting there.'

Friar Bunfold swiftly untied his apron and hung it up, wiping face and paws on a clean towel as he issued orders to Togget. 'Could you make up a tray and bring it to the gatehouse, my friend? Hot mint tea, a flagon of cold fruit cordial, some of those scones we baked this morning, oh, and a plate of the thin arrowroot and almond slices which the Abbess favours, there's a good mole!'

'Hurr that oi am, roight away, zurr Bunny!'

Togget's words were lost upon Bunfold; he and Heartwood were scurrying off in the wake of Abbess Meriam, who was gliding away from them rapidly.

Barlom was self-appointed as Gatekeeper – the gatehouse was one of the few places he could carry out his Recorder's duty in relative peace. A solid-looking squirrel named Sumin often dropped by to chat with him, and he was headed there that day on Barlom's request, to discuss the strange visitor's arrival.

Sumin arrived with the Abbess and, in his stout, no-nonsense way, held open the door for her, nodding curtly. 'Marm, 'tis a kestrel within your gatehouse, don't be feared. I'm sure he means harm to nobeast'

The Abbess gestured for Sumin to enter. 'Mayhap you should hear what this bird has to say. Please come in with us, my friend.'

When Bunfold and Heartwood arrived they entered also, leaving the gatehouse door ajar. The fierce, handsome kestrel was perched on a chairback, watching all with keen golden eyes. As Meriam introduced herself and the others, the hawk watched them in silence, his head coming up sharply as a knock sounded on the door, followed by Togget's voice.

'Yurr's drink'n'vittles furr ee goodbeasts insoid o' thurr!'

Heartwood took the tray and closed the door. The food was placed before the kestrel, who dipped his beak courteously, and said, 'My name is Skarlath. I serve Sunflash the Mace, Lord of Salamandastron, a great warrior!'

Meriam held her paws outward, a sign of peace. 'You are welcome within our walls, Skarlath. Redwall Abbey is open to all goodbeasts who come seeking rest and food.'

Hunching his wings, the kestrel leaned forward. 'My thanks to you, Abbess, but I have time for neither food nor rest. I felt duty bound to bring news when I saw your Abbey. My Lord Sunflash has a great and merciless foe, Swartt Sixclaw the ferret Warlord. They are sworn enemies for many long seasons now.'

Meriam poured herself a little mint tea. 'We have heard often of Salamandastron – it is a place that stands for freedom and justice, protecting the far coast. Though you will forgive me for saying that we have no

153

knowledge of Sunflash the Mace, or of this Swartt Sixclaw. What have they to do with us, Skarlath?'

The kestrel opened one wing and pointed north. 'Even as I speak, Swartt is coming this way with his great horde of vermin. Your Abbey lies in his path. I came to give you warning. Sixclaw is strong and evil, and, though he seeks Sunflash, I am certain that he will try to conquer Redwall if he sets eyes upon it.'

Sumin was well experienced; he had spent many seasons ranging Mossflower country. He nodded in agreement with Skarlath. 'You are right, friend, this is always the way with vermin, especially those who travel in great bands. But what would you have us do? Salamandastron is too far away to ally ourselves with your Lord.'

Skarlath swooped from the chairback to the door. 'If Swartt comes to Salamandastron, Sunflash is well able to deal with him. I do not know the strength of your warriors here, so I cannot suggest your course of action – I merely come to warn you of the danger. Now I must be gone; my Lord will want to know of the ferret's movements. Seasons and fates be with you!'

Without further ado, Skarlath unlatched the gatehouse door and soared off. The Abbey dwellers stood in the doorway, watching the hawk's flight, south by west. When he had been swallowed up by the blue vault of the sky they went indoors to hold counsel.

Abbess Meriam looked from one to the other. 'Friends, this is serious news. Redwall appears to be in great danger. What do you think?'

Barlom spoke up. 'Where is this ferret Warlord and his horde? Skarlath didn't say, exactly. One day away, two, maybe a week . . . or just a few hours, who knows?'

'Then we must find out straight away.' Heartwood's voice held no hesitation. 'I say we raise our own army and train them. Swartt won't get Redwall without a fight.'

Friar Bunfold stamped his footpaw angrily. 'Aye, we'll show the vermin a thing or two!'

'Wait, not so fast,' Sumin interrupted the irate Friar. 'You talk as if Redwall were full of trained warriors and fighting beasts, but I doubt if any of us but Bella has ever seen a real vermin horde, or realize the damage and slaughter they could inflict upon Redwall!'

Barlom thumped the tabletop, sending quill and parchments fluttering, then he banged the table once more for effect. 'What's to stop us training our own army? Better that than to sit about waiting for a Warlord's horde to conquer us!'

Meriam placed a restraining paw on her Recorder's shoulder. 'Shouting will get us nowhere, Barlom. I think we should hear more of what Sumin has to say.'

The sturdy squirrel outlined a plan that had been forming in his mind. 'What if this Swartt never gets as far as our Abbey, what if he has to take a different route to Salamandastron?'

Heartwood looked mystified. 'Why should he do that, mate?' he shrugged. 'You heard the hawk say Swartt was headed down the path towards us. Why should he change course?'

The Abbess placed a paw to her lips. 'Sshh! Listen to Sumin and find out! Carry on, friend.'

The squirrel outlined a bold and daring scheme. 'Squirrel archers an' otter slingthrowers, that's what we need: I'll bet me an' Heartwood could raise a goodly band of 'em from around this part o' Mossflower. Now, we take them north up the path an' intercept the vermin, stayin' on the east side of 'em all the time. Then we hit an' run, all the while stayin' out o' sight, so Swartt doesn't know what numbers he's up against. A good squirrel archer or otter slinger who knows the lay o' the land can make himself seem like six, workin' undercover. We strike an' hit an' keep on strikin' an' hittin', dodgin' an' hidin' all the time! Make the ferret realize he can't stay out on the path in the open, force him off into the woods on the west side so the vermin have t'take to the west shores an' follow south lookin' for Salamandastron. That way Swartt won't use the road an' he'll never know the Abbey is here!'

Barlom was quivering with eagerness. 'You're right, Sumin, I'm coming with you!'

The strong squirrel shook his head decisively. 'No, Barlom. I take only squirrels who can vanish into trees or otters who can fly underwater – an invisible army!'

Bunfold bit his lip in disappointment. 'Why can't *we* go an' strike a blow for Redwall an' freedom? Me'n Barlom would make good warriors!'

The Abbess placed her paws around both their shoulders. 'Of course you would, that's why you'll be needed back here. If Sumin's plan fails, I'll need fighters on our walls to defend the Abbey. I'd like you and Barlom to be in command of Redwall should the need arise.'

Bunfold tried to swell his chest, but only succeeded in puffing out his stomach. Barlom quivered slightly with pride, and busied himself rearranging his parchment and quills.

'Nobeast in Redwall must know of Swartt and his horde,' Abbess Meriam cautioned her friends. 'What passed between us in this gatehouse remains secret. I will not have panic in my Abbey – most unseemly. We carry on with the feast this evening as planned.'

Friar Bunfold noted the sad looks of Sumin and Heartwood. 'Don't worry, brothers, you won't miss anything. When you return from defeatin' the vermin I'll make you both a special welcome-back victory feast with my own two paws!'

20

That evening the Abbess stood up on the west battlements of the outer wall to watch the sunset. Bryony accompanied her; the two were special friends. Meriam turned from the evening sky and viewed her Abbey.

'What are you thinking of, Mother Abbess? You look sad,' said Bryony, tugging the wide, pale-green habit sleeve.

The calm eyes blinked momentarily, slightly moist. 'I was thinking of our long-gone heroes, little one, how they helped to build this beautiful place from rose-coloured sandstone. Your own great grandsire, Gonff the Mousethief, and his goodwife Columbine were part of it all. See the wonderful Abbey building beyond the gardens and lawns? It soars to the sky, oaken doors, stained glass windows and carved stone. Every room inside, from the wine cellars to the kitchens and larders, Cavern Hole where the Dibbuns play on winter nights, Great Hall where we go to feast this evening, the dormitories, sickbay, passages, stairs and corridors, all, all were built for us and otherbeasts who will come after.

'Nothing must happen to this wonderful place – not to the pond, the orchards behind our main building, or even the gatehouse, set in the side of the main gate over

157

which we stand on these ramparts. Look at this great wall, battlemented and constructed to keep out fear and famine. See how it stands open to the west flatlands, bordered by the great trees of Mossflower Wood on three sides. You and I and others to come will add to it. One day when these stones are old, Redwall shall have a belltower and a bell, libraries, tapestries and a schooling place. Is that not wonderful, Bryony?'

The little mousemaid looked up into Meriam's face. 'Wonderful indeed, but you still look sad, Mother Abbess.'

Meriam smiled one of her rare smiles. Taking Bryony's paw, she led the way down the gatehouse steps. 'Sad? Why should I be sad – we're going to a feast together! What happier occasion than that, my pretty one?'

The mousemaid laughed aloud then, for the great Mother Abbess of all Redwall Abbey did a most unlikely thing. Picking up the hem of her gown in one paw she skipped across the lawn with Bryony, the two of them giggling and chuckling like a pair of Dibbuns escaping on bath night.

As they entered Great Hall a chorus greeted them; the young ones were impatient to get started.

'Cut the cake, cut the cake,
Cut the cake for goodness sake,
Me an' my mate have each got a plate,
An' here we have to sit an' wait.
So cut the cake, say the grace,
Let's get cream upon me face,
An' sticky paws as a slice I take,
Oh cut that cake for goodness sake!'

Gliding across to her big chair the Abbess put on a mock frown. Silence fell in the hall like a stone.

Meriam waited until two small fat moles pulled her chair back so she could sit. Tucking paws into her sleeves she remained standing, gazing out across the foursquare set tables. Candle and lantern lights twinkled against spotless white linen, posies of buttercup, kingcup, daisy and apple blossom lay wreathed amid the festive fare. Bunfold's great cake dominated all; it stood above the fresh loaves of wheat, oat and barleybread, goldenbrown crusts glowing. Cheeses lay sliced and quartered, coloured from deep yellow through to pale white. Woodland trifles, topped with honeycream, jostled for position among carrot flans, watershrimp and mushroom pasties, spring vegetable soup and the favourite of moles, deeper'n'ever turnip'n'tater'n'beetroot pie. Latticed fruit tarts sat alongside fruit pies and applecream puddings. To refresh the palate there was old cider, October Ale, cellar-cooled mint tea, fizzy strawberry cordial and dandelion burdock cup.

And still all was silence as Abbess Meriam stared severely about her, repeating aloud the Redwall grace for the occasion.

'This feast we've made to remember you,
Who made our Abbey great,
Comrades, stout of heart and true,
Belov'd by valorous fate.
Dinny, Gonff and Columbine,
Good Martin and Abbess Germaine,
I raise to you this glass of wine,
And to others, too many to name,
So join me friends, this toast I call.
Redwall heroes one and all!'

The last line was echoed by everybeast; a sip was taken from each drink. Still the silence held under Meriam's stern gaze. Suddenly she winked and flashed a swift smile. 'Well, I don't know about you lot, but I'm starving!'

Amid applause and roars of laughter she sat down. Then the feast of the Redwall Heroes was begun.

Not half a league away, the night foliage of Mossflower rustled and a streambank came alive. By the light of a silver half-moon a hundred creatures readied their weapons. Heartwood turned to a huge brawny otter who had sprung from the water armed with javelin and sling. 'Yore warriors ready, Skipperjo?' he said.

Rocks clacked in the big fellow's slingpouch as he patted it. 'Right as rain an' fierce as thunder, matey!'

Sumin patted the shoulder of a small but extremely fierce-looking female squirrel. 'What d'ye say for your lot, Redfarl?'

She licked the barbed tip of an arrow, grinning in anticipation. 'Anything for Redwall an' a chance of a vermin scrap. You point the way, bucko, we'll be there before ya!'

'I say, old thing, goin' t'be a minor tussle, wot?'

Sumin peered through the gloom and was surprised to see a lanky hare carrying an immense bow and a quiver of arrows bigger than any he had ever seen. The squirrel blinked in surprise, but Redfarl merely waved her bushy tail, saying, 'He's all right, we found him wandering lost a few seasons back. Best shot I've clapped eyes on, though his arrers are like spears. Would y'believe, he wants to be a squirrel like us? Great fighter though, but sometimes I've got my doubts, he fights like ten an' eats like twenty!'

The hare was indeed a curious sight; his short bob tail was looped around with a cord which led up his back and was fastened to his ears. The normally taciturn Sumin hid a smile as he whispered to Redfarl, 'What's his name?'

Redfarl shook her head. 'You don't want to know.'

Sumin coughed to disguise a giggle. 'Yes, I do.'

The squirrel warrior smiled wryly. 'Go on then, ask him.'

Sumin pointed at the strange creature. 'What's your name, hare?'

Bending his lanky legs the hare stooped and then shot up, landing in the lower branches of a stunted oak. 'Got the species wrong, old thing. I'm a squirrel now, doncha know. Oh, don't tell me, I've got the bally old body of a hare, but here, where it counts, in the head'n'the heart, I'm a blinkin' great treewalloper, a squirrel!'

Sumin tried not to look astounded. 'I never asked your species, hare, er, squirrel, I asked your name! What is it?'

The squirrelhare leapt to a higher branch, missed it and fell flat on the ground in front of Sumin. 'You don't want to know!' he said.

'Yes, I do!'

'Oh, all right, then. M'name is Wilthurio Longbarrow Sackfirth Toxophola Fedlric Fritillary Wilfrand Hurdleframe Longarrow Leawelt Pugnacio Cinnabar Hillwether . . .'

'Stop, stop! You were right, I don't want to know!'

The squirrelhare twanged his bowstring musically. 'But you can call me Judd. D'you want to know what that's short for?'

Redfarl gave the creature an exasperated glare. 'No, he doesn't. Come on – let's get goin'!'

The bushes rustled, there was a small splash in the stream, and a moment later the woodland was quiet as the warriors vanished like smoke on the breeze, heading northward to where Swartt Sixclaw the Warlord was camped with his horde.

21

All through that dreadful winter, heavy grey-green seas pounded the rime-crusted shores, and immense rolling waves hurled themselves high above the tideline. Sometimes the breakers nearly touched the mountain itself, but the extinct volcano stood solid, proof against all weathers since the dawn of time. Inside Salamandastron, for the main part, it was dry and warm, particularly the inner chambers of the honeycombed rock. Hares of the redoubtable Long Patrol had made it so; it was not just a fortress, but a home in which they could rear their families in comfort.

A young and very shrewd female hare named Sundew was Sunflash's constant guide and companion throughout the winter. She saw that all the badger's needs were catered to with the minimum of bother. His personal living quarters were quite high up in the levels of mountain chambers. They were big and comfortable in a rough way, as befitted a Badger Lord.

Sunflash had woken with a start on his first morning, then, realizing where he was, he rolled in a leisurely way from the cushion-strewn rock ledge which served as a bed. Throwing wide the wooden shutters of a long rectangular stone window frame, he gazed out at the restless sea and dark, cloud-scarred sky, illuminated by that pale dusty lavender light which often heralds the oncoming of winter. Hearing the thick cedar door creak open behind him, the badger did not turn, but remained staring out to the horizon.

Sundew stood beside him, paws cupping her chin, as she leaned on the sill, watching the birth of a new day. 'Goin' t'be a jolly hard old winter, m'Lord,' she said.

Sunflash glanced sideways at her. 'Indeed it is, Sundew, and harder for me than most creatures, for I have a lot to learn about this place.'

'Then let us go and have breakfast. When you have eaten, I will show you around your mountain and try to answer all your questions, Sire.'

The dining chamber was a scene of chaos. Hares are reputedly mighty eaters and it was as if each was trying its hardest to live up to that reputation. Long trestle tables were packed with hares, from lanky tough old males, through to formidable-looking harewives, leverets of both sexes who fluttered their eyelids at one another whilst stuffing food shamelessly, and little ones with atrocious table manners who gorged and fought alternately. The food was good, but not fancy: autumn pears and russet apples, nuts and berries, hot oatmeal, soft white bread, cheeses and herb tea, with flagons of cordial for those who wanted it.

As Sunflash entered an immediate silence fell upon the diners. He shunned the huge carved chair that was the seat of the Badger Lord, choosing to sit by a young male leveret instead. Hurriedly the servers set out food and drink before him.

Sunflash broke bread and winked at the leveret, asking, 'What's your name, young un?'

'Bradberry, Sire, but the chaps call me Bradders, doncha know.'

The badger looked across the table to a female leveret

who was twitching her nose and fluttering her lids at Bradberry. 'Well, I tell you, Bradders, that young hare-maid yonder looks as if she's trying to tell you something.'

A chubby young hare seated the other side of Bradberry stopped sucking oatmeal from a bowl long enough to comment, 'That old gel's Fordpetal – she's jolly deep in love with Bradders. Silly as brushes the pair of 'em, Sire!'

Bradders wiggled his ears so hard with embarrassment that they almost twisted into a knot. He averted his eyes shyly, paying detailed attention to some crumbs on the table. 'Yah, go stuff nuts up your nose, Porty. Soppy ole haremaids, always pullin' faces an' wigglin' eyes at me!'

Sunflash stifled a smile as he bit into a russett apple. 'You shouldn't be so good looking, then! Try to seem a bit ugly and battered, like me.'

Fordpetal's big brown eyes widened, and she leaned over towards Sunflash smiling boldly. 'Oh, Sire, how could you say that you're ugly'n'battered? I think your golden stripe is very pretty – matter of fact, you're a very good-looking badger, if y'pardon me sayin', wot!'

Sunflash rose hastily from the table, taking with him a hunk of cheese and another apple.

'You're right, Bradders,' he said. 'She is pretty soppy! See you later.'

Sundew took Sunflash through the cellars, where he inspected the drinking stock, stopping to sample from different barrels with a small tasting ladle.

'Hmm, I like this one, very fruity and warm!'

'So it bally well should be, Sire; that's old elderberry wine, been sittin' there fifty seasons, they say. Very good for colds'n'chills, but two beakers of it'd blow your ears off!'

He was shown through the bachelor hare barracks,

sickbay, larders, dormitories, meeting chambers and nursery. Next came the armoury, cells and lookout caves; practically that whole day was given over to viewing all Salamandastron had to offer. Sunflash began to realize that he was Lord over what amounted to a town inside a rock.

When they were above the level of his own accommodation, Sundew stopped, and said, 'Only you may go here, Sire; few hares have been allowed this far.'

Turning to ask her the reason why, Sunflash found himself alone. Sundew had vanished downstairs. Walking down a broad passage, Sunflash came to a hanging curtain; he pulled it aside and discovered a great forge room. There was a forgefire at its centre, with bellows, a stock of timber and seacoal, and nearby stood a mighty, horned anvil. Spears, daggers, lances and arrows, javelins, heavy slings and clubs lined the walls. A gigantic broadsword hung from metal pins; the badger took it down, surprised at its weight, but delighted by the balance of the fearsome battleblade. His grandsire, Boar the Fighter, may have wielded it, or his great grandsire Lord Brocktree. Sunflash put the sword aside and picked up his own weapon, the mace; it felt better suited to his paws. Several sets of finely-made badger armour stood about: deep-chested breastplates, shining steel greaves and warlike helmets, and there were shields too, with heroic devices graven upon them.

Passing through the forge room Sunflash wandered, upstairs, around corners, down passages, until he felt completely lost and overawed at the vastness of the mountain's interior. Then he came to a dead end: suddenly the corridor ran out, and he was facing a bare rock wall. Sunflash inspected it and noticed in it a crack, little more than a claw's thickness. Setting his own claws into the crack he tugged sideways, and the rock gave a bit, grating noisily. He pulled harder, until the crack widened sufficiently for him to wedge his mace handle in. Setting his shoulder to the macehead Sunflash gave a mighty shove and the crack opened wide. One more hard push and the whole wall started to swing outward. The secret doorway was open.

Flint, steel and tinder lay on the floor inside, along with several torches of dry brush. Swiftly he struck flint to steel, blowing the sparks which had landed on the tinder into life. A small flame appeared. Sunflash lit a torch, and walked to the narrow hall.

Then, with a roar of shock the badger staggered back, dropping the torch. Swiftly he' retrieved it, sparks showering around him like fireflies as he held it high. There at one end of the hall was a fully armoured badger seated upon a throne! Immediately he knew that this was his great grandsire, Old Lord Brocktree. The hairs on Sunflash's back stood on end as he walked forward to stand in front of his ancestor. The vizor of the splendid warhelm was closed over the Badger Lord's eyeless sockets. Sunflash's paw trembled as he traced it through the dust on Brocktree's burnished breastplate. He knew that inside the armour there remained nought but a skeleton of the once great warrior, but there was no denying that their blood was one and the same. Sunflash knelt and wept then, for the heavy burden fate and seasons had placed upon his family.

The guttering torch brought him back to reality and he looked about for something to keep the light going. There beside a great wall covered in carvings, he found a hammer, chisels and a lantern. Gratefully he lit the lantern from the dying torch and sat upon the floor staring at the rows of curious pictures graven across the wall. Sunflash breathed in the sweet-smelling smoke from the lantern; it was not an unpleasant aroma. Gradually he leaned over until he was lying flat on the cool floorstones; they felt good, restful. He put aside the smoking lantern with its dim golden light. A great desire to sleep overtook him; closing his eyes he listened to a soft voice, singing to him from afar. The corridors of his mind became one with the dim incense-wreathed hall and its music.

Rest awhile, sleep awhile,
Here where the warrior stays,
Old as the dust of seasons,
Soft as the call of lost days.
Mountain Lords marked out by fate,
Watch o'er great seas forlorn.
You are the heart of this ancient rock,
Where mighty legends are born.

Pale shades of bygone Badger Lords, hares in battle formations, searat galleys, vermin hordes and the clangour of war, mingled with pounding surf in the dreams of Sunflash the Mace. Louder and louder the pounding grew. Sunflash came awake in darkness; the lantern had gone out. Somebeast was pounding against the far wall from its other side. Dim cries reached the Badger Lord's ears.

'Sire, are you there? Answer if you can hear us!'

Sunflash stood upright, bellowing aloud, 'I'm in here, wait!'

Groping his way to the wall, he felt around until he encountered a deep crack. Sunflash pulled both ways, gouging huge blunt claws into the stone rift, and the entire wall moved fractionally. Howling his warcry, the badger pitted his strength in one colossal effort against the groaning rock.

'Eeulaliaaaaa!'

The wallrift opened full three pawlengths. Shaking dust from his eyes, Sunflash kicked his mace into the gap, wedging it open. Sundew and several other hares were on the other side in the forge room. They shouted out in relief.

'Oh, thank the fur an' fates you're all right, Sire!'

'Whew! When you go missin', you make a proper job of it, wot?'

'What's that sweet smell? Whew, what've y'been cookin' in there, m'Lord?'

'Must've eaten somethin' t'keep him goin' three days, wot!'

Sunflash could scarce believe his ears. 'Three days? You mean I've been in here three full days?'

Sundew's paw came through the opening, and she patted Sunflash's face, as if to reassure herself that it really was him. 'Rather! An' three nights, doncha know, this is the morn of the fourth blinkin' day, Sire. I'd have never forgiven myself if we hadn't found you, worried out of m'mind I was!'

Sunflash interrupted her recriminations. 'Is there a lantern or a torch in there? Pass me a light through, hurry!'

There was a few moments' scratching about, then a flaring, resin-soaked torch with a metal sconce ring on it was thrust through the opening. Sunflash took it, saying, 'Stay where you are, I won't be long. There's something I must see.'

The carved wall was covered with pictures of badgers and battles, searats, vermin bands – they were all there. Sunflash recognized a figure near the end; it was obviously his grandfather, Boar the Fighter, armour-clad, armed with a great battleblade, putting searats to flight. Curiously, the next figure was very small, but quite heroic. It was a mouse, carrying a broken sword hung about his neck on a cord, and there were other smaller figures accompanying the mouse on a journey towards the mountain. Next was a likeness of the same creatures leaving Salamandastron, though this time the mouse was wielding a bright new sword of great beauty. Beyond that was a small space. Sunflash caught his breath. Carved into the wall was a clear picture of him-

-self, carrying his mace over one shoulder, walking towards the mountain.

22

In the forge room, the hares sprang aside as the wallgap rumbled wide. Sunflash opened it by using his great mace as a lever, then he squeezed through and pulled the mace after him not a moment too soon. The rock rift ground back into place closing the gap in the forgeroom wall. They stared curiously at the Badger Lord as he stood there calmly, a faraway look in his dark eyes.

Sundew was profuse in her apologies. 'Beggin' your pardon, milord, we should never've ventured this far into your personal quarters, but we were so worried!'

Bradders had also come along with the search party. 'I say, Lord, you must be absolutely starvin', old Sire. The last mouthful of scoff you had was breakfast, three flippin' mornin's ago – must make a chap jolly hungry, that sort of thing!'

Sunflash rubbed his eyes and shook his great head to bring himself back to normality. He patted Sundew's paw. 'You did the right thing, young un. Bradders is right though, I'm really hungry. Is breakfast over?'

Porty, the fat young hare who was Bradders's pal, nodded. 'Not a bally crumb left, old lad, er, I mean Sire.'

Sunflash could not help chuckling at the tubby hare. 'I couldn't imagine there being much left on any table once you've had your fill, wobblechops. Never mind, I'll fix something for myself in the kitchens.'

Sundew whispered in Sunflash's ear. 'First you must come to the sickbay – there is an urgent matter that can't wait.'

Sunflash recognized the two slight figures laid in twin beds immediately. He went to them and took their paws. 'I remember you two – it's Breeze and Starbuck. You're the two elders who met me when I arrived here that first day.'

Starbuck blinked his rheumy old eyes and coughed fitfully. 'Aye, Sire, that was us. Do you know, we both served under your grandsire Boar the Fighter.'

Sunflash looked closer at both creatures. It was then that he realized just how old they really were. He turned to Sundew, saying, 'If this is right they must have more seasons on them than anybeasts I have known.'

The young hare dampened a cloth and wiped the wrinkled brows of both the ancients. 'They speak true, Lord. These two are the only ones left who fought alongside your grandsire, and how they lived this long nobeast knows. Every last day of autumn season since the death of Boar the Fighter they have both stood in the main cave entrance by the shore, as if awaiting your coming.'

Breeze pressed Sunflash's paw feebly. 'Lord Boar told us of a dream he had, he told us to watch for the gold-striped warrior. You came, now our waiting is at an end – is that not so, Starbuck?'

The old male smiled weakly and managed a nod. 'Aye, 'tis so, sister, our duty is done now. We go to the dark forest. Lord Boar will have a great feast prepared in our honour.'

Sunflash pressed Starbuck's paw gently. 'Tell me about my grandsire,' he said.

Starbuck gazed at his small withered paw, almost lost

in the badger's massive one. 'What is there to tell, Sire? Boar was a mighty fighter. None could stand against him when the bloodwrath took him. He was a true Badger Lord, and so are you. I see it in your eyes, feel it in your paw. You will be a mighty warrior, even greater and more fearsome than you are now, eh, Breeze?'

The old female tightened her hold on Sunflash's paw. 'Aye, that is true, but you will fare better than Lord Boar, because you love young ones and babes, I know this. The young will always befriend and admire you. Boar was a lonely creature; the only babe he ever spoke of was your mother Bella. She was his babe, but all the young ones of the earth belong to you in friendship. Be good to them.'

Sunflash and Sundew stayed with Starbuck and Breeze until they fell asleep, then they left the room quietly and went down to the kitchens. Sunflash felt two things: hunger, and the need to cheer up after his long sojourn in the secret chamber and the saddening experience of sitting with two old creatures whose seasons had run out. The cooks looked up from their steaming pots and bubbling concoctions as Sunflash entered. They bowed briefly, and the head cook, a fat, bad-tempered bachelor hare, enquired, 'Do you require food, Sire? I will cook your meal myself.'

Sunflash lifted the lid of a pot and sniffed its contents, saying, 'Hmm, porridge again! Don't we ever have anything more exciting?'

Clang! The head cook slammed his ladle down on a panlid. 'Sire, you are in my domain now, the kitchens. You are also in my way – kindly take yourself off somewhere!'

All work in the kitchens stopped; the younger hares, who were minor cooks and helpers, held their breath momentarily. The head cook was something of a tyrant, and they wanted to see how the new Badger Lord fared against him.

Sunflash could have cowed the head cook with a single glance, but the badger never used bullying tactics. Instead he began peeling a big russet apple, smiling at his opponent. 'What d'you put in your porridge, friend?' he asked.

'Salt, oats'n'water – what else would y'put in porridge, eh?' the cook replied snappishly.

The badger began tipping the ingredients in the pot as he spoke. 'A lot more oats to thicken it up, less salt, more greensap milk than water, a good portion of honeycomb, maybe some dried fruit, apple rings, hazelnuts. Don't let it cook too long, turn it out onto a tray to cool, slice it up in squares and you've got good sweet oatcake, best eaten warm from an oven.'

An instant round of applause went up from the kitchen helpers. The head cook turned on Sunflash, furious at having another experimenting with his porridge. 'That's not the way I'd make porridge, Sire. Who taught you to cook, if I may make so bold as to ask?'

Sunflash finished peeling and coring the apple. 'Moles and hedgehogs, friend – the best cooks I ever knew. See this apple? Stuff the corehole with candied chestnuts and a dribble of honey, bake it in the oven, then serve it piping hot with meadowcream – ever tried it?'

The cook thrust out his chin defiantly. 'No! And what's more I wouldn't want to!'

'H'I would, Sir, frizzle me paws, it soun's wunnerful, it do!'

The head cook glared at the young hare who had piped up.

Sunflash strode over and shook the keen-eyed youngster's paw. 'What's your name, mate?' he said.

'Bloggwood, Sire!'

'Well, I like the look of you, Bloggwood. Are you a good cook?'

'As good as any, Sire, an' willin' t'learn. I likes t'cook!'

'And tell me, Bloggwood, if you were in charge round

here and somebeast came to you with a tasty recipe, what would you do?'

'Well, h'I'd 'elp 'em t'cook it an' see if 'n we c'd make it taste even better!'

With a few deft movements, Sunflash snatched the head cook's tall hat and placed it on the young hare's head, then, lifting Bloggwood with one paw, he set him on top of a table.

'As Badger Lord of Salamandastron I appoint you, Bloggwood, new head cook in my kitchens. The rest of you – will you help our friend to produce good and tasty meals?'

Ladles and aprons were hurled high in the air, and the helpers and assistants cheered aloud.

The former head cook stood in front of Sunflash, hatless and bewildered by the sudden turn of events.

'But what about me, what'll I do?' he cried.

Sunflash threw a friendly paw about his shoulder, saying, 'Well, you've never liked cooking, have you?'

'Of course not, but it's a job, somebeast's got to do it.'

'Right, but you didn't like doing it, so you don't have to do it any longer. What d'you *really* like doing, friend?'

'Well, er, I've always been interested in brewing ales, cordials and wine. Here, would you like to try some of my cowslip wine, Sire?'

The hare opened a cupboard and pulled out a flagon and beakers.

Sunflash watched him pour two beakers full, and said, 'Why not, I'll try anything once.' He sipped and rolled his eyes appreciatively. 'This is excellent! Can you make fizzy strawberry cordial for little ones?'

The hare winked and snorted, 'Can I make fizzy strawberry cordial? Listen, matey, er Sire, I can make it so fizzy it'd curl your fur!'

Sunflash shook him heartily by the paw. 'Well said! Go and see our cellarkeeper and tell him his workload is halved, because I've just appointed you joint Chief

Cellarkeeper and winemaker brewer of Salamand-astron!'

As Sunflash and Bloggwood produced a tasty giant turn-over of leek, carrot, mushroom and dark gravy between them, word got around. Hares came filing into the kitch-ens with requests and observations, knowing the new Badger Lord would give them a fair and good hearing. He did!

Within the space of a half morning, Sunflash the Mace had appointed an assistant cellarbeast, two flower gar-deners, a new sickbay assistant, a carpenter, banquet arranger and a whole host of young ones who wanted to be armourers and forge assistants to the Badger Lord.

Later, Sundew sat with Bloggwood and some others, as they helped themselves to an impromptu lunch of the big turnover, which had been named a Bloggflash Special.

The badger put aside two slices, rich dark gravy seep-ing from them onto the plates as he popped them in the oven.

'Keep an eye on them slices, Sundew,' he said, 'they'll do for Starbuck and Breeze's supper tonight. The old uns'll enjoy my turnover.'

Sundew wiggled her ears in admiration of the Badger Lord. 'Well, well, Sire, you've certainly made some jolly old changes round here. I'd say you're doin' a spiffin' job, wot!'

Sunflash shoved her lightly, almost sending her sprawling. 'You can stop wiggling your ears at me, missie – besides, you'll have to show a little more dignity now that I've decided to appoint you as my confidential aide.'

Skipping and laughing, Sundew almost collided with Porty, who was holding up a chubby paw for Sunflash's attention. 'I say, old Sire, can I be official food taster? I'd be jolly good at that I think.'

Sunflash roared laughing until he had to hold his sides.

At suppertime, Sunflash and Sundew took the turnover slices up to the sickbay, only to find Dewfleck, a quiet older hare, whom Sunflash had appointed as sickbay assistant that morning, sitting weeping on the top stair. Her face was buried in her paws as her whole body shook fitfully.

Sadly the badger set down the two plates and sat on the stairs next to her. 'It's Breeze and Starbuck, isn't it?' he asked.

She nodded, sobbing brokenly. 'Oh, Sire, they was 'oldin' paws, just lyin' there all peaceful like. I thought they were 'avin' a little doze, but ole Breeze an' Starbuck, they was . . . Boohoohoohoo!'

Sunflash dried her eyes with the corner of a kitchen apron he had been wearing all day. 'There, there, hush now, those old uns were looking forward to meeting their friends in the dark forest, they told me that only this morning. Isn't that right, Sundew?'

The young hare sniffed as she wiped her eyes against the apron. 'Absolutely, Sire. They'll never have t'face a rotten ol' winter again, they're both happy now, along with your grandsire.'

Throughout that long winter the hares of Salamandastron came to know and love their new Lord. Sunflash was all things to them, friend to the old, counsellor to the young and playmate to the babes, who were his constant delight. He looked forward eagerly to the spring, when he planned to take up farming once more. Often on dreary winter afternoons the forge room was alive with helpers as Sunflash and his blacksmiths turned out spades, hoes, rakes and trowels, in readiness for the coming season's planting and cultivation. The badger had almost forgotten about his foebeast Swartt Sixclaw, and would not think of him until the arrival of Skarlath in the early spring.

23

The vermin horde found the path broad, smooth and easy to march on, and good progress was made on the first day travelling south. That evening, they camped in an untidy sprawl, right across the path and on both sides of it. Tender young shoots and new green foliage, which would have been shunned as food any other time, were welcomed after their winter starvation.

Next day blustered in bright and breezy, lightly warm with random fleece clouds scurrying across spring skies. Swartt was in a good mood, pleased with the ground he had covered the previous day. Muggra the weasel Captain was still out in front of the army, dragging himself painfully along on all fours, his injured footpaw causing him great pain.

Pitilessly, Swartt marched hard behind Muggra, watching him crawl as he spoke to him in a cruel voice of mock reason. 'See now, friend, you could've been marchin' upright an' brisk like the rest of us if you 'adn't chosen to argue wid me. Come on now, don't go sulkin' an' mopin', apologize t'me like a goodbeast an' ask me fer mercy.' He kicked the Captain, sending him sprawling on the road.

Muggra spat earth as he whimpered, 'Mercy, Lord, I was wrong to argue with yer!'

Swartt laughed harshly, stepping on Muggra's back as he passed him. 'Get out o' me sight, y'snivellin' craven, an' thank yer lucky stars I'm in a good mood t'day!'

Sssssthunk!

A javelin came streaking out of the blue and buried itself deep in the path, in front of the Warlord. It stood quivering as the ferret fell back and seized Nightshade's paw. 'Where in the name o' blisterin' blazes did that come from?' he cried.

The vixen tried desperately to extricate her paw from the ferret's vicelike grasp. 'I don't know, Lord, but it looks to me like some sort of warning that we should go no further!'

Swartt held on to the paw, glaring at her. 'Tell me true, fox: did you 'ave any visions or dreams about this?'

Nightshade wrenched her crushed paw away, shaking her head. 'None, Sire, I saw nothing!'

Tugging the javelin loose, Swartt broke it across his mailed paw. 'One javelin ain't goin' t'stop this horde. Forward march!'

The Warlord stood still, allowing the marchers to walk past him. Screams rang out as the foremost three vermin fell, two pierced by arrows, the other felled by a hefty rock. Suddenly the horde was in disarray.

'They're in the woods on the east side!' Swartt roared. 'Scraw, charge 'em with spears, wipe every last one of 'em out! Aggal, Nightshade, line some archers up, here – jump to it!'

Redfarl watched the spearbeasts charge into the woodlands, letting them get sufficiently far from the path before nodding to a score of squirrels perched in the treetops. Half of the vermin were cut down by a hail of arrows, the rest, turning to run back, were set upon by otters whirling heavy loaded slings, which they used as clubs. As quickly as they struck, the attackers faded into the woodland.

On the path all Swartt heard was a few distant screams, then silence. He held up a warning paw, saying, 'Stretch those bowstrings; be ready; keep yer eyes peeled on them woodlands!'

Still not a sound. Then Swartt heard a strange noise and saw the bushes shake not far from the path. 'Shoot at those bushes!' he said, pointing.

A volley of barbed shafts shredded the foliage and the rat Captain Scraw toppled out, already wounded by a squirrel arrow, but now transfixed by seven more from his own side. Swartt performed a dance of rage, whirling his sword wildly. Horde archers ducked to avoid the blade.

'Idiots, did none of y'think to look before shootin'?' he yelled. 'Put up those bows until we can see 'em!'

As the vermin archers relaxed their bowstrings there was a shout from the east woodlands. A whistling rain of rocks and javelins hit the unsuspecting archers, and one large stone caught Swartt a glancing blow, stunning him. Nightshade signalled four vermin to carry him to safety, as she called out to the rest of the horde, 'Into the woods on the west side of this path – hurry!'

The vermin needed no second bidding. They hurled themselves at the bushes, helped on their way by a shower of missiles from the hidden attackers.

The old rat carrying Swartt's son was hit. Clutching at the javelin protruding from her side, she tugged at the backsling. Tearing loose the carrying cradle she dropped it, babe and all, into a shallow ditch bordering the west pathside. She crawled painfully after the retreating horde and was trampled by other vermin in their haste to escape death.

Down in the ditch the ferretbabe wriggled from its restricting sling and began gobbling a mess of frogspawn from a muddy pool. It fed voraciously, neither whimpering nor crying.

Nightshade pressed cobwebs and damp leaves to the side of the Warlord's head. Swartt gritted his teeth and staggered upright, grabbing a weasel as it sneaked past. 'You! Did yer see 'em, who were they, 'ow many . . .'

The unfortunate weasel's reply was cut short by a gigantic arrow, which silenced him for ever. A jovial voice rang out from somewhere deep in the woods. 'I say, top marks there, Jodders. Good shot, wot?'

Swartt looked around wildly. He could not stop the horde retreating deeper into the words; they ignored his commands.

'Halt! Stop there!' he yelled. 'What are ye runnin' from – some ragtailed little bunch o' woodlanders? Stand an' fight!'

Another spearlike arrow thudded into the trunk of a sycamore, right near the Warlord's head. Silently, he decided that discretion was the better part of valour and fled too.

The great otter Skipperjo was left in command of the path. His otters crouched in the foliage on the west side, ready to deal with any vermin who tried to regain control of the road. Sumin and Redfarl pursued the horde; travelling high in the trees, they picked off stragglers. The vermin ran as if chased by unseen demons, each trying not to be at the back of the horde, which was the most vulnerable position. Gradually they slowed, weariness taking toll of their trembling limbs.

Late afternoon found them in a deep natural hollow, somewhere in the west reaches of Mossflower. Swartt sat, allowing the vixen to bandage his head with a mud and leaf poultice.

He glared at the silent horde, venting his spleen on them.

'Squirrels an' otters, that's all they was, a bunch o' mis'rable squirrels an' otters, an' you beauties ran from 'em. Tell 'em, Nightshade – you saw them, didn't yer? Squirrels'n'otters, that's all they were!'

A surly voice called out from the horde, 'I never seen squirrels shootin' arrers as big as that'n wot wiped out pore Grinflit!'

Swartt's head was aching; he was too tired to reprimand the culprit. Instead he beckoned his Captains and they gathered round as he lay back, covering his eyes with his mailed paw. 'Well, what've you lot got t'say fer yerselves, eh?' he growled.

The replies were what he expected.

'No point in gettin' slain for trespassin' on some other-beast's road, Chief.'

'Keep travellin' west, that's what we were doin' in the first place.'

'Aye, you can't slay an invisible army. We lost a good number today, an' didn't even see who did the killin'!'

Swartt stood up, shaking his head sorrowfully, but secretly glad that his Captains had provided him with an excuse not to turn back and seek retribution on the foebeast. 'Huh, the backbone's gone from you lot, yer a load o' jellyfish. Ah well, I s'pose we'll keep goin' west through this forest if yer all too scared to go back an' avenge yer dead mates.'

Redfarl perched in the low branches of an elm nearby, listening to what was going on. Her tail shot upright, a signal to the waiting squirrel archers stationed in the trees not far from the horde. They fired a line of shafts into the ground, not a pawsbreadth from where the vermin sat. Slightly further back in the woodland cover, Jodd lay flat on the earth, his head inside a great hollow log. The hare's voice echoed and boomed as he called slowly in a loud sepulchral voice, 'Begone from our land while you still live! Worms feast upon any who try to stand against us; their bones rot upon the territory of the phantom slayers! Go noooooooowww!'

All the squirrels in the trees, plus a few otters who were with Jodd, echoed the mournful howl. 'Go noooooowwww!'

Nightshade could be heard shouting as the horde took to their heels and charged westward into Mossflower, the speed of panic urging them on.

'Carry Lord Swartt, he is injured! See the line of arrows, it is a warning, the phantom slayers have spoken. Let us go!'

The vixen found she was talking to herself; the horde had gone. Without a backward glance she dashed off after them.

Some of the squirrels nearly fell from the trees laughing. Jodd was still lying with his head in the hollow log, calling mournfully, 'I'm starving, wonder what's for bally supper, us phantoms have t'jolly well eeeeeeaaaaattttt!'

Sumin gripped Redfarl's paw gratefully. 'We did it, thanks to you an' Skipperjo. Redwall Abbey is deep in your debt. We will hold a feast for you all!'

The squirrelhare's voice boomed out from below. 'That's the ticket, a great feast! Soooooooooper!'

Skipperjo met them back at the path, and there was much paw-shaking, tail-wagging and back-slapping.

'Never lost a one of my otters, we tricked 'em good, mates!'

'Aye, all my archers are accounted for, not a scratch on any of 'em. We did a great thing here today, eh, Sumin?'

The sturdy squirrel beamed proudly. 'We did that, it was risky an' darin', but we pulled it off. A good yarn to tell the young uns, Skipperjo!'

The brawny otter held up a paw. 'Oh, talkin' about young uns, matey, lookit what I found.'

He signalled to a female otter, who came forward bearing a small bundle, which she carried in two slings tied together across her back.

The lanky Jodd peered into the improvised cradle. 'Great fur'n'feathers! It's a jolly little junior vermin. Yowch! The bounder chomped m'paw. Good appetite, wot?'

Sumin watched as the otter placed the squirming ferretbabe on the soft grass at the pathside. Skipperjo shook his head, saying, 'Pore liddle thing, looks 'arf starved. What'll we do with it?'

Sumin waggled a paw at the ferretbabe, and it snarled. 'Suppose we'll have to take him back to the Abbey an' let Abbess Meriam sort it out, that's unless anybeast here fancies adoptin' 'im?'

There was silence. Redfarl touched the ferretbabe gently, and it bit her. Stonefaced, she watched the small creature licking its teeth, savouring the taste of blood, and said, 'I know 'tis a hard thing to say about a babe, even a liddle vermin, but let me tell you, no good will ever come of this one. Don't ask me why, I just feel it in my fur!'

24

Towards evening Abbess Meriam stood on the north wall battlements with Bryony. They had been waiting and watching for days, but Meriam had not told Bryony why. The sounds of singing drifted to them on the twilight breeze, and the Abbess leaned across the battlements, smiling with relief. 'Listen, Bryony, friends are coming to Redwall!'

Lantern lights showed like fireflies and, as they drew closer, rousing voices could be heard singing a quick marching song.

'Oh we chased 'em off the highway,
They fled off to the west,
We sent 'em every whichway,
Our warriors are the best.
They'll never see ole Redwall,
'Cos they were forced to flee,
Sent on their way by shaft an' stone,
From every greenwood tree.
Bad luck attend the vermin beast,
Who came out of the north and east,
We'll give 'em blood'n'steel'n'stone,
Until they leave our land alone!'

Abbess Meriam cupped paws around her mouth and called, 'Who goes there?'

There were chortles and guffaws as Jodd replied, 'Just some jolly ole phantom warriors who need fattenin' up, m'dear. Did my sufferin' ears hear mention of a whackin' great feast at your splendiferous Abbey, wot?'

Meriam's voice shook with laughter as she shouted back, 'No, they didn't, but come in anyway and we'll see what we can do to silence your grumbling tummies!'

A hearty cheer went up from the marchers.

The tale was told and retold over the banquet board, of how a small determined force sent the horde of Swartt Sixclaw, the ferret Warlord, running defeated into the west. Dibbuns watched open-mouthed as the squirrel-hare Jodd demolished everything edible that came within his reach.

'I say, this Spring Salad's absolutely top hole! Eh, what's that, marm? Oh yes indeed, pile it on here, m'dear, nothin' like apple pie'n'meadowcream to clear one's palate y'know. Er, excuse me, young molechap, pass yon turnip'n'tater'n'whatever they call that bally great pie you coves eat. Thank y'kindly, no, leave the jolly old dish, might want some for afters, wot!'

The leader of the Redwall mole contingent, whose title was always Foremole, winked at the mole who was serving Jodd. 'Hoo arr, that'n be an 'arebeast, you'm b'ain't see'd any h'aminal eaten 'til you'm see'd an 'arebeast, burr no zurr!'

Friar Bunfold dashed about, topping up all the beakers with good October Ale. 'A toast, friends, to the good-beasts who saved Redwall!' he called.

Beakers were raised, cheers rang to the rafters.

'The goodbeasts who saved Redwall! Hooray!'

Amid much whispering and giggling a steaming caul-dron was wheeled in by Togget, Bryony and Friar Bun-fold. The hogwife Myrtle announced to one and all,

185

'Now I don't take no blame fer this concoction, 'twas a thingummy created by these three 'ere, in honour of our guests this eve. Oh, you tell 'em, Bryony – I gets all muddled!'

'Well, we know that otters like their hotroot soup with watershrimp, leek, onions and plenty of hotroot,' Bryony explained to the feasters, 'but we have our friends the squirrels to consider. Their favourite is the treetop broth made from maple tips, acorns, beechnuts, green apples and horse chestnuts. So, my friends and I combined both, adding a few ingredients of our own. Two beakers of parsley wine, a touch of ramson and some winter rosehips. We hope you enjoy it – our phantom warrior soup!'

It proved to be a great favourite: hot, spicy, sweet and also strong. Some said Skipperjo ate the most, though Jodd was only a fraction of a ladle behind him.

'Mmmm, mm, quite tasty, very nice, though I do like that deeper'n'thingee pie the molechaps make. Who knows, when I'm fed up bein' a squirrel I might join up an' become a bally mole.

Foremole shook his velvety head vigorously. 'Oh, nay, zurr, 'tis a turrible loif us'n's lead, you'm far better orf bein' a squirrelbeast, you'm lukk more loik one.'

Jodd was quite flattered by this remark, and he hitched hard at the cord tied from his bobtail to his long ears. 'I say, d'you think so really? Actually, I do meself. In fact I think I look quite like a jolly old treewalloper these days. Tied the old tail to me ears so it'll stretch an' grow long'n'bushy, same as a squirrelchap. D'you think it's workin'?'

Foremole gave Jodd's tail a tug and winked at Togget. 'Whoi oi do berleev 'tis gettin' gurt'n'bushy, eh, maister?'

Togget nodded solemnly. 'Much longer an' et'll be a curlen o'er onto ee nose, zurr!'

The banter and chatter went on late into the night amid an abundance of good food, firm friends, and a general feeling of thankfulness and wellbeing. Skipperjo, Redfarl and Jodd raised beakers to the Abbess.

'If we're to be rewarded with such a splendid spread every time we defend yore Abbey, marm, then we 'opes the next passel o' villains is headin' down the path tomorrer!'

Meriam shook her head. 'Fate and fortune forbid such a thing, my friends. You do not need to fight for food at Redwall; our table is here for you any time you call by our gate. You are always welcome.'

As the night wore on, Meriam took Bryony to one side and led her from Great Hall, saying, 'Come with me missie, I have something to show you – a surprise.'

Together they mounted the stairs and made their way to a chamber close by the sickbay. Meriam tapped upon the door. Bryony thrilled to the mellow sound of a deep voice, that of the beloved Redwall Badger Mother, Bella.

'Enter please, there are no locks on my door.'

Bella was massive with age. Her silver fur shone in the lantern light, almost creating a nimbus of radiance about her. Raising a huge, ageworn paw, she adjusted small thick crystal glasses from her muzzletip up to her eyes.

Arranging a shawl about her friend's shoulders, Meriam whispered, 'I thought you might be asleep, Bella. Are we disturbing you?'

The great shining head shook slowly. 'No, no, not at all. There's no need to whisper, Meriam – I sleep when I like and stay awake as I want to these days. Hello, Bryony, my pretty little mousemaid, come and sit with old Bella.'

Bryony sat upon the broad soft lap, her favourite place since she had been a Dibbun, and she looked questioningly at Meriam. 'What is the surprise, Mother Abbess?'

Meriam placed a paw to her lips. 'Sshh! Not so loud, missie.'

Bella nodded to a cradle within easy reach of her paw. 'Oh, don't worry about him. He's wide awake and taking all in.'

Leaning over, Bryony saw what the cradle contained. She jumped from Bella's lap and swept the babe into her paws, hugging it. 'Oh, it's a babe, a little one! Is it male or maid? What's it called? Whose is it? Where did you get it from? Oh, Mother!'

Meriam allowed Bryony to hold the babe. 'Not so fast, missie, maybe you won't be so quick to cuddle him when I tell you. He is the young of a vermin, abandoned when they retreated from the path, a male ferretbabe.'

Bryony continued nursing the ferret, rocking back and forth. 'Poor little thing! He looks so alone and lost! Is he not beautiful, Bella, see!'

The ancient badger smiled wisely, saying, 'All little creatures are beautiful, Bryony, every living thing when it first sees life is born in beauty. What they grow to be is a different matter. I have given the ferretbabe a name; he shall be called Veil, because there is a veil over his life before he came here. We know nothing of him.'

Bryony looked down at the little ferret. Its sharp slitted eyes were watching her intently. She tickled its nosetip gently with her paw, saying, 'Veil, Veil, it's a lovely name, hello little Veil. Owch!'

Bella exchanged glances with the Abbess before speaking. 'He has bitten you, Bryony.'

The mousemaid sucked her paw briefly, smiling. 'No, not really, it was more of a nibble. Perhaps he's hungry.'

Bella closed her eyes and leaned back. 'Some creatures are always hungering after one thing or another. I have a feeling about this one, and if I am proved right in the seasons to come I will tell you why I really called him Veil. But it is far better now to hope for the best that can happen, so we will say no more about it. You are a good mousemaid, Bryony, that is why the Abbess and I decided that you shall have Veil, to bring up and care for. He may benefit from you.'

Bryony's eyes were shining, and she hugged the small bundle close. 'Oh, Mother Abbess, is it true? I will be like his mother, no, more like his big sister, no, more like his good friend!'

The Abbess smiled at her friend the mousemaid. 'Make your mind up, missie. Best be a little of all, mayhap that's what Veil will need to grow up good. Put him back in his cradle now and take him up to the dormitory with you. Bella is too old to care for him and I have my Abbey to look after. From this day forth he is your responsibility.'

When Bryony had taken Veil and gone from the room, Abbess Meriam stooped and dabbed a tiny spot of blood from the rush mat. It had spilled from the mousemaid's paw when the ferretbabe bit her. She sat on the arm of Bella's chair, staring at the crimson dot, and said, 'Did we do the right thing, old friend, or will this ferret cause more blood to be shed in Redwall?'

The great silver badger bent down and wiped away the speck with her apron corner. 'Only time will tell, Meriam!'

25

As the earth turned slowly, time passed and season followed season many times. Swartt Sixclaw and his horde wandered the land, through woodland, across rivers, over mountains, often lost and frequently sidetracked by dissent and mutiny. But his obsession, to avenge himself upon the badger who had maimed and deadened his famous sixclaw, drove the Warlord onward.

Many things happened to swell the infamy of Swartt's name. He lost some of his horde in marsh country, fighting a long and protracted battle against toads and reptiles, emerging victorious but with a depleted horde.

Then chance brought him into an alliance with Captain Zigu and his Corsairs. Zigu was a ferret like himself who, having lost his ship on the rocks in foul weather, was forced to range the coasts with his motley band of vermin, some searats, but mainly Corsairs, creatures of any species that chose the marauding life. Zigu was no stranger to Salamandastron; he had seen it from the sea and knew its exact location. He was a valuable, if untrustworthy, asset, and joining forces with him meant that the horde would be lost no more. For Swartt, this sealed the pact.

Southward down the coast the horde ranged, being

joined by deserters, mutineers and other vermin who had been marooned by their searat brethren. Swartt sat upon the beach one morning at the start of summer, picking at a roasted mackerel. He glanced across at Nightshade who was tossing shells into the air and watching in what position they fell upon the sand.

'Never mind the stupid shells, vixen, look at my horde – just cast yer eyes over 'em. Every one a murderer, they'd slit their own mothers' gizzards over a morsel of food, hah! 'Arf of 'em prob'ly did, killers all! Now I'm a real Warlord, the best of a bad bunch, an' I could lick any six of 'em single-pawed!'

Nightshade went back to her conjuring. 'Aye, Lord, we'll do great things together. Shells are magic, they don't tell lies. See these here, they are our horde. But see this big curling conch; you can hear the tide come and go if you put it to your ear. Look though, it fell standing straight up in the sand – it's the mountain. See the distance from it that the horde lies; we cannot be far from it now.'

Swartt shook his head, as if in disappointment at his seer. 'You know that because of what Zigu told you – he knows how close to Salamandastron we are. Go on, then, if your shells are so clever, what else do they tell you? That little red shell that fell far apart from the rest, what does that say?'

The vixen looked at the small red shell and shrugged. 'Lord, though it doesn't *say* anything it tells me a great deal. Remember you once had a babe, a male? This shell represents him, and you would do well to beware of it.'

Swartt stared at the little red shell, his lip twisting contemptuously. 'Oh yes, I remember the brat, but that was long ago, he's probably dead by now. We lost him after the battle on the path.'

Nightshade narrowed her eyes, staring hard at the shell. 'You never really lost him. See – he's come back!'

Swartt kicked sand at her. 'Idiot! How can a little red shell hurt me?'

'Pick it up and see, it's not so little any more.'

Swartt picked the shell up and found it was quite a big one. In falling it had been almost covered by the soft sand, allowing only a small part of it to remain visible.

The vixen nodded. 'It was a little shell once, but it has grown, Lord. Beware of it I say. Turn it over and look.'

The ferret turned the shell over and scrutinized it, saying, 'A few markin's on it, like scratches. So?'

'Six marks, Lord; six scratches representing six claws!'

Swartt spat on the shell and threw it into the sea. 'Stupid rubbish! If that's the best ye can do then 'tis a pore show. Fall in with the rest an' git marchin'. Swartt Sixclaw decides his own destiny – only fools believe what they see in shells!'

Zigu the Corsair strode out on the right flank of the horde, along with his former bosun, a stoat called Welknose. Both could see Swartt marching at the head of the horde.

The bosun had taken a dislike to Swartt and made no secret of it. 'Warlord, huh! That'n ain't no Warlord, more like a puffed-up toad swaggerin' out front there. You c'd take 'im, Cap'n, easily, I knows yer could!'

Zigu was an unusual Corsair. Tall and saturnine, he dressed plainly and affected the manner of a gentlebeast. Despite this, he was shrewd and ruthless, and feared by many among the searat fraternity for his skill with the deadly long rapier. His paw resting on the fine basket hilt of the weapon, he strode at a leisurely pace, regarding his bosun's angry outburst with faint amusement.

'Lack a day, Welknose, shame on you for speaking of our beloved leader in such a dreadful manner. Tell me, pray, why should I "take 'im", as you so quaintly put it?'

'So that you kin be the boss of all this lot, Cap'n. Yer

kin bet an oyster to a lobster they'd foller a finebeast like yerself if 'n yer tickled Swartt to death wid yer rapier!'

Zigu smiled benevolently at his companion. 'Hmm, yes. I see what you mean. Mayhap all of these vermin would benefit from my leadership – but later, my friend, later.'

The stoat wrinkled his long lumpy nose and scratched one ear, saying, 'Later, Cap'n, why later?'

Zigu shrugged expressively. 'Why *not* later, prithee? Let our barbaric ally lead his horde against the Badger Lord an' his mountain; one would imagine fierce battle and bloody slaughter on both sides. Just before I slew him, my old father used to have a saying:

Where fate is sealed on battle's field,
And many low are laid,
The wisest mind says stay behind,
And let the fools get slayed!'

'Haharr haharr hohoho!' Welknose broke into raucous laughter. 'Yer a caution, Cap'n, an' no mistake. I see wot yer means, we let ole Swartt get hisself killed an' then we steps in an' takes command!'

'Roughly put but apt, my lumpnosed confederate.'

Welknose grinned fondly up at the tall Corsair. 'Yore a real gennelbeast, Cap'n. You talks fancy but fights dirty – that's real quality, an' no mistake!'

At the front of the horde Swartt was busy plotting with Nightshade against his Corsair ally.

'Lord, this Zigu creature,' said Nightshade, 'I do not need shells or omens to tell me that he will slide that thin blade of his into your back one night if he is not dealt with soon.'

'Oh, don't worry yerself, vixen, I've got me eye on Zigu, but we need 'im to take us to the mountain. He knows where it is, an' the best way of approachin' it.'

'And after that, Lord, what then?'

'Simple, we let everybeast know 'ow brave our Corsair is, then let 'im take the honour of leadin' a dangerous charge. If he dies, well an' good, but if he wins the day an' comes out alive, you know wot t'do, don't yer.'

'Aye, Sire, we hail him as a hero and let him drink fine wine from the silver chalice, like Bowfleg and Damsontongue.'

'Right, we can't let bravebeasts go thirsty, 'twouldn't be good manners!'

Skarlath was too high up to hear what went on below. A mere hovering speck, he noted the moving horde on the shore before winging off towards Salamandastron.

26

The great mace now hung in the forge room. Sunflash no longer carried it everywhere looped on his paw; it had become a hindrance to his new occupation. Clad in a flowing smock and wearing a woven straw hat, the Badger Lord had become the perfect farmer. Every available surface of the mountainside was cultivated; berries and hardy little fruit trees flourished on the leeside, root crops in the deeper-soiled hollows of the south face, and cereals on the front where the dark ancient volcanic soil was more sandy and shallow.

Sunflash sat with his hares on a high ledge. Their chores for the day completed, they were enjoying a picnic. Filling his beaker with pennycloud cordial, the badger pointed out an area below them, and said, 'We'll have to shore the edges of that salad garden with rocks, stop the rains washing the soil away. Leave a few small gaps for drainage though.'

The fat Porty saluted furiously, tugging his eartips and imitating rustic molespeech. 'Hoo urr, zurr Sunnyflasher, roight ee be farmer, burr aye!'

Sunflash chuckled as he flung his straw hat at the cheeky hare. 'When you get weary of being a mole, let me know, you impudent young rip. I'll teach you how to become a gull and we'll see how well you fly, from here down to the shore!'

Sundew and a hare called Fleetrunn appeared from a side tunnel carrying a cloth-covered tray between them. Bradberry sniffed, and said, 'I say, somethin' smells jolly good!'

Sundew twitched her ears severely at Bradders. 'Keep your grubby paws away from this, gannetface, it was made specially for Lord Sunflash.'

Uncovering the tray, Fleetrunn set it before the badger. A heavy dark cake still warm from the oven gave off fruity aromas. The golden stripe quivered as Sunflash's muzzle twitched. 'Bradders is right, it does smell nice! Cut it up quickly – hungry farmers don't like to be kept waiting!'

'It's a plum and almond cake,' Fleetrunn explained as she cut it into dark, fragrant slices. 'Bloggwood used old cider to mix it with; it had to be baked slow to keep it moist.'

'Kreeh! Cake is good for hungry birds!'

Suddenly, Skarlath landed on the Badger Lord's broad shoulder and started in on the slice that Sunflash held up to him.

'Well, my faithful friend,' said the badger, 'it's over a season since you last visited me. Eat your cake before you tell me the news.' Sunflash blinked as crumbs flew left and right. 'Now I know what somebeasts mean when they say "hungry as a hawk". I don't suppose you get fresh-baked cake often.'

The kestrel's throat bulged as he swallowed the last morsel. 'It is good cake, I will take some when I go. News is all bad, friend. The Sixclaw is three days from here with a great horde. There are no young ones and families with him now. These are fighting vermin: Corsairs, searats, marauders, plunderers, the rakings and scrapings of sea and shoreline, as many as leaves in an autumn gale!'

The big badger's jaw tightened. 'What of our friends, Tirry and Bruff and their families; did Swartt find their dwelling cave?'

Skarlath's fierce eye winked. 'No, they are safe. The horde entered Mossflower further south. Tirry and Bruff are out of their path, more northerly.'

Suddenly, the cake was forgotten. Sunflash rose, taking the hawk with him, and said, 'Come to my forge room, Sundew, and tell the Officers of our Long Patrol to meet me there urgently. This is a counsel of war.'

A dozen or so big lean hares of both sexes gathered in the forge room for the counsel of war. These were the Officers of the Long Patrol, tough and skilled in the fighting arts. Sunflash sat on the window seat, and Skarlath perched on the sill. The Badger Lord let his kestrel speak.

'This ferret has a horde greater than any ever seen, far too big to be met in the open. You have not got a quarter of their numbers, but I have been busy raising help – that is why I got here so late.'

A hare carrying a long sword spoke out. 'Help, old chap – what sort of help?'

Skarlath pointed north with his outspread wing. 'Guosim shrews; their Log a Log has promised me six logboats of shrew warriors, to come in from the sea and strike at the rear of the vermin when they arrive on the beach.'

Sunflash nodded his approval. 'That is good; if the horde of Swartt is as large as you say, we will need all the help we can get. Have you any other ideas, Skarlath?'

The kestrel preened a few crumbs from his pinions, saying, 'Give me the talisman you wear about your neck, Sunflash, and I will seek the help of otters and squirrels.'

'Take it and fortune fly with you, my good hawk!' said the badger, as he looped Elmjak's greenstone leaf about his friend's neck.

Skarlath bowed his head slightly to the Officers, then he was gone, shooting like an arrow through the open windowspace.

Then Sunflash addressed the hares.

'Our main fighting will be done from the mountain. We have supplies here, food and water to last us, and that puts the foebeast at a disadvantage. Their provisions are carried with them and cannot last long. Now, is there anything we can do to harass them while they are down on the shores in front of here? I am open to suggestions.'

Sabretache, the hare who carried a long sword, put forward an idea that had worked in the past against invading searats. 'Milord, we can dig long trenches, line 'em with sharpened stakes an' cover 'em with rush mats disguised by sand, wot?'

'Good idea, but surely they'll see them.'

A female hare called Hedgepaw held up a light javelin. 'Not if me'n'a few jolly old Sleepers give the blighters a taste of these, they'll run straight into the blinkin' pits.'

The badger looked puzzled. 'Sleepers?' he asked.

The most senior hare, a rangy male named Colonel Sandgall, winked knowingly at Sunflash. 'Sleepers, sah, take too bally long to explain what they do, but rest assured that each of these blighters, who fondly call themselves Officers, have a job t'do an' can do it rather well, doncha know. Beggin' y'pardon, milord, but if you concentrate your efforts fortifyin' all entrances an' exits at ground level then we'll see to the rest. Actually, I think the right form for the present is to marshal an' arm all the troops, wot?'

Sunflash was impressed with the confidence and ingenuity of his hares; he knew that despite their affected speech manner they were dangerous beasts and expert warriors. But he had a final word. 'Good enough, I'll leave you Officers to it. However, stay away from the Warlord, Swartt Sixclaw – he's mine!'

Every hare in the forge room knew by the look on the Badger Lord's face that he would brook no interference in the matter of his sworn enemy. They saluted smartly and went off about their duties.

Overnight, Salamandastron was transformed into a military garrison. The hares emptied both forge room and armoury of weapons; and bows, arrows, slings and rocks were stacked at every rock slit and window in the mountain. Young ones were taken deep inside to the central inner caves. Old ones took over the forge, repairing, sharpening and creating weapons. Random trenches were dug halfway up the shoreline; sharpened stakes stuck up from the trenchbeds. Boulder piles began to grow from halfway up the mountain, ready at the removal of wedges to topple down on any foebeast.

Sunflash worked with a team he had selected. They moved around Salamandastron's base, blocking off entrances and exits with boulders cemented together by powdered limestone and sand mixed with water. The main entrance was blocked by a large, rough-timber gate. Old harewives began baking extra food, readying the sickbay for wounded and manufacturing poultices.

In the midst of all this activity Sunflash stopped for a moment, to gaze sadly out at the areas he had cultivated. The salad garden had been stripped bare to allow the hares to set up a large, timber-framed rock catapult. He shrugged, sighing deeply. All this peace and beauty that he was trying to create would be ruined by war.

A war which began two dawns later.

27

'Where has my little blue honeypot gone?'

Friar Bunfold wandered distractedly around Redwall's kitchens, mixing batter in a bowl that he carried as he went, searching hither and thither. 'Sister Orris, watch those pasties, they're beginning to leak gravy on the floor. Has anybeast seen my blue honeypot? I had it with me on the cooling slab, just after breakfast. Bryony, did you move my honeypot, you know, the small blue one?'

Bryony placed a tray of scones on the windowledge to cool. 'No, Friar, I'm sorry, I haven't seen it. Maybe you left it in the wine cellars when you went down for damson juice.'

Bunfold beat the mixture in the bowl furiously with his ladle. 'No, it never leaves this kitchen. That pot was very special. It belonged to my mother, and she gave it to me when I became Friar here. Ahh! Young Veil, c'mere, where's that honeypot, eh?'

Bunfold put aside the bowl and caught the ferret by one ear, shaking him vigorously.

'Yeeeaah! Lemme go! Yowch!' Veil squealed. 'I don't know anythin' about your ole honeypot! Aaaaargh! Bryony!'

The mousemaid was between the two like a flash, pulling Veil from the wrathful Friar's clutches. 'Leave him alone this very instant, Friar Bunfold! How dare you treat Veil like that! Why should he know anything about your honeypot? You're *always* blaming him if anything goes missing!'

Sister Orris looked up from her pasties. 'That's probably because Veil is usually the one responsible!' she said.

Bryony turned on the Sister. 'That's not fair, he's changed! Veil only did things like that when he was a Dibbun!'

Myrtle the hogwife shook her paw disapprovingly at the ferret. 'Aye, well, he ain't a Dibbun no more, but things're still goin' astray.'

Veil ran behind Bryony and, poking his head over her shoulder, he stuck out his tongue at Myrtle. 'Yah, fatty ole spiky, go an' boil your snout!'

'What in the name of goodness is going on here, may I ask?' Abbess Meriam had glided in unnoticed. Silence fell in the room. She looked from one to the other. 'Please explain all the noise and shouting.'

The explanations came thick and fast, everybeast trying to get their say in at once.

'That liddle robber, he's taken my honeypot!'

'No, he never, Abbess, they're always blaming Veil!'

'That's 'cos he's always to blame, missie!'

'No, he isn't, you're all against him!'

Meriam held up a paw for silence. 'Friar Bunfold, did you see Veil take the honeypot?' she asked.

'Er, well, no, I didn't, Mother, but I know it was him!'

'He never, Mother, he never!'

'Keep out of this, Bryony! Veil, did you take Friar Bunfold's honeypot?'

'No, Mother Abbess, I never took it, an' he twisted my ear!'

Meriam pursed her lips at the Friar. 'Please, do not

ever do that again. There will be no violence in this Abbey. Come immediately to me if you have a grievance against anybeast.'

She turned away from the chastened Friar and placed a paw under the ferret's chin, lifting his head. 'Look me in the eye, Veil. Now tell me, and I want the truth, you have nothing to fear, did you take the pot?'

Veil blinked back tears as he tried to return Meriam's gaze. 'I never took it, Mother Abbess!'

Meriam's paws disappeared automatically into her wide sleeves. 'Then the matter is finished and done with. Nobeast saw Veil take the pot; he should not have been accused without proof. I believe him when he tells me he did not take it. As for your honeypot, Friar, I know it is valuable to you, so we will instigate a search right away. Togget, you will recruit any Redwaller who is not busy at the moment, bring them here and let the search begin.'

Bryony felt so angry at Bunfold and Myrtle that she could not bring herself to help with the search. Putting a paw around Veil's shoulders, she led him out into the orchard. The fruit trees and berry bushes were still; not a single leaf moved in the shimmering warmth of midday. Bees humming and the muted sounds of birdsong from beyond the walls in Mossflower added to the tranquillity of the verdant glade. Bryony sat beneath a gnarled apple tree. The Abbess's reprimand to stay out of the dispute weighed like a stone on her heart.

She patted the grass beside her, saying, 'Come and sit by me, Veil.'

The young ferret remained standing, pulling the leaves, one by one, from a redcurrant's foliage. 'We've missed lunch y'know,' he sniffed.

Bryony folded her paws and hunched forward, head down. 'I don't know how you could even think of food at a time like this, I'd be sick if I tried to eat anything. Take an apple if you're so hungry.'

Veil plucked a rosy apple that was ready to drop from a low bough. He bit into it, spat out the piece and flung the apple away rebelliously. 'Don't want one! They're all against me in this Abbey!'

He dashed off out of the orchard. Bryony half rose, calling after him anxiously. 'Veil, come back, I'm on your side, you know that!'

But he was away, dashing off to the bushes near the south wall stairs, a place he often went to in times of trouble.

Bryony sat alone, her mind in a turmoil. Since Veil had been a Dibbun things had gone missing, and each time she had defended him, never able to believe he was the thief. Often he was caught red-pawed, then she would apologize for him, lectures would follow, then tears and solemn promises from Veil that he had changed his ways. Bryony knew he had not, but she had cared for him, nursed him and comforted him; the mousemaid loved Veil as if she were his real mother. Standing upright Bryony wiped her eyes and clenched her paws resolutely. Today would begin a new era. She would assure Veil of her faith in him, show him that others could like and trust him if he was honest with them. He would discover happiness through goodness, and together they would learn to shake off the clouds of mistrust, until Veil earned the respect of all Redwallers!

The young ferret was growing tall and strong, lithe and sinewy like the father he had never known. He sat in the cover of the bushes alongside the south wallsteps, tossing the blue honeypot in the air and catching it skilfully with his agile, sixclawed paw. Smiling craftily, he licked the last of the honey from inside the pot's rim. Maybe he might have sneaked it back into the kitchen when it was empty. But no! Friar Bunfold had twisted his ear; the fat stupid mouse would pay for that, by never again seeing his beloved blue honeypot.

Bryony knew where Veil would be. She climbed the east wallsteps in the afternoon heat and wandered slowly along the battlemented top of the outer wall, hoping to catch a cooling breeze. Seeing the bushes moving in Veil's hiding place she remained silent, peering down to see what he was doing. The blue honeypot rose above the bushes as he threw it high and caught it. Bryony held her breath and ducked low, and she bit her lip hard to stop herself crying out.

Holding the pot close in to his side, Veil hurried over to the Abbey pond. Nobeast was there to see him, they would all be inside the Abbey at lunch. Bryony had watched him from her position on the walltop; now, scurrying bent low, she dashed around the battlements, descending the wallsteps at the southwest corner. Arriving at the opposite side of the pond, she peered through a screen of rushes at Veil.

He filled the pot with water and spoke to it. 'Thanks for the honey, always tastes sweeter when it's stolen. Nobeast will ever see you again, just think, I'm the last creature on earth to touch you. Goodbye, little blue pot!'

He threw it high over the pond, drawing in a breath sharply as he realized that he had thrown it too hard. The pot flashed blue in the sunlight as it splashed down at the far side, right in the centre of the rushes. Bryony crouched low, watching Veil.

He stood on tip-paw, peering across the pond, not able to see the pot. Then the young ferret laughed, shrugged, and ran off towards the Abbey, thinking that perhaps there would be some lunch left.

It was mid-afternoon when Togget found the pot, nestling in the top of an open sack of hazelnut kernels. Friar Bunfold was overjoyed, though Abbess Meriam tapped her footpaw thoughtfully. Why had the Friar's pot reappeared empty, clean and washed?

Bryony could not bring herself to face Veil, because she knew he would deny everything. Either that or he would wheedle and weep, explaining it all away until everybeast in Redwall, with the exception of himself, was to blame. The mousemaid felt an awful sense of guilt, but she could not have left the pot in the pond, knowing how much Bunfold valued it. Returning it secretly was the only thing she could do in the circumstances. Sighing heavily, Bryony tried putting the entire incident to the back of her mind. The mousemaid loaded up a tray with cooled mint tea, damson preserve and some scones freshly baked that day, adding a scoop of meadowcream.

Bella watched the doorlatch rise and the door swing slowly inward. Bryony entered, tongue sticking from one side of her mouth as she balanced the tray she was carrying. The ancient silver badger beamed fondly at her friend. 'What a good little mousemaid you are, bringing noontide tea to a helpless old fogey like myself!'

Setting the tray down, Bryony arranged the old badger's shawl snugly about her huge shoulders and opened the window to let in a breath of fresh summer air. She poured tea for them both, and set out the rest of the food. Then she perched up on the arm of Bella's chair.

The ancient sipped tea, watching Bryony over the top of her tiny spectacles. 'So, my friend,' she said, 'what's troubling your little heart?'

'Oh, this and that. Bella, have you been good all your life?'

The badger's chuckle sounded like a deep rumble. 'Bless you, no, sometimes I've been quite naughty, like now, piling all this damson jam and cream onto one scone. Shame on me!'

Bryony laughed as she watched the scone vanish in

two bites. Wiping cream and preserve from Bella's lip, the mousemaid continued, 'What I mean to say is, d'you think anybeast could be naughty all the time and never be good at all?'

Bella took another sip of tea. 'Ah, that's the difference, pretty one. Most creatures can be good most of their life and naughty sometimes, just like you and me. Others are good and never naughty, like Abbess Meriam. But then there are the other kind, those beasts who never do good, because they don't know how to and won't listen to any advice from goodbeasts. Naughtiness can grow and grow, like a marshweed, until it turns to badness, then if it continues there is only one name for it. Evil!'

Bryony put aside her scone and tea. 'Have you ever known an evilbeast, and if you did, well, did they change and become goodbeasts?'

The old badger shook her head. 'Questions, questions, why all the questions, my little flower? You should be out in the sunlight, enjoying your seasons with the other young Redwallers. Wait, let me guess. Do you know somebeast who is evil, is that why you ask me?'

Bryony got down from the arm of the chair. 'No, Bella, I don't know anybeast who is evil, a little naughty maybe, but not bad or evil. I think that others can drive a creature to naughtiness, always accusing and blaming them. After a while it must make the creature unhappy and drive him, er, or her, to be naughty, because nobody expects them to be good, that's what I think.'

A heavy paw descended gently on Bryony's shoulder. 'I think we both know the creature you are talking about, little one. Maybe it is the fault of Meriam and myself for accepting such a one into our Abbey.'

The mousemaid began fussing with the shawl and plumping up cushions around her friend. 'You're wrong, Bella. I know you are old and very wise, but you're wrong. I don't know who you're talking about. Time for your afternoon nap, marm. Shall I leave the window open?'

The great silver badger closed her eyes, saying, 'Whilst there are creatures like you on earth there is hope for others, my young friend, but don't waste your youth and kindness upon hopeless cases.'

Bryony touched a paw to Bella's lips. 'Sshh! Enough now, you need your sleep.'

Leaving the room quietly, the mousemaid closed the door carefully behind her. Noticing that the door to the sickbay was ajar, she looked in, expecting to see the slender mouse Sister Withe, the Infirmarykeeper and Herbalist.

Veil was in the sickbay; he had his back to Bryony, unaware of her presence.

'Veil! What are you doing in here?' she said, sharply.

Veil started at the sound of her voice. Bowls and jars clattered and fell as the ferret stammered, 'Er ... er ... Nothing! I ... I ... er, I was just looking around.'

Bryony pointed to the door, eyes alight with anger. 'Get out of here this instant before I report you to the Abbess.'

Veil pushed past her, protesting his innocence. 'I wasn't stealing anythin', honest I wasn't!'

Bryony's love was temporarily clouded by contempt. 'Hah! Just like you never stole the blue pot, eh? I'll bet you were surprised when it showed up again – if you'd had your way it would have been at the bottom of the pond!'

The ferret's eyes radiated hatred at the mousemaid who had reared him since infancy. 'Yah, go on! Blame me, you're like all the rest. I found that pot by the south wallsteps, but I couldn't return it, could I? Everybeast would say I told you so, it was Veil. I was too scared to take it back, so I chucked it in the pond.'

Bryony softened towards him and, taking his six-clawed paw, she tried reasoning with him. 'I took it

207

back, Veil, but *you* could have taken it back, then it would have proved to them that you weren't a thief. Can't you see, I did it to help you!'

Veil tore his paw from the mousemaid's grasp. 'You were spyin' on me, just like you were a moment ago, Miss Goody Goody. I hate you!'

He dashed off down the stairs, leaving Bryony dumbfounded with a large teardrop trickling down each of her cheeks.

28

That same evening, Skipperjo the otter and Redfarl the squirrel brought their warriors to supper at the invitation of the Abbess. It was a jolly meal and the food, as usual, was excellent. A large redcurrant, apple and blackberry tart graced the centre table, surrounded by small bowls of gooseberries and cream, a strawberry syllabub and wild cherry flans. Servers went around with large jugs of dandelion fizz, specially brewed by old Bral Hogmorton, the cellarkeeper, and his friend the Foremole. It was an instant success, especially with the Dibbuns, many of whom fell about chuckling when the bubbles fizzled in their mouths.

Jodd the squirrelhare set about demolishing an immense deeper'n'ever pie, made for him by a group of moles, who betted each other that it was too big for him to finish. The Foremole had wagered that he could. Smiling from ear to ear he collected candied chestnuts from the gaping moles as Jodd licked the deep pie plate clean.

'Hurr hurr ahurr hohurr! Ee should never bet agin 'ow much yon 'arebeast can put aways, ee'm a champeen scoffer, ho urr!'

Jodd wiped his chops delicately on a white serviette.

209

'My word, 'ceedingly tasty! Right ho, chaps, what's the jolly old main course look like?'

Abbess Meriam shook with stifled laughter. 'No more for you until you've given us a song, sir.'

Jodd was immediately up, cavorting around the tables and twanging on his bowstring as he launched into a comic ditty.

'Oh the reason why I sing this ballad,
Is 'cos I wish I were a salad,
If I were a salad, a great big one,
I'd lick the plate when I was gone!
   But merrydown derrydown, I don't care,
   I'm hungry as a good old hare.

So all you frogs pay heed to me,
A pudden's what I'd like to be,
All full of plums an' steamin' hot,
I'd scoff me in a flash, eh wot?
   But merrydown derrydown, no not me,
   A good old hare is what I'll be.

Then if I were a great fat fish,
The frogs would lay me in a dish,
And when they all sat down to sup,
With knives an' forks they'd cut me up.
   So merrydown derrydown, lack a day,
   A hungry hare is what I'll stay!'

Amid the laughter and applause, a mole who was on kitchen duty tugged at the Abbess's sleeve and whispered urgently, 'Cumm yurr, mum, ee 'ogwife be sicked in ee kitchen!'

Meriam got up from her chair and glided to the kitchen with Bryony in her wake questioning the mole.

'Myrtle sick? What seems to be the matter with her, Figgul?'

The molemaid Figgul spread her digging claws, mystified. 'Oi doan't be knowen, missie. Furst she be a tum-
mypainen, then groanen an' a moanen sumthin' orful,
et quoit upset oi, ho urr!'

Friar Bunfold was wringing his paws helplessly when
they arrived. Myrtle lay doubled up on the floor, shivering. Others crowded into the kitchen as Abbess Meriam
knelt over her, saying, 'Skipperjo, Jodd, clear that table,
lift her up onto it, gentle now. Myrtle, what is it, my dear?'

The old hogwife was decidedly pale, and greenish
around her lips. 'Ooooohhh! 'Elp me, marm, the pain,
the agony!' she wept. Then, mercifully, she passed into
unconsciousness.

Sister Withe pushed her way through to the table and
swiftly she inspected the hedgehog, feeling her brow,
sniffing her breath.

'Looks like she's been poisoned to me!' the mouse
announced.

A look of horror passed across Bryony's face.
'Poisoned?'

Sister Withe questioned Friar Bunfold. 'What's she had
to eat and drink lately, Friar?'

Bunfold waved his ladle distractedly. 'Nothin' we
haven't all eaten tonight, as for drink, well, there's that
jar of cold water sprinkled with oats and powdered
barley. I drink quite a bit of it, because of the heat in
here – gets quite hot when we're cookin', Sister.'

Withe took the jar, then she sniffed it, dipped a paw in
and tasted a drop. Pulling a wry face she spat it out, saying,
'Has any of this been drunk by you or the kitchen helpers?'

Friar Bunfold shook his head. 'No, the helpers have
all been drinkin' dandelion fizz. Myrtle didn't usually
drink the oat'n'barley water, said she wasn't sure if she'd
like it, 'owever, I drink lots of it, an' I told Myrtle to
drink some, as it'd do her good in this heat.'

'But you didn't drink any, Friar?'

'No, I was goin' to when Myrtle drank some as I

211

advised her . . .' The ladle clattered from Bunfold's paw as realization struck him. 'That was meant for me to drink!'

Myrtle was carried up to Bella's room by Skipperjo, Jodd and Redfarl. The Abbess and Sister Withe went with her. They laid the hogwife on Bella's bed as Withe prepared an antidote, speaking her thoughts aloud as she worked.

'Wolfbane, the hooded plant that kills. She must have drunk only a small sip – if Myrtle had taken a proper mouthful she wouldn't be with us now. Crushed mustard seed, lots of it in water, that should bring it up – what d'you think, Bella?'

The silver badger answered without hesitation. 'Aye, lots of it, you're right. Better hurry!'

In Great Hall, Bryony and Togget were helping to clear the tables. Veil began stacking dishes beside them; he looked puzzled. 'Bryony, what's all the fuss about, why's the feast stopped?' he asked.

'Didn't you hear? Myrtle's ill, they say she's been poisoned.'

Veil sat down, disbelief written across his face. 'Poisoned? Myrtle? But why?'

Togget picked up a great pie dish. 'Aye, poisinged, maister, tho' she'm aloive, thank guddness!'

Veil grasped Bryony's paw, his lip quivering. 'Poor Myrtle, who would do such a thing?'

Bryony watched tears pop out onto the young ferret's cheek. She hugged him, glad that he could show such tender feelings for the old hogwife. 'There, there, she'll be right as rain in a day or two, you'll see. They never said anybeast did it, perhaps it was just an accident, something got into the water jar somehow, who knows?'

The mousemaid felt sympathy for Veil, he looked so upset, and she sent him off to bed.

Myrtle was out of danger. Sister Withe had administered

the remedy, and Myrtle reacted favourably. After a further treatment of camomile tea, she had fallen into a peaceful slumber.

Later, in Bella's room, a meeting was held. Abbess Meriam looked sternly at her friends. 'There was no way that wolfbane could have found its way into the kitchens, I'm certain. We must face this fact, somebeast put it there, possibly to harm Friar Bunfold. We have a poisoner in Redwall!' The friends looked at each other, shaking their heads at this announcement.

Skipperjo addressed Sister Withe. 'Beggin' yore pardon, marm, but this wolfbane – d'you keep any in yore herbstocks?'

The good Sister pondered a moment. 'Wolfbane hmm, ah yes, I did have some, though I don't think I ever found a use for it; old Brother Farrow who used to be the herbalist left it there.'

Redfarl nodded towards the infirmary. 'I'll wager it ain't there any more. Go an' take a peek, Sister.'

Withe was away and back in a short time, crying, 'You're right, it's gone!'

Bella tapped her paws on the chair arms. 'So, we've got a poisoner in the Abbey. What's to be done about it? Nothing like this has ever happened before.'

Jodd the squirrelhare bowed elegantly. 'Permit me, m'dears. I am afflicted with a wise old head on young shoulders, y'know. Subterfuge is called for here, wot. Leave it to us squirrels an' otters, marm, I have a ruse or two up m'sleeve that I wager will lay the villain by his – or her – paws before the summer is much older.'

Redfarl winked at the Abbess. 'Aye, ole Jodders might talk like a mole with a gobful of roses, marm, but y'can trust him to solve yer problem.'

Abbess Meriam tucked paws into sleeves and bowed lightly, saying, 'I leave it in your capable paws, my friends!'

29

Next morning at breakfast, Great Hall was abuzz with the events of the previous night, though nobeast could venture an explanation or solution to it all. When the meal was finished, Abbess Meriam rapped the table with a spoon, calling the Redwallers to order.

'Silence please. Stay where you are, everybeast, I have something to say to you all, and to one in particular. A terrible thing has happened. Never, in the history of our Abbey, has anything like this ever occurred. Last night our hogwife Myrtle was very close to death. She had been poisoned, but not by any accident. It is my opinion that Myrtle was poisoned by somebeast sitting here in our midst this morning!'

An uproar and clamour arose until Skipperjo thwacked the oak tabletop several times with his hefty rudderlike tail. 'Order, mateys! Give order an' let the Abbess marm 'ave 'er say!'

Meriam continued in a loud clear voice. 'There is a poisoner among us, but whatever beast did this awful deed will not escape justice. Sister Withe!'

The slender mouse stood up, trembling slightly; she was not accustomed to public speaking. She piped up in a reedy voice, which grew bolder as she proceeded.

'Whoever poisoned Myrtle used wolfbane, a plant that I know much about. If our poisoner knew much about wolfbane then he, or she, would have used gloves. Let me tell you why. Two days ago I picked the wolfbane, but I forgot to wear gloves to protect my paws. This morning when I woke to come down to breakfast I looked at my paws. See!'

Withe held up both paws for all to look at. They were a deep crimson red, as though they had been dyed. She explained to the hushed audience. 'If you hold wolfbane with bare paws it will permanently stain them within two days of holding the plant. Luckily I learned to make up a herbal wash to remove the stain; I have a basin of it in the infirmary. After breakfast I will wash away the scarlet stains in my solution, but the poisoner has no such wash to do this simple task. So, friends, within the next day, or by early tomorrow, we will know who the poisoner is!' Withe held up her reddened paws again.

'The creature with paws that look like this!'

Veil let his paws drop slowly below table level, though he dearly wished that he could have raised them, to wipe away the sweat that was beading upon his nose. Chairs scraped and dishes clattered as the Redwallers rose to go about their day's chores and pastimes. Veil remained seated. He felt stunned – this time he would not be able to deny his guilt. Unless he could sneak up to the infirmary and wash his paws in the special herbal bath.

Bryony and Togget practically leapt up from the table, skipping from Great Hall as they called to Veil.

'Come on, Veil, the strawberries are ready to pick!'

'Hurr, ee Froir Bunny said us'n's c'n gather straw-bees, tho' ee doan't loik us to eat 'em all, hoo hurr!'

'C'mon, Veily, is your bottom stuck to that seat?'

The young ferret was gazing at his paws as he replied, 'You go, I'll catch you up later.'

By mid-afternoon Veil was convinced that his paws were beginning to redden. He had rubbed them hard on the grass by the south wall, scrubbed them more than a dozen times in the pond, and at one point even used a piece of sandstone to scour at them. His paws were sore, and the more he looked at them, the more he believed they were turning red. More than once he had wandered near the stairs to the infirmary, only to find squirrels and otters sitting, chatting on them. They showed no signs of moving, and the young ferret had to make himself scarce, or they would be suspicious.

At supper Veil's seat was empty. Bryony leaned across to Togget as he shovelled up woodland trifle with all the gusto of a hungry young mole. 'Have you seen Veil? It's not like him to miss supper,' she said.

Togget paused to down a half beaker of pear cordial. 'Ummm, ee'm wurn't lukkin' too gudd this arternoon.'

Heartwood the old otter joined the conversation. 'That young Veil you're talkin' about, meself an' Brother Barlom saw 'im not an hour since, sittin' in the bushes o'er by south wall. I tell you, he looked a bit pasty to me'n'Barlom, we sent him off to bed. Hah! Looked to me like he'd been eatin' too many strawberries.'

Bryony helped herself to some woodland trifle. 'Oh, is that all. He'll be all right after a good night's sleep. Did you send him off to his room?'

'No, we let him have the little foldin' bed in the gatehouse, nice an' quiet in there if yore not feelin' up t'the mark.'

After supper Bryony and Togget walked across the Abbey lawns to the gatehouse. The mousemaid knocked, calling, 'Veil, it's me, Bryony. Can I come in?'

The reply was loud and surly. 'No y'can't. Go 'way – I'm trying to sleep!'

'B'ain't you well, maister?' Togget called back. 'Zurr 'eartywood ee said you'm eated too many strawbees, hurr, oi never can eat enuff of ee strawbees, oi dearly do luvs em!'

Something struck the other side of the door. It sounded as if Veil had thrown a beaker. 'Go away, I said. Go away! Why can't you leave me alone?' His voice was shrill with temper.

Pressing her face to the door, Bryony spoke softly. 'Poor Veil, I'm sorry we disturbed you. Have a nice sleep if you don't feel well; see you in the morning. Good night.'

There was no reply, so the mousemaid and her mole friend made their way back to the Abbey.

It had long gone midnight, and the skies were cloudy and moonless. A faint chill breeze caught Veil as he stole quietly from the gatehouse, a length of rope over one shoulder. Silent as a fleeting shadow, the young ferret crossed the Abbey lawns, rounding the south side of the great building. Veil stood back and looked up to the sickbay window. It was shut. He gnawed at his lip, looking desperately for a way in Then he saw it. Bella's room was next door to the sickbay and the window was half open.

Veil was strong and agile, and he found he did not need the rope. There was a small corner angle where the stonework was bumpy and rough. Wedging his back against one side and jamming his body into the wall angle, Veil found he could climb quite easily. There was no lack of pawholds, and soon he was up to the broad first-floor sandstone ledge which served as one long windowsill for all the rooms at that level. The stone here had been cut and dressed smoother than at the base. Veil lay flat and crawled along until he reached the open window. Holding his breath the ferret inched it open wider. It creaked slightly, but not very loud; he slipped inside.

Myrtle lay on the bed, covered by a quilted counterpane. Bella snored gently, lolling in the deep armchair that she seldom left these days. Veil stood on the cushioned windowseat and allowed his eyes to adjust to the gloom inside. He saw a faint strip of light coming under the door, and slowly, softly, he made his way to it, taking care not to knock against any object he felt in his path. Then he was outside in the small corridor, which was dimly lit by a single lantern on a wall bracket. Closing Bella's room door carefully, he turned his attention to the door of the sickbay, which was slightly ajar. Veil put his eye to the space and peered in.

The sickbay was still and quiet, and it seemed unoccupied. For the first time that day a sly smile was on the young ferret's face. Luck was finally with him.

There in the dim shaft of light thrown from the barely-open door he could see a table. A glint of copper told him that the basin of herbal solution stood on the tabletop. He opened the door wider and paused a moment – still no sound from within the sickbay. Good! Placing one footpaw carefully in front of the other, Veil made his way slowly to the table. With a deep sigh of relief he let his paws sink into the dark, cool herbal mixture; now he was safe.

'Give 'em a good scrub, old lad – nothin' worse than guilty paws. Wot, wot!'

Veil went stiff with shock!

Before he could make any movement the door banged wide open and the sickbay was flooded with light. Abbess Meriam, Skipperjo and Redfarl strode in, lanterns held high. Jodd was already in the room, sitting on a bed with a pillow plumped up behind his long ears. He winked at Veil. 'Caught red-pawed I'd say, laddie buck!'

Veil's paws were indeed red, as deep a red as Sister Withe's paws had been at breakfast last morning. The herbal mixture was red too, a dark, purple-tinged crimson. Sister Withe entered the sickbay and, brushing past Veil, she dipped a paw in the mixture and licked it.

'Beetroot juice, not very herbal, but it dyes red, as you've just found out. *Poisoner!*'

Veil snarled and launched himself at her, teeth bared. Jodd moved like a blur; one swift hard kick from his long footpaw connected with the ferret's chin, knocking him spark out. They moved aside as Bella shuffled into the sickbay, and glanced at the prone figure on the floor.

'So, the trick worked,' she said. 'Our culprit fell into your trap, Jodd. Well done!'

The squirrelhare made an elegant leg. 'All done by brains and beauty, marm. Where'll we put this foul felon until you're ready t'deal with him, eh?'

Abbess Meriam took a key from her rope belt. 'Bral Hogmorton our cellarkeeper has cleared out one of his storecaves. Lock him in there for tonight.'

Meriam escorted Bella back to her room, and the silver badger plumped down wearily into her armchair. 'It seems we made a wrong decision all those seasons ago, Meriam. The ferretbabe grew up bad.'

The Abbess glided over to sit on the edge of Myrtle's bed. 'So he did, but we tried our best. It's Bryony I feel sorry for. She reared Veil, and no matter what he does, she still has very deep affection for him. We should never have let her raise him; he will break her heart.'

Bella nodded sadly. 'What could we have done, friend? Neither you nor I would have refused to take a helpless babe into this Abbey. I think we both saw him as Bryony did, a pretty little thing, like all small creatures. Though I remember my father, Boar the Fighter, he used to say, when rocks have crumbled to dust, vermin will still remain vermin.'

Meriam sat with Bella until the ancient badger fell

asleep. Before she left the room, the Abbess picked up a faded scrap of parchment from where it poked out beneath the rush floormat. She stared at it.

Give him a name and leave him awhile,
Veil may live to be evil and vile,
Though I hope my prediction will fail,
And evil so vile will not live in Veil.

30

Even as the servers laid breakfast places early next morning the news was out, starting as a whisper and growing like a grassfire until it was common gossip throughout Redwall Abbey.

'The poisoner has been caught in a trap – it was Veil!'

Abbess Meriam saw no point in discussing the dreadful affair; she would speak of it when the time was right. Meanwhile, she sat calm and pensive at table, her mood affecting the many Redwallers until breakfast in Great Hall became a hushed and sombre meal. Many looked towards Bryony's empty place. They nudged one another and shook their heads sympathetically; the good mousemaid would be feeling very sad this day.

When the meal was finished the Abbess rose to make a short speech.

'Please go about your work as normal and try not to gossip too much about last night's events. This afternoon when tea is finished I would like you all gathered on the lawn in front of the gatehouse.' To lighten the mood, Meriam smiled one of her rare smiles. 'It is a beautiful morning outside and I'm sure everybeast has something to do. Come, cheer up now, Redwallers, and let's not have any creature injured in the rush for the door!'

Grinning sheepishly the diners rose and ambled slowly out.

Togget, Jodd and Barlom had put together a plate of food and a beaker of dandelion fizz. They placed them on a cloth-covered tray, with a posy of summer flowers arranged in a small jug. Bryony was sitting beneath her favourite apple tree in the orchard, head bowed. She looked up as her molefriend placed the tray in front of her.

'Coom on, missie,' he said, 'eat ee up an' smoil, lookit that gurt long face, ee'll 'ave et rainen afore long, hurr!'

The mousemaid let out a long shuddering sigh. 'Oh, why, oh why did he do it? How *could* he? To try to poison . . . oh, I can't bear to think of it. He must have known that he'd be caught sooner or later.'

The squirrelhare waggled his ears playfully. 'Sooner, the way I planned it, jolly good ruse, wot!'

Jodd was silenced by a glare from Barlom. The kindly mouse pushed the tray forward encouragingly, saying, 'Eat something, pretty one. You won't solve anything by starving yourself. Come on, just a morsel.'

Tears sprang to Bryony's eyes as she grasped the Recorder's paw. 'I'm sure Veil didn't *mean* to do it, Barlom. What will they do to him?'

Barlom dabbed at her tears with a spotted kerchief. 'Bryony, don't waste your grief on Veil, he will only break your heart. You have a life of your own to live. Whatever punishment he receives will be according to the rules of our Abbey. There is nothing you can do to change that.'

Veil hammered and banged at the thick, elm-planked door of the storecave, his voice hoarse from shouting.

'Let me out of here, d'you hear me? Open this door!'

Clenching his beetroot-stained paws, he battered the door afresh. 'You're only a bunch of stupid mice, you ain't got no right to keep me locked up, get this door open. Now!' Flinging himself down on a straw pallet, he sobbed.

Skipperjo had taken charge of the storecave keys, and now the brawny otter unlocked the door, following Friar Bunfold inside as he delivered the prisoner's lunch. At the sight of the food Veil stopped weeping; he threw himself at the tray and began tearing ravenously at his meal. The Friar turned his head away in distaste as the young ferret slopped and gurgled, half-chewed food and hastily-swigged drink spilling from his open mouth.

Veil's eyes narrowed, and he glared hatred at his captors. 'Well, what're you two thick'eads gawpin' at, eh?'

Skipperjo shook a warning paw at Veil. 'Mind yore manners, ferret, or I'll mind 'em for ye!'

Veil bared his needlelike teeth at the otter. 'What'll you do, streamdog? Knock me out like that big daft rabbit pal of yours did last night? Well, go ahead, everybeast in this Abbey wants to beat me up, or pull me ears off.'

He switched his wrath to Bunfold. 'Oh aye, I won't forget you, fatbelly. Found your precious blue jar, did you, eh? After blamin' me for pinchin' it. Everybeast in this lousy place hates me, I never had a chance from the first day I was brought here as a babe!' He went back to eating, snuffling and weeping around mouthfuls of food.

'I know that Bryony put the pot back secretly,' Friar Bunfold squeaked sternly, 'but I didn't say anything for fear of getting her in trouble.'

Veil began chuckling through his tears; it was not a pleasant sound. His eyes shifted cunningly around the storecave. Skipperjo moved to block the half-open door as the ferret held up his crimson-stained paws, laughing. 'Heeheehee! Nearly got you, Friar Fatbelly, didn't I? Pity silly old Myrtle never drank enough to finish her off. Oh, but don't worry, I'll get you all before I'm finished. Heehee! Veil the red-pawed poisoner, eh! Well, next time it won't be just poison I'll use, it'll be a noose, a rock, a dagger, anything I can lay my blood-coloured paws on. Heeheehee!'

Friar Bunfold drew back fearfully from the grinning ferret; Skipperjo shepherded him out and turned the key in the lock, saying, 'Something'll 'ave to be done about that beast, he's crazy!'

Mid-noon saw a visitor to the Abbey, a tawny female-owl called Wudbeak. She visited Redwall every summer, to exchange news and gossip with her Abbey friends, but also to satisfy her craving for candied chestnuts. Abbess Meriam, assisted by Jodd, Redfarl and Sister Withe, had helped Bella down from her room, and along with many other Redwallers they sat on the banks of the Abbey pond. Wudbeak ate a great many of her favourite nuts from the improvised picnic that had been spread in her honour.

Jodd watched her, frowning slightly. 'By the left an' centre! Where's she puttin' them all?'

Redfarl whacked him in the stomach with her bushy tail. 'Exac'ly the same place you'd be stowin' 'em if we let you loose on those nuts, you great walkin' stomach!'

Having finished eating, the owl sucked dandelion fizz through a hollow cornstalk, to clear her mouth for speaking. 'Ah very nice, so 'twas indeed! Now, me fine Abbess, 'tis yerself sittin' there like an ould stone wid ears, waitin' on me news.'

Meriam was used to Wudbeak's odd accent, and she nodded quietly as the owl took another suck at the straw before continuing. 'D'ye not know a fierce-lookin' kestrel bird called Skarlath?'

'Yes, he has visited here once before to warn us of an attack.'

'By the faith'n'feathers, that's the very feller, a fine hawkbird. Well, now, not five days since, no, I tell a lie 'twas six. Anyhow, there's meself, sittin' on an ould mossy log countin' me feathers an' who should fly up but himself, the hawk that is. Sez he t'me, are there many otters'n'squirrels in this part of the woodlands? So sez I t'him, well yes'n'no in a roundabout sort o' way, there's treejumpers an' waterdogs aplenty, if you was t'take the time t'be lookin' for the beasts, why d'you ask? Well sez he, because I carry this amulet round me neck, to show them, they're to come to the aid of my Lord Sunflash at the mountain of Salamandastron on the far west shores. Well now, isn't that the wonderful thing, sez I t'him, an' who, me bold bird, is yer Lord Sunflash when he's at home? Marm, sez the hawk t'me, he is the great and mighty Badger Lord Sunflash the Mace!'

Bella cast off her shawl and stood up. 'Sunflash the Mace, Lord of Salamandastron! Oh, thanks be to fortunes and fates! Did the hawk say what he looked like?'

Wudbeak cocked her head on one side thoughtfully. 'Why no, ma, he didn't, but why d'you ask?'

Bella sat back down, her great silver face wreathed in smiles. 'Because he is my lost son. Now I know that my dreams were not just imagination. I have looked upon his face and talked with him as I slept.'

Heartwood pulled Barlom to one side, whispering to him, 'Stripe me! We forgot to tell 'er about Skarlath's last visit, he mentioned Sunflash to us then!'

Barlom kept his voice low as he replied, 'Aye, but Bella wasn't feeling too well at the time, and the Abbess told me not to mention Sunflash in case she got upset. It would have done Bella no good at all had it turned out that Sunflash was some other badger and not her son. No harm done, friend, at least she knows now for certain that he is.'

From behind Bella's back, Meriam winked slowly at them and held a paw to her lips, before turning back to the owl. 'Pray continue, my friend.'

'Right, where was I? Oh aye, well it seems that there's this dreadful ould ferret, a sixclawed vermin they call

Swartt. Do ye know what the villain's up to doin'? I'll tell yer, so I will. This Swartt has gathered a mighty horde of vermin, oh the rakin's an' scrapin's of the earth they are, and he's after attackin' the mountain of Salamandastron! That's why the hawk was lookin' for otters an' squirrels, to help out his Lord the badger. So, that's me news, ma.'

Wudbeak went back to devouring candied chestnuts as the Abbess bowed to her. 'Thank you, my friend, you are welcome to stay as our guest. When you are ready to leave I will have Friar Bunfold pack a good supply of chestnuts for you, the harvest was very good to us last autumn. Wonderful news for you, Bella?'

The silver badger was nodding as Skipperjo and Redfarl helped her to her feet. 'Nobeast can know just how wonderful, Meriam. So, my son fights a war against some vermin horde, that is the way of the warrior. Badger Lords are never satisfied until warfare touches them. This Swartt, no matter how great his army, will be defeated and slain by Sunflash. My son carries the blood of Boar the Fighter in his veins, and it was he who helped our warrior Martin.'

Abbess Meriam walked alongside her old companion. 'But do you not fear or worry for him?' she asked.

'All my life, Meriam. He is too far away for us to do anything for him, but I can dream, and the spirit of Boar will aid him, and that of his sire and great grandsire. Who knows, maybe even the voice of our own warrior Martin may reach my son. How can he lose with such allies to advise him? My only wish is that one day he might walk through our Abbey gates before my seasons have run.'

The Abbess felt immensely relieved. 'Don't go up to your room yet, Bella,' she said. 'Stay down for afternoon tea. I will need you to support me in the unpleasant task I must carry out.'

Bella stared at Meriam through her crystal glasses.

'You have enough to worry about as Abbess of Redwall. I feel better today, stronger. Leave the business to me; you will need to comfort and reason with Bryony.'

Throughout the afternoon tea Togget tried his level best to cheer Bryony up, but to no avail. The mousemaid sat stone-faced, neither touching food nor talking to anybeast. There was only Veil that she wanted to see, but the otter Skipperjo had banned all from seeing the ferret, save for himself and those who brought him his meals. Platters of fruit scones, wedges of white, nut-studded cheese, blackberry tarts, honey, meadowcream, new cider and mint tea, passed in front of Bryony, their delicious aromas not even tantalizing her. Two of Redfarl's squirrels did a hobjig with a pair of Skipperjo's otters, whilst the molemaid Figgul beat a small drum in time with Sister Withe's herbsong. It was all done for the mousemaid's benefit, though Bryony paid no attention. Sister Withe got her voice around the tongue twister admirably:

'See all the plants of the woodland are mine,
Gilliflow'r, nettle, dock and columbine,
Good Nature provided these things for my own,
The speedwell, fine cottongrass, and the cockscomb,
They grow and they flourish in sunshine or rain,
Groundsel, rush, hemlock, soapwort and verbane,
Some in the summer and others in spring,
Whilst others in autumn do cause me to sing,
Yarrow and arrowroot, bracken and bramble,
Pennywort, chervil, marestail and eyebright,
Teazel and thistle and ivy to ramble,
Whilst lily and violet await morning light,
Mint, borage, fennel and basil are mine,
Like lavender, rosemary, thyme and woodbine!'

The good Sister took a deep drink of cold mint tea

and held a paw to her heart. 'Phew! I'm glad I don't have to sing that twice!'

Nothing seemed to cheer Bryony up, but she leapt to her feet immediately when Jodd poked his head around the doorway of Great Hall.

'Attention, chaps an' chapesses, Abbess wants every-beast out on the lawn by the gatehouse soon as y've finished vittles!' There was an immediate exodus from the tables, with Bryony in the lead, her face a picture of anxiety.

Bella stood on the lower wallsteps by the gatehouse, supported by Abbess Meriam, the owl Wudbeak at their side. Ancient as Bella was the recent events at her beloved Redwall had driven her to speak. Every Abbey creature sat on the lawn facing the three. There was a profound silence over the gathering, then heads turned to see Skipperjo and Redfarl escorting Veil from the main Abbey building. Bryony drew in her breath sharply. Jodd was walking in front of the prisoner, but she could see Veil's paws were bound in front of him. He jumped and snarled, biting at his guards, as they hauled him along to the bottom step.

Bella came forward, spreading her silver-furred paws. 'First, let me say that I take responsibility for what will happen here today. Any resentment or grievance you hold must be against me, and not our Mother Abbess.' Bella looked directly at Bryony. 'Is that clear?'

Bryony nodded, looking stricken, and the ancient badger continued. 'You see before you a young ferret called Veil. I gave him his name when he was brought to this place many seasons ago. Abbess Meriam, myself, and one other, our friend Bryony, aye, and all of you for that matter, showed him every kindness. The goodbeasts of Redwall helped Veil to grow from a Dibbun to a youngbeast, trying to teach him the values of the life we live here, to honour, help, befriend and never to harm others. Sadly he ignored all advice and went his own way, lying, cheating, stealing and creating bad feeling among otherbeasts. All this could have been forgiven, and has been countless times in the past. However, now Veil has passed the point of forgiveness. He tried to kill one of us, and there is no absolution whatsoever for a creature who would do this to a Brother or Sister of Redwall. Had he lived among badgers, who have a far more rigid code, I tell you, he would have been slain instantly. But this is not the way at our Abbey, though nothing as terrible as this has ever before occurred here.

'Therefore I must say something to you, Veil, that has never been said to another creature within these walls so far, and it is a hard thing for me to say. You are no longer one of us: there is no place for you at Redwall; once you are put on the path outside the Abbey, our gates are closed to you for ever. Veil, you must go now. I declare you Outcast!'

A cry, like that of a wounded animal, broke the silence. Bryony dashed forward, trying to get hold of the young ferret. 'No, no! Not my Veil, please let him stay, I'll look after him, he'll change, you'll see, I'll talk to him . . .!'

Meriam got to Bryony before she reached Veil; wrapping her in the folds of her gown the Abbess hugged the mousemaid tightly. 'Hush now, be still, little one, he is a poisoner and would have murdered had he not been stopped. There is nothing more you can do for him!'

Veil looked stunned as Jodd cut the bonds from his paws, and he stared at the old badger on the steps, crying, 'What about me? Where'll I go now? I've got no family, I'm alone, what'll I do?'

Seizing both the ferret's paws in a vicelike grip, Skipperjo brought his face close and said through gritted teeth, 'Little sixclaw the poisoner, eh? I knowed who you was, matey, from the day I picked you up suckin' frogspawn in a muddy ditch! Yore the whelp of that other sixclawed vermin, Swartt the Warlord. Aye, the one who's over at Salamandastron mountain right now fightin' the great Badger Lord. Why don't yer travel over thatways, due west and through the mountains they say, an' take a look at some real slayin', or would 'onest warfare be too noble fer a sneakin' poisoner!'

Then, dragging Veil by both paws, the big otter lugged him through the gateway and flung him on the path. 'Go an' work yore evil someplace else, scum!'

As the gates of Redwall slammed shut on him, Veil stood quivering with rage, shaking his sixclawed paw at those inside. 'Stupid oafs!' he yelled. 'Bumblin' fools! You ain't heard the last o' me! See these paws, well, you dyed them red, an' red they'll stay, to remind me that someday I'll be back! Aye, with my own horde, I'll tear this Abbey apart, stone by stone, then I'll slay every livin' one of you, I promise!'

Inside on the lawn, Bella and the Abbess held Bryony close between them as she pleaded, wept and begged for them to give Veil one last chance – Veil, the ferret she had reared and loved from a babe, despite all his evil ways.

BOOK THREE

The Warrior's Reckoning

31

The absolute size and majesty of Salamandastron staggered Swartt Sixclaw when he first saw the mountain. From behind a rocky groyne which stretched lengthwise across the shore, the Warlord sat in counsel with his Captains, whilst the horde sprawled across the sands, eating, relaxing and readying their weapons. Zigu could not resist sneering at Swartt's strategy, which was to take the mountain from behind in a pincer movement. The Corsair ferret lolled indolently against the rocks, making parries and thrusts at mid-air, practising with his long, basket-hilted rapier.

'Zounds! Listen to him – attack the mountain from behind. Methinks I've heard some halfwitted schemes in me time, but strewth, this'n takes the biscuit!'

Swartt faced the sardonic Corsair, holding his temper level. 'Well, you were clever enough t'lose yer ship on the rocks, let's 'ear yore plan if'n you don't like mine, Cap'n Zigu.'

Stung by the barb about the loss of his ship, Zigu sketched a swift plan on the sand with his rapier point. 'Right you are, Warlord, here's my scheme. The sea at our back is a natural ally; wait until the last of ebb tide, then form the whole horde up in ranks below the

233

tideline. Obviously the defenders of yon mountain have nothing like the numbers we possess, and mayhap Salamandastron will fall to us by a mere show of power. When they see the might of our horde advancing up the beach, perhaps their nerve will fail.'

A murmur of approval rose from the Captains, but Swartt drew a line through Zigu's plan with the tip of his curved sword. 'What was wrong with my plan, why's yores any better?' he said.

Zigu was enjoying his verbal victory over Swartt, whom he considered a savage clod. 'The fault with your strategy, my good Warlord,' he said condescendingly, 'is that we leave our backs unguarded. Who can tell what lies in the hills behind the mountain – we could be attacked by those who are friendly neighbours to the Badger Lord. However, if you take my way it is a two-edged blade: first, we have nothing to lose by a show of strength; secondly, it will put fear into the hearts of our enemy.'

The horde Captains nodded vigorously; they liked Zigu's idea. Swartt gestured at the mountain with his chainmailed paw. 'Fair enough, but what if they ain't scared of us, what do we do then, march up'n'down on the shore lookin' fierce? That ain't goin' to conquer no mountain. Yore plan ain't bad, Zigu, but it needs a bit of work doin' on it.'

The Corsair sheathed his rapier and performed a flourishing bow in Swartt's direction. 'Be my guest, Sirrah, by all means. Plan away!'

Playing him at his own game, Swartt bowed back. 'Righto! If'n they don't come flockin' out terrified an' surrenderin' like you say they should, then 'ere's wot we do. Split up an' attack, usin' the pincer movement I was goin' to use from the back, this time at the front, but wid a difference. This time we mount a charge, straightforward at the front entrance, same time as the pincers hit both sides. Now, it'll need a clever an' fearless beast t'lead that frontal charge. Captains, who d'you say it should be?'

The Captains replied en masse without hesitation, 'Zigu!'

The Corsair smiled and saluted them with his rapier, inwardly seething that he had allowed himself to be outwitted by Swartt.

The midday sun was at its zenith. Sunflash the Mace stood at his bedchamber window with Colonel Sandgall, Sundew and Sabretache. Together, they watched the seemingly endless ranks of hordebeasts marching out to line up below the tideline. Wardrums pounded relentlessly and conch shell trumpets brayed aloud, over the barbaric banners streaming high over glinting spearheads.

Colonel Sandgall watched them coolly through his monocle. 'D'you know, I do believe the blighters've brought enough troops along t'make a decent scrap of it, eh, 'Tache?'

Sabretache the swordhare tutted indifferently. 'Tchah! Let's hope they fight better'n they drill, sloppy lot, no right markers, no proper dressin' from the right. I'd smarten 'em up if I were their Captain, believe you me!'

Sunflash smiled at Sundew. 'Afraid, missie?' he asked.

She looked up at the Badger Lord, his golden stripe showing through the open vizor of a high black war helmet, massive chest covered by a fine chainmail tunic, and the great mace balanced easily over his broad shoulder.

'Not while you're around, Sire!' she said.

Now the horde was fully marshalled with the neap tide protecting their rear, and a forest of spears and lances pointing skyward. Hordebeasts stood shoulder to shoulder, covering the whole lower beach, so that not even the sand below the tideline was visible. Swartt came to the forefront, flanked by Zigu and the stoat Captain Aggal. The Warlord's face and teeth were freshly stained with bright plant dyes, a multicoloured cloak swirled about him, and his heavily chainmailed sixclaw glittered brighter than the long curved sword thrust into his snakeskin belt. He drew his blade and pointed at Salamandastron. That was the signal. The horde began marching slowly forward, splitting into three groups as it did, Swartt leading the left, Aggal the right and Zigu the centre.

Sunflash had sighted his lifelong foe. He hurried from the chamber, threading his way through the mountain passages to the left side, where he knew Swartt was heading. Back in the chamber, Colonel Sandgall took a whistle from his tunic and blew three sharp blasts. The hares of the Long Patrol went into action.

Zigu's command were hardly upon the soft sand above the tideline, when the ground rose up in front of them. Thirty hares leaped from a shallow trench covered by sand spread over the top of rush mats – these were the Sleepers that Sandgall had spoken of. They sprang up from hiding when the front line of vermin was less than twenty paces away. A wild cry went up as they launched javelins into the front marchers.

'Eeulaliaaaaa!'

Completely taken by surprise, half the front rank were slain. Hedgepaw and her Sleepers fled back to the mountain, taking care to leap over the disguised trench which contained the sharpened stakes. Zigu flung himself to one side, avoiding the rain of javelins, then, leaping upright, he drew his rapier.

'After them. Charge!'

The words had scarcely left his mouth, when the sand another score of paces away heaved upward. Bradberry spat out grit as he called to his two dozen archers, 'Quickfire, chaps!'

Again Zigu's lightning reactions saved him. Flinging himself flat, he heard the screams and felt the thudding weight of two horde soldiers, as they fell dead on top of him. Pushing the bodies roughly aside the Corsair sprang up and, grabbing a spear from one of the slain vermin, he hurled it at the fleeing backs of the retreating Sleepers. It was a lucky throw. Fordpetal, the young female hare with the fluttering eyelashes, went down with a scream, the spear sticking out of her back.

Zigu looked around for another spear to throw as the hordebeasts charged past him. Fifty paces further on they vanished into the covered stakepits; agonized yells rent the hot air as vermin soldiers plunged onto the sharpened stakes.

Zigu roared at those still alive, 'Back! Back, you fools, can't you see it's a trap?'

As they retreated, the Corsair ran to where Fordpetal lay groaning. His face tight with rage, Zigu lashed at her with the long blade of his rapier.

'Hit and run, eh, hare! Well, I'm hitting now, let's see you run!'

She screamed as he lashed her mercilessly with the thin blade.

'Hey, filthface, why doncha try doin' that to somebeast who can hit back!'

Zigu looked up to see the Long Patrol Captain Sabretache striding purposefully towards him. The Corsair grinned evilly, calling to his hordebeasts, 'Leave this one to me, he carries a blade!'

Ignoring the gaping hordebeasts, Sabretache leapt the stakepit. Drawing his sabre he confronted Zigu.

Nobeast had ever bested the Corsair in swordfight. Flexing the long steel blade between his paws, he stared contemptuously at the hare, who stood alone before him, and said, 'Zounds, you're a bold bunny and no mistake. Come and be spitted!'

The hare shot forward, his narrow curving sabre striking the rapier blade with a force that sent shockwaves tingling through his opponent's paw. He smiled recklessly. 'Defend y'self, ferret!'

Balancing lightly on their footpaws both beasts took up the *en garde* position, swordpoints flickering like snaketongues as each sought an opening. Momentarily the frontshore of Salamandastron grew silent. Hordebeasts on the sand and defenders from the mountain stood stock still, watching the two swordbeasts battle to the death.

Zigu pressed forward, step, step, step, his rapier seeking the elusive foe. Sabretache backed and went sideways, the sabre a bright blur as it slashed and took the ferret's ear. Scarcely believing what had just happened, Zigu clapped a paw to the side of his head, glaring venomously at the hare. One paw behind his back, Sabretache stood with his legs bowed, sabre in the salute position as he kissed its hilt. 'Can y'still hear me, old chap, hard luck, wot?'

With a roar of rage, Zigu charged, flailing the rapier in front of him. The two blades met, and sand flew about their nimble footpaws as they locked in a dance of death. Blade clashed upon blade as they battled across the beach. Zigu managed to grab Sabretache's swordpaw with his free one, and as the hare pulled away the Corsair struck a downward slash at his head, hissing triumphantly.

'Sssssdeath!'

Sabretache flicked his head to one side, avoiding the blade slicing at his throat. He came up smiling, running a paw along the fine scar tracing his cheek.

'Not quite, old lad, try again, eh!'

Zigu plunged forward once more, but the hare was ready. Locking hilts with the ferret, he wrenched down and gave a powerful twist upward. The rapier described a glittering arc in the noon sun as it left Zigu's paw, then a swift kick to the stomach left the Corsair sprawling, unarmed. Sabretache leaned on his sabre as if it were a walking stick, and he nodded towards the rapier as the horrified ferret scrambled to get out of blade range. 'Pick it up, vermin!'

Zigu was scared, he knew he was facing a swordmaster, but the Corsair still had a trick or two in him. Reaching down to retrieve his blade, he snatched up a pawful of sand and hurled it in his opponent's face. As Sabretache's paw shot up to his eyes Zigu bulled forward, throwing himself upon his foe, and they went down together. However, the hare was not finished. His long legs shot out like two pistons, catching the ferret in his stomach and sending him flying over Sabretache's head. He landed with a bump that winded him. The hare was up; pawing sand from his eyes he went for the ferret. Zigu staggered upright in time to raise his blade, but not to stop the lightning attack. He staggered backward, blade clashed upon blade as thrusting, hacking and swinging the hare drove his foe skilfully around the stakepit, manoeuvring the ferret until he was backed up to a rock. Then both blades locked, sabreguard against basket hilt. Eye to eye, whisker to whisker and jaw to jaw they swayed.

Panic glistened in Zigu's eyes, he had met his match. Gasping for breath he pleaded for his life, 'Sirrah, a boon, a boon, spare me!'

There was no mercy in the face of the Long Patrol Captain. He knocked the rapier to one side and thrust forward with the curving sabretip. 'You ask for mercy, ferret? You who moments ago whipped a wounded creature with your blade! Tchah! You have lived the life of a coward, now learn t'die like a soldier, sir!'

Zigu slid lifeless to the sand. Sabretache tucked the sword beneath his elbow like a pace stick and marched boldly off. Whilst the fight had been in progress Bradberry and Bloggwood had sneaked out and retrieved Fordpetal's body.

Aggal and his band came marching around to the sloping right side of the mountain. It was completely deserted. The stoat Captain had expected to meet some resistance, but there was nothing, just a solid rock face soaring upward with no sign of entry visible. A weasel called Bandril shrugged his shoulders in bewilderment, and said, 'Well, we're 'ere! Wot d'we do now, Cap'n?'

Aggal cuffed the hapless weasel a quick clip over his ear. 'Do, what d'yer think we do, peabrain? We climb up an' try t'find a way in o' course. Now git climbin', all of yeh!'

Encumbered by spears, shields and various weapons, the hordebeasts began clambering, not too enthusiastically, up the rockface. Aggal was well ahead of the rest, energetically scaling upward and calling back in a loud whisper, 'If we kin find us a window or some way in we'll battle our way down t'the main entrance an' unblock it fer Cap'n Zigu.'

Bandril lagged at the back of the climbers, waiting for an even tardier rat to catch up with him. 'C'mon yew, move yerself,' he called down. 'Keep yer eyes peeled fer entrances!'

The rat gave him a withering glance and climbed slower. 'Entrances, y'must be daft as a bat if you think I'm goin' to climb inside o' there, the place is fulla badgers an' 'ares!'

Bandril sat down on a grass-covered ledge. 'Yore like meself, mate, not soft!'

32

High up and hidden from view, Porty and an old campaigner called Floke risked a quick peep over the edge at the vermin climbing upward.

Floke squinted. 'Do yer think they're sufficiently far enough h'up, master Porty? Yore h'ossifer material, h'it's yore decision.'

Porty scratched his chubby stomach reflectively, and looked up from the climbing vermin to the huge pile of boulders artfully held in position by one long aspenwood wedge. 'Hard t'say really, actually I think it's a bit thick layin' decisions on my doorstep, old chap. I mean, you're supposed to be senior wallah round here.'

Floke placed his footpaw against the wedge. 'Well, yore a right young corker, you are, master Porty. Colonel Sandgall said you was trainee h'ossifer in charge o' this h'operation, yore supposed t'give the blinkin' orders!'

Porty pulled a face. He felt hungry and peeved. 'Oh, right ho then, it's jolly hot out here an' I'm starvin'. Away wedge, Floke, an' that's an order!'

The older hare chuckled. 'That's wot h'I likes ter see, a young h'ossifer in command.'

One swift kick from Floke's footpaw sent the wedge

sailing into space, closely followed by a great shower of boulders.

Aggal pawed sweat from his eyes as he shielded them and peered upward. 'Bound ter be a openin' up there . . . Yaaaaaarrrrgh!'

Had not the boulders bounced out from the face there would have been total slaughter among the climbers, but as it was nearly half their number were wiped out by the falling rocks, Aggal being the first to go.

Floke watched the scene from his high perch, shaking his head and muttering, 'Serve youse right for attackin' us in the first place, ain't that right, master Porty. Master Porty, sir?'

But the hungry young hare had gone inside, never having once missed afternoon tea since his hero, Lord Sunflash, had introduced it a couple of seasons back.

Sunflash was down and waiting in the shelter of the base at the mountain's left side. He watched as the hordebeasts rounded a bend in the rock. Suddenly he saw Swartt, as usual, letting the others go in front of him. All the Badger Lord's previous plans deserted him at the sight of his hated enemy; Sunflash felt the blood-wrath rise within his brain. Throwing caution to the four winds he swung his club and came charging out of cover.

'Eeulaliaaaaaaa!'

It was a frightening sight to the foebeasts; a giant badger clad in chainmail, helm, and wielding a mace the like of which few of them had ever seen. They turned and ran, Swartt with them. Roaring his warcry, Sunflash pursued them recklessly.

Sabretache was back up at the chamber window with Colonel Sandgall and Sundew, all of them watching the progress of the battle on the shore below. Zigu's command had been taken over by a weasel called Bleeknose, an active quick thinker. He had led his troops into the staketrench, where they had smashed the wooden spikes, piling them with the carcasses of the slain on the edge of the trench and covering them with sand. The result was a good trench fronted by earthworks, from which the horde could send arrows, spears or sling-stones against the mountain defenders.

Colonel Sandgall sent a despatch runner to the lower windows and openings. 'Tell the squads t'come up here, perfect spot for shootin' down into that trench, wot. All the harder for the bally vermin to send blinkin' missiles this far up. What d'you say, 'Tache, old lad?'

Sabretache groaned aloud at what he saw below. 'Oh my giddy aunt, take a look at this, sah!'

There was Sunflash, alone and unprotected out on the shore, roaring his defiance in the face of the enemy. Swartt had fled almost to the sea, leaving most of the horde as a barrier between himself and his foe.

Sandgall squinched his brow down hard on his mon-ocle. 'Instant calamity, wot! Lordship's goin' t'get himself massacred, there's enough vermin down there t'kill ten badgers! Bloodwrath or no blinkin' bloodwrath, they'll have 'im. Calls for swift action, 'Tache, jump to it!'

Sundew stared anxiously at the lone figure down on the shore. 'They're shootin' arrows at him!' she cried.

Swartt was angry with himself. He had come all this way for vengeance, only to turn tail and run at the sight of Sunflash. Breathlessly he splashed through the shallows to the line of rocks that stretched from shore to sea.

Nightshade could see what had taken place, and art-fully she soothed the Warlord's bruised ego. 'Nobeast could stand against the badger in his madness, Sire. You did well to escape him; besides, I know you want to take him alive so that you may have your revenge bit by bit, you always said that.'

The ferret ceased pounding his mailed paw against

the rocks, and looked hopefully at his seer. 'You've got a plan, vixen, tell me!'

'We'll snare him like a fish in a net, Lord.'

'Fool, where is there a net big enough to hold him? We don't 'ave any such net.'

'No, but we still have a few big tent canvases. . . .'

The Warlord's face split into a huge grin. 'Of course! He can't club 'is way through canvas. Once we bag the badger, those hares'll fold like dead bark!'

Sunflash was beset on all sides. He whirled and roared in a fury, unable to get at his attackers. The vermin kept their distance, slinging rocks and firing arrows. The heavily meshed mail tunic and iron war helmet were weighing the Badger Lord down, but he could not chance removing them. His paws sunk deep in the soft sand, and bellowing and howling he shook the big mace.

'Eeulaliaaaaaa!'

Rocks and shafts clanged and thudded against the enraged Badger Lord. The vermin circled like small vicious predators trying to bring down a big beast, hurling their missiles and keeping out of his range. Sand was in every crevice of his chainmail. The iron helmet, hot from the sun's rays, caused sweat to trickle over Sunflash's head, into his mouth, down his ears, blinding and stinging his maddened eyes. Nowhere through the small vizor slits could he see his enemy Swartt. He began floundering, and an arrow thudded deep into his unprotected paw. With a roar he tore the shaft out and, snapping it in two, he hurled it at his unseen tormentors. A spear raked his footpaw as he lifted it from the entrapping sand. Blundering and staggering, he tottered towards the rocks, not knowing in which direction he was moving.

Then the canvases trapped him like a great fish in a net.

Suddenly Sunflash felt the enveloping weight fall on him, driving him down on all fours into the sand. Everything went dark. As he fought blindly against the tough, unyielding canvas, he could vaguely hear Swartt's voice.

'Keep those blades away, I want him alive! Jump on that canvas, pile sand on it – we've got 'im!'

Completely stifled and overburdened, the badger's helmeted head hit the soft sand, his senses swimming as he fought for breath.

33

It was an hour after dawn when Abbess Meriam discovered Bryony had left the Abbey. Sadly, she sat on the empty truckle bed, looking at the disarrayed sheets and touching the dented pillow where her friend's head had lain.

Meriam read again the note that Bryony had left. 'Redwall will not be the same without our little flower,' she whispered, and turned to see Bella standing in the doorway.

'Alas, no, my heart will be heavy each time I see her empty place at table,' said the ancient silver badger, as she sat beside Meriam on the bed. 'Do you think she will ever return?'

'Oh, yes. One day when Bryony is older and wiser we will see her walking back through our gates, of that I am sure.' Then the Abbess's paw clenched, and her voice became harsh. 'Unless some bad fate befalls her as she follows Veil – trouble pursues that vermin like winter follows autumn. A young maid alone . . . we should send someone after her.'

Bella rose slowly. 'No, Meriam,' she said gravely. 'The path that Bryony follows was marked out for her by fate and seasons long ago. All we can do now is send our hearts and feelings out to her, wherever she is.'

Bella leaned on Meriam's paw, and the two friends quit the deserted room, which seemed emptier than it had ever been before.

Grasshoppers chirruped their ceaseless dry cadence; somewhere high in the cloudless blue a skylark trilled; bees droned busily from kingcup to meadow saffron, and butterflies perched upon scabious flowers, their wings like small, still sails on the calm air. Bryony stopped awhile, enjoying the feel of dry curling grass underpaw as she got her bearings. The sun was still easterly and climbing towards high noon. She moved until it was against her right shoulder, striding off after Veil. She had overheard Skipperjo's challenge to the ferret and knew that the great mountain lay somewhere due west.

It took Byrony some time to shake off the feeling of depression she had encountered when leaving Redwall. All morning she kept looking back at the Abbey, watching it diminish in size as she got further away. Finally she crossed a long rolling hill and Redwall was lost to sight. The mousemaid knew what she must do: find Veil and bring him back, even though he had been made Outcast and sent away. Bryony had been forming her own plans for both of them. Her Mossflower friends would help; together they would build a small dwelling in the woodland, close to Redwall. There she would live with Veil, teaching him to behave well and showing all at Redwall how he had changed for the good. Maybe, just maybe, Bella would one day regret her decision, and allow Veil to return to the Abbey. Cheered up by these thoughts and her resolute optimism, Bryony strode onward, singing an old Abbey ballad.

'I search for the summer o'er fields far and still,

Though seasons may take me wherever they will,
Cross vale and o'er hill as the warm winds blow
  down,
'Twas there I found autumn gold, russet and brown.
I wandered the lands 'neath a misty morn sky,
'Til the frost rimed a small icy tear from my eye.
O winter, cold winter turns short days to night,
And dresses the lea in a gown of pure white,
So windswept and sad until yon comes the day,
A pale morn of sunlight melts snowflakes away.
See greenshoots a pushing to pierce the bare earth,
Bringing fair coloured flowers to herald springbirth,
As spinney and woodland grow leafier each day,
Young birds sing that summer is soon on its way.
I'll find me the glade that my heart recalls best,
In my soft summer dell I will lay down to rest.'

It was mid-noon before Bryony decided to take a break
and eat something. Choosing a shaded patch on the side
of a broken hill she sat down and opened her haversack.
Pouring pennycloud cordial into her beaker she selected
a russet apple, and recalled helping to store the apples
in dry straw, at the end of the previous autumn's harvest.
It was only when she took out one of Friar Bunfold's
home-baked oat scones from the pack that emotions
overcame her. There was nobeast around to see, so the
mousemaid gave full rein to her grief, weeping
unashamedly as she drank cordial and ate her scone.
Memories of Redwall flooded over her, like spring tide
hitting a dry beach. Teardrops spattered onto the half-
bitten apple and dampened her travelling habit.

'Er, hrumm, hrumm, I'll 'ave that if y'don't like it,
mouse!'

She looked up to see a very fat robin watching her. It
nodded at the scone. 'Y'don't 'ave to eat that if'n it
makes y'cry. Give it t'me, y'll feel 'appier, I know y'will.'

Bryony tried wiping her eyes on her sleeve, but the

tears kept rolling down unchecked. She broke off a piece of the scone and tossed it to the robin. 'H . . . h . . . here, n . . . now g . . . go 'way and leave m . . . m . . . me!'

The robin pecked at the scone critically, bobbing its head. 'Mmm, mm, very tasty very nice. Gone an' give y'self hiccups now, haven't you, should never whinge while eatin', bad f'you!'

Bryony turned her head away, still trying to stem the tears. 'I'm n . . . not whingeing, j . . . just l . . . leave m . . . me alone p . . . please!' She broke off another piece of scone and gave it to the nosey bird.

Huffily he seized it and fluttered off slowly. 'Chipp! Not very good company, are y'mouse?'

Bryony got her hiccups under control and shouted after the bird, 'You didn't see a ferret pass this way, by any chance?'

The robin flew swiftly back, eating his piece of scone before he ventured a reply. 'Might 'ave. Give me the rest o' that cake an' I'll tell you. Cake's no good t'you, on'y makes y'cry.'

Bryony passed over the remainder of the scone. The robin began pecking it thoughtfully, head on one side.

'Got any more o' these in that bag?'

The mousemaid sniffled away the last of her tears angrily. 'No, I have not. Now will you please tell me if you saw the ferret pass this way!'

The robin nodded. 'Yes, ferret passed this way las' evenin'.'

'Well, which way did he go, please?'

One wing shot out pointing west and slightly south, the exact direction in which Bryony was travelling.

'That way! Bye bye, crymouse!'

He flew off fast with Bryony shouting after him, 'And goodbye to you, greedybeak!'

Suddenly the mousemaid felt drained and tired, exhausted by the long walk and her emotions. Curling up, she fell asleep in the twinkling of an eye.

A breeze, or an insect, or something tickling her whiskers, brought Bryony back to wakefulness. Slowy, she opened one eye. Immediately she closed it, fear making her lie very still. There in front of her eye, she had seen a huge flat paw with big blunt claws.

'Wake ee oop, missie, et be only oi!'

Pushing the footpaw away from within a hairsbreadth of her face she sat bolt upright, crying, 'Togget! What are you doing here?'

The mole wrinkled his button nose and shrugged. 'Watchen ee sleepen, yurr, you'm an orful snoarer, Broinee.'

Bryony stood up, brushing herself off indignantly. 'I do not snore!'

Togget put down his haversack, chuckling, 'Ahurrhurrhurr, that's 'cos ee never be'd awake to 'ear eeself, 'ow you'm knowen if'n you'm snoar if'n ee be asleepen?'

The mousemaid stamped her footpaw. 'Never mind whether I snore or not. I asked you what, pray, are you doing out here? Why did you leave the Abbey?'

Togget took her paw. 'You'm moi gudd friend, missie, Togget wuddent leave ee to go off a surchin' for ee maister Veil all alone, burr no!'

Bryony seized Togget and hugged him. 'You're a true friend, Togget, a good loyal companion, thank you!'

Togget covered his face with his great digging paws, as moles will do when embarrassed by anything. 'Hurr, oi'll go straightways back to ee h'abbey if'n you'm goin' to be a squeezin' an' 'uggin' oi!'

Bryony understood, and without another word the two friends set off together travelling southwest.

It was evening, still light, but getting on to dusk, and Veil was hungry. The ferret had only eaten a few young dandelion shoots and some edible roots all day. Sucking a flat pebble to ward off thirst he carried on across the darkening landscape. After a while he noticed a faint glow from some hills to the north of his route and, overcome by curiosity, he sneaked silently over. As he drew nearer the hill he could tell the glow was being made by a fire in a small hollow at the hill's base. Flattening himself belly down against the grass, the ferret wriggled forward quietly. When he was close enough, he lifted his head and looked.

It was an old male dormouse with two little ones, sitting around the fire roasting apples. To one side lay a homely looking cottage loaf and a big wedge of dark yellow cheese. Veil noted that the old dormouse carried a knife, which he used to cut the bread, and that there was also a stout walking staff at his side. Veil walked into the firelight with both paws spread wide and a disarming smile upon his face.

'Pray, friends, don't alarm yourselves,' he said, keeping his voice soft and low. 'I come in peace.'

The old dormouse inspected him critically. 'In peace, aye, an' in hunger too by the looks of ye. Sit ye down, there ain't much, but yore welcome t'share supper with me'n'the grandmice. Last bad winter took their parents, an' I'm the only one left to look after 'em, pore mites. We're travellers, livin' where we can, starvin' when we have to.'

Veil sat opposite the oldster, accepting a slice of cheese, a hunk of the loaf, a roasted apple and a large seashell filled with water from a flask. He ate gratefully, improvising a pack of lies to the kind dormouse.

'My name's Bunfold, I'm the same as your little ones, lost my mother an' father, aye, an' a sister, too, last winter. I've been on my own ever since, wanderin' field an' forest.'

The old dormouse stared into the flames. 'The babes are called Hoffy an' Brund, same as their parents. I'm Ole Hoffy. Arr, Bunfold, 'tis a hard life for porebeasts without a dwellin' place. See the little ones are asleep already, wore out, just like their paws, from trekkin' an' livin' rough. Here, young un, cover y'self with this against the night chills.'

He dug out a ragged blanket from a bark carrier and tossed it to Veil. The ferret wrapped himself up and snuggled down, saying, 'Sleep well, Ole Hoffy. Who knows, mayhap tomorrow'll bring us all good fortune an' a bit o' luck, eh?'

The dormouse threw some twigs on the fire before settling. 'We could certainly do with it. G'night, Bunfold!'

Veil lay with his eyes half closed, listening to the crackle of the fire and waiting his chance.

Togget was awake before Bryony the next day, unpacking food for them both from the haversack he had made up before leaving the Abbey. Picking a kingcup, he placed it gently between the mousemaid's folded paws.

'Wake ee oop, 'tis a bran' new day,
Or oi'll eat all ee vittles an' run away!'

Bryony sat up staring at the flower. 'Where did this come from?'

Togget busied himself slicing cold deeper'n'ever pie. ''Ow shudd oi know, missie, et be thoi own biznuss if you'm want to roam roun' all noight a picken flowers, hurr aye!'

Bryony curtsied prettily to her molefriend. 'Thank you, sir. Ooh! Deeper'n'ever pie with dandelion and burdock cordial, what a good breakfast!'

They dallied awhile after the meal, enjoying the bright summer morn. Then, packing their gear, Bryony and Togget set off still trekking southwest. About mid-morn they reached the top of a high grassy hill and stopped momentarily to enjoy the breeze.

The mousemaid looked around. 'You know, if this hill were any higher I'll bet I could see the tip of Redwall Abbey from here. It's not that far away really, only just over a day's journey.'

Togget was looking the other way. Shading his eyes against the sun he peered southwest before scanning all the land around. 'Yurr, missie, lookit, thurr be somebeasts a wanderin' o'er yon!'

Bryony looked hard in the direction he was pointing; she could make out a huddle of dark shapes. 'Well, I don't think it could be Veil, he'd be travelling the wrong way. Can you make out how many of them there are?'

Togget had exceptionally good eyes for a mole. 'Lukks loik two, nay three, aye, et be three. Yurr, wot if'n they be foebeasts or villyuns?'

Bryony decided that they should lie flat, so that the otherbeasts could not easily see them. Stretched out on the hilltop, they watched until the trio drew closer. Bryony stood up. 'They're mice, looks like two of them are only small. Come on, Togget, they won't harm us. Let's find out what they're doing in this country.'

The two little dormice were weeping piteously, clinging to the blanket draped about Ole Hoffy's shoulders. He had a wound on his head, crusted with dried blood around a swelling lump. Staggering crazily towards Bryony and Togget he fell, pushing the babes from him as he toppled over.

Bryony was at his side in an instant. 'Oh, you poor thing! What happened?' she cried. Damping a cloth she bathed the dormouse's head as he relayed a halting account of the previous night.

'Ferret, said his name was Bunfold, camped with us, gave him supper an' a blanket to sleep. Must've rolled over an' burnt my paw in th' fire embers, woke me up this mornin', head achin', food gone, knife an' staff gone too. Huh, ferret gone an' all!'

Bryony looked at Togget and shook her head.

'Bunfold! That could only be Veil. Build a fire and take care of the babes, Togget. I'll see what I can do for this old fellow. Hmm, he's not badly injured, he should be all right.'

Togget issued the little dormice with a slice of deeper'-n'ever pie apiece and some dandelion and burdock cordial. He also dug out a packet of candied chestnuts for them. They had not eaten since the previous night, and both fell gratefully upon the food.

The mole patted their heads. 'B'ain't much wrong wi' these two gurt rascals, they'm a vittlin' oop loik a pair o' 'arebeasts!'

Bryony soon had Ole Hoffy feeling better; she cleaned and dressed his wound and fed him. He told her of his life so far and the hard times he had experienced with the two babes. And the mousemaid came up with a solution that would solve all the dormouse's problems.

'You must carry on walking east for a day, or a bit more, and then you will see a path. Once on that path you will be close to Redwall Abbey – go there with your babes. Tell the Mother Abbess Meriam that Bryony sent you. Redwall Abbey is a place where all goodbeasts are welcome; you may live there in peace and plenty. The babes will be brought up well, never again knowing hunger or want. You will all find the love of good friends there. Have a safe journey, and fortune attend you and your grandmice, Ole Hoffy.'

The dormouse did a little jig, surprising for one of his long seasons, then he bowed to the two friends as he took the babes' paws. 'Good comes out o' bad, some say. Last night that villain wished me good fortune an' luck on the morrow. Who'd have thought that a bad ferret's wish brought me'n'the babes good!'

Calling loud farewells they went their separate ways, but not before Bryony and Togget had donated one of their food haversacks to the dormice, more than enough to see them to the Abbey.

There was no talk of Veil between the two friends. Bryony set her face, and refused to discuss what he had done to the good dormice. In silence, the two set off tracking the ferret once more.

Veil was back on the southwest trail again. Armed with a knife, staff and food, he had cut the blanket up to make a cloak for himself. Finding a patch of wild strawberries he ate as many as he could, streaked his face and renewed the red on his paws with the juice, then stamped the remainder into the ground until the strawberry patch was a sludge of red fruit and bruised leaves. Blissfully unaware that Bryony and Togget were less than a day behind him, he strolled off in search of the great mountain of Salamandastron and the father he had never known. He wondered occasionally if his parent, the one called Swartt, was as cunning and tough as himself. Mentally Veil wagered that he wasn't.

34

Sunflash the Mace was down. Vermin crowded to jump and stamp on the sand-heaped canvas bundle, screaming and yelling with triumph. Swartt stood imposingly on top of the rock groyne, hero of the hour. Up at the chamber window Colonel Sandgall leaned far out over the sill, anxiously watching the threshold of the main mountain entrance.

Sundew stood alongside the Colonel, beating the rock sill with her paws. The young hare was trembling, and sobbing, 'Oh help him, help him! Where are they?'

Sandgall replied without looking at her, 'Steady in the ranks, m'gel, stiff upper lip an' don't let the side down, wot. By thunder! Here they come – listen!'

A band of hares came bursting through the main entrance, Sabretache at their head, swinging his long sabre like a drum major's baton. Two stout Captains, Fleetrunn and Rockleg, flanked him, and behind them bounded fifty hares of the famous regiment, all armed with lances and short slings, loaded with iron lumps from the forge.

'Long Patrol, give 'em blood'n'vinegar! Eeulaliaaaa!'

Soaring through the air like hungry eagles, they cleared the horde-filled trench in a mighty leap, and went crashing into the midst of the startled vermin surrounding Sunflash. Swartt vanished down the far side of the rocks and ran towards the sea as if pursued by demons.

Hordebeasts fell like leaves before a winter gale. The veteran warriors of Salamandastron took no prisoners; javelins flashed in the sunlight, and metal-filled slings thudded savagely into their targets. Sabretache took a tattooed rat through his midriff with the sabre, yelling as he did, 'Cut through the canvas – free Lord Sunflash!'

Swiftly the vermin who were left alive fled, and a tight circle of hares, javelins pointing outwards, surrounded the big canvas bundle. Then keen-edged hareblades sliced the canvas to shreds. Sabretache and his Captains pulled Sunflash from his stifling prison. The badger was limp and unconscious; Fleetrunn was at his side, unhinging the helmet roughly. Supporting the Badger Lord's head she called to Bloggwood, 'Bring water, hurry!'

Swartt had regained his courage. Gathering a crowd of hordebeasts, he led them up the back of the rock groyne and around to the front of the mountain. They massed across the big rough timber gate at the main entrance, blocking the way back into the fortress.

Swartt issued orders to his archers in the trench further down the sands. 'Don't let 'em pass, drive 'em down to the sea with yore arrows!' He turned his attention to his own group. 'About turn an' give those in the mountain plenty o' rocks an' shafts, that'll keep their heads down!'

The Warlord was trembling with frustration. He had almost taken Sunflash and won the battle; but the badger would not elude him a second time. The ferret's plan was simple and good; once he had the Badger Lord and his hares up to their waists in seawater, he could slay them at his leisure.

Fresh water splashing over the gold-striped face

brought Sunflash slowly back to his senses. Bruised, scarred and weakened, he lay still, allowing Fleetrunn to pour the life-giving water over his head.

The female hare Captain allowed him a few sips. 'Let it wash over you, Sire, don't drink too much or y'll feel pretty bad. That's the ticket – just wet y'mouth, eh.'

Sabretache rapped out commands as a hare fell beside him, slain by a barbed shaft. 'Keep y'heads down! Back up to the rocks, troops, they're shootin' at us from that flippin' trench!'

Dragging Sunflash with them, the Long Patrol hares fought their way to the line of rocks stretching from the mountain to the sea. Swiftly digging the sand with their long legs, they formed a temporary barricade, a low sandy hump between themselves and the vermin archers. Arrows hissed viciously, some burying their points in the sand, others hitting the rock, while some found targets among the beleaguered hares.

Colonel Sandgall had to draw back from the window: arrows and slingstones from Swartt's hordebeasts were whistling through the opening, ricocheting around the chamber.

He sniffed disdainfully and, adjusting his monocle, he waggled one long ear at Sundew. 'Out y'go, missie, no sense in gettin' y'self injured here, wot. Go an' make y'self useful elsewheres, there's a good gel.'

Sundew had collected the slingstones that came in, and now she was sending them out with a vengeance. Whirling her own sling she dashed at the window and hurled down a quick one at those below. 'I'm stayin' here with you, sah,' she said. 'They won't make me shift!'

Sandgall took a bow from a wallpeg and, notching one of the fallen shafts to its string, he nipped smartly to the window and fired, nodding as he was rewarded by a scream from below. 'Good gel! True blue'n'never fail, eh! Come on, let's return fire with their own gear.

Long time since I put ash to yew an' twine. Never forget the old skills – good show!' Squinting through his monocle he loosed another arrow.

Sabretache crouched low with Rockleg at his side, assessing their perilous situation. 'Looks bad, old chum, the blighters have got us well pinned down here. Not much chance of gettin' back to the jolly old mountain either, just look at that evil rabble all ganged up in front of the main gate! Absolute rotters!'

Rockleg twitched an ear in the direction of the sea. 'Right y'are, 'Tache, y'see their strategy, doncha, they want to drive us down to the water, stop us gettin' back to the mountain. Huh, look at that dirty great mob of vermin, waitin' for us on the waterline. Bad show if y'ask me. They've got us trapped here like frogs in a bucket!'

Sabretache flicked his head to one side as an arrow whizzed by. 'We'll just have t'sit it out old boy, wait until Lord Sunflash is up to the mark again an' hope for some sort of a miracle t'pull our chestnuts out of the fire, wot.'

Sunflash had begun to tear at the confining chainmail tunic; Fleetrunn tried to hold his massive paws still. 'Best leave it on, Sire,' she said. 'Better feelin' a bit uncomfortable than bein' stuck all over with arrows.'

As if to confirm her words, a shaft glanced off the chainmail and buried itself in the sand. She winked at the badger. 'No disrespect, Sire, but y'see what I mean now!'

Evening shades began to fall; the hot day cooled with a breeze from the incoming tide. Still trapped against the rocks, the hares crouched and waited. The arrows and slingstones had slowed somewhat, though now the horde in the trench were sniping, taking more careful aim. It was a frustrating and dangerous time. Rockleg poked his head over the sandy barricade and took a quick peek seawards.

'Oh dash it all!' he groaned. 'That lot down by the water are startin' to sneak up here. Stand by, chaps, I think we're about to be ambushed shortly. It'll soon be dark – that's when they'll come.' Licking a wound on his shoulder he poured dry sand on to seal it.

'Logalogalogalogaloooooog!'

Sabretache's ears shot up. 'What'n the fur was that?'

Sunflash struggled upwards and grabbed his mace. 'It's the Guosim shrews! They've arrived by sea!'

'Guosim, Guosim, Guosim! Logalogalogaloooooog!'

Rockleg pointed with his javelin. 'Look, they're givin' those blighters down by the water a hard time of it. Up here, chaps! Up here!'

Sabretache turned towards the mountain. 'Hurrah!' he cheered. 'Look, there's a gang of otters'n'squirrels batterin' the livin' daylights out of the vermin!'

A great roar went up from the warriors at the mountain front.

'Heyaaah! Hoyaaah! Firjak Greenstone! Whump! Whump! Whump!'

The otters and squirrels had come around the mountain from both sides, hurling themselves on both flanks of Swartt's hordebeasts with clubs and spears. Guosim shrews charged up from the tideline, cutting a swathe through the vermin pack with flashing rapiers.

With the blood of his ancestors rising in his veins, Sunflash came bulling out at the head of the hares. Joined by the shrews they went crashing heedlessly over the heads of the trench archers, scattering vermin left and right.

Swartt took flight once again and the demoralized hordebeasts broke and fled, rushing straight to the safety of the rocks or the tide shallows. The rough-timber gates swung open. Sunflash stood by them, brandishing his mace until everybeast was inside and safe. Sentries were posted at every lookout post to watch the horde, while the rest crowded into the banqueting hall.

Food was rushed in to the returning warriors and their allies, the best that Salamandastron could serve. Mounds of pasties and great barrels of Mountain Ale, thick seasoned stews, crusty hot bread and new cider were carried to the tables, and full justice was done to the victuals that night.

Sunflash sat with Colonel Sandgall, Log a Log, the two otters, Folrig and Ruddle, Sabretache and the other Captains. Sandgall wagged a reproving paw at the Badger Lord. 'Ahem, Sire, y'll kindly let us know before you go chargin' off again to take on a whole filthy horde single-pawed.'

Sunflash shook his head, as if disapproving of himself. 'I'm sorry, Colonel, but I am not myself sometimes.'

Sandgall winked at the badger and patted his paw. 'Hmm, the ol' bloodwrath, wot! It's that an' a Badger Lord that've kept these shores an' this country safe'n'-free, don't apologize for it, sah. But us hare chaps are here to protect you as much as you protect us, so it's nice t'be able to return the favour. Now then, Log a shrew an' you otter types, that was a bally clever show you put up out there today, eh!'

Log a Log explained how it had come about. 'It was simple really. We arranged it between us – sent out a few spies to see what was goin' on, then we put a plan together. I landed the logboats further up the coast before sunset and we waded along through the shallows, round the rocks an' charged 'em. My call was the signal to attack.'

Folrig took up his side of the campaign. 'We came in from the backway, me'n'ole ugly mug Ruddle with Lady Firdance an' her gang . . .'

Firdance, a big rangy squirrel, with a deep scar running from ear to nosetip, interrupted in her husky voice, 'Aye, we split up an' worked the old pincer movement, caught the scum nicely in between an' gave 'em some buryin' t'do!'

Bloggwood caught Sunflash's eye. He sidled over and whispered in the Badger Lord's ear. 'Sire, can yer come'n' 'ave a word or two with Bradders? Pore feller, 'e's proper cut up about Fordpetal.'

'Why, certainly, friend – what's up with Fordpetal?'

'Foller me an' I'll show yer, Sire.'

Sunflash excused himself from the company and followed Bloggwood; they threaded their way through the packed hall. As they went the banter of old warrior friends having a reunion was thick upon the air.

'Gully, y'old treeflyer. I thought you was slain seasons ago!'

'Well, I'm still here, matey, an' eatin' aplenty t'prove it!'

'Haharr, Munga, 'ow is the shrew logboat business goin'?'

'Saves gettin' your paws wet like you otters, Reedtail.'

'Ahoy there, Floke, we pulled yore chestnuts out of the fire just in time for yer today, didn't we?'

'Aye, matey, an' yer cracked a few nuts on the other side too!'

It was cold and silent in the vaults beneath the mountain where Bloggwood led Sunflash. They went through to a long torchlit cave where the hares who had been slain in battle that day were laid out on stone slabs, each one wreathed in fresh mountain flowers. Bradberry was standing by the body of Fordpetal, his head bowed. Sunflash dismissed his guide with thanks and went straight to the young hare.

He placed a paw comfortingly around Bradberry's shoulders. 'Bradders, I'm sorry, I didn't know . . .'

The hare buried his face in Sunflash's chainmail tunic and wept. 'She wasn't really soppy, was she, Sire?'

The Badger Lord swallowed hard. 'No, just young and

262

very pretty, and she knew we were only joking when we said that. Let's hope that we have somebeast as thoughtful and tender hearted as yourself to weep for us some day.'

The young hare turned his tearstained face up to Sunflash. 'Why do creatures have to have wars and kill one another? Why can't everybeast live in peace and be contented? I was just thinkin' before you came, Sire, Fordpetal won't ever see another summer day or laugh an' smile again. Why?'

Sunflash led Bradberry slowly away from the vault. 'Why? It's a question I've often asked myself, Bradders, particularly when the life of a young one is wasted. Over quite a few seasons now I've found myself wanting to be only a farmer and grow things, but there are evil ones in the lands. One day when all the evil is gone, maybe then we'll be able to find peace and watch things grow. Until then it is up to the good ones, like yourself, to fight against evil. Fordpetal was doing just that today. War is a terrible thing, but until something arrives to stop the fighting, we must endure it, and battle harder to make sure that good wins.'

In the banqueting hall the warriors were singing an age-old song they always sang after battle.

'Oh here's to the comrades who fought the good
      fight,
On the field where their valour was won.
They gave their lives hard to defend what was right,
Let us drink to the warriors who've gone.
They stood shoulder to shoulder, there's none who
      were bolder,
And many's the foebeast we slayed,
We'll remember our friends who will never grow
   older,
Alas what a price that they paid.

For the word has been spoken, the sword now is
  broken,
When we're old we will sit, and tell tales of their
  days.'

35

Swartt Sixclaw sat roasting a mackerel by a fire, far down on the tideline close to the rocks. Over one third of his great horde had been lost that day, but victory had been nearly within his grasp. The groups of hordebeasts crouched around their fires were too weary to do anything but eat, sleep, or lick their wounds. Swartt stared up at the rock, racking his brain for a solution. Within the next hour it presented itself in the form of a weasel whom Nightshade brought to him.

Swartt found that he had to keep his eyes trained on the skinny, undersized creature. It was mottled, whether naturally or by skilful dyes, he could not tell, but it was only by watching its pale eyes that the Warlord could tell where it stood. The weasel had only to stand motionless against rock or sand and it almost vanished. It was sandy-coloured – or was it rock-hued? – with grey, dirty white and dark brown flecks, the strangest-looking creature he had ever witnessed.

Swartt looked at the vixen. 'Where'd you find that thing?' he snarled.

'Lord, he is called the Wraith. He is not of our horde, I do not know where he comes from, though you would be wise to listen to his offer.'

Swartt looked back and found he had lost sight of the Wraith. 'Stan' still, weasel, where are yeh?'

He tried not to start with shock as the voice came from behind the back of his neck.

'Me herrrre, Sirrrre!'

The Wraith flitted round in front of him and sat by the fire. He spoke in a most peculiar manner, extending his 'r's. Swartt kept his gaze fixed on the Wraith's eyes, the rest of his body kept disappearing and reappearing in the flicker of the firelight.

'Sit still an' tell me why yer came here,' said Swartt.

The speckled mouth opened, revealing two rows of toothless gums. 'Wrrrraith hearrrr you have enemy, me kill him forrrr you.'

Suddenly Swartt was interested. The idea of an assassin had not occurred to him before. He would have liked to take Sunflash alive, but in the end one way of winning victory was as good as another. The Warlord pointed his mailed paw at the pale watery eyes. 'An' what d'you get out of it, eh?'

The soft rolling voice replied, 'Me think you know that. Half, Sirrrrre!'

Swartt knew what he meant – he had dealt with rogues and villains all his life. Half meant half of every-thing he stood to gain, but really it meant all: assassins who offered their services were always over-ambitious. Swartt shrugged. 'Half seems fair enough. See yon mountain, there's a badger inside o' there they call Sun-flash the Mace. Bring me back the great mace that never leaves his side an' you get yer half!'

The Wraith vanished. Swartt looked around and saw the creature was sitting behind him, holding something in its claws, hissing, 'Just strrroke badgerrr with me Kisserrrr!'

It was a tiny knife, carved from some strange type of mottled stone, almost the same colour as its owner.

Swartt curled his lip at the undersized weasel with

266

his minute blade, 'Yore goin' t'kill a Badger Lord wid that toy?'

The pale eyes narrowed in a mocking smile. 'See that rrrat yon, sitting by his firrrre? Watch!'

The rat was wearing a bright red bandanna, so he was hard to miss. Swartt watched him sitting by the fire with some others. He had lost sight of the Wraith, so he kept watching the rat. Then the Wraith's voice came from beside him; the thin weasel was sitting warming himself by the flames.

'One strrrroke from my Kisserrrr, that one is slain.'

The Warlord continued to watch the rat, his voice laden with sarcasm as he spoke. 'Huh, he don't look so dead t'me, chewin' on a mackerel there as if there weren't no tomorrer.'

'Rrrright, Sirrrre, no tomorrrrow forrrr him!'

Without warning the rat leapt up and, clapping a paw to the side of his neck, he staggered about gurgling for a moment, then fell to the sand as if poleaxed. Swartt stared in astonishment, listening to the others from the company, as they left the fireside to crowd around their companion.

'Wot's wrong wid ole Glimpy?'

'Hahaha! Can't yer see he's takin' a nap, mate!'

'Mebbe it's somethin' 'e ate?'

'Come on, Glimp ole mate, gerrup!'

A stoat knelt at Glimpy's side and inspected him. Suddenly, he cried, 'Glimpy's dead, mates. Ain't that awful, sittin' scoffin' fish one moment, nex' thing 'e's pegged it!'

A fox spat mackerel into the fire and rubbed his mouth. 'Phtooh! I ain't eatin' no more o' this fish, mates!'

The Wraith had shifted position. He smiled at Swartt from across the fire. 'Now Sirrre believe me, just one strrroke, not even a rrrreal cut. Me Kisserrrr neverrrr fail!'

The Warlord nodded his head in admiration of the

deed. 'The Wraith, eh? Well, the job's yores, Wraith. When do I expec' to see yer again?'

'You don't see me if Wrrrraith not want you to. I will find you when it is done!'

Then the Wraith vanished, melting into the night.

Swartt threw the vixen a roasted mackerel. 'Good work, at last y've done somethin' right. Stripe'ead is as good as dead, I'd say. Oh, when the Wraith gets back, you know what t'do.'

'Aye, Lord. I know exactly what to do!' Nightshade replied.

36

It was the evening of the day Veil had robbed the dormice of their food and possessions, and the young ferret was not finding the going too easy. He chose a thick copse of pines for his camp. He brushed away the pine needles and dug a shallow hole, then he put steel to flint and made a small fire. Squatting by the flames, he ate some bread and cheese whilst roasting an apple. He was dozing, half asleep, warmed by the blazing pine cones and dead twigs, when two foxes arrived. At first Veil chose to ignore them. Though he was a bit startled and unsure of himself, he put on a tough face, making sure his knife and staff were clearly in evidence. Equally, both foxes feigned indifference to him. They squatted on the other side of the fire wordlessly. They were old and ragged, but sly looking. One carried a spear, the other a sling and pouch of stones. Drawing their tattered cloaks about them they sat silent, casting the odd cunning glance towards the lone ferret.

Veil began to feel more uneasy, and he tried striking up a conversation with his uninvited visitors. 'Where did you come from, friends?' he asked.

The taller of the pair spat into the flames, narrowly missing Veil's roasting apple.

'Nosy young snip ain't 'e, Brool?'

The other smiled nastily, his eyes never leaving Veil. 'Aye, stoopid too, we saw 'is fire from a good way off. Look, he's got bread'n'cheese an' apples, a richbeast, eh, Renn!'

Veil decided he could let the situation go no further. Holding his stave ready and brandishing the knife, he stood up and shouted, 'Keep yer mangey paws off my vittles, I'm not scared of you two ol' ragbags!'

The foxes worked their way around the fire until they were either side of him. The one called Brool bared his few blackened tooth stumps. 'Young uns these days ain't got no respect, eh, Renn. Mangey ol' ragbags? We got a cheeky one 'ere, no mistake!'

The one called Renn neatly stabbed the roasting apple with his spear tip and, pulling it from the fire, he blew on it and took a bite. 'Mmm, 'e cooks a decent apple though . . .'

Veil grabbed at the spear, his voice shrill with anger. 'You leave my apple alone, you dirty old . . . Unnhh!'

The young ferret had made the mistake of turning his back on Brool. The fox's sling, loaded with a heavy pebble, cracked down on Veil's head from behind, laying him flat.

He came to his senses slowly, groaning at the trip-hammer throb in his skull. Both his paws were hoisted high, tied to an overhanging pine bough.

The two foxes were eating Veil's food, cramming bread and cheese ravenously into their mouths. Brool took a drink from the flask; pulling a face he spat it out. 'Yerk, water! Ain't you got no good wine or ale, young un? Cold water don't sit easy on my stummick these seasons.'

Renn sorted roughly through the travelling bag Veil had stolen from Ole Hoffy. 'Nothin' much in 'ere, Brool, jus' a thin blanket an' a few more apples. Not very considerate of yer, ferret!'

Struggling against the tight bonds, Veil glared hatred at them. 'Blunderin' ol' fools, don't yer know who I am? I'm Veil Sixclaw, son of Swartt the Warlord!'

Renn tore a strip from the blanket and did a low servile bow. 'Oh, fergive us, yer 'ighness! Yaaahahahah!'

Then he gagged the young ferret firmly, boxing his ears and pulling his nose painfully. 'Son of a Warlord, y'don't say! I'm the cousin of an eagle an' a great fish meself, wot about you, Brool?'

'Who, me? Oh, I'm the Queen o' the flowery dell, pleased t'meet yer majesty I'm sure!'

Both foxes fell about cackling. Forced to stand on tip-paw, bound and gagged, Veil could only glare at them and make whining sobs of rage.

An even shade of grey washed the dawn sky, bringing dun-hued clouds and a steady downpour of rain. Bryony and Togget gathered up their belongings hurriedly from their camp on the open hills. The mole did not like rain.

'Yurr, us'n's be soaken an' cold if'n ee doan't foind shelter missie, on'y fishes do loik ee rain!'

The mousemaid pointed to the distant pine grove, saying, 'Come on then, let's make for there, we can camp in the trees until the rain stops.'

Togget took off, both paws over his head, calling back to Bryony, 'Hoo aye, maken ee foire an' git brekkfist a goin', oi'm gurtly 'ungered furr ee vittles!'

The mousemaid ran after her companion, laughing. 'Slow down, you great Dibbun, the rain won't melt you!'

'Hurr, so ee says, missie, tho' oi b'ain't too sure!'

It was dim and dry in the half light of the close-growing pines. They shook themselves off and began opening their pack. Bryony stopped, sniffing the air.

'Smoke, I can smell burning,' she said.

Togget's small button nose twitched. 'You'm roight, Broinee, sumbeast got flames burnen sumwheres.'

The mousemaid fastened the haversack and

shouldered it. 'It may be Veil, but then again, it may not be. Go quietly, Togget, make no noise. Let's see who the fire belongs to.'

Following the aromatic smell of burning pine cones, the two friends stole silently through the grove.

Bryony was first to spot the glow of flames between the trees. Taking care not to crack twigs underpaw, they stole forward, then, bellying down in the springy carpet of pine needles, they peered over a fallen trunk at the scene in a hollow below.

Brool and Renn were breakfasting off what was left of the bread and hurling apple cores at the bound figure dangling from a pine bough.

Bryony seized Togget's paw. 'Look, it's Veil, those two foxes must have captured him!'

'Hurr, but they'm looken loik narstybeasts, wot can us'n's be a doin' to 'elp maister Veil?'

Bryony studied the situation below before answering. 'Hmm, they're armed, we couldn't risk an open fight. But I think I might have an idea that will work. Here's what we do!'

Renn the fox threw some twigs on the fire and sprawled on the ground, eyeing Veil. 'D'you suppose this Swartt Warlord would pay a bit o' ransom to 'ave his darlin' son back in one piece, mate?'

Brool looked at his companion pityingly. 'You gone squishy in th' brains, Renn, the only thing a Warlord would give you for takin' 'is kin prisoner would be yore own 'ead on a plate . . . Yowp!'

A hard, green pine cone struck the fox on his nose, followed a moment later by another which bounced off his partner's jaw.

Renn grabbed his spear, snarling, 'Who's slingin' cones? Owch!' Another solid green cone hit him in the eye.

Brool was about to take his sling out when a green cone stung his paw. 'Owowow! Hoi! Stop chuckin' those things willy . . . Agh!' He fell back clutching his mouth as he spat a broken tooth out.

Cones began whizzing in thick and fast and accurate. The two foxes were battered and bewildered; the missiles seemed to be coming from everywhere. Renn could hardly see, having been struck in both eyes. Brool had been belted over the head five times in quick succession by cones and was feeling very sore and dazed. They huddled together, crouching to escape the stinging rain of hard green cones, but the cones kept hurtling in, thwacking them hard as ever, bouncing off their skinny backs and bottoms until Brool howled out, 'Stoppit! Stoppit! We're goin'!'

Thwack! Ping! Thud! Clack! The green cones continued. The two foxes could bear it no more. 'Yaaaah! Let's get outta . . . Yeeek! Ooh! Yowp!' They fled through the woods, away to where it was open ground, regardless of rain, limping and hopping in pain.

Togget rolled down into the hollow and sat with his paws hanging limply by his sides.

'Wo'urr, moi ole paws'll drop off if 'n oi flings jus' one more of they poiney cones, wo'urr!'

Bryony stretched painfully to reach the ropes binding Veil's paws to the bough. 'Veil. Poor Veil,' she cried.

The moment Veil's paws were free he tore away the gag from his mouth and yelled angrily at the mousemaid, 'What in the name of blood'n'fur are you followin' me for?' Ignoring the hurt in Bryony's eyes, he continued. 'Still spyin' on me, eh! Why don't yer jus' leave me alone?'

Bryony was dismayed and puzzled at Veil's attitude. 'But . . . but . . . we saved you from those vermin! They might have ended up killing you, Veil!'

The young ferret stormed about the hollow, rubbing life back into his paws, which were still numb from being bound. 'Well, I didn't need savin', see! I was ready to slip those ropes and grab the spear. I can look after meself without you an' that stupid mole runnin' around tryin' to nursemaid me.'

Togget shook a heavy digging paw at him. 'You'm watch ee tongue, maister, you'm a gurtly ungrateful furret. Missie Broinee never did ought but good to ee!'

Veil slumped beside the fire. 'Well, where was she when they chucked me out of Redwall, eh?' he sneered. 'I'll tell yer, sidin' with all her goody goody friends, that's where she was. Outcast they called me; nobeast raised a paw to 'elp me then.'

Bryony placed a paw gently on his shoulder. 'Oh, Veil, you're so wrong. I've always been your friend, I care for you more than any creature living!'

He shook her paw off and leapt up, grabbing his staff and belongings. 'Get away from me, both of you! Go on, get back to your precious Abbey and spend your nights talkin' about me an' what a bad lot I was. Aye, Veil the vermin Outcast!'

Togget ran between Veil and Bryony and shoved the young ferret backwards, away from the mousemaid. 'Harr, you'm nought by a villyun, wi' all yore bad talk!' he shouted.

Veil rushed forward. 'Out of my way!' he snarled, pushing Togget roughly to the ground. The mole fell, hitting his head on a jutting rock.

Immediately Bryony was pummelling Veil with both paws. 'You stupid beast! Me and Togget are the only friends you have in this world! Don't you see?'

But in his rush to escape, Veil hurtled on, knocking her flat. Crawling on all fours, Bryony dragged herself to the stricken mole's side. 'Togget, are you hurt? If you've harmed this good creature . . .' But she was talking to thin air. Veil had grabbed their remaining haversack of supplies and dashed off into the pines.

Bryony sat by the fire, cradling her molefriend's head in her paws and weeping. Togget's eyelids flickered, then weakly he raised a digging claw and brushed a teardrop from her nosetip. 'Oi thort et were a rainen again, hurr moi ole 'ead do be 'urted gurtly.'

The mousemaid wiped away her tears and hugged him. 'Oh, Togget, thank goodness that you're alive!'

'Hurr, 'tis a wunner oi am, missie, layin' yurr wi' a lump loik a mounting on moi 'ead, an' ee crushen moi ribs t'bits!'

Out on the hills, the rain had stopped. It was a breezy midday when Veil sighted the two old foxes up ahead. At the point where hills met flatlands, a river, swollen by the rain, ran its winding course out onto the plain. The foxes were camped at its edge, using wet grass poultices to bathe the injuries from the sharp green pine cones. They did not see Veil until it was too late. Swinging his stave down hard with both paws he hit Brool a vicious blow to the base of his skull. Then, grabbing a spear sticking into the ground next to Brool, he drove it into Renn. Rolling both foxes into the river, he watched them being borne away on the flow.

'When you get to Dark Forest tell them Veil the Outcast sent yer!'

The river was flowing in a westerly direction. Veil followed its banks until he found what he was looking for, an old willow trunk, washed up there after winter. Levering it into the water with the spearbutt he waded in and boarded it. Straddling the trunk, the young ferret made a meal of scones and crystallized fruit from the haversack as he was borne westward. Far in the distance he could see mountains.

37

Bryony would not let Togget travel until mid-afternoon. When they quit the pine grove she made a compress of rainwet dock leaves and bound it to his forehead. Hungry and dispirited, they pressed onward. Bryony had to put up with listening to a relentless menu of Togget's favourite foods; she let him ramble on, knowing he was trying to forget the ache in his head. He trudged by her side, arranging meals.

'Oi loiks damsen pudden wi' lots o' meadowcream on et, an' oi favours noo-baked bread, hurr, wi' ole yellow cheese an' a gurt Summer Salad. Ho, but deeper'n'ever turnip'n'tater'n'beetroot pie, hoo urr! Oi'd swap moi tail furr one roight naow, wi' gudd mushyroom gravy poured thick atop of et!'

The visions conjured up by Togget's descriptions soon had Bryony comparing her favourite dishes with him. 'I'd like a beaker of strawberry cordial and a big pastie, a mushroom, potato and onion one, after that I think I'd go for some hot apple and blackberry crumble, with sweet white arrowroot sauce poured all over it. Then I'd have a wedge of whitecheese, the one with almonds and hazelnuts in it, and one, no two, of Friar Bunfold's fresh oatfarls, straight from the oven. Yummy!'

Togget held one paw to his forehead and the other to his stomach. 'Aow, missie, do be soilent, oi'm turrible 'ungry!'

'Well, you started it, moleyface! Look, there's a river!'

They made camp on the riverbank, and Bryony redampened Togget's poultice with riverwater. Nowhere was anything edible to be found. The country ahead of them sloped slightly downward, running off to a flat plain, grassy and deserted. Behind a small hillock they snuggled down on the lee side; away from the breeze, it was quite sunny and warm. Togget was snoring gently and Bryony's eyes were beginning to droop when she heard a deep bass voice singing:

'One day in spring I said to me wife,
"Though we're close together as fork'n'knife,
An' I've loved y'dearly all of me life,
Still I'll have to follow the wateeeeeeer!"

She yelled at me an' took up her broom,
An' chased me twice around the front room,
Shoutin', "That ole river'll be yore doom,
Think of yer son an' yer daughteeeeeecccr!"

So I said to her, "O love dearle me,
I must follow the river right down t'the sea,
'Tis the only way a beast can be free,"
An' I ran 'cos I couldn't have fought heeeeeeer!

She said t'me, "Now listen you,
Me an' the young uns are all comin' too,
On board of a raft you need a good crew,
It'll make the journey seem shorteeeeeeeer!" '

A large untidy raft hove into view round the bend, smoke curling from the chimney of a hut built at its centre. A fat, jolly-looking hedgehog was leaning on the tiller; over his head a line was strung between two poles set for'ard and aft, with gaily coloured washing fluttering from it.

Bryony ran into the shallows waving her paws. 'Hello there, I mean, ahoy! Could you take two passengers?'

The fat hedgehog grinned from ear to ear, revealing a wonderful set of even white teeth. 'Ahoy yoreself, mousey, gangway while I brings 'er inshore!'

He steered the raft into the shallows, almost grounding it, and asked, 'Two y'say, where's t'other one, missie?'

'Yurr, surr, tho' oi'm nought but a pore damaged molebeast!' Togget came ambling around the hillock holding his head.

A small wiry female hedgehog came bustling out of the hut on the raft, her skirt billowing over a welter of petticoats. 'Corks an' crivvens!' she exclaimed. 'Wot 'appened to yore nut, mole? Did yer fall on it?'

Togget tenderly rubbed the poultice on his forehead. 'Oi'd tell ee, marm, but oi'm far too 'ungered furr gossip.'

Immediately the hogwife gave her husband a mighty shove. 'Ducks an' drakes! Don't stan' there lookin' ornamental, Duddle Pollspike, git the pore mole an' the mousemaid aboard an' let's feed 'em!'

Duddle tugged his headspikes respectfully. 'Wotever you say, Tutty, my liddle bankblossom!'

The cabinhut was very chintzy, with gaily coloured tablecloth and curtains, thick, bright-dyed rushmats and a large square stove on which various dishes bubbled and stewed. Bryony and Togget were seated at a semi-circular window table and given beetroot and raspberry wine in small mugs to revive them. Tutty Pollspike busied herself at the stove, whilst her husband Duddle shooed their two young hoglets, Clematis Roselea and Arundo, out of the way.

'Landing party, my darling ducklings, play ashore

awhile until yore dear mama an' my goodself get the vittles ready.'

Bryony and Togget introduced themselves and told their story while Duddle and Tutty prepared the meal. Duddle tasted soup on a spoontip, smacked his lips several times and muttered, 'Needs more fennel, splendid herb, always like it. Well, let me tell you, young uns, yore ferret has prob'ly taken the river route if he has a grain of sense, it's the only way t'travel. Easy on the paws, never goes uphill, an' y'can take the home too.'

Tutty placed fresh bread on the table, smacking Togget's paw away. 'Crabs an' clawlegs! Yore worse'n my Duddle. You can travel with us for as long as you pleases, may'ap you'll find yore ferret. But if'n you touches any vittles afore the table is set, I'll chop off yore tails afore you can blink. Got that?'

She fixed Togget with a warning stare as he nodded, and said, 'Got et, thankee, marm, you'm be a cutten off ee tailers if us'n's be a touchen afore vittles be ready. Ho urr!'

The two hoglets were called in from play when the meal was ready. Duddle poled the raft from the bank and it drifted downriver, with the tiller lashed in position whilst they ate.

There was thick watercress and turnip soup, warm brown wheatbread, a deep dish of cheese, mushroom and leek bake, and a blackberry jam roly poly pudding with meadowcream. Afterwards they sipped borage and rosehip tea. Duddle went out on deck to tend the tiller, whilst the friends were entertained by young Clematis Roselea, who recited a poem taught by her mama.

'I have learnt to wash my paws,
An' say sir an' marm,
An' don't act daft, when on this raft,
Lest I do come to harm.
To sit up straight at table time,

An' go to bed when told,
Mama says I'm a precious hog,
In fact I'm good as gold . . . So there!'

Young Arundo was about to flick an apple pip at her,
when he caught his mama's stern eye, and he shrugged
philosophically instead. 'Thorry! I don't want my tail
cut off with a thingle thwipe!'

'Ahoy in the hut, mole'n'maid, all paws on deck an'
see this!'

At the sound of Duddle's voice from outside, Bryony
and Togget left the table and went to see what he had
found. Tutty set her stern gaze on the hoglets, who
had half risen from table. 'Rhubarb an' rosebuds! Did
anybeast tell you two to move?'

Arundo settled back glumly, making a chopping
motion with his paw. 'Thame old thtory, chop off our
tailth!'

The bodies of the two old foxes were caught up in the
branches of a half submerged bush in a shallow cove
beyond a curve.

Duddle pointed them out to the friends. 'Dreadful end
for anybeast, even two villains like them. How d'you
figger it happened?'

Togget nodded knowingly. 'Oi'll bet an acorn to an
apple 'twere maister Veil did et!'

Bryony wagged a reproving paw at the mole. 'Oh,
Togget, how could you say that? Veil wouldn't have
killed them, perhaps it was just some kind of nasty
accident!'

Togget turned away and trundled back to the hut,
muttering, 'Aye, an' p'raps 'twill snow this evenin', et
bein' midsummer!'

Sometime during the next night, when Veil lay sleeping
on the willow trunk, a sidestream came up and flowed
off on a slight slope. Not being awake to control the log,

Veil slept on, unaware that the current had steered his craft off the main river. The willow trunk drifted silently into the slipstream, bearing the sleeping ferret away towards the distant mountains, and fast-running rapids which led to a waterfall.

38

The same wet dawn which had sent Bryony and Togget scurrying for the pine copse broke over Salamandastron. Rain sheeted out in curtains over the still waveless sea; hordebeasts huddled miserably among the rocky outcrops on the tideline, protecting smoky fires from guttering in the downpour. Swartt crouched with several of his Captains and Nightshade, their fire sheltered by an old tent canvas pegged to the side of the rock groyne. Those around the Warlord remained silent, not knowing which mood chose to possess their leader on such a cheerless day. Neither the ferret nor his vixen had spoken to anybeast of their latest plan.

Both watched the mountain, its top shrouded in mist. Though Swartt and his seer did not speak, both their minds were concentrated on the same thing. Was the Wraith inside the caves and passages of Salamandastron, stalking their enemy Sunflash with his lethal stone blade?

Wraith lay panting on a narrow ledge halfway up to the window of the Badger Lord's bedchamber. Though the weasel could move speedily over short distances he had never been a strong creature. Granted, he was endowed with a natural cunning and the fantastic power of camouflage, but there his powers ended. He lacked strength and stamina. Wiping rainwater from his pale eyes, he glanced upward. Sounds of breakfast bustle and banter reached his soaking ears. Checking that his deadly stone knife was dry and safe in its sheath, Wraith hauled himself wearily up the rainslicked mountainside as the downpour continued its relentless course.

Folrig and Ruddle were merciless jokers, and wherever the opportunity presented itself for a bit of fun the two otters were certain to be involved. Unwittingly, the fat, food-loving hare Porty had presented himself as an easy target. Sunflash had pointed him out at breakfast.

Folrig and Ruddle came bounding into the dining hall, hungry from dawn sentry duty. Roughly they elbowed their way in beside the Badger Lord and began helping themselves to his hot oatcakes.

'Move over, ole frightface, make way for two starvin' riverdogs! We're fightin' fit an' ready to eat anybeast to a standstill!'

The big badger pushed hot blackberry pie and mint tea in their direction, commenting drily as they ate ravenously, 'You two uglymugs are mere babes when it comes to victualling. See that fat young hare over there, Porty? Now there's a bucko I'd call a good scoffer – why, he'd eat you two out of house and home while he was waiting to be served. Watch him!'

Both otters did, their own food forgotten as they observed Porty with fascination. In rapid order a full apple pie, a plate of dried fruits, a big pitcher of strawberry fizz and an enormous carrot and mushroom pastie were devoured by the insatiable hare. Mopping up the gravy from the pastie with half a crusty loaf, Porty eyed his neighbour's plate covetously. 'Mmmf grmmmf snch! Er, I say, old lad, if y'can't tackle that measly bowl of pear crumble then chuck it along this way, wot?'

Ruddle shook his head in admiration. 'Wot a beast! C'mon, mate, we've got to meet that furry feedbag!'

After breakfast Sunflash went up to the bedchamber window, where he stood with Sabretache and Colonel Sandgall. They viewed the rainswept beach and the saturated hordes gathered round their sputtering fires amid the rocks. Polishing his monocle, the Colonel twitched an ear to the sky.

'Good ol' rain, wot! Nothin' like it for dampenin' vermin spirits, give 'em a chance to reconsider their bally position. Wet'n'worried, I'd say, by the look of the blighters!'

Sabretache clapped paw to the hilt of his fighting blade. 'Mayhap, sah, but what about when the jolly old precipitation ceases, what then?'

The Colonel stared at him blankly. 'Precipitation ceases? Explain y'self, laddie buck!'

Sabretache gave Sunflash a quick wink. 'Beggin' y'pardon, sah, I mean, what happens when the rain stops?'

The Badger Lord answered before Sandgall had a chance to. 'We attack! Leave the bare minimum of defenders at the mountain here, the rest of us put on full battle gear and take the fight to the enemy. This is the best chance we'll have: our numbers are bolstered by shrews, otters and squirrels.'

Squinching the monocle into his cheek, Sandgall agreed. 'Excellent plan, milord, was just about to suggest it m'self!'

The Wraith was directly below the broad windowledge. He lay breathless in the rain, listening to what was going on. A quick peek reassured him that Sunflash was standing close to the windowspace. The weasel planned to make his move as soon as he regained his wind and felt fit enough for a burst of speed. Drawing the poisoned stone blade he sheltered it carefully against the rain with his paw. All it would take was a quick leap onto the windowsill and a swift strike at the unsuspecting badger.

Chuckling and chortling, Folrig and Ruddle came bounding into the bedchamber. They dashed about searching frantically in the nooks and corners.

Sunflash could not help smiling at the two funsters. 'Excuse me, you two frog-frighteners, but what are you doing chasing round my bedchamber, eh?'

Between gusts of laughter they explained.

'Yahahaha! You shoulda seen ole Porty's face!'

'Whoohooheehee! We pulled the ole rockcream trick on 'im!'

'Haha! Aye, we told 'im that otter rockcreams were the most delicious thing anybeast 'ad ever tasted. So, that greedy Porty, couldn't wait to get 'is paws on some!'

'Right! Then we nips out t'the kitchens an' covers a few rocks wid meadowcream. Otter rockcreams, see?'

Sunflash stifled a chuckle. 'He didn't eat any, surely?'

Folrig and Ruddle leaned on each other for support, helpless with mirth. 'He, he, heeheehee! Pore old Porty 'ad bolted one down afore we could stop 'im, shoulda seen 'is face, hahahahaha!'

Colonel Sandgall twitched his eye, making the monocle wiggle. 'Hmm, very droll I'm sure, but if I were you chaps I'd scoot fast or hide. I can hear young Porty comin', an' he don't sound greatly pleased or amused by your jape!'

'Gloggle! Yarggh! I'll rockcream the bounders! Where are the flippin' plank-tailed villains, I'll skin 'em alive!'

Folrig and Ruddle shot around Sunflash, attempting to hide themselves behind the badger's broad back. Porty came thundering in, cream all around his mouth and an otter rockcream cake in each paw, his face a picture of comic indignation.

'Come out, you rotten otters!' he yelled.

A loud giggle from behind Sunflash gave them both away. The outraged hare saw that the Badger Lord suddenly appeared to have six footpaws. Porty raised the rockcreams to throw. Sunflash saw what was about to happen and dropped flat to the chamber floor, leaving Folrig and Ruddle exposed to Porty's vengeance.

It was not a lucky day for the Wraith. The mottled weasel sprang upright in the windowspace, wielding his deadly stone knife, triumph shining in his pale eyes. At that exact moment Porty flung the cream-covered rocks and the otters ducked with lightning speed.

Splakk!

Both missiles scored a direct hit on the Wraith's face.

Instinctively, the weasel's paws flew up to his mouth, and he plunged silently backward into space, the dagger sticking in his jaw. The last sound the Wraith made was when his falling body thudded against the rocks far below. Draped limply across the rain-soaked stone with both eyes closed, the carcass of what had once been the weasel Wraith was almost invisible.

Sabretache fixed Porty and the two otters with the haughty glare of an outraged officer. 'I'm goin' to count to three now, an' if you chaps haven't found someplace else to play your silly tricks by then, you'll all be on a fizzer, double guard duty for three nights. Understood?'

Three hasty salutes, a patter of footpaws and the slamming of the door announced tranquillity had returned to the bedchamber.

Colonel Sandgall polished furiously at his monocle. 'Must be somethin' wrong with this bally contrivance, wot! D'you know, I thought I saw some type of vermin standin' on that windowledge, not a moment ago, confounded strange, eh, wot?'

Sunflash coughed politely, catching a nod from Sabretache. 'Did you really, Colonel? I'm sure I saw something there, too; must've been a trick of the light, reflection off the sea or something. What d'you think, 'Tache?'

The hare leaned out over the windowsill. 'Oh indeed,

286

sah, stranger things have been seen around this mountain more times than enough, wot! I say, the jolly old
rain's startin' to pack in, see, there's the sun comin' out!'

Steam rose in wisps from the sand as the midday sun
rose high to warm the earth. Swartt Sixclaw stood rapping his gauntleted paw against his swordhilt.

'We should've heard somethin' by now. Surely if this
Wraith beast is as good as 'e's supposed ter be, the
badger must be dead?'

Nightshade moved artfully out of paw range. 'We'll
just have to wait and see, Lord.'

Swartt turned on her, snarling as his temper rose. 'Let
me 'ear you say that jus' once more, vixen, an' you'll be
wearin' yer tail round yer neck fer a scarf!'

He transferred his attention to the hordebeasts, who
were leaping about in the shallows, trying to catch mackerel from a shoal that had ventured in too close. 'Huh,
will yer lookit that slab-sided lot o' bumpkins, they make
better fishers than fighters. See that the best of their
catch is sent up to my fire. Where in the name o' tripes
an' tendons 'as that Wraith got to?'

Silently the warriors of Salamandastron stood ready as
the rough-timber gate at the main entrance creaked
open. Sunflash the Mace led them out, clad only in his
chainmail tunic and carrying the mace loosely at his side.
Lady Firdance, the squirrel leader, took the left flank
with Folrig and Ruddle. Log a Log took the right
flank with Fleetrunn and Hedgepaw. Sabretache and
Rockleg took the centre slightly behind Sunflash. Javelins, bows, spears, slings and rapiers were clutched
tight in every paw as they skirted the deserted trench
in front of the mountain. Quietly, grimly they strode,
squirrels, otters, hares and shrews, hard eyed, tight
jawed, their paws making no sound in the sand.

Swartt had turned away; he sat with his back against

the rocks, eyes half closed, enjoying the warmth and gentle breezes after the morning's rain. A stoat was emerging from the shallows, a flapping silver-banded mackerel impaled on his spearpoint. Suddenly, he glanced up the beach and froze. Fish and spear were forgotten as he stood pointing and yelling, 'Look, they're comin'!'

Swartt sprang upright, yanking out his sword. 'Captains to me! Get out of that water! Everybeast stan' to arms! Battle stations, the lot o' yer!'

Bradberry was marching alongside Porty. He heard the shouts lower down the beach and saw hordebeasts from afar, dashing hither and thither, and said, 'Well, they've seen us now, Porty old lad.'

Keeping his eyes front, Sabretache gave orders calmly. 'Don't run, me beauties, not yet. Shoulder t'shoulder, that's the stuff, keep those weapons down, don't want to stab the chap in front of you. Ready, milord?'

Sunflash's deep grunt was heard throughout the ranks.

'Ready! Follow me!'

The horde massed on the tideline, spears bristling, drums banging, conch shells blowing, banners fluttering out on the noon breeze. Swartt moved to the rear and, climbing up on a rocky outcrop, he spoke down to the vixen. 'Well, we lost some yesterday, but now I can see what their strength is. Hah! We still outnumber 'em three to one. I see the badger still lives, so I can stick t'the oath I swore. It'll be me, Swartt Sixclaw, who slays 'im, an' no otherbeast!'

Porty grasped Bradberry's paw firmly. 'Here we go, Bradders. Good luck, old chap, give 'em what for!'

Sunflash half raised his mace. 'March at the double now!' he ordered.

The pace speeded up, Sabretache and other officers calling, 'Keep those lines straight, weapons down. Wait for it!'

Sunflash raised the mace higher, and shouted, 'Forward at the half run now!'

The paws of the advancing warriors broke into a fast lope.

'Archers ready at flanks and rear. Fire!'

A broad half moon crescent of shafts cut into the blue afternoon air, whirring angrily over the advance at the front ranks of the waiting vermin.

Sunflash swung his mace high.

'Chaaaaaaarge!'

Breaking into a headlong run, the warriors from the mountain brought their weapons up. Spears and javelin-tips glinted, swords and rapiers flashed. Amid the thunder of paws, wild warcries and battle shouts rent the summer air.

'Eeulaliaaaaa! Logalogalogalogaloooog! Firjak Greenstone! Whump! Whump! Whump! Blood'n'vinegaaaaar!'

The hordebeasts banged their shields and yelled back.

'Swartt! Swartt! Sixclaaaaaw! Kill! Kiiiiiillll!'

Like a tidal wave against a rocky shore, Sunflash's command crashed into the horderanks, the shock of the impact driving the vermin back full ten pawlengths. Like a madbeast the Badger Lord plunged deep into the enemy lines, his mace whirling as he fought towards the distant figure of Swartt perched on the rock at the rear. Sabretache led his troops in to protect the badger's back. Already limping from a spearwound, the sabre master dealt death to any who came within range of his curving blade. Arrows and slingstones from the rear of both forces zinged overhead like maddened wasps.

The might of the horde, having taken the initial shock of the charge, now began pressing forward, and many a good warrior fell to vermin spears and cutlasses. Lady Firdance was having more success than most; forming a fighting triangle with Folrig and Ruddle she hit hard at the horde's right flank, driving deep in an effort to meet up with Sunflash, whose huge form could be seen like a landmark as he ploughed forward. Bradberry went down with an arrow in his shoulder, and Porty stumbled and tripped, falling upon his friend. He turned to rise as a searat swept a large scimitar at him; the rat gave a shriek and fell dead at his side. Folrig pulled his javelin free as Ruddle assisted both hares up, winking at Porty.

'Up y'get, matey, must've been the weight of that rockcream pulled you down. Get Bradders be'ind our archers, see yer later, good huntin', eh. Whumpwhump-whump! Firjak Greenstone!'

The vermin on the opposite flank charged the shrews gleefully. Attacking small creatures with small swords was better than facing hares. They did not reckon on an old shrew manoeuvre known as the Guosim Windmill. Three tight circles of shrews in one, whirling madly, some cutting low, others at stomach height, whilst more worked at head and neck level, the vicious little rapiers went in and out, round and round, scything at every-thing in their path, while a row of Guosim shrews at the centre of the ring continuously slung rocks over their comrades' heads.

Swartt stood tip-pawed upon his rock, shouting, 'We're pushin' 'em back, vixen, I told yer, we've got the numbers on our side!'

Nightshade climbed up to appraise the situation. 'Aye, but only in the centre, Lord, and that's because the badger made his move too early and allowed them to close in around him. See the flanks, the horde is crum-bling and giving way on both sides. We may have the numbers, but they've got the heart!'

Swartt sent her flying with a kick. 'When I want yore opinion I'll ask fer it. Get me that bow an' arrers, the badger'll soon be in range!'

Sunflash was like a great seabeast surrounded by waves of foebeasts, but all he could see through the red mists of bloodwrath was the ferret, perched on the rock down by the tideline. His great speed with the heavy mace was causing destruction among the horde. Up and down, left and right, swinging in a huge blur the mighty warclub battered horde vermin, sword, spear and dagger without regard to any. Snapped blades, shattered hilts and splintered hafts flew high in the air around him. Sabretache wisely kept his force behind the berserk Badger Lord. Rockleg fought alongside Hedgepaw. Both would take a short run, vault high on their spearshafts and come down with long hindlegs kicking savagely into the faces of the vermin.

The hordebeasts fought fiercely, with the strength of desperation. Most were experienced warbeasts, determined to push through their attackers and gain the mountain, where there would be shelter, food and plunder. But Nightshade's judgement had been correct: the mountain warriors all had brave hearts. The tide of the battle began to turn when the Guosim shrews broke through to the centre and joined up with the hares and Lady Firdance's squirrels, who had been holding the middle with the otters. Now the flanks of the horde had been well battered and the attackers massed in the centre. Leaving any vermin who had broken past them to be dealt with by the rear lines of archers, the entire force turned to fight their way through to Sunflash, raising one mighty cry. 'Eeulaliaaaaaa!'

Swartt cursed as his arrow took a searat in the back of the skull instead of striking Sunflash. He notched another shaft to his bowstring and fired. This time he did not miss: the arrow pierced the Badger Lord high on his shoulder, where the chainmail tunic ended. Still swinging the mace, Sunflash gave a deep roar and tore the arrow out with his teeth. Spitting the shaft away, he waved the battleclub in Swartt's direction, his voice thundering out over the melee.

'I'm coming, Sixclaw, wait there!'

Then the horde broke and began retreating, battered and defeated by the relentless mountain warriors.

Sunflash was suddenly knocked down from behind as milling, panicked hordebeasts fled towards the sea. Sabretache stood with one footpaw on the Badger Lord's back, wielding his sabre like a maddened drum major as he shouted orders.

'Up an' at 'em! Forward to the sea! Chaaaaarge!'

Hedgepaw and Rockleg were at his side in an instant. Between them they managed to drag the dazed Sunflash upright. Rubbing sand from his eyes, the badger bellowed furiously, 'Where's Swartt?'

The rock stood empty. Swartt Sixclaw and his vixen had gone!

39

Evening crimsoned into purple; on the horizon, a blood-coloured sun dipped slowly into the dark, tired sea. Spears with thick rush torches tied to them stood upright in the shore along the tideline. Sunflash the Mace sat with his head buried in both paws; his war weapon lay on the sand beside him. Colonel Sandgall had come down from the mountain; he threaded his way through the exhausted warriors, shaking paws, patting shoulders and giving credit where it was due.

'Well fought! Good show! Stout feller! Brave gel, wot!'

Sabretache was cleaning off his blade in the sand. He stood smartly to attention, saluting the old Colonel.

Sandgall nodded. 'Did any of 'em surrender? Prisoners?'

The hare Captain's sabre pointed to the sea. 'None, sah, 'fraid not, it was a no-surrender situation. Most of 'em retreated too far an' too fast, dragged out by the undercurrent. As for our own, we got off surprisin' light, sah, though they're still takin' count on wounded an' slain.'

Sunflash joined them. The red light of bloodwrath had faded from his eyes, though they were still dark and troubled. 'Sixclaw wasn't lost in the sea, I'm sure of it, he's too cunning for that. Swartt has escaped, and he can't have got very far. It's my job to go after him and finish what he started!'

Sandgall gave his monocle a quick polish and looked the badger up and down from head to footpaws. 'If I may make so bold as t'say, milord, you're in no fit condition to go chasin' off anywhere. Headwound, arrow hole in y'left shoulder, spear thrust to footpaw, deep slash across mace paw. How far d'you think you'll get in that state, eh? Sundew, Ryeback, fetch your box of medical tricks an' patch this beast up!'

As the hares ministered to his wounds Sunflash protested, 'Don't you see, I must go after Swartt. The more time I spend dawdling here, the further away he's escaping!'

But Colonel Sandgall would brook no argument, not even from the Badger Lord of Salamandastron.

'Tomorrow our Long Patrol will pick up the ferret's trail, then you can face the bounder an' settle up your score. But if you try to go it alone tonight, sah, then I'm afraid I'll use our warriors to stop you. It is my duty as Colonel and Senior Offisah at Salamandastron to protect my Badger Lord, beggin' y'pardon an' hopin' you understand. Sah!'

Sunflash nodded. 'I understand. Ow – that hurts!'

Sundew chided him as she rethreaded a fishbone needle with a long hair plucked from the badger's own back. 'Keep the ol' head still then, Sire, how's a body supposed to stitch up this headwound if you keep nodding like a woodpecker at an oak?'

When the hares had finished, Sunflash stood up stiffly. Stitched, poulticed and cleaned, he strode off with a slight limp towards the mountain and his bedchamber.

'Tomorrow then, Sandgall! I'll be up at crack of dawn; have your Long Patrol waiting, ready to travel!'

'If he's up at crack o' dawn it'll only be to sleepwalk,'

Ryeback whispered to her friend Sundew. 'I gave him enough slumberin' draught to knock three out!'

With his vixen and about thirty other vermin, Swartt had waded off through the shallows in the thick of the retreat. Striking north and east he crossed the shore on the mountain's south side, up into the high hills behind Salamandastron. The ferret knew that making camp or sleeping was out of the question; he had to get far away from Sunflash the Mace. Breasting the first hill, he paused and watched those behind him struggling and panting as they strove to reach the top.

'Move yerselves if you want ter stay alive, y'rot-pawed, maggot-backed ditherers!' Swartt berated them. 'Step lively or sit'n'weep here 'til the badger an' those hares track yer down!'

Nightshade brought up the rear. The vixen seer was puzzled. Her dreams and visions all showed Sunflash falling at the battle in front of the mountain, and twice it had almost happened, but at the last moment her visions clouded and Sunflash was replaced by an ancient female badger. The vixen was baffled, because all of her dreams ended with Swartt standing on top of a mountain, laughing and victorious. Wearily she cast all omens aside, banishing dreams from her mind as she followed the leader she felt fated to serve.

Dawn had long dispelled the sea mists, and the sun was already beginning to climb in the sky when Skarlath landed on the windowsill of the badger's bedchamber. Cocking his head curiously on one side, the kestrel's keen eye watched the Badger Lord sleeping. The mace still hung from its cord on Sunflash's paw, and his mighty chest rose and fell to the echo of rumbling snores. Skarlath spread his wings wide and tilted his fierce curved beak upward.

'Kreeeeeh! Does my friend sleep his life away? Kreeeeh!'

The big badger sat bolt upright pawing at his eyes. 'Where, what? I've been asleep . . . Skarlath!'

The kestrel swooped in, landing on Sunflash's shoulder. 'So, my gold-striped friend, it must have been a good, hard day's battle to keep you so long abed this morn . . .'

The Badger Lord tore at the bandages and poultices restricting his limbs, flinging them from him. 'Crack o' dawn, eh? Well, where are they, the Long Patrol trackers? Swartt escaped. I've got to go after him!'

Skarlath flew back to the windowsill. 'The hares are down there by the sea, burying their comrades who were slain in battle. I know that Sixclaw got away, I picked up his tracks south of here at dawn. His band numbers three and thirty. He is heading north, taking a wide easterly loop, travelling light with few rest stops.'

Shunning the chainmail tunic, Sunflash chose an old woven tabard, smiling grimly as he donned it. 'So, it all comes full circle. That is about the number he had when we used to hunt one another in younger days. Come on, my hawk, let us go hunting again one last time, just the two of us!'

The burial party had completed their sad task, and they arrived back at the dining hall within the mountain to take lunch. Sundew, who had immediately gone to check on her patient, came bounding downstairs, shouting, 'Colonel Sandgall, sah, Milord Sunflash is gone!'

Sandgall slammed a flagon of cordial down so hard that it cracked and the liquid dribbled into his lap. 'Fur'n'botheration! I thought you said he'd sleep 'til noontide, marm! Sabretache, how's the old footpaw, ready to travel? Rockleg, Fleetrunn! Rations an' weapons for twelve Long Patrol. Pick up the tracks, follow His Lordship, quick's the word, sharp's the action. Dismiss!'

Within a remarkably short time twelve hares of the Long Patrol, headed by Sabretache, had found the distinctive pawprints of Sunflash, and set off fast after him.

High in the hills, with the hawk on his shoulder and the mace in his grasp, Sunflash followed the trail of Swartt Sixclaw, the lifelong enemy whom he had sworn long seasons ago to slay.

40

Bryony and Togget lay flat on their backs at the stern end of the raft, a jug of cowslip cordial and a deepdish pear and redcurrant tart between them.

The mousemaid dipped her paw overboard, allowing cool riverwater to caress it. 'Hey ho, Togget, this is the life for us, eh!'

'Bo urr, et surpintly am, Broinee, oi never gurtly was one furr sailen, but this be's most wunnerful, burr aye, so't be.'

The hoglet Arundo was hiding behind the hut, watching them. The sight of Togget's fat stomach sticking in the air was too much for him. Breaking cover, he dashed up and jumped on it. 'Heehee! I jumped onna moleth thtomach!'

Togget was too winded to express an opinion on the subject and Bryony was shaking with laughter along with Arundo. Tutty Pollspike was pegging out washing up for'ard; she had seen what took place and shouted dire warnings. 'Rushes an' riverbanks! Just let me catch either o' you jumpin' on that pore h'animal's stummick agin an' I'll chop yore tails off, d'ye hear me, you two?'

Bryony sat up indignantly, pointing at Arundo. 'But it wasn't me, it was him!'

Arundo pointed back at her, still giggling. 'Heeheehee! Mouthemaid tol' me to do it!'

Duddle emerged from the cabin, stretching after his mid-morning nap. 'Now then me bold beasties,' he said, 'what's all the kerfuffle out here? Still mindin' the tiller for me, Togget?'

Remembering the duty he had been allotted, Togget got up and, rubbing his stomach, leaned against the tiller. 'Aye, zurr, ee tiller ain't been gone nowhere's since oi been mindin' et.'

Duddle took command of the tiller, saying, 'Have to be careful on this stretch, there's a slipstream off to the south comin' up shortly. Rapids an' waterfall down that way, dangerous, 'stremely perilous, mmm, ain't that right, my little river lily?'

Tutty passed the washing basket to Clematis Roselea. 'Rocks an' rapids! We'd do well t'stay away from that lot. Keep tight 'old of that tiller, Duddle!'

'Never fear, my darlin' damselfly,' the fat smiling hedgehog reassured her. 'I have it within my vicelike grip, no harm will befall the family. Hmm, just a thought, Bryony, but d'you think yore friend the ferret may have drifted that way? He could very well have strayed into the slipstream, not bein' used to the currents'n'flows.'

Bryony looked up from a piece of pie. 'Do you think so, sir? If he did, how would we find out?'

Duddle indicated a spot on the left bank further along. 'That's where the slipstream is, we'll pull over an' hove to land when we get past it. I'll ask Ilfril, a mean-tempered creature if ever there was one – best let me do the talkin'.'

It was a difficult business keeping the raft in midriver while passing the slipstream. Bryony helped Duddle to control the tiller. When they were safe downriver from the side-pulling current, they hauled the raft into the high bank, securing it to a crack willow with a stout rope. Duddle Pollspike led them back along the bank until they reached the slipstream. It flowed on a slight downhill gradient, very fast and smooth, losing itself as it twisted and turned into the distance, where a big greensloped mountain stood out clear against the cloudless sky. Duddle tapped the side of his nose, cautioning them to be silent. Planting his bottom firmly on the edge of the bank, he dangled both footpaws in the water and spoke aloud as if to himself.

'Perfect day for a spot o' fishin'!'

A squeaky, ill-tempered voice answered him. 'Clear off! You're not fishin' on my stretch of river!'

The overhanging plants on the bank's edge parted and a sourfaced bankvole clambered out and waved a knobbly stick at Duddle. 'Hah! I should've known it'd be you, Pollspike. Now go on, shift yerself off my bank!'

Duddle grinned from ear to ear, teasing the bankvole. 'Oh, cheer up, Ilfril, an' give us a smile, you know I'm not fishin'. Come on, laugh, yore face won't crack.'

The bankvole scowled and swiped at the reeds with his stick. 'What d'you want around here, then?'

'Lookin' for a ferret, friend o' the mole an' mousemaid yonder. Did he pass along this stretch perchance?'

Ilfril scratched his stubby chin thoughtfully, saying, 'I don't give information freely to trespassers, y'know.'

Tutty Pollspike produced a thick wedge of the pear and redcurrant tart from beneath her apron. 'Parsnips an' periwinkles! We didn't expect nothin' for nothin' off you, ole crabapple face. Take this, it's more'n the likes o' you deserves!'

Ilfril grabbed the slice of pie, his eyes darting hither and thither as if somebeast was trying to trick him. 'Ferret eh, saw 'im last night, late on, sittin' astride a willow log. Dozy oaf! Fast asleep, didn't 'ave the sense to rouse 'imself an' keep to midriver. Shot off down the slipstream snorin' like an 'edge'og. Huh! That un'll get a rude awakenin', I can tell yer!'

The bankvole clambered back into his den, dragging

the pie slice with him, muttering and complaining. 'Got what y'want, now make yerselves scarce an' give a creature a bit o' peace.'

Duddle placed a friendly paw on Bryony's head. 'So, there you have it, my little bank blossom, yore ferret has taken a turn for the worse. This is where our paths must part, I couldn't risk life'n'limb takin' my family down the slipstream, 'tis a wild an' dangerous waterway. I wouldn't advise any creature to follow it.'

Togget gazed at the swift-flowing water. 'Hurr, nor wudd oi, zurr, but missie Broinee, she'm bounden to foller ee rascal, tho' oi doan't knows why.'

Tutty agreed wholeheartedly with the mole. 'Fiddles an' follies! After wot you've told me about that ferret I wouldn't pass 'im the time o' day nor a piece o' pie. Why does an 'onest mousemaid like yoreself go chasin' after such an evil vermin?'

Bryony gave the only answer she could. 'Because I'm responsible for him. I've cared for Veil since he was a babe and bad or good I cannot desert him.'

Tutty gave Bryony a careful embrace, as is the way with hedgehogs, overcome with admiration for the mousemaid. 'Summers an' strawberries! This earth'd be a better place if there were more like yer, missie!'

Veil was enjoying himself. It was early morn with the sun rising hot, and flickering light patterns danced on the fast current as the boughs of graceful alders from either bank formed a canopy over the stream. The young ferret ate some candied fruit and an oatfarl from the haversack, scooping up the clear rushing water in his paws to drink. Not knowing he had veered from the river, he leaned forward on the willow trunk, allowing the spray to wet his face. The stream was deep, smooth and swift, and wherever he was bound it was better than plodding by paw. Sometimes he drew his knife and slashed through the green-shaded waters at passing fish, but they were far too quick for him. Veil was about to lie on his back and take a nap, when an unexpected turn in the streamcourse made him grab tight hold of his log.

The willow began to bump up and down on the widening stream, and he had to start fending off rocks which sprang up in his path. Leaving the shelter of the trees, the dashing water bounded through a high-walled gorge. The log struck an underwater ledge and bounced high, coming down with a juddering splash. Veil began to feel frightened. He clung grimly to his perch in the splayed fork of the willow trunk, thoroughly drenched and shivering from a combination of fear and cold water. Steering the log to the bank was out of the question; it bucked and rolled as it plunged headlong into a series of rapids. Blinded by the spray, Veil gripped the bark until his paws were numb, while the deafening noise of rushing water pounding in his ears drowned out his own screams. Blinking furiously, he made out a mist-clouded rainbow ahead, then the log struck a rock and turned sideways, slowly at first, then picking up speed on the boiling current until it was spinning around like a top. Then it turned over and Veil was in the water, screeching, yelling and choking on icy mouthfuls. Clunk! The butt end of the willow trunk struck his head. Unaware of the unearthly roar and awesome drop, the senseless ferret hurtled over the cascading top of the waterfall.

Bryony and Togget stood waving on the bank, a bulging haversack between them. Pulling out into midriver the big untidy raft sailed off, its line of washing fluttering like stately banners. They shouted their goodbyes to the Pollspike family, who were grouped around the tiller at the after end of the flat craft.

'Thank you for everything, friends, fortune sail with you!'

'Goombye, zurr Duddle an ee famberly, thankee gurtly!'

The hedgehogs waved cheerily, returning the farewells.

'Seasons be good to you, we'll meet again I hope!'

'Rocks an' rivers! Of course we will, take good care of yoreselves, an' give that ferret a kick from me!'

'Yeth, cut hith tail off with a thingle thwipe!'

The last thing they heard was young Clematis Roselea, as her father held her up high, singing aloud:

'If I'm very, very good my mama bakes me pies,
Hogmaids never should bring tears
To their dear mamas' eyes.
I scrub my face quite hard each morn,
And keep my dress so clean,
And to my little brother dear,
I'm never ever mean!'

Togget waved at the receding raft, pausing to blink away a tear. 'They'm vurry dear beasts, oi diddent moind ee liddle un a jumpen on moi stummick, hurr no!'

Making fair progress on the sloping streambank, the two travellers strode easily along through lush grass and sheltering foliage towards the mountain, following the course of the stream. Before they left the trees at midday Togget discovered blackberries, their stalks winding around a thick lavender clump. Dangling their footpaws into the water, Bryony and Togget sat on the bank, sharing a heap of the dark juicy berries. A flicker from the far bank caught Bryony's eye; she saw a small bankvole watching them from the shelter of some overhanging ivy.

The mousemaid smiled and waved at the little creature. 'Hello there, it's very beautiful around here. Would you like some blackberries? Here you are!'

She threw the berries across the stream, and the bankvole quickly gathered them and stuffed his face greedily. He stood watching for more, his mouth and chin stained purple. Bryony threw him a few more and enquired after Veil. 'Did you see a ferret pass this way on a log?'

Immediately the tiny creature began dancing up and down the bank, pointing animatedly and gibbering. 'Yis yis! Ferret, went down tharraway, right down ferret went! Yeeheehee! Ferret'll go bumperty bump bump! Can't stop down tharraway, ferret'll go yaaaaargh! Right over top o' th'big wateryfall! Yaaaaargh! Ferret'll be smashed t'bits yeeheehee!'

Bryony stopped throwing the berries and stamped her footpaw on the bank, looking sternly at the grinning little bankvole. 'Don't say such awful things!'

This seemed to encourage the tiny creature; he leapt in the air, waving his paws wildly. 'Ferret smashed inta likkle bits! Yeeheehee! Lotsa bits! 'Ead one place, paws anuther, fur everywhere, tail inna nundred bits. Smashed ferret! Yeeheeheehee!'

Bryony gathered the remainder of the blackberries huffily. 'Come on, Togget, we're leaving here. That impudent creature isn't getting any more berries – we're going!'

The little bankvole pursued them, shouting from the opposite side as he skipped and danced along. 'All smashed inta ferrety bits! Yeeheehee! Belly smashed, dinner all over'a place, teeths everywhere, eyes smashed, eeyukka! Nose in bits, blood too, allover allover alloveraplace. Blood's everywhere off smashed ferret! Yeeheeheehee!'

He continued in this manner until Togget put both digging claws into either side of his mouth, pulled his lips wide and stuck out his tongue, and made a grotesque face at the bankvole. Still jumping and skipping the little bankvole returned the insult, squinching his nose and waggling his ears. Unfortunately, he did not look where he was going and went smack into an alder. Sitting flat on the ground he nursed a bruised jaw and set up a fearful yowl. 'Waaahaaah! 'Urted me face! Waaahaaahaaah!'

Bryony shook her head reprovingly at her molefriend. 'Tut, tut, really, Togget, did you have to?'

'Hurr, hurr, at least et stopped 'im a goin' on abowt bits o' furret, missie, oi wurr beginnin' t'feel quoit ill.'

When they reached the gorge top the afternoon grew hot, but as the sheer sides lessened, spray from the rapids hit the two friends like a welcome, cooling drizzle. Bryony looked at the wild rapids, foaming and leaping as they dashed downhill towards the mountains.

'Look at that water! No wonder Duddle said he wouldn't dare take the raft down this way, it's dreadful!'

Togget pointed ahead. 'Yurr oi think et wursens yonder, 'ark at ee roaren et makes!'

A short distance further on they saw the mist-shrouded rainbow and the roar increased in volume until they had to shout aloud at each other to be heard above it.

Soaked and bewildered they found a small cavelike crevice to one side of the waterfall's edge. Crouching inside, Togget dug out a turnip and watercress flan, and they shared it, together with a flask of cowslip cordial. They peered in fascination at the colossal torrent, falling so far down that it was lost in an almost solid white spray of mist.

'Whurr do et all go to, miz Broinee?'

'I'm not certain, Togget, but I think it must fall into some big lake below and stream off into the mountains.'

Bryony suddenly realized how close to the mountains they were; the falls seemed to drop into their very side. 'Well, I'll have to figure out a way to get down there to the bottom of this waterfall. If Veil was here, he couldn't avoid going over. What an awful thing to happen to anybeast, Togget.'

'Hurr aye, missie, oi knows 'tis 'ard, but us doan't 'spect to foind maister Veil still aloive, do us?'

Bryony clasped the mole's paw earnestly. 'You don't have to go down there, Togget. I won't have you risking your life to find Veil.'

The good mole's face was earnest as he replied, 'Oi doan't go, then you'm b'ain't goen. Oi cummed this furr with ee, Broinee, burr, an' oi b'ain't aven ee riskin' yore young loif furr ee wuthless vurmin alone, no zurr!'

It was evening before they were ready to descend the slippery rocks. The two friends were ill equipped for their task; after an exhaustive search of the area all they came up with was a few short lengths of vine. Using their belts and the haversack sling they knotted them all together. Bryony fastened one end to Togget's waist and the other round her own, and wordlessly they set off down the slick, waterworn rockface, with the deafening din of the torrent ringing in their ears. Bryony went first, Togget taking the strain as she scrabbled and slid to a smooth ledge. She waited until he had scrambled down beside her before taking a look around.

There seemed no way off the ledge, except for a series of rocky protuberances on one side, half covered by the falling water. Carefully the mousemaid lowered herself to the first one, feeling Togget slip slightly as he was pulled by the tension on their lifeline. He waved a digging claw to show he was all right and she began the descent to the next. Suddenly a chunk of driftwood hurtling past on the waterfall struck Bryony, and she slipped, but managed to grab on to a spur. Battered by the falls and fighting for breath she hung on tight, barely able to hear her molefriend above the pounding cascade.

'Oi'm cummen, missie, 'old on!'

As Togget climbed down to her he edged too near the waterfall; it caught him and swept him away like a leaf in a gale. A split second later, Bryony screamed as the

improvised rope tautened like a bowstring and cata-
pulted her off the spur after him. Bound together both
mole and mousemaid were carried off by the raging
waterfall.

41

Swartt had been going long and hard. He had cleared the big hills behind Salamandastron in two days, without either food or sleep, but now he had to rest, to stop awhile before he dropped. The Warlord crouched beside a stream flowing out onto the heathland, his tongue lolling from one side of his mouth. Panting like a winded dog, he awaited the arrival of the rest. The vixen fell in a breathless heap alongside him and splashed water into her open mouth with both paws.

Swartt kicked her. 'S'bad for yer, it'll make yer sick, y'won't be able to run!'

Nightshade lay back, her flanks twitching and quivering. 'Makes no difference now, Lord. I'm old, I can't run any more, whether you want me to or not!'

The ferret pawed water over the back of his neck. 'So, what're you goin' t'do, vixen, stop here an' be slain by the badger? That's what'll happen if yer don't move.'

Nightshade watched the rest lolloping up and dropping exhausted by the stream. 'I've got a plan, Sire, listen. You take five and twenty with you, leave me the rest with some bows and arrows. Look to the east there – see that fringe, it's woodlands. Keep low and stay in the stream; 'tis only shallow, but the water will cover

308

your tracks. Once you make it to the trees, wait there for me. I still have poison. We will lay an ambush; those who are hunting us will be coming fast, with the badger in the lead. They won't be expecting a sudden shower of poison shafts. We'll let fly at them, then we'll use the streambed to follow you. I think my idea is our best hope.'

Swartt stared curiously at his seer. 'Yer an odd one, vixen, why would you do this fer me?'

Nightshade closed her eyes. 'You are not defeated yet, Lord. I follow my visions. I see the badger laid low at your footpaws, you standing atop of a mountain, smiling and victorious . . .'

Swartt's eyes lit up, and he leaned towards Nightshade. 'More, tell me more, what d'you see then?'

The seer opened her eyes and shrugged. 'Then it gets hazy and I see an old female badger, silver with seasons, very ancient and wise looking, then I wake.'

The Warlord brought his chainmailed sixclaw down hard. 'The badger laid low, me victorious. This is a good dream – it's not over yet. As for your old silver female badger, when I've finished with Sunflash I'll find her an' slay 'er!'

Nobeast was more surprised than Sunflash the Mace when Rockleg and Fleetrunn caught up with him. He was facing the bottom of the final hill when the two hares came loping swiftly along and saluted him.

'Splendid day for huntin' vermin, Sire, wot!'

The badger halted, his chest heaving as he sucked in air. 'Where in the name of fur did you two spring from?'

Fleetrunn gestured over her shoulder. 'Actually, there's more followin', we're the jolly old front runners, makin' the pace, scoutin' ahead an' so on.' She unslung a canteen from her back. 'Here, Sire, care for a drop o' the ole oat'n'barley water, rather good in this hot weather, y'know.'

Gratefully, Sunflash took a brief sip, scanning the sky. Skarlath came soaring out of the blue and landed beside him. 'Kreeh! Eight vermin and the vixen are awaiting your arrival over this hill, they are laying an ambush, with archers!'

'Well sighted, my friend. What of the Sixclaw, where is he?'

'Swartt and the rest are following a shallow streambed towards the forest to the east, staying in the water so that they cannot be tracked.'

Sunflash turned to the two horses. 'Here is what we'll do. You wait here until the rest of your Long Patrol arrives, I'm going off to skirt this hill and pick up the streambed south of here. Watch the sky; when you see Skarlath dive then you may charge the vermin, but do it carefully, keep out of arrow range. When you hear me attack then come in fast. Take your Long Patrol to this hilltop and watch for my hawk's signal.'

It was hot and uncomfortable in the depression around the stream, and those with Nightshade were anxious and impatient. The shallow water had been warmed by the sun and the presence of the vermin caused a cloud of midges and gnats to descend upon them. Nightshade swatted at the insects, sweat blurring her vision as she tried to focus on the hillslope in front of her. A quarrelsome rat drank some streamwater and spat it out, complaining, 'Yurk! Doesn't taste too good after twenny odd pair o' dirty paws 'ave been sloshin' through it!'

Tension hummed on the air as the vixen snapped at him, 'Then don't drink it, fool, keep your eyes on the slope and your claws on that bowstring. Lord Sixclaw wants no slip-ups.'

A burly weasel scoffed as he spoke his thoughts aloud. 'No slip-ups eh? Lissen, mate, it's been one long round of slip-ups since I took up with this lot, an' who was

310

the one who did all the slippin' up, eh? Ole Sixclaw, that's who!'

The vixen stared hard at the burly weasel. 'I'll tell Lord Swartt you said that when we catch up with him in the forest – or would you sooner tell him yourself? You look like a big brave beast.'

The rat who had complained about the water signalled the vixen. 'Look, atop of the hill, I kin see those 'ares, they're watchin' us!'

Nightshade could barely see a few javelintips and long ears poking over the hilltop. 'Aye, they're up there sure enough. Strange, I wonder what they're waiting for?'

The burly weasel ventured an opinion. 'Some sorta signal maybe?'

Then the vixen spotted Skarlath, hovering halfway between the streambed and the hares. 'That's it, the badger's hawk, it must be able to see something that we can't. I'll stop it spying on us!'

Wiping the moisture from her eyes, the vixen rubbed dirt on her paws to prevent them slipping. She selected an arrow, sighting down the shaft to make sure it was straight and true, from feathered flight to poisoned barb. Testing the air with her eartip, Nightshade noted with satisfaction that there was not even a slight breeze to ruffle the still summer noon. Notching the shaft to her bowstring she took aim and drew the arrow back until the yew wood bow bent almost to a perfect semicircle.

Then Skarlath dropped from the sky, giving the signal.

Nightshade was quick, she dropped her aim instantly and fired. The arrow struck home. Skarlath gave a piercing cry, and his wide wings flopped loose as he tumbled to earth.

The vixen turned in triumph to the others when she saw Sunflash charging along the streambed from around the bend in the hill. Her courage drained from her. The huge Badger Lord pounded towards her, bellowing out his grief and rage. Dropping the bow she fled, deserting the vermin in the depression. They turned too late. Sunflash was amongst them with an earsplitting roar.

'Skarlaaaaath!'

On top of the hill Sabretache heard the Badger Lord's anguished cry and saw the hawk lying halfway down the hill, a bundle of feathers and a broken arrow. The hare Captain drew his sabre.

'Long Patrol! Eeulaliaaaaaa!'

The hares came charging down the hill, dust rising in clouds from their paws, weapons at the ready. With a bound they sprang into the depression. The stream was slowly being dammed, choked by dead vermin and smashed weapons. The berserk Badger Lord had done his work, and now he was gone. Sabretache signalled them forward, and they rushed off in a spray of streamwater, following the shallow bed towards the distant forest.

Nightshade ran as she had never done before. Paws pounding, brushy tail standing out behind like a streamer, her heart banged like a triphammer as she fought to suck in the hot air. The wound in Sunflash's footpaw had reopened, tingeing the streamwater red as he sped roaring in the wake of the beast who had slain Skarlath. Terror lent speed to the vixen; she dashed for the shelter of the forest, well ahead of the badger, though a quick glance over her shoulder confirmed that he was beginning to shorten the gap between them. Blinded by tears and aching all over from battle wounds, the Badger Lord pursued his enemy doggedly, determined to catch up with the lighter, swifter fox.

Swartt was well within the woodlands, ravaging a wild cherry tree with the rest of his vermin. He turned swiftly at the approaching patter of paws. It was a stoat he had left on watch at the forest edge.

'Lord, I climbed a tree and saw your vixen,' gasped the stoat. 'She is running fast towards these woods, with the badger hard on her tail. There are no others, he must've slain those you left to ambush him, it looks like Nightshade escaped! There are hares too, more than half a score, coming up fast!'

The Warlord did not hesitate. He took off north into the trees taking his band with him. 'The vixen bungled the ambush,' he growled. 'If the badger catches her, well, that's 'er lookout. If not she'll pick up our tracks an' find us. But that badger an' his hares can track too, so move yerselves if you want ter stay alive!'

Nightshade made the forest cover on trembling limbs. Expecting Swartt and the others to be waiting there, she slowed her pace as she dashed into the trees yelling for assistance. 'Lord, the badger's after me! Get him! Cut him down!'

But no help was forthcoming. Staggering with exhaustion the vixen loped off through the woodland. The crash of heavy footpaws pounding through the undergrowth in her wake caused Nightshade to turn her head fearfully. She tripped over an exposed tree root and fell flat. She managed to scramble halfway up before a huge footpaw knocked her down again. Sunflash the Mace stood over her, tears coursing down the golden stripe, his massive paws shaking with fury as he raised the great warclub. Nightshade scrabbled against the earth. 'No, Lord! Mercy pl. . . Yaaaaaggh!'

Sabretache leapt over the carcass of the dead seer, following the trampled undergrowth to where the badger lay, too exhausted to rise and shaking with grief, now that the bloodwrath had left him.

'Skarlath,' he wept. 'Skarlath, my true friend.'

The hare sheathed his blade, speaking low to his followers. 'Camp here tonight, it'll be twilight soon. Rockleg, Fleetrunn; attend to Lord Sunflash, rebind his wounds. Hedgepaw, see if you can fetch some clean water from the stream, the rest of you stand easy. We'll pick up the ferret's trail at dawn.'

Refreshed by his rest in the woods while waiting on the results of the ambush, Swartt drove his band hard. Soon after dawn he came across a wide river flowing down through the trees. Halting his band for a short rest he drank sparingly and waded in to test the depth of the water. The weasel called Grayjaw waded into the shallows beside him. 'It looks deep in the middle, Chief. Wonder where this river goes?'

Swartt was not listening. He was facing upstream, staring at the green slopes of the distant mountains.

'Up on yer paws, you idlers,' he shouted to the horde. 'That's where we're bound, the mountains upriver. Stay in the shallows, stick t'the water, it'll make trackin' difficult fer the badger. Come on!'

Grayjaw splashed alongside the Warlord. 'But Chief, what about Nightshade, you said she'd be able to follow our trail?'

Swartt looked pityingly at the weasel. 'If the vixen was goin' to catch us up she'd 'ave done it durin' the night. Ferget that one, I'm more concerned about that badger an' his hares. If we can make it t'those mountains I'll think up a good plan to deal with 'em.'

Sunflash and the Long Patrol were a day behind Swartt and his band. They arrived at the river in the late evening and made camp on the bank.

Sabretache inspected the bruised and broken overhead foliage of the trees that dipped to the water's edge. 'Hmm, about a score an' five of 'em, tryin' t'put us off the trail by takin' to the water. See here – willow branch cracked, leaves bruised an' damaged on that rowan further along. Hmph! One of 'em even stepped ashore for a while an' left a few pawprints on the bank edge, see, a stoat.'

Sunflash had waded in almost waist deep, wanting to feel the cold current pushing against him. He stared up at the mountains, distant in the gathering dusk of the dry summer day. 'We'll take only a short rest now and travel by night,' he said. 'It's cooler and we don't need to track any longer. Swartt has gone to the mountains, I feel it in me. When he attacked Salamandastron I thought we would meet there, but it was not to be. Still, one mountain is as good as another when there's a score to be settled with a sixclawed ferret!'

42

Bryony regained her senses in a pale flickering world. Somewhere close by, the sounds of the waterfall carried to her, echoing all around. She was draped across a rock slab, up to her waist in water. Togget's face was next to hers; he was still unconscious, but breathing slowly. Surprised that she was still alive, the mousemaid stood swaying groggily with the water lapping gently around her. As she heaved Togget's limp body up onto the rock, she noticed that the lifeline had held. Unfastening it from both their waists Bryony coiled the line and shouldered it.

She climbed up on the rock slab alongside the mole and took stock of their surroundings. It was a gigantic cavern inside the mountain. Redwall Abbey would have easily fitted into it with room to spare. The waterfall formed a broad river, dotted with rock islands and natural stepping stones. Luminosity from the river flickered all round, forming shifting liquid light patterns on the high rock walls and surfaces. It was a timeless world where neither night nor day held sway, forever bathed in its own pale radiance, constantly echoing to the sound of water everywhere, flowing, falling or trickling.

Their food haversack came floating gently by. Bryony hooked it out and emptied the contents onto the rock slab. The fruit was all right; she wiped off an apple and took a bite.

Togget stirred, opening his eyes slowly. 'Yurr, be this place Dark Forest? 'Tain't loik oi 'magined et t'be. Broinee, be us'n's dead or still a livin'?'

The mousemaid chuckled and unstoppered a flask of dandelion and burdock cordial. She passed it to Togget, who sat up blinking like an owl and drank deeply. 'Hoourr! That's betterer, missie. Yurr us'n's shorely landed en a roight strange burrow.'

The mousemaid relieved him of the flask. 'Well at least we're still alive. Most of our food is ruined by the water, though – a bit of fruit and this cordial seems to be all we have. Rest a while here, then we'll search for Veil. If we've survived the waterfall then I'm sure he did.'

Togget wrung moisture from his tunic. 'Burr, wot if'n ee diddent survoive?'

The mousemaid was unwilling to contemplate such an idea. 'Don't say that, Togget. He is alive, I'm almost certain he is.'

The faithful mole shook his velvety head. 'Hurr, Broinee, you'm wasten yore luif a chasen after yon furret, ee'm a badbeast an' will bring you'm nought but 'arm!'

Bryony packed what little food was still edible into the wet haversack and started the search. 'Veil wasn't always bad. Remember when he was a tiny Dibbun? He was such a nice babe. He'll change one day, you'll see.'

Splash!

A large rock hit the water nearby. 'He'll change! He'll change!' a voice echoed eerily. 'Hahaha! Are you fools still followin' me?'

Bryony whirled and looked upward. Veil was standing on a ledge behind them, the luminescent light playing oddly across his face. He waved a crimsoned paw at them and vanished into a dark crack in the cave wall.

Bryony clambered over the wet rocks, with Togget following. She shouted as she made her way to the spot where Veil had been. 'Wait, Veil, please wait for us! He's alive, Togget, I knew it!' The crack turned out to be a concealed entrance to a winding tunnel. Hurriedly the two friends pursued Veil into the dank musty darkness.

The young ferret crouched in a niche, hidden from Bryony and Togget. They dashed by, bumping and stumbling blindly, trying to catch up, as they thought, with Veil. Sniggering silently to himself, the ferret listened to their footpaws recede down the dark tunnel. It had been easy to trick them. He made his way back out onto the ledge, intending to run off and leave them searching the winding tunnel for him.

Then he noticed the slab. It was a broad, heavy oblong of rock precariously perched higher up on the brink of another ledge. Veil climbed nimbly up to it, and found that he had only to lean on the slab and it rocked. Rubbing his paws together delightedly, he began rocking the big flat piece of stone. The harder he pressed and jerked both paws on it, the more it rocked. With a groan it slid forward and downward a little. Veil could hear Bryony and Togget calling him; they were obviously coming back to the tunnel entrance. He jumped wildly on the tilting rock, bouncing up and down for all he was worth; the rock wobbled perilously on the brink of the ledge, inching forward, then it went altogether. Veil threw himself from the teetering slab; sitting down hard on the ledge he watched the stone slip over the edge. It slid down, stopping only when it reached the lower ledge, blocking the crack which formed the tunnel entrance. The ferret's face was a picture of fiendish delight as he climbed down to survey his work.

The slab was wedged immovably into the crack, sealing the tunnel. He leaned his back against it, laughing. 'Hahaha! Now try an' follow me, Abbey oafs!'

He could hear the frantic scratching from the other

side of the slab. Bryony's voice was shocked and reproving. 'Veil! What have you done? Let us out of here. Please!'

The young ferret turned and walked away. 'Why don't yer try movin' it with kindness? Goodbye an' good riddance to the both of yer!'

'That was neatly done!'

The big lean ferret, surrounded by a score or more heavily armed vermin, stood paw on swordhilt watching Veil. He came forward, walking around the young ferret, inspecting him curiously from ear to footpaw.

'Friends of yores, were they?' he said

Veil eyed the other coolly. 'Don't have friends – they were my enemies!'

One or two of the vermin hordebeasts, who had followed Swartt since the early days, began nudging each other and nodding towards the two ferrets. Apart from their age difference they were almost identical, the one being almost a younger edition of the elder.

Swartt fixed the young ferret with his piercing gaze. 'What's yer name, an' how did y'get 'ere?'

The young ferret stared boldly back at the Warlord. 'I came in over the waterfall; they call me Veil Sixclaw the Outcast!'

There was an audible gasp from the hordebeasts as Veil continued, 'I know who you are, you're Swartt Sixclaw the Warlord!'

They stood with their eyes locked, staring each other down.

Swartt smiled mirthlessly, his voice heavy with sarcasm. 'Yer a hardfaced brat, aren't yer? Veil – who gave you a name like that?'

Before Veil could reply, Grayjaw came splashing along from the far end of the cave, shouting, 'Chief! The badger an' those hares are comin' upriver, they'll be 'ere in a couple of hours!'

Swartt pointed to the ledges and craggy galleries leading into the darkness overhead. 'C'mon, let's see which way that takes us!'

Veil stood in Swartt's path. 'What about me? I can fight.'

The Warlord brushed him aside contemptuously. 'Stay out o' my way, brat, I got enough trouble t'deal with!'

Veil smiled thinly. 'Aye, so it seems. Looks like the badger defeated yer an' yer on the run. Huh, some Warlord!'

Swartt almost lost his balance. Stung by the insult, he shot a venomous glare at the young ferret as he began climbing. 'Step careful around me, whelp – a smart tongue could be the death of yer!'

43

Sabretache stood out in the shallows, peering at the dark, shaded cave where the river exited from the mountain. He signalled to Rockleg and Fleetrunn. 'Scout it out, chaps, go easy, see the villain hasn't laid any traps, ambushes or nasty surprises.'

The hares sat on the bank, making a hasty meal whilst they awaited the return of the Long Patrol scouts. Sunflash sat apart from them, the food by his paw untouched, two great rivulets scored deep from eye to jaw where his tears had run. Bradberry sat next to Sabretache, watching the Badger Lord from the corner of his eye.

Sunflash took a leaf, split it and pressed it to his lips, then he blew, producing a long, high-pitched whistling sound, then he dropped the leaf and watched it float away downriver. A great shuddering sigh ran through him as he buried his gold-striped face in both paws.

Bradberry whispered to the hare Captain, 'What did he do that for?'

'That was the way he called Skarlath sometimes, old lad. They were t'gether a jolly long time, doncha know. It'll take some seasons before he stops grievin', poor chap.'

It was not long before the scouts were back. They reported the way clear. Weapons drawn, the hares entered the cave, wading through the river with Sunflash in the lead. Once inside the scouts went ahead again. Sunflash and the others gathered on a rock islet in mid-river. Standing silently, they stared into the pale, eerie stillness of the huge cavern.

Sabretache drew his blade. 'Hist! What's that noise?'

It was a clack clacking sound, as if somebeast were knocking one rock against another. Bradberry murmured to Hedgepaw, 'It could be them, layin' a trap for us, maybe. Where's the sound comin' from?'

Hedgepaw looked about and shrugged. 'Hard t'say, too much echo an' waternoise in here. I say, is that Rockleg an' Fleetrunn comin' back?'

Rockleg made his report to Sunflash. 'Thumpin' great waterfall back there, they never went that way.'

Sunflash looked up at the high ledges and galleries winding away into the darkness above, and nodded. 'Then they're in here somewhere. Sabretache, take the Long Patrol outside and climb to the top of the mountain. It's my guess that's where Swartt will be making for. I'll stay in here and find my way up from the inside; we may be able to trap them in between us. Those are my orders. Go!'

The hare Captain saw it was useless arguing, but he tried. 'Sire, p'raps you'd best take Rockleg an' Fleetrunn with you.'

The Badger Lord splashed into the water and began wading to the side of the cave where the ledges began. 'I'll be all right on my own. Do as I say!'

Sabretache decided it was better not to argue further.

When the hares had gone, Sunflash stopped a moment. The clacking noise could still be heard echoing amid the watersounds of the cavern. He climbed onto the first ledge and the sound seemed to grow closer.

Moving along the natural rock step he stopped by a large slab.

Clack! Clack! Clack!

Sunflash pressed his muzzle to a narrow crack between the slab and the ledge. 'Is there somebeast there?' he shouted.

The noise stopped and a voice called back, 'Burr aye, thurr be two of us'n's trapped en yurr!'

The badger gave the rock a few solid thumps with his paw. He felt a very slight movement. 'I'll try and get you out of there, stand back!'

Climbing onto the ledge above, Sunflash found he could reach the top of the slab with both footpaws. Bracing his back, he pressed his full weight upon the slab and began pushing outward. The slab keeled forward then jammed. 'I've pushed the top away a bit,' he called down. 'Climb up the slab, you should be able to squeeze out over the top. Here, get hold of this.'

Holding his mace upside down, he thrust it in the space with the handle cord dangling down. Bryony's voice reached him. 'I've got it – can you give me a tug out, please?'

Sunflash hauled her swiftly out. Togget took a bit longer because of his plumpness, but he finally popped out like a round furry stopper.

As introductions were being made, there was a screech and something splashed into the river. Sunflash waded in, and came out carrying a bat with an arrow piercing its wing.

Bryony came forward to help him. 'Oh the poor creature, lay him down here, sir!' she cried.

Fortunately the shaft had done no great damage, merely piercing the filmy wing membrane. Bryony snapped the shaft and drew the end carefully out, speaking gently. 'There, that didn't hurt, did it. You'll soon be as good as new when it heals.'

The bat bared its small fangs, in what appeared to be

a smile, thanking the mousemaid in a soft sibilant whisper. 'My thanks, thanks. I am Lord Duskskin, ruler of Bat Mountpit, Mountpit. Up above is my territory, territory. Wicked creatures are there, they are armed, armed, my bats can do nothing against them, nothing against them.'

Duskskin gave them a brief description of his encounter with Swartt and the hordebeasts, with his curious, echoing speech. Sunflash interrupted him. 'The vermin are my enemies. I am sworn to slay them. Can you show us the way up to where they are, Lord Duskskin?'

The ruler of Bat Mountpit blinked his tiny pinpoint eyes. 'You are a mightybeast, carry me, carry me, I will show you.'

High above in the far upper reaches of the mountain a dozen or more bat corpses littered the rock ledges. Swartt and his beasts had stopped to rest briefly, ducking their heads as angry bats homed in on them. A rat let fly an arrow and it bounced off the stones, dropping out of sight into the dizzying chasm below.

Veil watched the rat notch another shaft to his bow. 'Do you always let them waste arrows like that upon creatures that can't harm yer?' he sneered.

Swartt aimed a glancing blow at a passing bat. 'Keep yer mouth shut, brat, 'cos if a bat don't fly down it then my blade will!'

Veil looked up at the slender shaft of sunlight coming from somewhere above them. 'Well, you sit 'ere thinkin' up clever insults an' lettin' these wall-eyed idiots waste their arrows. I'm climbin' up ahead to see where that light's comin' from.'

Swartt snarled, half drawing his sword as Veil pushed past him. The young ferret grabbed a hefty chunk of rock and tossed it threateningly from paw to paw. 'Draw that blade an' I'll let daylight into yer skull!'

Swartt did not attempt to pull his sword out; he sneered upward as Veil began climbing. 'Hah! Big talk fer a pup still wet be'ind the ears. Once I'm done wid the badger I'll fix you, that's a promise!'

Veil smiled easily down from a crag he had just surmounted. 'Talk's cheap, deadpaw – we'll see who fixes who in the end!' Without a backward glance he continued his ascent.

The rat was about to fire another arrow, when Swartt laid him flat with a blow from his chainmailed sixclaw. 'Stop wastin' those shafts, maggotbrain, you couldn't hit the sea if you was standin' on the edge of the shore!'

Youthful agility soon brought Veil up to the source of the light. It was coming from a knothole of a small timber door set into the rock. Pulling aside the bar that held it closed, he kicked the door open and crawled out. Blinking in the sunlight, Veil found himself looking down from the mountaintop. He walked around a flat plateau.

Far below the hares could be seen, toiling upward through the steep, bush and shale coated mountainside. It was but the work of a moment for Veil to tumble loose chunks and slabs of the shale down at them. He watched, sniggering like a malicious Dibbun, as the missiles started up small avalanches of loose scree and rock. Hares dived for cover and hung on to the deeper rooted bushes, helpless because of the distance and unable to return arrow, slingstone or javelin at their tormentor. Veil chuckled to himself; this was real power. He loosened more slabs and watched them hurtle and bounce off down the slopes in clouds of reddish dust. The young ferret wished fervently that it might have been Redwallers and not hares that he held at his mercy.

Meanwhile, Sunflash climbed stealthily up through the rocky galleries, holding the Bat Lord Duskskin on one shoulder and listening to his whispering repetitive directions. Bryony and Togget were no trouble; the big badger lifted them up onto the rocks ahead, one in each paw, as if they weighed nothing at all.

Togget was staggered by the might of their gold-striped friend. 'Yurr, ee be's a gurt strong un, oi feels loik a liddle pebble bein' chucked abowt, hurr, ee'm gentle tho'!'

Duskskin cautioned the mole to be silent. 'Quiet now, quiet. Foebeasts are not far above us, far above us.'

Unfortunately Swartt had already heard them, as the echoes of their voices bounced up from the lower galleries. Since Veil had opened the door at the mountaintop, there was a fair-sized shaft of light beaming down. Swartt looked up, judging the distance he had left to climb, an idea forming in his mind. He chose the rat he had chastised and three others – two stoats and another rat, all armed with bows.

Keeping his voice to a bare minimum the warlord whispered, 'You four stop here awhile, and take care o' any bats or small beasts that're followin' behind. I'll be up on the mountaintop with the others. Come an' join us there when the coast's clear down 'ere. That's a nice soft job for ye, eh!'

Silently Swartt led the other vermin off towards the high exit.

Sunflash had just placed Togget on a rocky outcrop above his head when an arrow came hissing down like a snake and struck the mole in his shoulder. Swiftly the badger lifted the mole down and placed him alongside Bryony, saying, 'He's been wounded, take care of him and don't make a sound!' Then, laying aside his mace, Sunflash selected two good-sized throwing rocks and popped his head out into full view. The rat saw him and fumbled to get shaft onto bowstring as Sunflash flung a rock, hard and accurately.

Thud!

It struck the rat, knocking him off his perch. Silently he fell, bumping off ledges until he was swallowed up into the dark void of Bat Mountpit. Far below there was a splash.

A stoat showed himself, not far from where the rat had been. 'Wot's 'appened to Buskit? Anybeast seeeeeeeee!' The second rock knocked him flying into space.

The remaining stoat and rat glimpsed the great striped head as the badger stooped to pick up more rocks, and panic gripped them.

'Let's get outta 'ere, mate, it's the badger!'

Stumbling against each other, they scrabbled upwards towards the hole. Bats flew out, attacking them as they climbed.

Sunflash turned to Bryony and the Bat Lord. 'Stop here and tend to Togget. I've got to catch those two before they raise the alarm. Don't try to come out onto the mountain until I give you the all clear!'

Leaving his mace, Sunflash sped off after the two vermin, heaving his huge frame upward, paw over paw. His legendary swiftness had not deserted him; swinging from rock to ledge, jumping and pulling himself upward, the Badger Lord pursued the pair. The rat was scrambling up a smooth stone incline when the relentless paw of Sunflash grabbed his tail and swung him off. He fell, screeching.

Outside, the shades of twilight were beginning to fall. Swartt strode around the plateau, watching as his remaining hordebeasts sent rocks, arrows, spears and slabs of shale hurtling down the mountainsides, to batter the gallant but beleaguered hares, who were still striving to climb up and reach the foebeast. Veil stumped to the edge, staggering under the weight of a jagged slab. He hurled it gleefully down and dusted off his paws.

'Wot's the matter, scared o' gettin' y'self dirty?' he said insultingly to Swartt. 'Huh, some Warlord you are, I've seen more action from a squashed frog!'

'I dunno about squashed frogs,' Swartt gritted back angrily, 'but you'll be a squashed ferret if y'talk like that to me, spindleshanks!'

The Warlord left his vermin to their own devices. Crouching next to the opening, he listened intently. He heard the screech of the rat and then the agonized yelling of the remaining stoat as Sunflash caught up with him. Swartt chanced a quick peek into the opening and saw Sunflash, head bowed as he pulled himself upward. It was too good a chance to miss!

Swartt grabbed a big rugged slab of shale with both paws and raised it above his head, rushing to the far side of the opening, so he would be behind Sunflash when he emerged. He was only just in time – the Badger Lord came up so fast that he was halfway out of the hole before Swartt came to a standstill. The Warlord brought the rock crashing down on the back of the badger's skull, hitting him so hard that it broke the slab into two pieces. Sunflash fell senseless, half in and half out of the hole. Swartt yelled to his hordebeasts, 'Grab him, get some rope! Pull him out of there and bind him tight! I've got the badger!'

44

Down on the rocky outcrop, Togget gritted his teeth bravely. 'Hoo urr, oi diddent know arrers 'urted so much.'

Bryony inspected the barbed point of the shaft she had removed from her molefriend's shoulder. 'Hmm, at least it's not poisoned. You're a lucky mole. Lie still and let Lord Duskskin's bats see to the wound.'

Togget watched as several bats gathered round him. They stopped the bleeding with skeins of spiderweb, binding the arrow hole with mountain moss and a paste made from some strange type of cave fungus.

The mole swigged deep from a pitcher of lilac-coloured liquid. 'Umm, this do taste noice, ee flyen mouses be guddbeasts!'

The bats' hissing laughter sounded like escaping steam. 'Flying mouses! Hihihihiss! Did you hear that, Lord Duskskin? The funnybeast calls us flying mouses, flying mouses!'

Lord Duskskin glanced up anxiously. 'It grows dark, dark. The mighty one has not called you, mousemaid. What is happening, happening?'

Bryony curtsied politely to the Bat Lord. 'Sire, will

you and your creatures take care of Togget until I return? I must go and see what is happening.'

The only protection Bryony had was the small knife that had been in their haversack. Gripping it firmly in her teeth, she began climbing slowly towards the exit hole.

A fire glowed in the centre of the plateau on the mountaintop. Sentries posted around the edge watched for any movement of the hares during the night. Not far from the fire lay Sunflash the Mace, still unconscious. The badger was bound between two broken spearshafts driven into the surface cracks, footpaws out straight and his forepaws stretched behind his head, the ropes cutting cruelly into them.

Swartt sat by the fire, hardening an ash javelin point in its flames. Veil crouched the other side of the blaze, watching the warlord. 'So, after many long seasons you've finally caught your enemy,' he said.

Swartt rubbed the smoking javelin end against a rock until it was like the tip of a great, dark brown needle, and snarled, 'Aye, many, many long seasons, longer than you've lived, brat!'

Veil enjoyed baiting Swartt. 'Just shows how clumsy you are, that badger'd 'ave been slain all those long seasons ago if he was my enemy.'

The Warlord smiled, refusing to rise to the bait. 'Addlebrain, 'ow many enemies have you ever 'ad, eh?'

Veil stared hard across the fire at Swartt. 'Oh, don't you worry, I've got a great enemy – the coward I've never called father, the slimy scum who ran off an' left me on a battlefield when I was scarce able to walk. Now that's an enemy whose grave I'll dance on an' laugh at!'

Swartt pointed the javelin at the inert form of the badger. 'Try it an' you'll die like this one will tomorrow, long an' slow, bit by bit, until he screams for me t'finish it!'

Bryony raised her head slowly and carefully, noting

every detail of the terrible scene on the plateau, from the sentries and the two ferrets at the fire, to the stillbound badger between two spearshafts. She knew she had to save Sunflash at any cost. Inching silently from the hole she flattened herself against the rocks and began squirming forward, the knifeblade gripped tight in her teeth. The mousemaid kept herself behind Swartt's back, shielding her body from the fireglow and Veil. All the sentries were looking down the mountain, one or two slumbering fitfully.

Something clacked faintly against Bryony's paw; it was a beaker, half full of whatever some hordebeast had been drinking. She paused; neither ferret had heard her over the crackle of the fire. Picking up the beaker, she circled, keeping on Sunflash's right side and out of the ferrets' vision. Inching stealthily forward the mousemaid reached Sunflash. Dark crusted blood stained the gold-striped muzzle; the Badger Lord lay quite still, his mouth slightly open. Holding the beaker up, almost too afraid to breathe, Bryony let the liquid trickle into Sunflash's mouth. Nothing happened for a moment, then the badger coughed and grunted. His head came up slightly, knocking the beaker askew so that the remaining liquid splashed in his face.

Bryony felt the shaft of the javelin strike her hard across her back. She was knocked flat.

'Hahah! Gotcher, mouse! What're y'doin' 'ere?'

Swartt seized her roughly and dragged the mouse-maid upright. Sunflash was coughing and gagging on the liquid trapped in his throat as Veil came racing around the fire.

'Yer scummy liddle sneak, you was tryin' to set 'im loose!' Swartt roared.

Veil struck Swartt hard in the face, tearing the captive from his grasp. 'Bryony, get out of 'ere. Run!'

Swartt flung himself on Veil and, while the ferrets fought, Bryony ran to where the knife had fallen from her mouth. Grabbing it, she began hacking at the ropes binding the Badger Lord's paws, screaming, 'Get up! Sunflash! Get up!'

Swartt threw his son down and raised his javelin for a throw he could not miss. 'The badger's mine!' he yelled.

Bryony turned and saw him throw the javelin. Something blurred across the front of her, shouting, 'Leave 'er alone! Uuuuuhh!'

Then Veil lay across her footpaws, the javelin protruding horribly where it had exited at his back. Bryony opened her mouth, but no scream would issue forth.

As Swartt ran forward, clawing at his sword, there was an earsplitting roar.

'Eeulaliaaaaaa!'

Both spearhafts snapped like twigs as Sunflash shot up from the rocks like a thunderbolt, eyes crimson, teeth bared, the ropes bursting as his huge chest swelled and he flung his paws apart. The sentries turned and, standing like frozen statues, they watched the awful conflict between Warlord and Mountain Lord.

Swartt's curved blade flickered in the firelight as he struck, gashing his enemy's side. Then he raised the sword and swung it a second time, aiming at Sunflash's head. Two great paws caught the blade in mid-air; the berserk badger tightened his grip on the blade, regardless of the blood that flowed as he did, the warrior spirit of his ancestors rising. The ferret stood open-mouthed as the badger snapped the swordblade, the sharp metallic clang echoing around the mountaintop. Still grasping both halves of the sword, Sunflash came forward with a bound, whirling both paws. He struck Swartt a blow that sounded like a plank hitting a rotten fruit. The force of the blow was so great that Swartt's footpaws left the ground, and he fell poleaxed. Nobeast could come near Sunflash the Mace; filled with the bloodwrath he seized the ferret in a grip of steel. Heaving Swartt high over his head, Sunflash stood at the plateau edge, bellowing as he flung his enemy out into the night.

'Eeulaliaaaaaaaaaa!'

The terrified sentries who had clambered over the plateau edge slid down the shale and scree on their tails. They were met by the vengeful hares of the Long Patrol, who had been racing upwards since the first sounds of combat from above.

Helped by several bats, Togget emerged onto the plateau and hurried to Bryony's side. The mousemaid was sitting with Veil's head resting in her lap. The young ferret's eyes were clouding over, his breath was hoarse and shallow; almost from the gates of Dark Forest he heard Bryony's voice echoing: 'Oh Veil, my Veil! You saved me . . . Why?'

'Go . . . back to your Abbey . . . shouldn't 'ave followed me . . . Go 'way . . . let me sleep!'

Bryony rocked him gently as she had done when he was a babe. The young ferret closed his eyes.

Thus ended the lives of father and son: Swartt Sixclaw the Warlord, and Veil Sixclaw the Outcast.

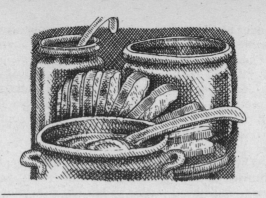

45

Three days they camped on the river's edge at the foot of Bat Mountpit, the full hospitality of Duskskin and his bats at their disposal. Wounds were dressed and weary limbs rested; they were brought fresh fruit, white mushrooms that had never seen the light of day, caveshrimp, and many other strange delicacies from the depths of the curious realm within the mountains.

Sunflash kept making Bryony and Togget repeat anything they knew of his mother, Bella of Brockhall, the great silver badger. He marvelled that she was still living and kept repeating her name over and over. 'Bella, Bella, I must see her, I will go to Redwall with you.'

For the first time in three days, the mousemaid smiled. 'What with my injured back, your cracked skull and Togget's wounded shoulder, we should just about make up one whole creature to go walking through Redwall's gates.'

Sunflash gave orders to his Long Patrol. 'Sabretache, you and Colonel Sandgall will command all at Salamandastron until my return. On your way back, search and find my hawk Skarlath, take him to the mountain and bury him high on a sunny slope, overlooking the sea. Rockleg and Fleetrunn, you will accompany me and our friends to Redwall Abbey.'

Lord Duskskin called them from the edge of the cave entrance. 'You will leave tonight, tonight. My scouts will go with you and guide you, guide you. I have sent out requests to my friends, friends. The Pollspike raft awaits you two days hence, two days hence. Go in peace, in peace!'

A full moon hung like a burnished shield in skies of deep velvet blue, watching the friends making their goodbyes. Togget had become very fond of the bats and promised he would return to visit them someday. 'Hurr, you'm watch owt furr Togget, gudd flyen mouses, burr aye!'

As they marched off on a secret route, which would take them around the waterfall, hundreds of bats wheeled around them in the night, whispering, 'Safe seasons, seasons. Goodbye friends, goodbye friends.'

Skirting the high rocks at dawn, Bryony looked back at the white mist with its rainbow. Sunflash helped her over a small gurgling brook, saying, 'Thinking of anything special, missie?'

Bending, the mousemaid let the brookwater run through her paws. 'Oh yes, sir, I'll never forget the waterfall as long as I live. It was so beautiful, but so dangerous. I'll hear those waters in my dreams for many a long season.'

The going was easy and late summer weather proved pleasant. A leisurely pace was dictated by their healing wounds, and the fact that Sunflash wanted to take cuttings and young plants from practically everywhere. Togget taught Rockleg and Fleetrunn to tug at their noses and speak in a rustic manner. Bryony could scarce stifle her laughter at the two hares and the mole, chewing on long straws and presenting the Badger Lord with

335

the strangest things, as they affected the tone of bumpkins.

'Oo arr, Lordy Sunnyflash, yurr be a wunnerful stone, may'ap if 'n ee plant it, 'twill grow into a bootiful pebblebush!'

Sunflash played them well at their own game, tossing the stone up and batting it out of sight with his mace, aping their speech: 'Whoi thankee, gaffer Rockleg, p'raps if yon pebble sticks up inna sky 'twill become a shiny star one night!'

Early in the morning of the third day they arrived at the junction of the river and slipstream. Immediately the bankvole Ilfril poked his head out in high bad temper. 'D'ye know you're trespassin'? Who are yer?'

The metal-studded end of a huge battle mace thudded down near the hole entrance, and Ilfril found himself staring into a great, gold-striped badger's face, whose voice boomed out: 'I am Sunflash the Mace, Badger Lord of Salamandastron, and I like a bankvole for breakfast each morn. Who are you?'

There was a frantic scuttle of paws as Ilfril fled down into his home, followed by a nervous squeak. 'Er, haha! Just a pore creature who lives down here an' minds his own business, Lord, feel free to walk anywhere!'

They sat laughing at the river's edge, watching the sprawling raft pull up to the bank. Duddle cried out heartily:

'Welcome friends, an' jump aboard,
Yore welcome to all we can afford,
There's the wife, two liddle uns an' meself,
An' plenty o' vittles upon the shelf!'

Arundo came dashing from the hut in the centre of the raft. He stared in awe at the badger, and said, 'Can I jump on yore thtomach, thir?'

Rockleg winked at the little hedgehog. 'Of course you can, ole chap, as long as y'let Lord Sunflash jump on yore stomach first, wot?'

Clematis Roselea came out to wag a paw at them. 'You know what will happen if my mama catches any of you jumpin' on each other's stomachs?'

Togget smiled and nodded. 'Aye, she'm cutten our tails off'n us wi' a single swipe, missie!'

Arundo confirmed this with a chopping sweep of his tiny paw. 'Thingle thwipe, thtraight off!'

Immediately they were aboard, Duddle cast off and lashed the tiller in position. Introductions were made all round and a happy band of voyagers retired to the cabin-hut, for a celebration breakfast.

Bryony thought the cabin seemed smaller, though it was only the massive presence of Sunflash within the confined space that created this impression. Even though the fragrant aromas arising from the stove in tantalizing wisps set his mouth to watering, Duddle Pollspike felt it was his duty to first make an announcement.

'Ahem! Good creatures all, before my goodwife Tutty an' m'self serve vittles, allow me to inform you about our course. I have charted a network of navigable waterways which will take us close to Redwall Abbey. So do not be alarmed, friends, you are in good an' capable paws. Now, my liddle riverplum, let us show these pore starvelings what a floatin' banquet looks like . . .'

Duddle was about to say more, when Tutty raised a ladle ominously. 'Faith an' fishgills, you ole windbag, are you goin' to blather on 'til suppertime? Stir yore stumps afore I chop yore tail off!'

Duddle draped a napkin over his paw, muttering as he gravitated between stove and table carrying heaped dishes. 'To hear is to obey, my violent violet, the banks'd be strewn with chopped-off tails if you had yore way. Gangway there, you ravenous rovers, make way for this wild cherry an' meadowcream pie, move that jug o' cowslip cordial, somebeast.'

Eyes widened as dish after dish was brought to table.

'One basin o' rivershrimp an' watercress soup!'

'Whitecheese with sage an' acorn, hot ryebread cottage loaf!'

'Almond an' chestnut slices with redcurrant preserve!'

'Damson an' greengage pudden. Been up since three hours afore dawn cookin' all this. Streambank salad with hazelnuts!'

Sunflash had both young hogs sitting on his lap. Clematis Roselea clasped his massive paw, cautioning him. 'You must be very good, sir, jus' like me. Don't dare touch anything until the table is set. Or else . . .!'

The Badger Lord pulled a frightened face and made the tail-chopping motion. Little Arundo nodded wisely. 'Ho yeth, my mama even chopth badgerth tailth off!'

Breakfast meandered on until past lunchtime. There was so much to tell: tales of mountain, waterfall and riverbank filled the cabinhut, and Arundo and Clematis Roselea listened open-mouthed, as their elders related stories, histories and reminiscences. Sunlight darted between the floating lilies of silent water meadows and shaded inlets as the raft cruised smoothly, wending its way down the broad river. It was, as Bryony later summed it up, 'A good time full of friends and fine food!'

Whilst Duddle went out on deck to tack into a north and east waterway, Rockleg persuaded Fleetrunn to sing a riddle song. She began by tapping a lively rhythm on the tabletop and, when they were all tapping in time with her, Fleetrunn sang.

'My first is in boulder and I have a stone,
My second is thrice in an apple alone,
My third may be found at the end of a hem,
My fourth starts a stick and a stop and a stem,

My fifth's in the middle of pop, but not pip,
My sixth is the second you'll find in a snip.
My first half can stop up a broad river's flow,
My second half no daughter, the other you know.
I'm found in pudden and pie and good wine,
And I know all your names, so can you tell me mine?'

There was much scratching of heads and gnawing of
paws as they tried to find the answer to Fleetrunn's
riddle song. Grinning cheerily, Duddle popped his head
in the window. 'Ahoy! I was listenin' to yore tune as I
was standin' at the tiller. Well sung, Fleetrunn, I ain't
heard the ole damson riddle song in many a season, my
ole dad used to sing it!'

Tutty flung an apple core at Duddle; he ducked and
came up still smiling, saying, 'Did I say something amiss,
my liddle flowin' duckweed?'

His wife stamped her footpaw, glaring at him.
'Flowers an' follies! You just told us the answer when
y'said damson riddle song; 'tis a damson, ain't it!'

Duddle climbed through the window and helped himself to a ladle of damson and greengage pudden. 'Right
first time, my winnowing willow, do I win a prize?'

The company fell about laughing as Tutty seized Duddle's ear. 'Pennycloud an' poppies! I'll give ye a prize,
you can wash all the pots'n'dishes, that's yore prize, you
great waterbumble!'

Throughout that day laughter broke out afresh as
Rockleg strode the deck of the raft, imitating Duddle
skilfully. 'Is it a damson, my delightful dandelion? Fetch
me a prize!'

46

Abbess Meriam was quietly enjoying the change of season. Paws tucked into her wide sleeves, she glided through the early morning mist which wreathed the orchard as if a cloud had fallen upon it. The coming days would see the beginning of harvest time, apples ranging from red to russet brown contrasted with mellow golden pears. Damp and dawn-dewed, the berries trailing from vine and creeper shone like jewels.

Meriam paused to look up at the vast Abbey rising from the mist; its warm red sandstone appeared softer, more dusky, in the day's first hours.

Without warning, the little molemaid Figgul came dashing through the misty ground swathe, and collided with the Abbess. Meriam steadied herself against a chestnut tree. 'Lack a day, little one, you nearly knocked the paws from under me. What is it?'

Figgul held up a fallen elm leaf excitedly. 'Hurr lookee, marm, ee leafs be turnen brown!'

Abbess Meriam smiled down at the mole, stroking her head. 'It's called autumn, the leaves become like this because trees do not need them in the winter season. You'll be able to help with the harvest, Figgul. I recall last autumn you were too small. Remember, Sister Withe let you sleep most of the day in an apple basket, but now you are big enough to help fill the baskets. Come on, we'd best go in to breakfast.'

Abbess and molemaid were soon swallowed up by the mist as they crossed the lawn towards Redwall's main Abbey door.

'Hurr, can oi cloimb to ee top of arpel trees, marm?'

'No, no, we don't climb the trees; if you shake the lower boughs the fruit that is ripe will fall.'

'Burr aye, then oi be a bough shaker an oi shake 'em gudd'n' 'ard!'

'You'll have to watch you don't shake any down onto your head. I remember a little mole named Togget doing that – he was knocked senseless by a big green pie apple.'

Hazy sunlight was dispelling the ground mist as Sumin the squirrel rapped his javelin on the threshold gate of Redwall. He had travelled through the night to reach the Abbey. He knocked once more. Barlom's voice called to him as he paced the path impatiently.

'Who goes there? Is it you, Sumin?'

'Of course it is, you know my knock! Open up, friend!'

The Recorder mouse swung the gates wide enough to admit the sturdy squirrel. Barlom brushed his paw along Sumin's tail. 'Tut, tut! Look at you, drenched in dew. Come and dry off.'

Sumin merely shook himself and strode purposefully off across the lawn towards the Abbey building. 'No time for that, mate – got news for the Abbess!'

Breakfast dishes were still being cleared; the servers dawdled close to the Mother Abbess's chair, staring curiously at Sumin, to overhear the news. Meriam fixed them with a cool glance as she rose from table, saying, 'Busy paws are far more useful than busy ears.'

Hurriedly, they resumed their duties. Meriam indicated by a flick of her eyelids that she would see Sumin in her study. When Sumin and the Abbess vacated the dining place, speculation broke out among the Redwallers.

'What d'you suppose it is?'

'Hope it's not vermin headed this way or anything nasty!'

'Ole Sumin looked as if he'd been travellin' hard, eh?'

Foremole spoke to them over the top of a tablecloth he was folding carefully into a neat oblong. 'Burr, ee be gurt gossipers! Oi 'spect ee h'abbess will tell you'm all when she'm gudd'n'ready, hurr aye, so she'm will.'

For what seemed an age the Abbess and Sumin remained closeted together, while the squirrel related news of the victorious battle. More Redwallers left off their chores and found excuses to be inside Great Hall, where they all stood about, doing nothing, yet trying to look industrious.

Friar Bunfold and Myrtle the hogwife came from the kitchens followed by a retinue of cooks and helpers. The Friar clapped flour from his paws and installed himself in the Abbess's chair. 'Might as well wait in comfort, come on, sit down you lot, no use pretendin' yore busy when you ain't. I'm plain nosey, always have been, make no secret o' the fact.'

Bunfold had just finished speaking when Meriam and Sumin entered. The Friar leapt up as if he had been sitting on a tack; vacating the Abbess's chair he began busily polishing an imaginary stain from the tabletop with a corner of his floury apron.

Abbess Meriam shook Sumin's paw heartily, smiling one of her rare smiles.

'Thank you so much, my friend. I'm sure there is lots of good hot food in the kitchens if you haven't eaten today.'

The stout squirrel needed no second invitation; he strode off eagerly. The Abbess flicked a little flourdust from her chair and sat, pausing to look around the waiting faces before she started speaking.

'By tomorrow noon I would like a feast set up. I know Redwall banquets have always been without equal, but let us try to make this particular one legendary!'

Myrtle raised a paw, trying to tease more information out. 'Er, 'ow many will we be cookin' for, marm?'

Meriam's answer set them wondering. 'Twice as many as usual should be adequate, Myrtle.'

Heartwood the old otter banged his walking stick down. 'Mother Abbess, will you please tell us what is going on here? Who are we expecting, why the legendary feast, tell us!'

A loud rumble of agreement echoed around Great Hall.

The Abbess held up her paws placatingly until silence fell. 'Please, friends, I know it looks as though I'm teasing you, but honestly, I'm not. All I can say is this. We are going to be visited tomorrow by friends, some old and others new to us. The reason why I can tell you no more is simply because gossip travels, and I do not want the surprise spoiled for a very dear friend, who shall remain nameless for the moment. So I appeal to you as Redwallers, do your job, well and silently, and I know you will be rewarded by a sight such as Redwall has never seen, the visitation of a great creature to our Abbey. I'm sorry, but that is all I can say for the present.'

Sister Withe banged the table so hard that everybeast jumped. 'Well, that will do me fine! Your word is good enough for me, Mother Abbess, and I'm sure I speak for all Redwallers!'

Everybeast hurried to agree.

'Aye, my lips are sealed!'

'Say no more, marm, nod's as good as a wink t'me!'

'You'm can trust us'n's, marm, ho urr!'

'Right! Let's get to it!'

343

'Aye, what're we all stannin' about like apples in an oven for? Come on, Redwallers, stir yore stumps!'

That day and the following night Redwall became a hive of activity. Flower gardeners staggered in under masses of blooms and blossoms, delivering them to mouse and molemaids appointed as table decorators. Otters performed acrobatic feats alongside squirrels, garlanding high wall- and windowledges with streamers, lanterns, flowers and flags. Crisp white table linen was unfolded and aired, embroiderers working on linen serviettes, and place mats. Fresh-dyed rush carpeting was spread on the twice-swept stone floors. Beeswax candles were trimmed and stuck in spiked sconces. Standing on a wide shelf in the kitchens, Friar Bunfold directed cooking operations, calling out in his high squeaky voice as he kept a professional eye on all.

'Bring more firewood, I need those ovens hotter than hot!'

Cooks called aloud to him as they worked.

'Will this be enough wild cherries an' almonds for the slices?'

'No, bring two bowls more, nothin' worse than skimped cherry and almond slices. You moles there! Make sure you lift that little un out of the deep bowl before you put in yore deeper'n'ever pie mixture, we don't want a small mole baked in a pie!'

'Hurrhurr, oi doan't moind, zurr, oi'd be warmed an' fed at ee same toime, hurrhurr!'

'Coom out'n thurr, Puckle, an' stop scoffin' ee pastry!'

'Big fruitcake's about ready for the oven, Friar!'

'Righto, Myrtle, start mixin' strawberries in with the meadowcream, not too many now, it's got to be pink, not red!'

'Watershrimps an' fresh button mushrooms, Friar, ottertwins just brought 'em in – where d'you want 'em?'

'Oh, right! Take them to Heartwood, and tell him not to let that hotroot pepper get near my hazelnut scones!'

'I 'eard you, Bunfold, the hotroot's goin' nowheres near yore scones; tell that squirrel to keep his honey away from my soup!'

'Brushtip, did you hear Heartwood? Mind what yore doin' with that honey – put plenty in the scone mixture. Oh, well done! That's a nice lattice tart cover, nothin' prettier than a blackberry an' pear tart with a good crisscross lattice of pastry on it. Open the top ovens, I can smell that bread, it's ready!'

'Friar, will you tell Brother Frimble that the cream is supposed to be piped onto woodland trifle in swirls, not blobs!'

'Oh, stop fussin', do it in swirls with blobs in between. Don't slice those candied chestnuts so thin, I like to see a fruitcake with chestnuts in big lumps on top, holds the maple syrup glaze better.'

Casks trundled out of the wine cellars, a Redwaller pushing each one, swerving and chuckling as they dodged others rolling cheeses from the storerooms. Trestles were set up to take the barrels of October Ale from the previous autumn, and jugs filled with cordials, fizzes and fruit cups were placed on serving trolleys. Window-ledges were lined with breads, cakes and scones, set out in rows to cool. Dibbuns waited as pails of crystallized fruits and nuts were opened, dabbing their paws into any of the thick syrup that overflowed onto the table-tops. Redwallers shuffled by each other on the dormitory stairs, some going down to work, others coming off duty to rest a few hours. It was activity the whole night through to next morning, two hours after daybreak.

The raft lay moored at a place named Wuddshipp Creek. Its passengers were met by a deputation of otters and squirrels, led by Skipperjo and the squirrel Redfarl. The warriors who had beaten Swartt off the path to Redwall stood lined on the banks as an honour guard. Pennants of bright hues tied to their lancetips and bows, they stared in open admiration as Sunflash the Mace came ashore. He was clad in a red cloak and wearing a tunic of creamy white belted by a woven green sash. He looked every inch the Badger Lord, from the mighty gold-striped head, which towered over even the long ears of his two hares, to the fearsome mace dangling from his massive scarred paws. When everybeast was assembled on the bank, Redfarl winked at Skipperjo; he cocked an ear, listened awhile, then nodded to her. 'Right y'are, marm, you do the honours!'

Redfarl bowed low to Sunflash. 'Sire, I beg yer, wait a moment, there are creatures comin' who have travelled far an' long to be with ye. Will ye tarry a moment, they'll be with us soon.'

The unmistakable voice of the squirrelhare Jodd sounded from beyond an ash thicket, further down the bank. 'This way, chaps, easy as y'go, wot. Ah, there they are!'

The lanky hare emerged leading a small band of creatures. 'What ho! Lord Sunflash, sah! An owl name o' Wudbeak told these goodbeasts you'd be comin' this way, and they insisted on journeyin' from their cave to be with you!'

Sunflash cast aside his mace and dashed to them, shouting, 'Tirry Lingl! Bruff Dubbo and Elmjak! Oh, my good friends! Dearie! Lully! Look at how your little ones have grown!' The two molemaids and the four young hedgehogs squealed with delight, threatening to topple the badger as they hugged his legs and footpaws.

Sunflash embraced the old moles. 'Uncle Blunn and Aunt Ummer, you look brisk as bumblebees!'

Whilst the Badger Lord was greeting his friends, Jodd wiggled his ears at Fleetrunn. He made an elegant leg at the pretty young hare, obviously stricken by her. 'I say, where'd you spring from, missie? You can call me

Jodd, all the chaps round here do. Er, would y'like to know my full name, miss?'

Redfarl shook her head at Fleetrunn. 'You don't want ter know that un's full name!'

Fleetrunn smiled coyly at Jodd. 'S'pose I'll get to know your full title soon enough, wot!'

Rockleg was an older hare and a confirmed bachelor; he winked at Skipperjo. The otter leader chuckled. 'Wait'll she sees ole Jodd tuckin' vittles away at table, that's enough to put anybeast off 'im fer life, matey!'

Skipperjo began bustling and hustling around the assembly. 'Stir yore stumps, me hearties, we can't dawdle 'ere all season, there's still a fair ways to go t'the Abbey!'

Dearie Lingl and Lully Dubbo extricated Sunflash from their young, who were swarming over him like ants.

'Bitty, Giller, Gurmil, Tirg, leave 'is pore Lordship alone, you'll 'ave 'im wore out afore he's much older!'

Lully called to her two daughters, 'Yurr Nilly, cumm Podd, show ee badger zurr wot us'n's bringed furr ee 'awkburd.'

She drew a small white cheese from under her apron and gave it to the molemaids, who presented it to Sunflash. The Badger Lord accepted it, shaking his head sadly. 'Come, friends, let's go to Redwall Abbey. I'll tell you some very sorry news as we walk.'

47

Sister Withe and Abbess Meriam were greatly surprised at what they found, on entering Bella's room, in the early morning of the day when Redwall was expecting its visitors. They were certain that nobeast had spoken of the coming festivities to Bella. Yet there she stood, shining silver from brush and comb, clad in a beautiful woven cloak of light purple, her head garlanded with a coronet of gillyflowers and young white roses.

Meriam bowed instinctively before the regal old badger, saying, 'Bella, you look magnificent!'

The silver badger picked up the carved, silver-mounted stick she used for walking. 'Thank you, Meriam, I felt that I must look my best on the day I meet my son the Badger Lord.'

Meriam gasped. 'But – how did you know? Who told you? Nobody but I knew—'

Bella sat in her armchair and shook the stick. 'Long before you knew of my son's arrival, I was told of it in a dream.'

Meriam nodded understandingly. 'Ah yes, your badger ancestors, no doubt.'

Bella beckoned to them both. 'Sit down, I have something to tell you. It was no long dead badger kin of mine that appeared in my dream, but one whom I knew well in the old days. Martin the Warrior, hero of Redwall and Chief Founder of this Abbey.'

Abbess Meriam's usual composure deserted her. 'Martin the great Mouse Warrior! He spoke to you?'

Bella closed her eyes, smiling happily. 'Yes, I can see him now. His message was not only for me, but for all Redwallers. Listen now. I was sleeping here in my chair, some moons ago, when he appeared before me. Full armoured and carrying his great sword, Martin told me of my son, of how he would defeat the Warlord Sixclaw and lose his friend Skarlath the hawk. He said that Sunflash would come to this Abbey when the leaves turned brown and that I would live to see him. He made me feel happy; a great peace, such as I have never known, filled my heart. Then he gave me this message to pass on to you . . .'

The two mice sat entranced as Bella spoke.

'Good creatures dwelling within these walls,
Be faithful, honest and true.
My spirit is near, when harm befalls,
I will comfort and counsel you.
Throughout all seasons, I will be here,
Fear neither evil, nor strife.
The Warrior protects all you hold dear,
To my Redwall comrades, long life!'

Soft morning sunlight flooded through the window, enveloping Bella in an aura of light, twinkling and sparkling off her ancient silver-furred form, clothing her in mysterious radiance.

Meriam's voice was hushed with wonder. 'Martin the Warrior is the spirit of peace and courage; our Abbey will remain safe for ever with him to guide us.'

Bella broke the spell, holding out her paws for assistance. 'Come on, you two young uns, help me up. Only a light breakfast today, save your appetites until after they arrive when the noon is high.'

By mid-morning everything was ready. Bella and the Abbess had pronounced the preparations well done and perfectly in order. Redwall's newest additions, Ole Hoffy the dormouse, with his grandmice, Young Hoffy and Brund, led the procession to the outer walltops. Banners and pennants fluttered in the breeze, flowers and vines were draped over the west and north-facing ramparts. Every Redwaller was scrubbed, brushed and wearing their festive finery. Sumin perched upon the northwest battlements, scouring path and woodland with his keen eyes, listening for any sound that would announce the arrival of visitors. A mood of gaiety prevailed; Dibbuns and young ones danced excitedly, their elders speculating eagerly.

'How big and fierce is a Badger Lord supposed to be?'

'Phwaw! Big as three of us stood atop of one another!'

'Aye, they'm sayen ee carry a gurt warclub, hurr, et'd take foive o' us'n's to lift it, they'm callen et ee macer!'

'Haha, if the Badger Lord's that big he'll take some feedin'!'

'Hurr oi wager ee'll eat more'n ten 'arebeasts cudd!'

Even Abbess Meriam's customary serenity was strained. 'Is it near midday, Barlom? I hope they'll be here soon. Can you see any sign yet, Sumin, do you hear anything?'

The little molemaid Figgul tugged Meriam's gown. 'Oi gets scolded furr arskin' too many questions, marm, moind ee owd badgermarm doan't send ee off t'bed, hurr!'

Bella pursed her lips in mock censure of the Abbess. 'She's right, Meriam, one more word from you and it's up the stairs and no feast! They'll come when they come, and not before, isn't that right, Friar Bunfold?'

'Right y'are, Bella marm, y'know what I always say:

Apples is ripe when they're ready,
When pears is ripe they'll fall,
What must happen will happen,
Or it won't happen at all!'

Heartwood glanced imploringly at the clear blue sky.
'Huh, that's a great comfort t'know an' no mistake.'

'Hist, there! Let me listen, quiet, everybeast!' Sumin
cupped a paw around his ear and, gripping the battle-
ment gable with his tail, he leaned outward facing north.
Silence fell over the Redwallers; every ear was strained
into the southerly drifting breeze.

Myrtle the hogwife coughed, and everybeast turned
to glare at her.

Then Sumin signalled wildly to Barlom. 'Throw open
the gates, it's them, I hear 'em comin'!'

Leading the column, Skipperjo stepped out of the
woodlands and onto the path, pointing with his javelin.

'There's the spire o' Redwall yonder, mates. Let's see
if 'n we can make 'em 'ear us. D'ye all know "Home
Returnin"?'

There was not a beast marching who had not heard
or sung the famous old marching song before. They
roared lustily:

'See the smoke curl from the chimney,
An' the mat beside the door,
On the path there stands the family,
Like you left 'em long before.
    Home returning, home returning,
    Seasons gone an' young uns grown,
    Home returning, home returning,
    Back to those I call my own!

There the fire burns and the ale brews,
And the bread bakes soft an' brown,
While my friends wait with the good news,

351

Bring my chair an' sit me down.
      Home returning, home returning,
      Comes the warrior from the war,
      Home returning, home returning,
      Home to wander nevermore!'

Voices rising to their limit, they sang the last chorus
over again, drawing out the last word with all their
might.

Bella gripped Sumin's paw like a vice. 'Do you see
my son? Where is Sunflash?'

The squirrel shook his head in admiration as he
pointed. 'I see him fine, marm! He strides out until they
run to keep up with him, he stands out like an oak
among ferns. Great seasons in the land! Now I know
what a Badger Lord looks like!'

The Abbess, Sumin and Ole Hoffy stayed to assist
Bella.

All the other Redwallers clattered down the wallstairs
to the main threshold gate, where they stood on the
path, waiting until Bella arrived, because it was her
special day above all days. The Abbey dwellers raised a
cheer as Bella stood out on the path, ready to lead them.
She turned smiling.

'Well, would you like to hear the warcry of a Badger
Lord? When I give the signal, shout out the word Eeul-
alia, but make it loud and long. Ready, set, go!'

'Eeulaliaaaaaa!'

Sunflash swung his mace in circles above his head
and, drawing air into his cavernous chest, he bellowed
back the badger warcry.

'Eeulaliaaaaa!'

Foremole clapped paws over both ears. 'Whurr, et
sounden loik thunder afore ee storm! Lookit, yurr he'm
a comen!'

Sunflash had caught sight of the silver badger leading
the Redwallers along the path. He knew it could be

only one creature, his mother, Bella. Passing the mace to Skipperjo, he ran the final distance, paws pounding the path like hammers, spurting dust up in a cloud, to the accompaniment of loud cheers from both groups.

He skidded to a halt and walked the last three paces slowly. There before him was the gentle old face he had seen in dreams. In the silence that followed, only two words were spoken.

'Mother.'

'Son.'

And that is how Sunflash the Mace, Lord of Salamandastron, came to Redwall Abbey and found his mother, Bella of Brockhall.

48

On that same hour of the next day, the feast was still in progress and showed no signs of slackening.

Bryony sat beneath her favourite old apple tree in the orchard with Barlom and Abbess Meriam. The Redwall Recorder had brought quill and parchment to document the mousemaid's story. She told it frankly, leaving out no detail. Abbess Meriam sat in silence until the recital was at an end.

The calm kind eyes of Redwall's Abbess met those of the mousemaid. 'So, Bella and I were wrong, there was some good in Veil, even though it cost him his life to show it. Can you accept my apologies, Bryony?'

The mousemaid kissed her Mother Abbess's paw respectfully. 'There is no need for your apology. Veil was bad, I know that now. Bella was right. Some creatures cannot help being the way they are. In all the time we knew him, Veil did not perform one act of kindness to any living creature. I have thought a great deal since he died and wondered if he would have saved me if he knew his father was really going to throw that javelin? I couldn't help loving him, because that's the way I am, but I know that the world is a better place without Veil or Swartt bringing death and misery to it.'

Meriam cast a knowing glance at Barlom before she replied, 'You have grown, Bryony. Your courage and compassion were never in doubt, but you have returned to us wiser and more sensible, far more mature than I ever was at your age. What do you think, Barlom?'

The Recorder finished rolling his scrolls. 'I think in the seasons to come Redwall will not lack a good Mother Abbess; that is, of course, marm, when you feel the need to pass on your title.'

Meriam placed a paw around Bryony's shoulders. 'I could think of no one better to be Mother of Redwall some day.'

Bryony could scarce believe what she was hearing. 'Me – Abbess of Redwall?'

'The same as Togget will be made Foremole when the time comes. You have both earned admiration and respect from many elders.'

Myrtle the hogwife trundled a fresh cart laden with hot scones, cheese and salad vegetables from the kitchens to the dining tables of Great Hall. Most of the feasters were resting, or playing with the young ones, but the die-hard core of trencherbeasts remained.

'Ain't you lot finished yet?' Myrtle groaned.

Rockleg smiled winningly at her. 'Not as long as there's such splendid food bein' served!'

Myrtle sighed, then sat down with them. 'Then I might as well join you; pass the mint tea please.'

Duddle Pollspike pushed it across obligingly. 'Mint tea, there you are, my chubby-cheeked chaffwarbler. It almost makes me wish I was a landlubber, dinin' in this wunnerful Abbey. What say you, my liddle larkspur?'

Tutty Pollspike looked up from a raspberry crumble. 'Lands an' lakes! 'Tis all very nice, but we've been water-beasts too long to change our ways now.'

Redfarl broke the crust of a pastie, letting the gravy

355

spill out. 'Wot about you, longshanks – thinkin' of changin' yore ways?'

Jodd cut himself a slice of fruitcake, a silly grin all over his face as he twisted his ears at Fleetrunn. 'Whazzat? Oh, er, rather! I'd sooner be a square any time than a hirrel!'

Fleetrunn giggled. 'Don't you mean you'd sooner be a hare than a squirrel, you great duffer? Fancy bein' called a squirrelhare, daft name!'

Jodd bolted the fruitcake reflectively. 'Oh, I dunno really. I don't mind daft names, as long as a chap has a good sensible real name. By the way, Fleetrunn, I never told you my real name, did I? Well, it's actually Wilthurio Longbarrow Sackfirth Toxophola Fedlric . . .'

Outside on the sunlit lawns of Redwall Abbey the happy laughter of old and young alike rose to mingle with high larksong on the warm autumn afternoon.

Epilogue

The young hare Burrbob twitched his nose inquisitively at Rillbrook the Wanderer.

'Is the tale finished? Oh, rats! I wanted it to go on an' on an' jolly well on f'rever!'

The old otter stood and stretched, balancing back on his rudderlike tail. 'Well, young cheekychops, y'know wot they say. There's bread an' cheese upon the shelf, want another story, tell it y'self.'

The harewife brought out rosehip and daisy cordial and some plum and damson cake. Together with the group of leverets she had been listening spellbound to the story, only absenting herself occasionally to bring food. Placing the cake and cordial in front of the old otter, she questioned him, 'What happened to Jodd and Fleetrunn? Did they marry?'

'Aye, and stayed on at Redwall. Rockleg didn't though, he came back to Salamandastron with Sunflash. But that was many seasons later, after old Bella had passed on to the Dark Forest. Sunflash would not leave the Abbey while his mother lived. She went peaceful and happy, long beyond her allotted seasons. They say no badger ever lived longer than Bella.'

'And did Bryony ever become Abbess?'

'Yes, she was in her middle seasons when Meriam retired and passed on the title to her. Togget became Foremole too. Now can I get on with this food, or are you goin' to ask me questions until I goes blue in me ole face answering?'

'Just one more thing. Is it true that Sunflash gave up being a warrior after he returned here? I have heard old ones say that he did.'

'No, he was always ready to defend the coastline or make war on searats and such vermin. Though he loved growing things so much that he was only known to his enemies as the Mace. Here at Salamandastron he cultivated the slopes of this mountain the way they are now, fertile and beautiful. As the seasons passed he became an expert farmer and creatures travelled from far and wide to learn from his great wisdom. In time, he changed his warrior name from Sunflash to the more gentle Sunstripe. Also he was the first Badger Lord to write poetry, an unusual quality in anybeast who was ever possessed by the bloodwrath.

'Here, come with me and I'll show ye something.'

Followed by a curious group of leverets, the harewife and Rillbrook made their way up a rocky path bordering a terraced garden. The otter halted at a stone slab seat. 'Watch now, I'll show you something my father showed me, just as his father showed him . . .'

The cheeky Burrbob muttered under his breath, 'An' his father showed him, just as his Auntie Bangtail showed him an' . . . Yowch!'

The harewife tweaked his ear warningly, and he fell silent as Rillbrook continued.

'There's not many seen this. My ancestors were showed it by an old Badger Lord who came after Sunflash. Here, watch now.' The seat was made by two flat slabs placed one on top of the other. He lifted the top slab to reveal the bottom stone beautifully carved in fine badger script.

Here I often gaze out o'er the seas,
When winter snows have gone to spring so fair,
Alone, except for butterflies and bees,
Remembering the times we used to share.
Your spirit soars o'er places where I'd walk,
Not holding any friend on earth so true,
Upon my shoulder, good and faithful hawk,
O Skarlath, there was never one like you!
With heavy heart I sit alone in grief,
Lord of the mountain, ruling over all,
Wishing I could split a single leaf,
To bring you back again, with our old call.

The harewife traced her paw over the letters carved countless seasons ago, saying quietly, 'A great and wise badger with many unusual qualities.'

The old otter leaned on his travelling staff, watching the young hares gathered around the stone reading the poem. 'Aye, Salamandastron flourished under his rule. It would be good for these young uns to learn from one like Sunflash.'

Burrbob looked up from the carved seat. 'There's not been a jolly old Badger Lord here for absolute ages, sir – well, not in my lifetime there ain't.'

Rillbrook put his paw around the young hare's shoulder, smiling and shaking his head. 'Great seasons, not in your lifetime? That must be a fair old span of dusty days!'

Burrbob looked hopefully up at the old storyteller. 'D'you think a badger will ever come to Salamandastron again, sir?'

Rillbrook sat the young hare down upon the stone seat. 'This mountain is never without a Badger Lord for too long. The warrior spirit seems to draw them here from afar. If you sit here for a short time each day and watch those shores below, some day you'll see that badger come striding along. Grow up strong and honest, all of you, and serve that badger well. It is the duty of Salamandastron hares to do this.'

Drawing his cloak about him, Rillbrook the Wanderer tapped his ashpole staff on the rock and set off on his travels. 'Farewell, my friends, and thank you for your hospitality, but the wayside beckons and the breezes call me away.'

As he picked his way slowly down the mountainside the harewife called after him, 'Wait on the shore below, I'll bring you a haversack of food!'

Rillbrook waved his staff in acknowledgement.

Remembering their manners, Burrbob and the young hares scrambled to assist the old otter down the slope.

'What ho, sir, lean on me!'

'Where do you journey to now, sir?'

Rillbrook winked at the pretty leveret who had asked the question. 'Why, to Redwall Abbey, where else? It will take me several seasons to haul my old carcass that far, but fate and friends have always been good to me. Never fear, I'll make it by next autumn. It's a pretty place to be at harvest time and the door is always open to friends. Maybe some day you'll visit there. I'm sure they'd make you welcome.'

The young hares and the harewife stood on the beach, watching Rillbrook the Wanderer growing small as he trekked off east into the golden afternoon.

Burrbob raised his paw. 'Let's send the old un on his way with a good ol' warcry.'

Throwing back their heads they roared out the time-honoured call of Salamandastron.

'Eeulaliaaaaaaa!'

Look out for the ninth thrilling Redwall adventure, PEARLS OF LUTRA by Brian Jacques, published in hardback by Hutchinson Children's Books, price £12.99 and coming soon in paperback in Red Fox in 1997.

The Pearls of Lutra

Far across the heaving deeps of restless ocean, some say even beyond the place where the sun sinks in the west, there lies the Isle of Sampetra. At first sight, it's a lush tropical jewel, set in turquoise waters where seasons never change from eternal summer. But a closer look would reveal that Sampetra is rotten as a flyblown fish carcass. It is a crossroads of evil, haven to the flotsam of the high seas. Corsairs, searats and all manner of vermin wavescum make their berth at Sampetra, the domain of a pine marten, the mighty Emperor Ublaz!

He is also known as Mad Eyes, though none ever called him that to his face and lived. He dwells in a palace built on a flat-topped escarpment at the island's southwesterly tip. Any ship entering the harbour must pay tribute to Ublaz, and captains who do not choose to anchor at Sampetra are considered to be foes of the Emperor. It is his decree that their ships and even their lives are forfeit; they are fair game to his followers.

Mad Eyes is cunning, all-powerful. Like a spider at the centre of a great web, he rules Sampetra. No trees grow upon the island but Ublaz has a vast timber stock in his courtyard. Wood for ship repairs is given only to those who pay him heavy tribute. The island is a good place for vermin from the seas to rest and roister: there are taverns dotted about the harbour area. Ublaz is served by a regiment of rats who carry long tridents as a mark of their rank; his Trident-rats patrol the harbour night and day. However, the most fearsome of his creatures are great flesh-eating lizards known as the Monitors, who have inhabited Sampetra for as long as anybeast can remember. Only the mad-eyed Emperor can control the dreadful reptiles, with the power of his hypnotic stare.

Conva the corsair captain was not a happy stoat as he watched his steersrat bring their craft, the vessel *Waveworm*, into the bay of Sampetra. On the jetty Conva could see lizards and Trident-rats waiting, and he knew what they were there for – to take him before the Emperor. Had the corsair known any pleas or prayers to the fates, he would have said them right then, hoping that Mad Eyes might have forgotten the treasure called 'Tears of all Oceans'. But then he recalled his meeting with Ublaz before the voyage, and the eyes, the strange mad eyes that had compelled him to return.

Sounds of singing, fighting and feasting drifted up from the taverns by the jetty as *Waveworm* hove alongside. Conva was relieved of his curved scimitar and marched off between two Monitors and two Trident-rats. The remainder of the guards boarded the ship, to make sure the crew stayed in their quarters until they received permission to come ashore.

As he was ushered into the throne room of the Emperor, Conva glanced around. It was the peak of barbaric splendour. There were silks, marble, rich velvet cushions and satin hangings, and the air was heavy with the scent of strange aromatic herbs smouldering in wall braziers. The Emperor was seated on a great carved cedar throne.

Though Conva feared Ublaz, he could not help but admire him. A big creature, this pine marten: strong, handsome and sleek, with fine brown fur from head to bushy tail, complemented by a creamy yellow throat and ears. He was clad in a green silk robe with a gold border; blue sapphires twinkled from the handle of a slim silver-bladed dagger thrust into a belt of shark's skin. The face of Ublaz was immobile. Savage white teeth showed slightly through a thin, almost lipless mouth, and above the curled perfumed whiskers and light brown nosetip, two jet-black almond-shaped eyes stared at the corsair captain.

All was silence. Conva stood riveted by the eyes; they pierced him to the core. Silent and mysterious Ublaz sat, transfixing the corsair with his gaze until words began flowing from the hypnotized captain.

'Mighty One who knows all, your commands were carried out. We raided the den of Lutra the otter on the far north shores. They were taken by ambush and slain, every one of them, and all that they possessed was loaded aboard my ship.'

For the first time Ublaz spoke, his voice scarce above a whisper. 'Tell me what you took, everything.'

The corsair repeated a list of spoils. 'Beakers set with coloured stones, platters also, carved bone tail- and pawrings, one gold neckband, a box of small purple pearls and another box made from a hinged scallop shell. This shell contained six large, rose-coloured pearls.'

The Emperor drew in his breath sharply. 'The Tears of all Oceans, you have them!'

Conva began to shiver visibly. He collapsed to the marble floor, his voice trembling with fear. 'Mighty One, they were stolen!'

Ublaz sighed deeply, slumping back on his throne as if the bad news came as no surprise to him. 'Tell me how this thing happened.'

Two Monitors entered the throne room bearing a litter containing the booty from Conva's ship *Waveworm*. At a nod from Ublaz they set it down in front of him.

The corsair continued his narrative in broken tones.

'Two moons after we slew the tribe of Lutra I charted a course following the coast south. I knew a stream of freshwater runs out across the beach near an area named Mossflower. We dropped anchor there and took on fresh water. When *Waveworm* was ready to get under sail again, two of my crew, both weasels, Flairnose and Graylunk, were discovered missing. So were the rose pearls in the scallop shell – they'd stolen them and jumped ship. I gave chase, tracked them, leaving behind only three to guard the ship. We found Flairnose wounded sore three days later. They had quarrelled over the pearls, and Graylunk had stabbed him. We searched Flairnose – he had no pearls, though before he died he told us that he'd given Graylunk a bad skull wound when they fought.

'Two days on, following Graylunk's trail, we came upon a big building called Redwall Abbey. I had my crew scout around it in a wide circle, but the only track of Graylunk we could find went straight to the main door. This Redwall is a large, well-fortified place, with many creatures living there. We did not let them see us; their numbers were tenscore more than ours.

'Graylunk is inside Redwall with the pearls, or if he has died from his wound then the pearls are still within the walls of that Abbey. I could do no more, Mighty One, not with the numbers I had. I made it back to my ship with all speed and hastened here to bring you the news.'

Ublaz moved smoothly around the booty on the litter, sifting through it with his silver-bladed dagger. 'Dented beakers, bone tailrings, gold neckband, huh, more like brass,' he said to himself. 'Small purple pearls, worthless musselseeds. Except for the rose pearls, the tribe of Lutra had nothing of value – they were poor as beggars!'

He ceased his examination and stood over the quaking corsair. 'And you, bold Conva, what shall I do with you?' The Emperor's fearsome eyes bored into Conva's mind.

His spirit completely broken with terror, the corsair grovelled shamelessly at the Emperor's footpaws. 'Mighty One, Great Emperor, spare me. I will gather more crew and the help of other captains. Give me a chance and I will go to Redwall and bring back the Tears of all Oceans.'

Ublaz stepped hard on the back of Conva's neck, trapping his head against the floor. 'Scum of the sea, fool who cannot control his own crew!' the pine marten said, his voice dripping with contempt. 'Do you think I would let an idiot like you travel half round the world to fight a war against Redwall Abbey? I have heard of that place. The bones of warlords moulder at its gates; more than one has tried to breach those red walls and died miserably. If I am to retrieve the Tears of all Oceans it needs cunning strategy.' Ublaz pointed his dagger at a Trident-rat guard. 'You, go and fetch my Monitor General!'

Leaning down, the pine marten nicked Conva's ear with his dagger. 'You I will let live, until I know the truth of your story. Take him away and billet him in the Monitor barracks.'

Conva knew it was pointless to beg for mercy. He had escaped instant death, but how long would he survive unarmed in the barracks of the strange, flesh-eating lizards? He was led off stunned, almost speechless with terror.

Lask Frildur the Monitor General stood before the Emperor, flat reptilian eyes unblinking, scales making a dry rustle as his heavy spiked tail swished lazily against the marble floor. Ublaz nodded approvingly. The Monitor General had never let him down; everybeast on Sampetra knew and feared the reputation of Lask Frildur.

'Does all go well with you, my strong right claw?' Ublaz said, as he poured wine for them both.

The Emperor turned his head from Lask's foul breath

as the lizard answered, 'Yarr, Mightinezz. Lazk Frildur awaitz your orderz!'

The mad-eyed marten took a sip of wine and wiped his mouth fastidiously on a silk kerchief. Good! I want you to take the ship of Conva and carry out an important mission for me.'

The Monitor General's eyes flickered momentarily. 'I will go to the endz of oceanz if Ublaz commandz!'

He accepted the goblet of wine that was pushed towards him, holding it at throat height. Lask never let his eyes stray from those of Ublaz; his head did not dip to the goblet, instead a long tongue snaked out and lapped at the wine as the Emperor gave his instructions.

'It is a long voyage to where the sun rises in the east, a place called the land of Mossflower. Take the *Waveworm* and her crew, with Romsca the ferret as captain, and a score of your Monitors. Here is what you must do . . .'

Outside the surf boomed on the sunwarmed rocks of the escarpment, and ships bobbed at anchor in the harbour. Sampetra shimmered under the midday sun, a once beautiful jewel of the oceans, now tainted by the evil of its ruler.

Don't miss Brian Jacques' debut picture book
The Great Redwall Feast
Coming soon from
Random House Children's Books!

The spell-binding world of Redwall, created by Brian
Jacques in his award-winning, best-selling novels, is the
inspiration for this glorious picture book for all Redwall
fans.

The creatures of Redwall Abbey are planning a surprise
feast in honour of their Abbot, and preparations in the
kitchens and cellars are in full swing. There are so many
kinds of sweet treats to be baked and beverages to be
brewed, *how* will it ever be ready on time?!

The warmth, spirit and fun of the Redwallers, so
perfectly captured in Brian Jacques' enchanting verse, is
magically bought to life by Christopher Denise's
charming illustrations – an exquisite gift for all occasions!

ISBN 0 09 972501 0   £12.99

If you would like a Brian Jacques goody or a Redwall poster, please write to:

Brian Jacques
Red Fox
PO Box 1375
20 Vauxhall Bridge Road
London SW1V 2SA

Humour and Adventure in the Redwall Series

Read the REDWALL adventures by master storyteller Brian Jacques –
an award-winning bestselling series of epic adventures based around
Redwall Abbey, home to a community of peace-loving mice.

REDWALL

As the mice of Redwall Abbey prepare for a feast, unknown to them,
Cluny, the evil one-eyed rat, is preparing for almighty battle . . .

ISBN 0 09 951200 9   £4.99

MOSSFLOWER

The gripping tale of how Redwall Abbey was established through the
bravery of the legendary mouse, Martin.

ISBN 0 09 955400 3   £4.99

MATTIMEO

Slagar the Fox is intent on bringing destruction to Redwall Abbey and
the fearless mouse warrior, Matthias. He'll stop at nothing – including
Mattimeo, Matthias's son

ISBN 0 09 967540 0   £4.99

MARIEL OF REDWALL

A young mousemaid is washed ashore on the fringes of Mossflower
country. Battered and bruised, she makes her way to Redwall Abbey,
where the story of her horrific ordeal unfolds.

ISBN 0 09 992960 0   £4.99

SALAMANDASTRON

Why did the sword fall from the Abbey roof? Who is the white badger?
And can the good creatures triumph over Ferahgo the Assassin?

ISBN 0 09 914461 5   £4.99

MARTIN THE WARRIOR

Bedrang the Tyrant stoat holds many creatures prisoner in his fortress
on the coast. But a young mouse, Martin, refuses to obey the Evil Lord,
and plans a daring escape.

ISBN 0 09 928171 6   £4.99

Humour and Adventure in the Redwall Series

THE BELLMAKER

Bar your doors! The Foxwolf and his horde of grey rats are coming to Southsward! After dreams of Martin the Warrior, old Joseph the bellmaker sets off with four young warriors to help friends abroad . . .

ISBN 0 09 943331 1   £4.99

THE OUTCAST OF REDWALL

Ferret Swart Sixclaw and arch enemy, Sunflash the Mace, swear to carry out a pledge of death – upon each other. Meanwhile a young creature is cruely banished from the Abbey – and a mousemaid finds her destiny linked to . . . the Outcast of Redwall.

ISBN 0 09 960091 9   £4.99

and coming soon in Red Fox . . .

THE PEARLS OF LUTRA

Far away, on the Isle of Sampetra, Emperor Ublaz, known as Mad Eyes, sends his fearsome lizards on a murderous mission to Redwall. Meanwhile, the abbey dwellers frantically race against time to unravel a fiendishly difficult set of riddles . . .

ISBN 0 09 963871 1   £4.99